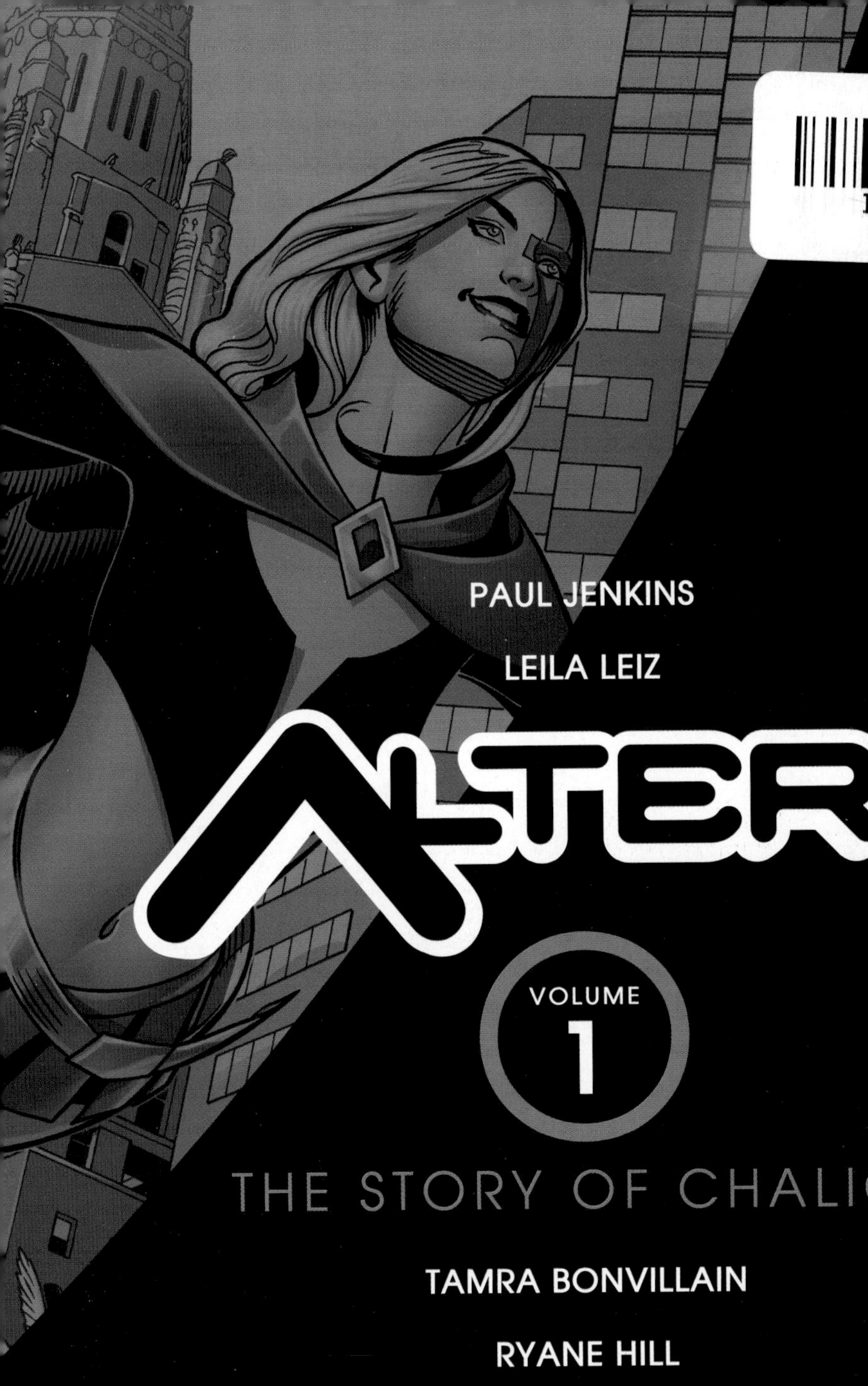

PAUL JENKINS

LEILA LEIZ

ALTERS™

VOLUME 1

THE STORY OF CHALICE

TAMRA BONVILLAIN

RYANE HILL

BRIAN STELFREEZE

AFTERSHOCK™

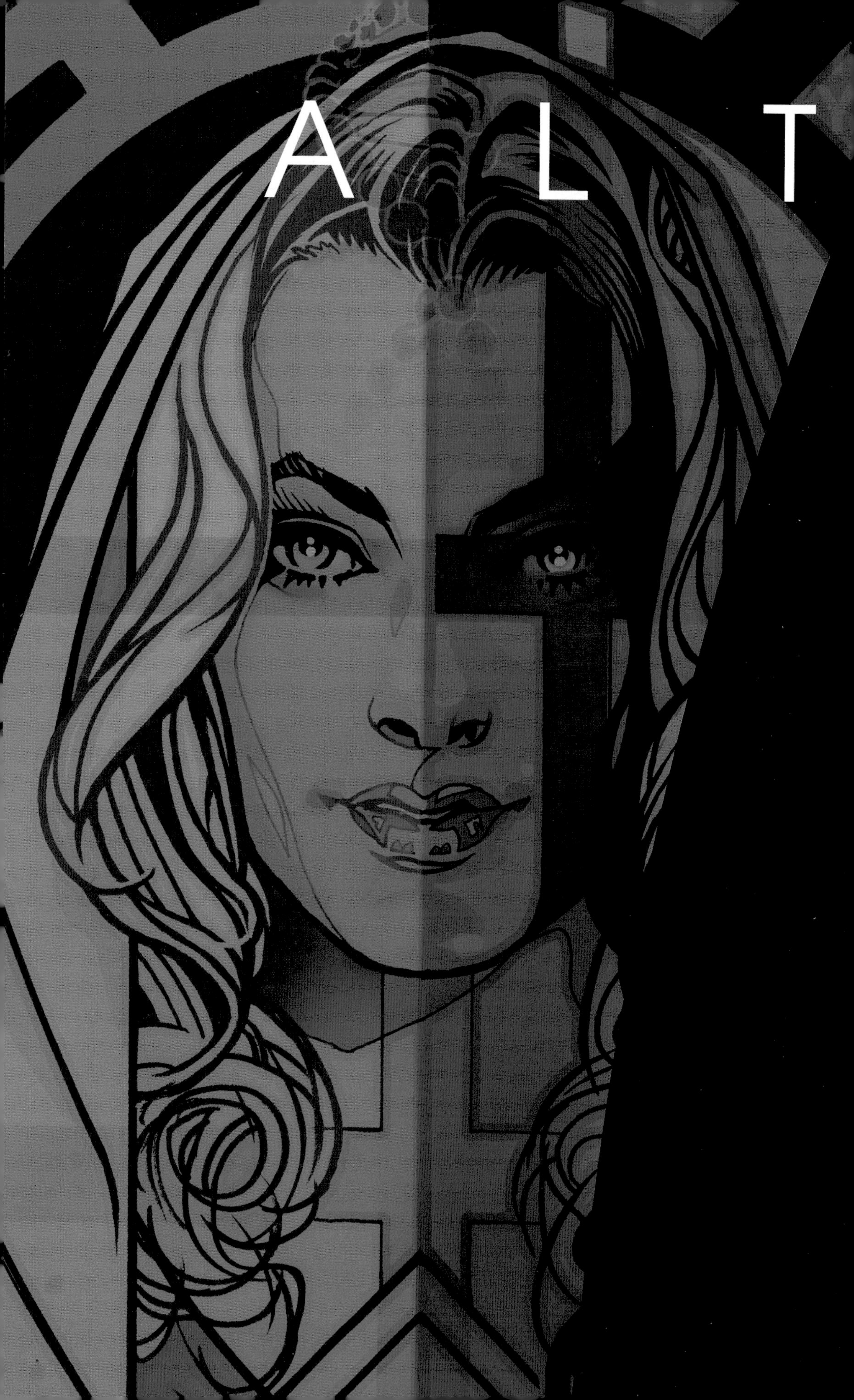
A L T

E R S

VOLUME 1

THE STORY OF CHALICE

PAUL JENKINS creator & writer

LEILA LEIZ artist

TAMRA BONVILLAIN colorist

RYANE HILL letterer

AFTERSHOCK GENESIS short story:
GEORGES JEANTY artist **DEXTER VINES** inker
ROB SCHWAGER colorist **CLAYTON COWLES** letterer

BRIAN STELFREEZE front & original series covers

JOHN J. HILL book & logo designer

LIZ LUU creative character consultant

JES GROBMAN special thanks

MIKE MARTS editor

NICK BRADSHAW, RICHARD CASE, TONY HARRIS, JOHN McCREA, CHRIS SPOUSE & **BRIAN STELFREEZE** variant covers

AFTERSHOCK™

MIKE MARTS - Editor-in-Chief • JOE PRUETT - Publisher/Chief Creative Officer • LEE KRAMER - President
JAWAD QURESHI - SVP, Investor Relations • JON KRAMER - Chief Executive Officer • MIKE ZAGARI - SVP Digital/Creative
JAY BEHLING - Chief Financial Officer • STEPHAN NILSON - Publishing Operations Manager
LISA Y. WU - Retailer/Fan Relations Manager • ASHLEY WYATT - Publishing Assistant

AfterShock Trade Dress and Interior Design by JOHN J. HILL • AfterShock Logo Design by COMICRAFT
Original series production (issues 3-5) by CHARLES PRITCHETT • Proofreading by J. HARBORE & DOCTOR Z.
Publicity: contact AARON MARION (aaron@fifteenminutes.com) & RYAN CROY (ryan@fifteenminutes.com) at 15 MINUTES

ALTERS VOLUME 1: THE STORY OF CHALICE Published by AfterShock Comics, LLC, 15300 Ventura Boulevard Suite 507, Sherman Oaks, CA 91403. Originally published as Alters #1-5 & AfterShock Genesis.
PRINTED IN KOREA. First Printing: April 2017. 10 9 8 7 6 5 4 3 2 1

AFTERSHOCKCOMICS.COM Follow us on social media

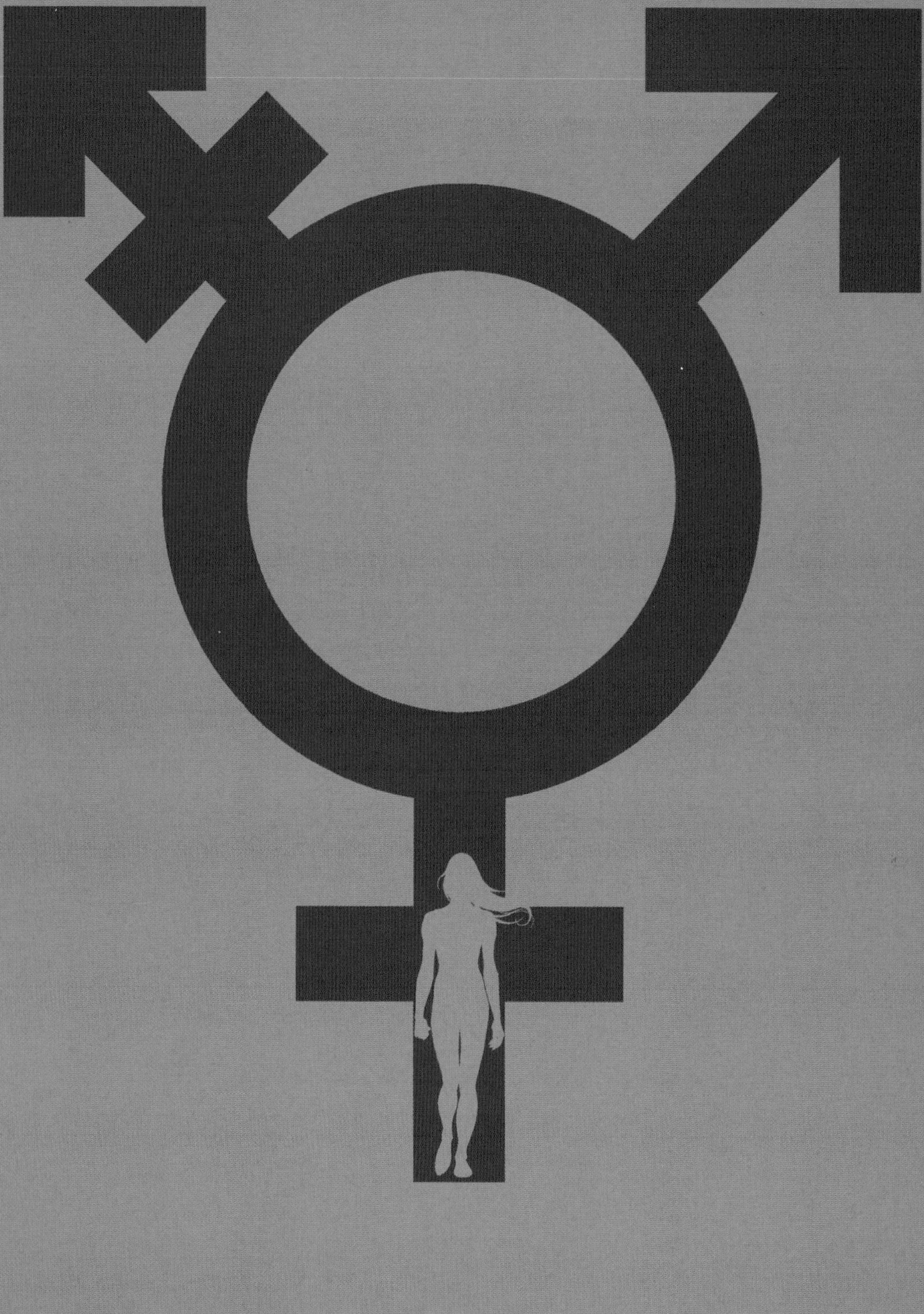

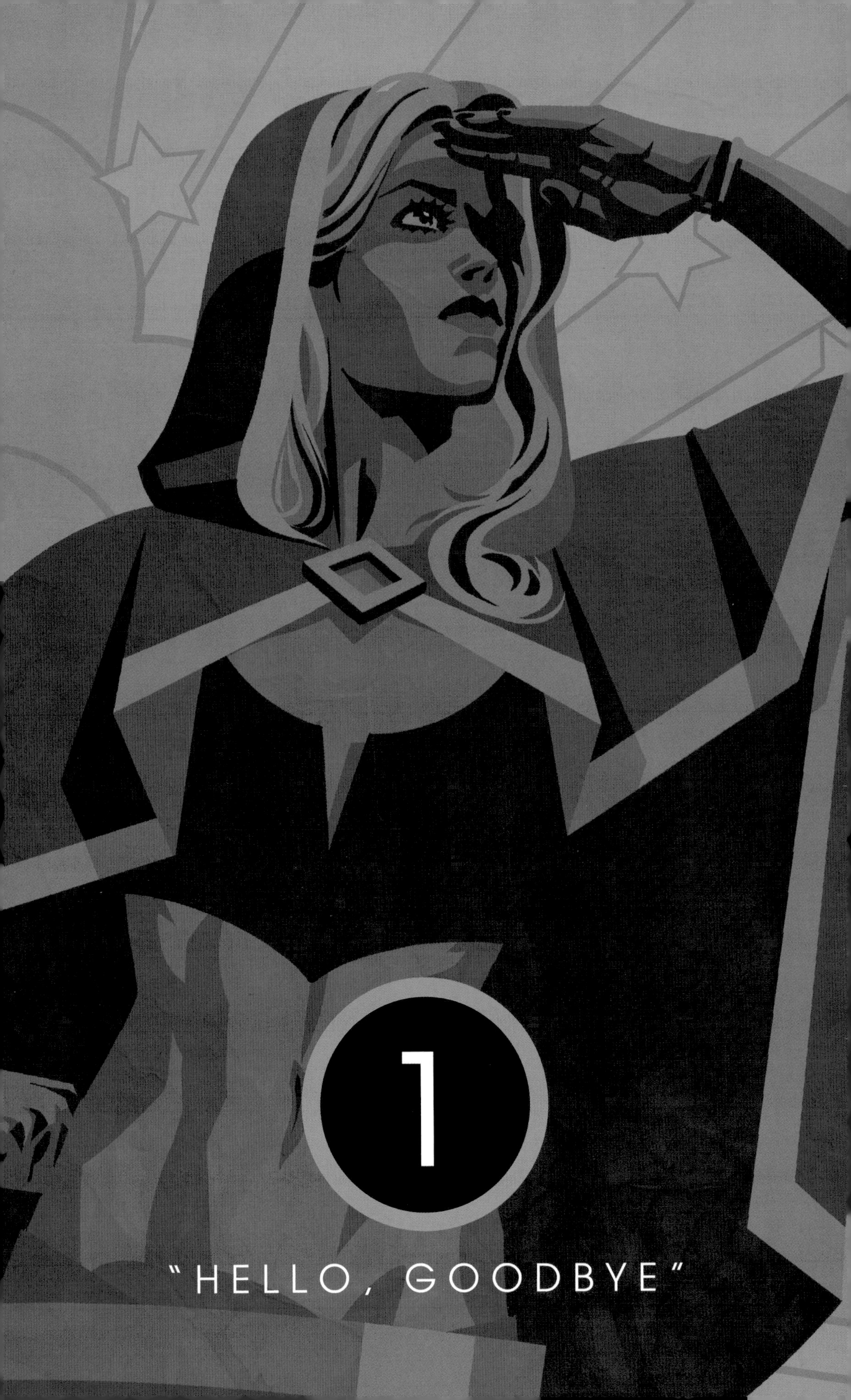
1
“HELLO, GOODBYE”

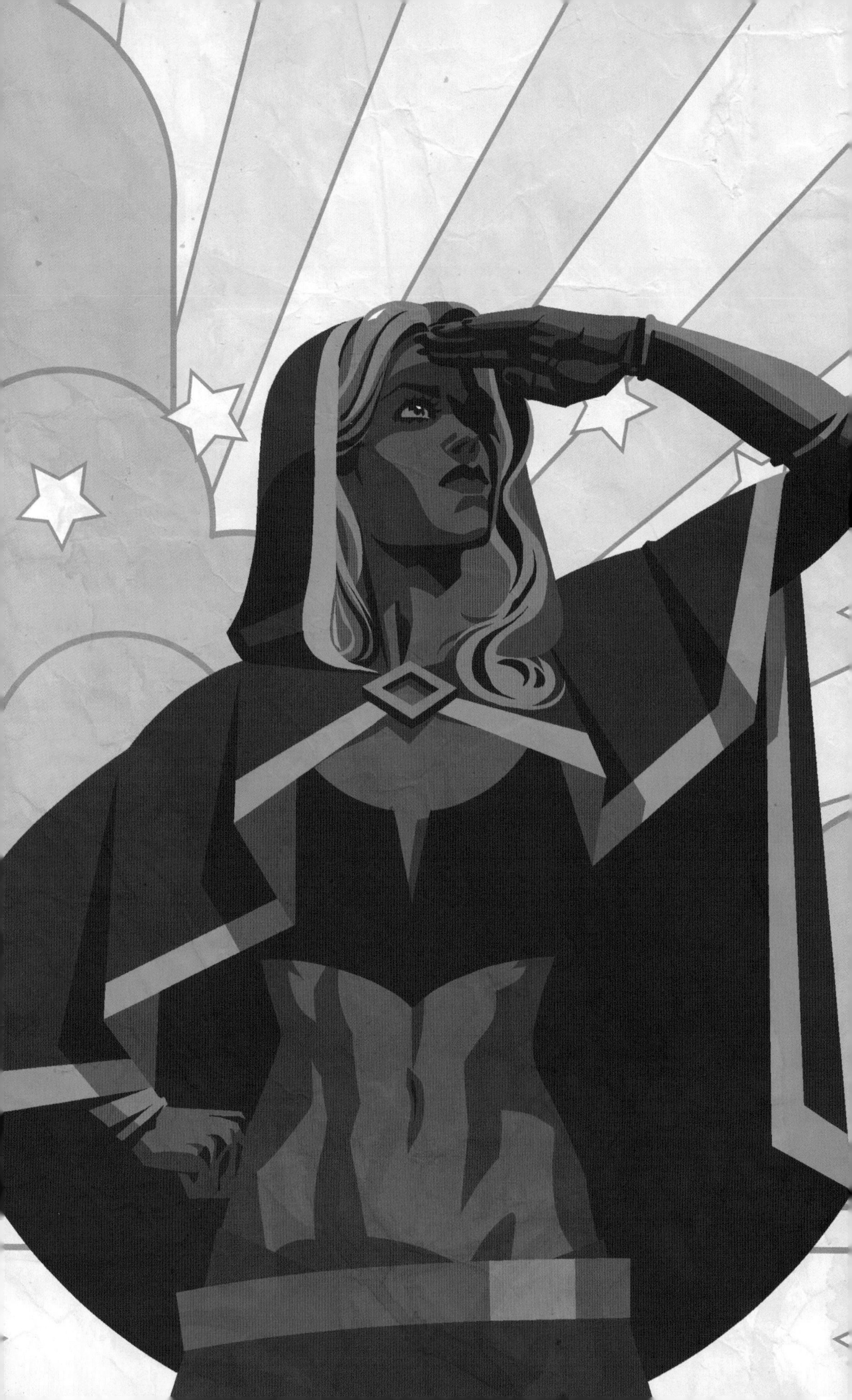

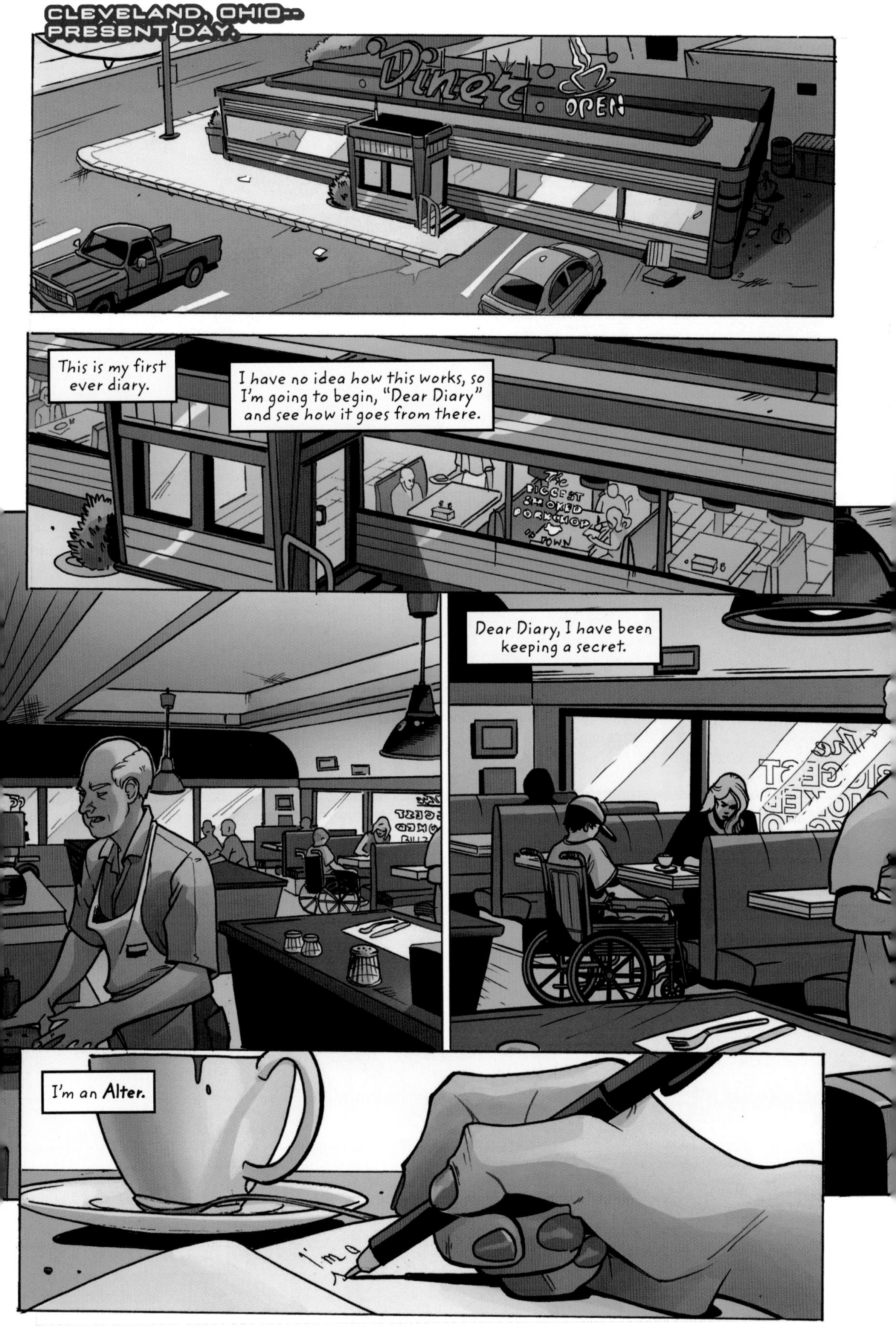
CLEVELAND, OHIO--
PRESENT DAY.
Diner
OPEN
This is my first ever diary.
I have no idea how this works, so I'm going to begin, "Dear Diary" and see how it goes from there.
The BIGGEST SMOKED PORKCHOP IN TOWN
Dear Diary, I have been keeping a secret.
I'm an **Alter.**

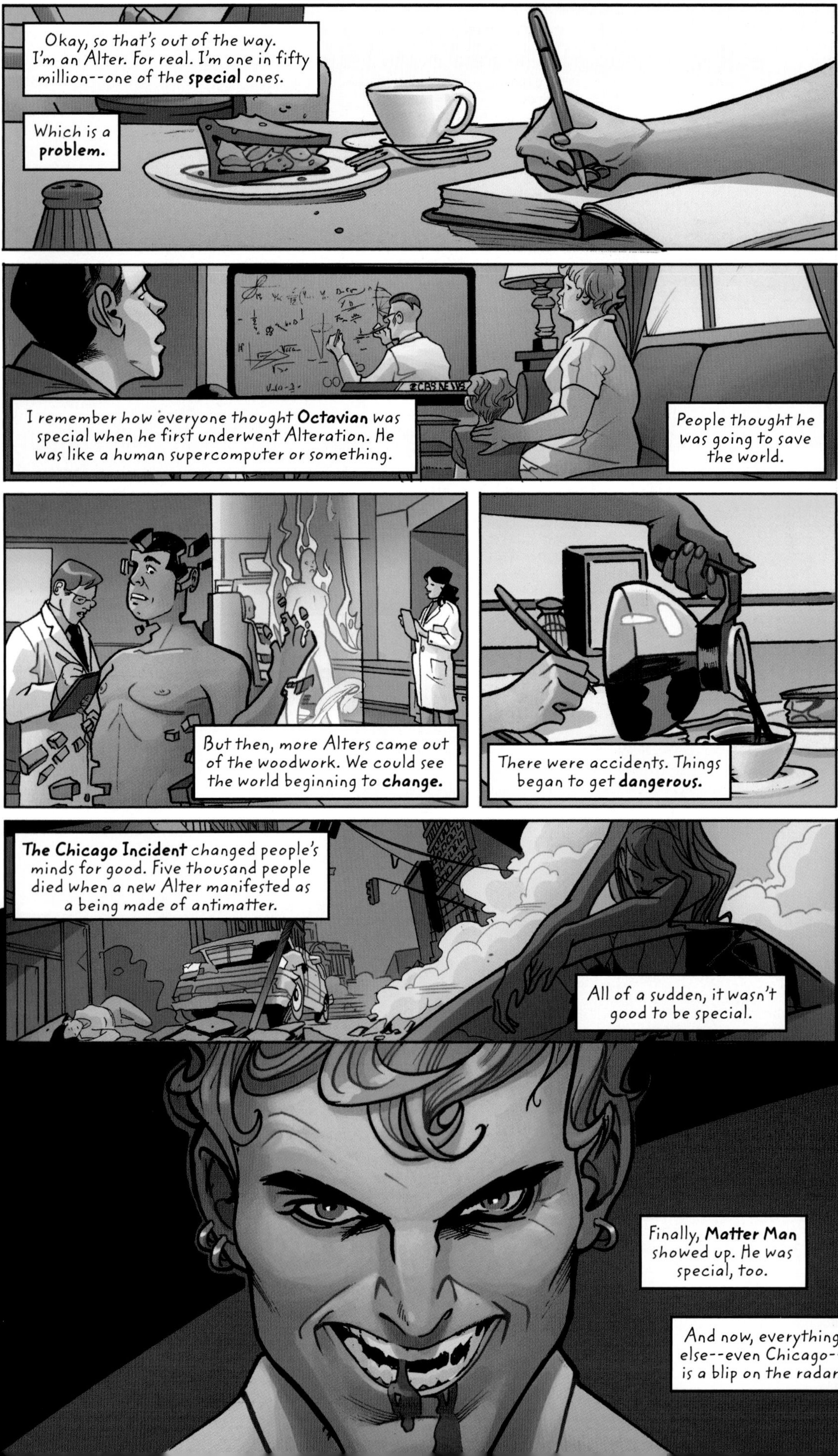

Okay, so that's out of the way. I'm an Alter. For real. I'm one in fifty million--one of the **special** ones.
Which is a **problem.**
I remember how everyone thought **Octavian** was special when he first underwent Alteration. He was like a human supercomputer or something.
People thought he was going to save the world.
But then, more Alters came out of the woodwork. We could see the world beginning to **change.**
There were accidents. Things began to get **dangerous.**
The Chicago Incident changed people's minds for good. Five thousand people died when a new Alter manifested as a being made of antimatter.
All of a sudden, it wasn't good to be special.
Finally, **Matter Man** showed up. He was special, too.
And now, everything else--even Chicago--is a blip on the radar.

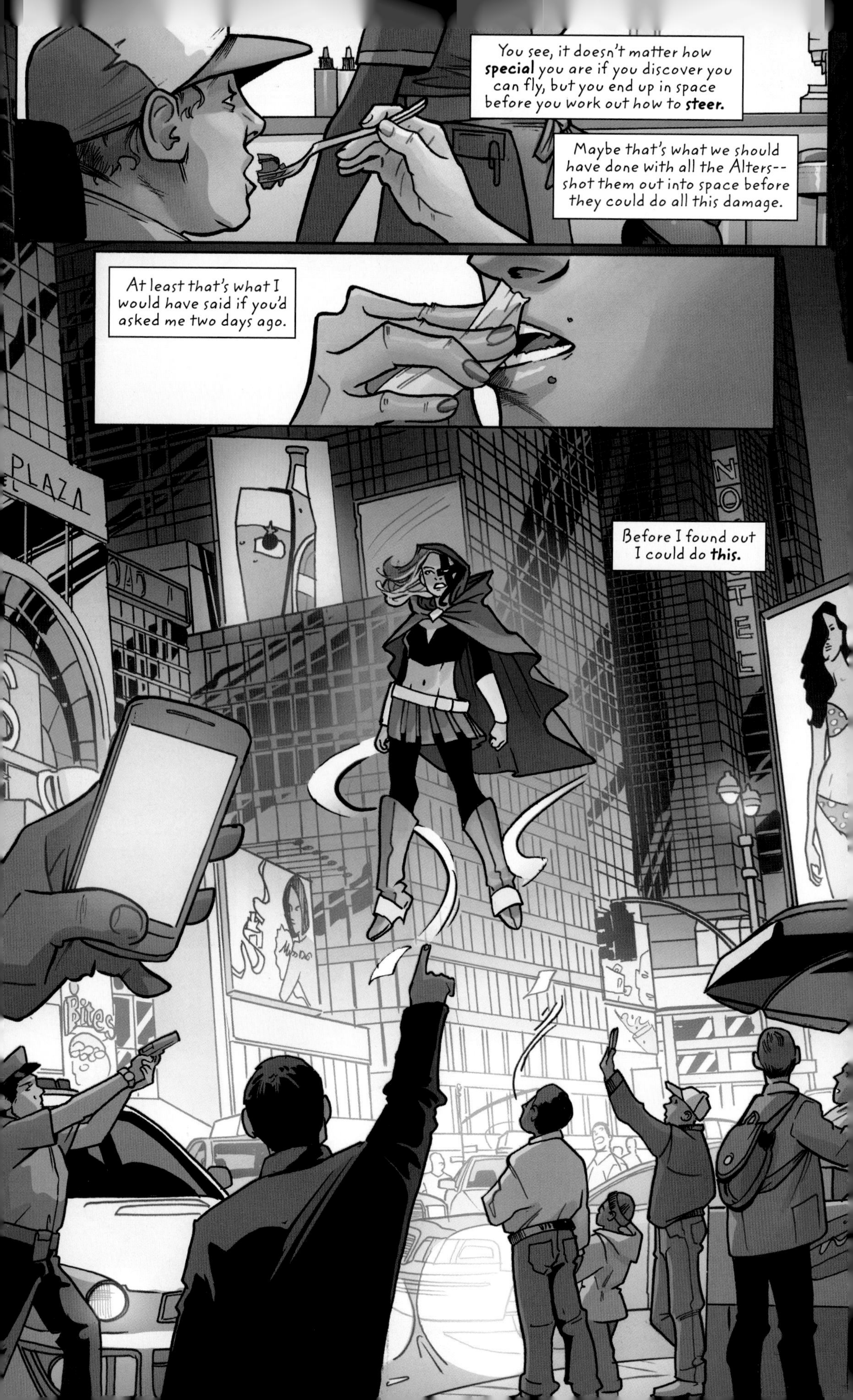

You see, it doesn't matter how **special** you are if you discover you can fly, but you end up in space before you work out how to **steer.**
Maybe that's what we should have done with all the Alters--shot them out into space before they could do all this damage.
At least that's what I would have said if you'd asked me two days ago.
PLAZA
Before I found out I could do **this.**

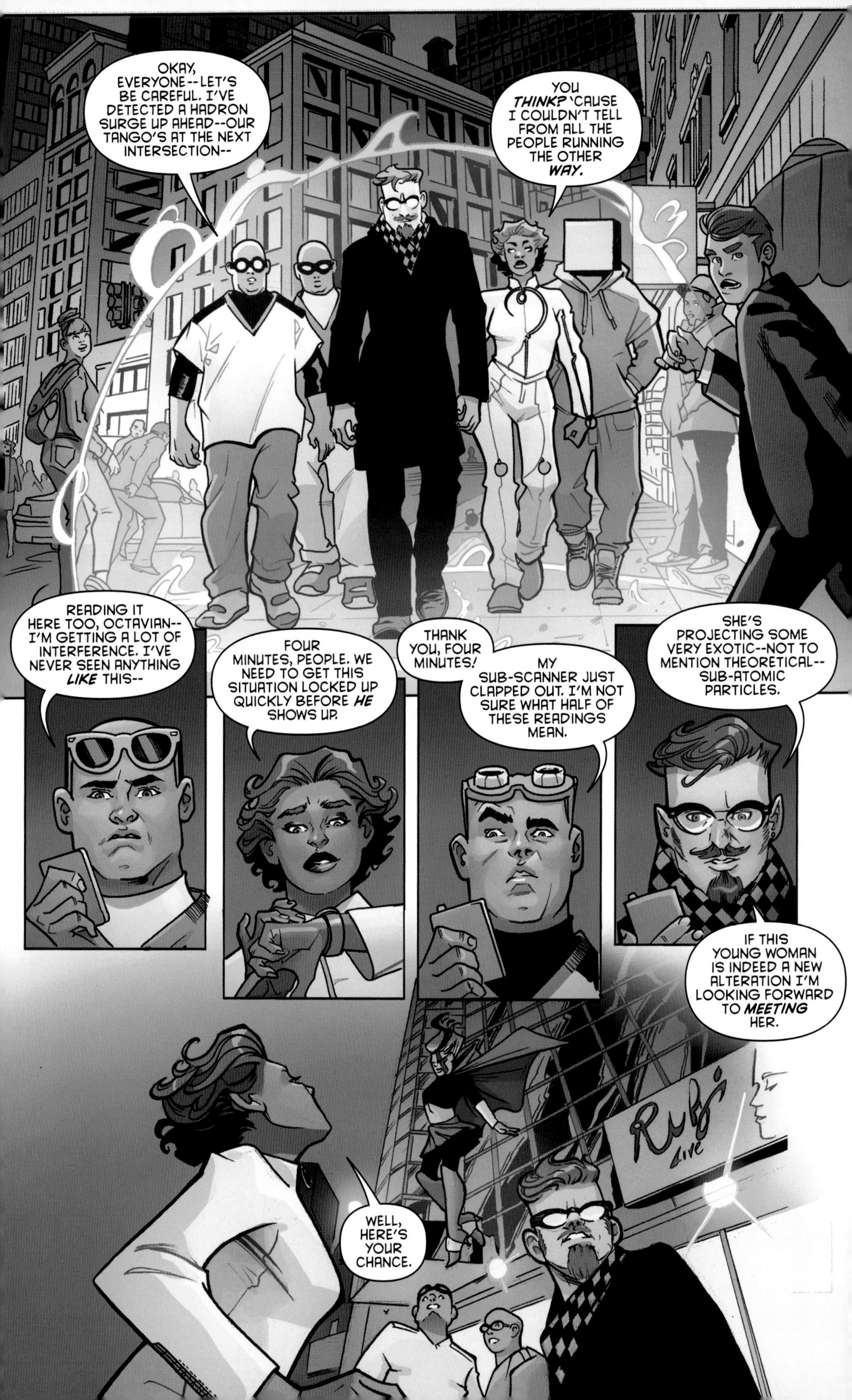
OKAY, EVERYONE--LET'S BE CAREFUL. I'VE DETECTED A HADRON SURGE UP AHEAD--OUR TANGO'S AT THE NEXT INTERSECTION--
YOU *THINK?* 'CAUSE I COULDN'T TELL FROM ALL THE PEOPLE RUNNING THE OTHER *WAY.*
READING IT HERE TOO, OCTAVIAN--I'M GETTING A LOT OF INTERFERENCE. I'VE NEVER SEEN ANYTHING *LIKE* THIS--
FOUR MINUTES, PEOPLE. WE NEED TO GET THIS SITUATION LOCKED UP QUICKLY BEFORE *HE* SHOWS UP.
THANK YOU, FOUR MINUTES!
MY SUB-SCANNER JUST CLAPPED OUT. I'M NOT SURE WHAT HALF OF THESE READINGS MEAN.
SHE'S PROJECTING SOME VERY EXOTIC--NOT TO MENTION THEORETICAL--SUB-ATOMIC PARTICLES.
IF THIS YOUNG WOMAN IS INDEED A NEW ALTERATION I'M LOOKING FORWARD TO *MEETING* HER.
Rufi Live
WELL, HERE'S YOUR CHANCE.

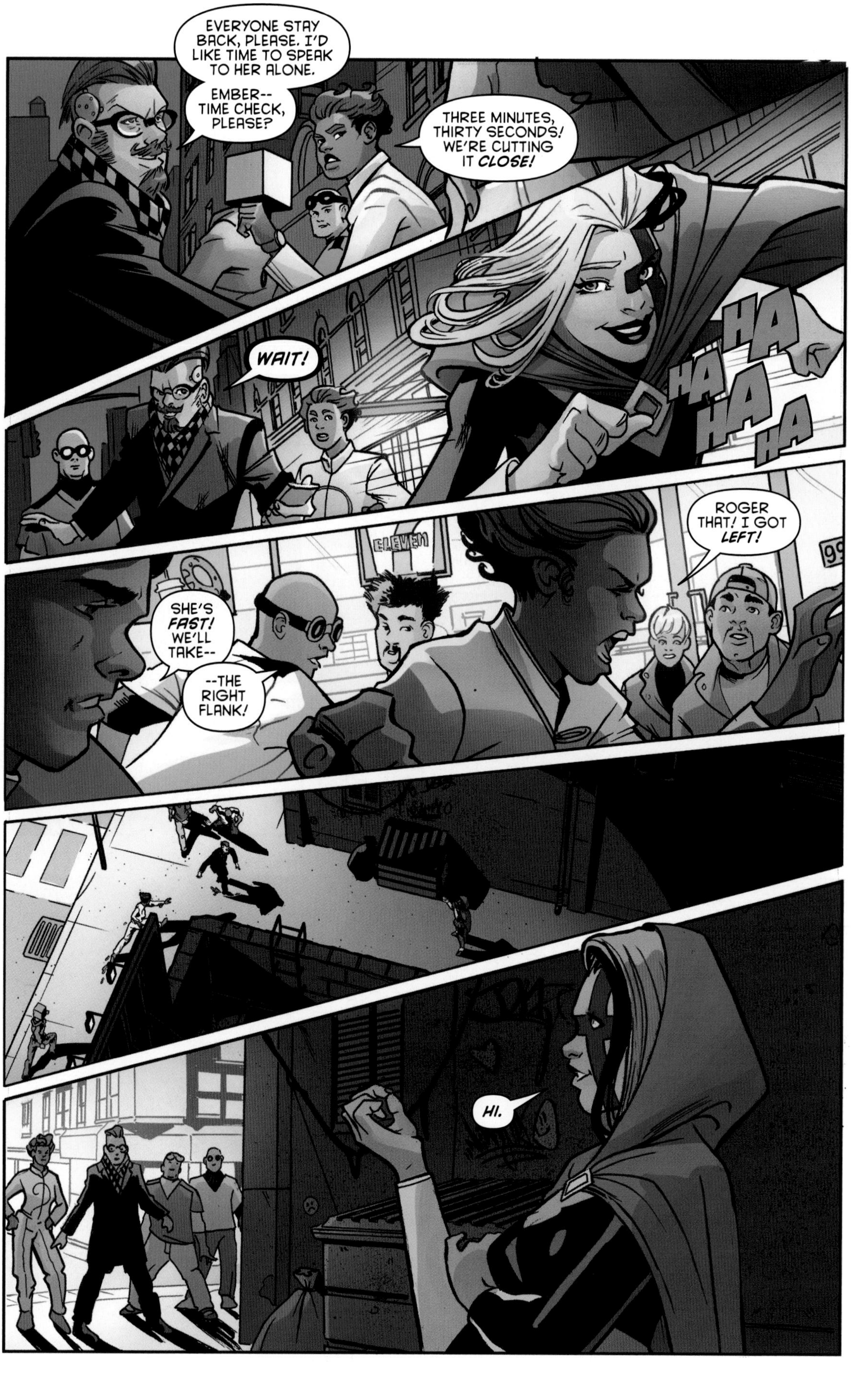
EVERYONE STAY BACK, PLEASE. I'D LIKE TIME TO SPEAK TO HER ALONE.
EMBER-- TIME CHECK, PLEASE?
THREE MINUTES, THIRTY SECONDS! WE'RE CUTTING IT CLOSE!
HA HA HA HA HA
WAIT!
ROGER THAT! I GOT LEFT!
SHE'S FAST! WE'LL TAKE--
--THE RIGHT FLANK!
ELEVEN
99
HI.

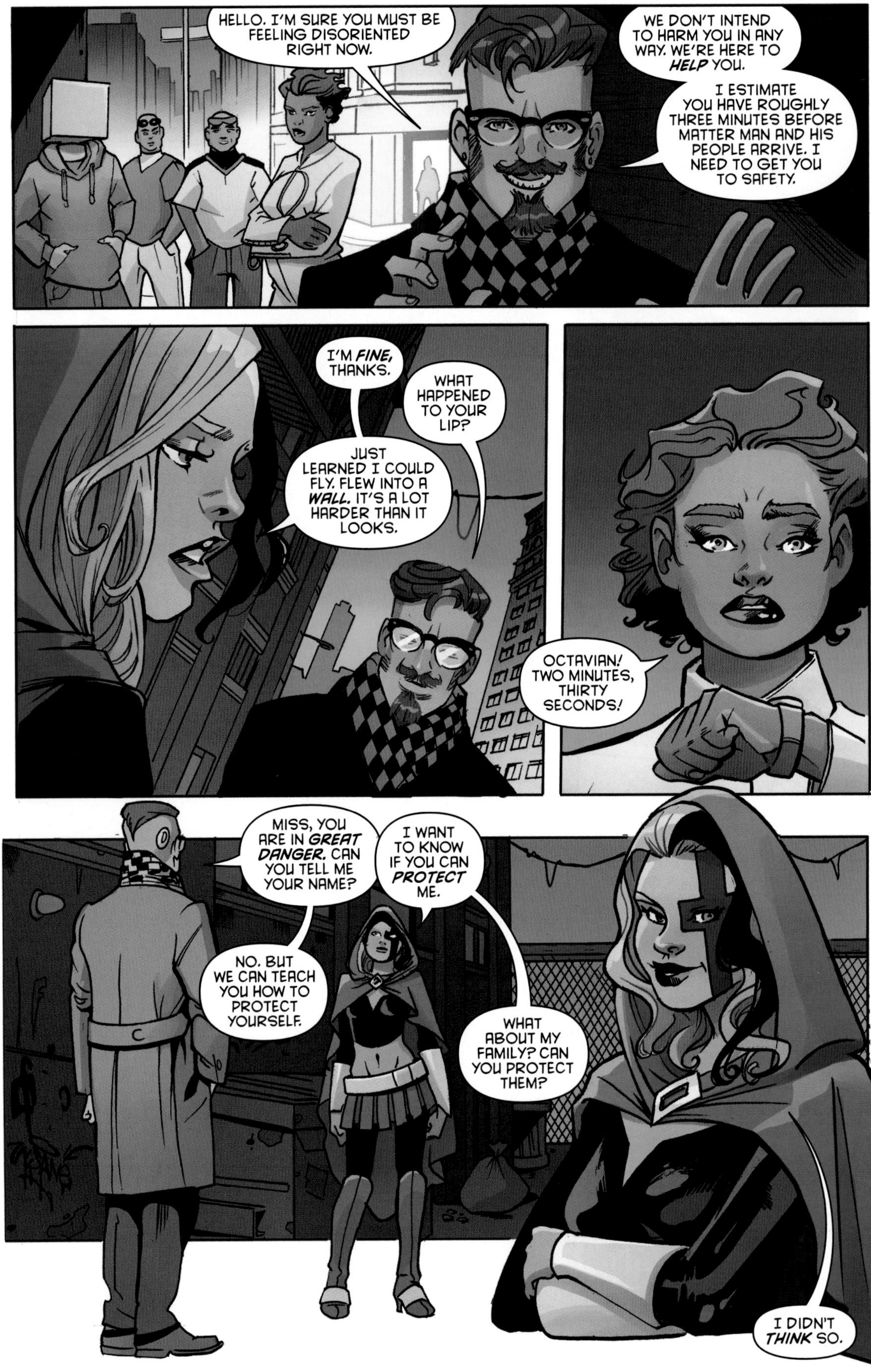
HELLO. I'M SURE YOU MUST BE FEELING DISORIENTED RIGHT NOW.
WE DON'T INTEND TO HARM YOU IN ANY WAY. WE'RE HERE TO *HELP* YOU.
I ESTIMATE YOU HAVE ROUGHLY THREE MINUTES BEFORE MATTER MAN AND HIS PEOPLE ARRIVE. I NEED TO GET YOU TO SAFETY.
I'M *FINE,* THANKS.
WHAT HAPPENED TO YOUR LIP?
JUST LEARNED I COULD FLY. FLEW INTO A *WALL.* IT'S A LOT HARDER THAN IT LOOKS.
OCTAVIAN! TWO MINUTES, THIRTY SECONDS!
MISS, YOU ARE IN *GREAT DANGER.* CAN YOU TELL ME YOUR NAME?
I WANT TO KNOW IF YOU CAN *PROTECT* ME.
NO. BUT WE CAN TEACH YOU HOW TO PROTECT YOURSELF.
WHAT ABOUT MY FAMILY? CAN YOU PROTECT THEM?
I DIDN'T *THINK* SO.

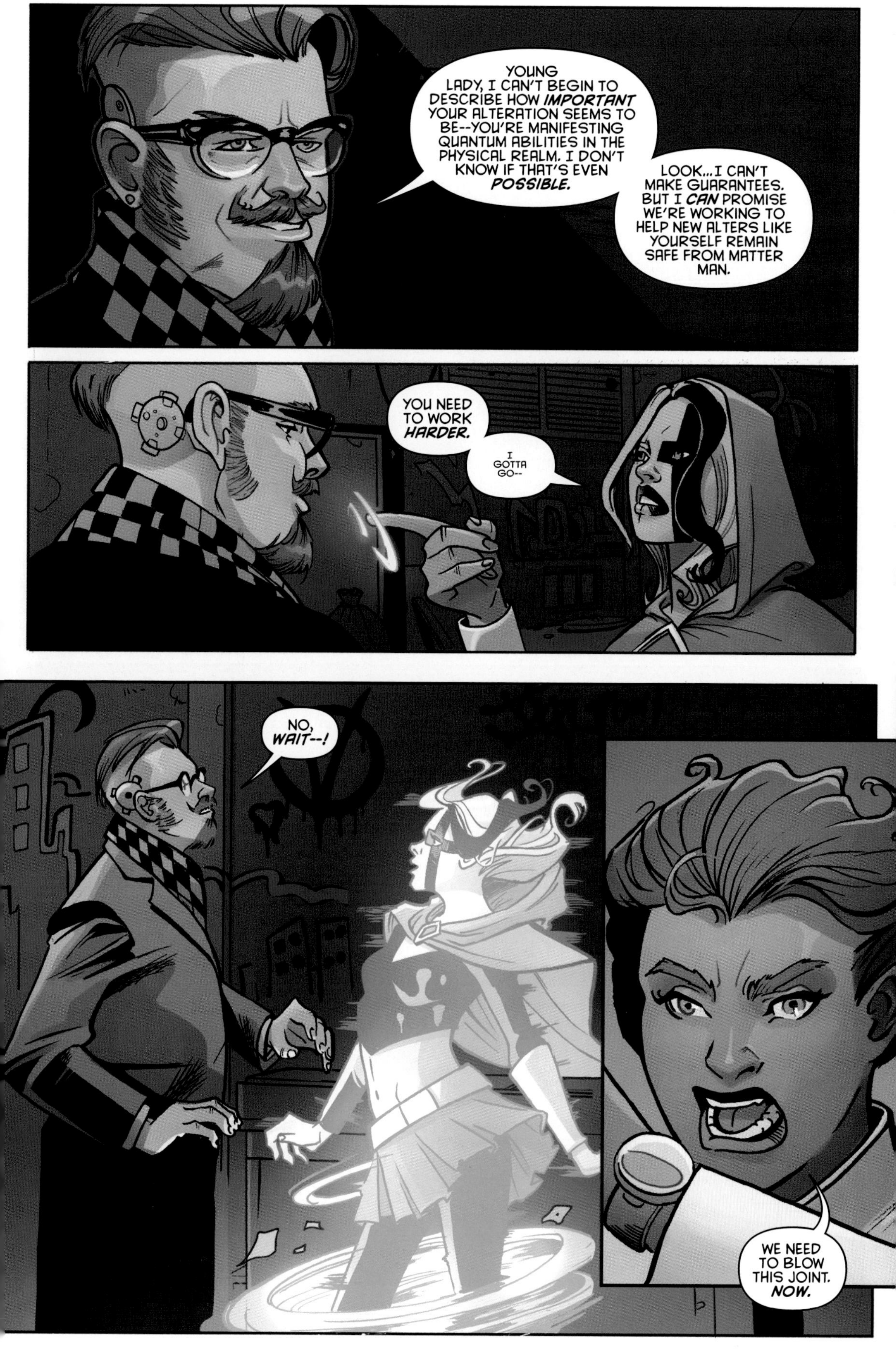
YOUNG LADY, I CAN'T BEGIN TO DESCRIBE HOW *IMPORTANT* YOUR ALTERATION SEEMS TO BE--YOU'RE MANIFESTING QUANTUM ABILITIES IN THE PHYSICAL REALM. I DON'T KNOW IF THAT'S EVEN *POSSIBLE.*
LOOK...I CAN'T MAKE GUARANTEES. BUT I *CAN* PROMISE WE'RE WORKING TO HELP NEW ALTERS LIKE YOURSELF REMAIN SAFE FROM MATTER MAN.
YOU NEED TO WORK *HARDER.*
I GOTTA GO--
NO, *WAIT--!*
WE NEED TO BLOW THIS JOINT. *NOW.*

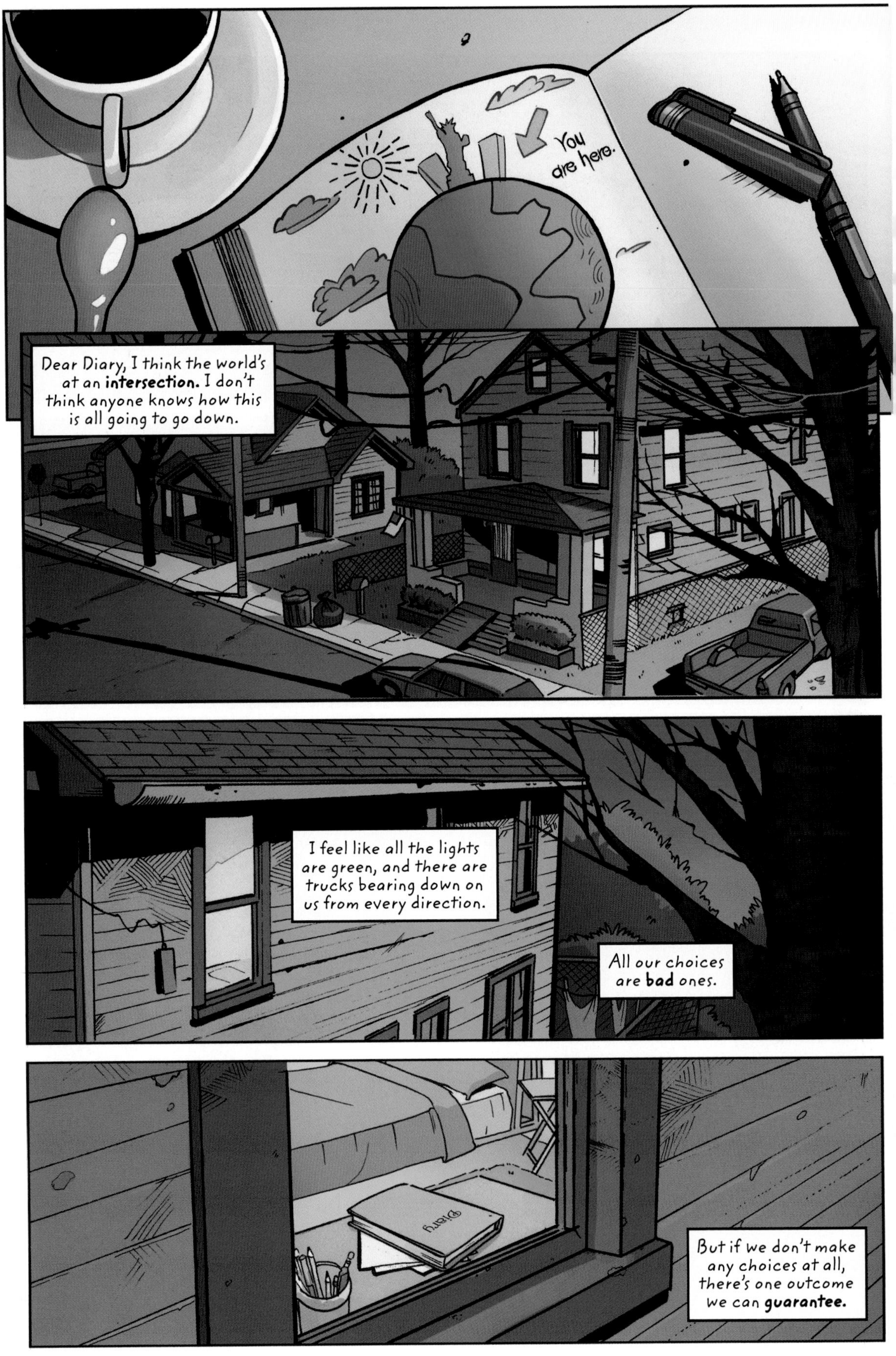
You are here.
Dear Diary, I think the world's at an intersection. I don't think anyone knows how this is all going to go down.
I feel like all the lights are green, and there are trucks bearing down on us from every direction.
All our choices are bad ones.
Diary
But if we don't make any choices at all, there's one outcome we can guarantee.

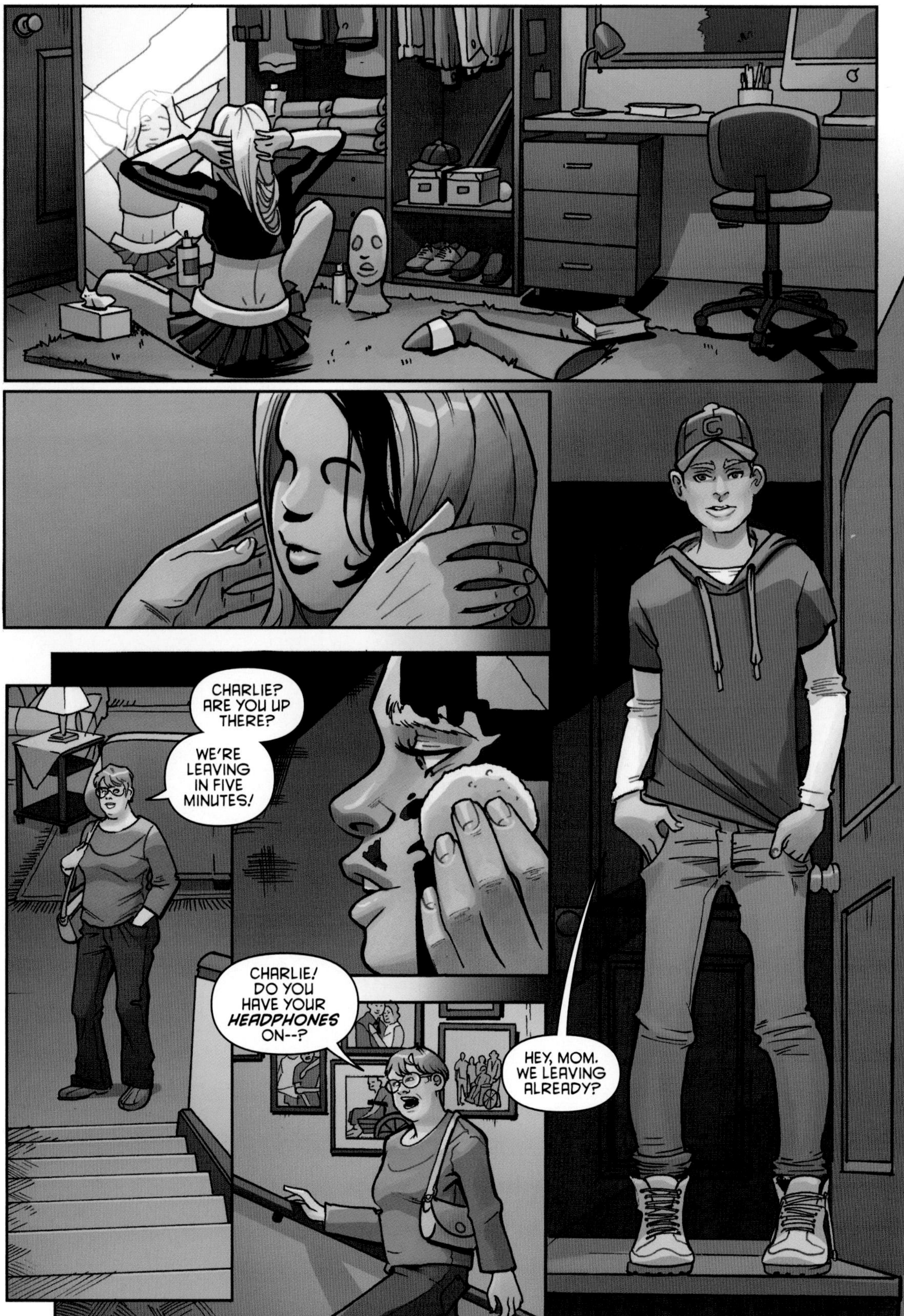
CHARLIE? ARE YOU UP THERE?
WE'RE LEAVING IN FIVE MINUTES!
CHARLIE! DO YOU HAVE YOUR HEADPHONES ON--?
HEY, MOM. WE LEAVING ALREADY?

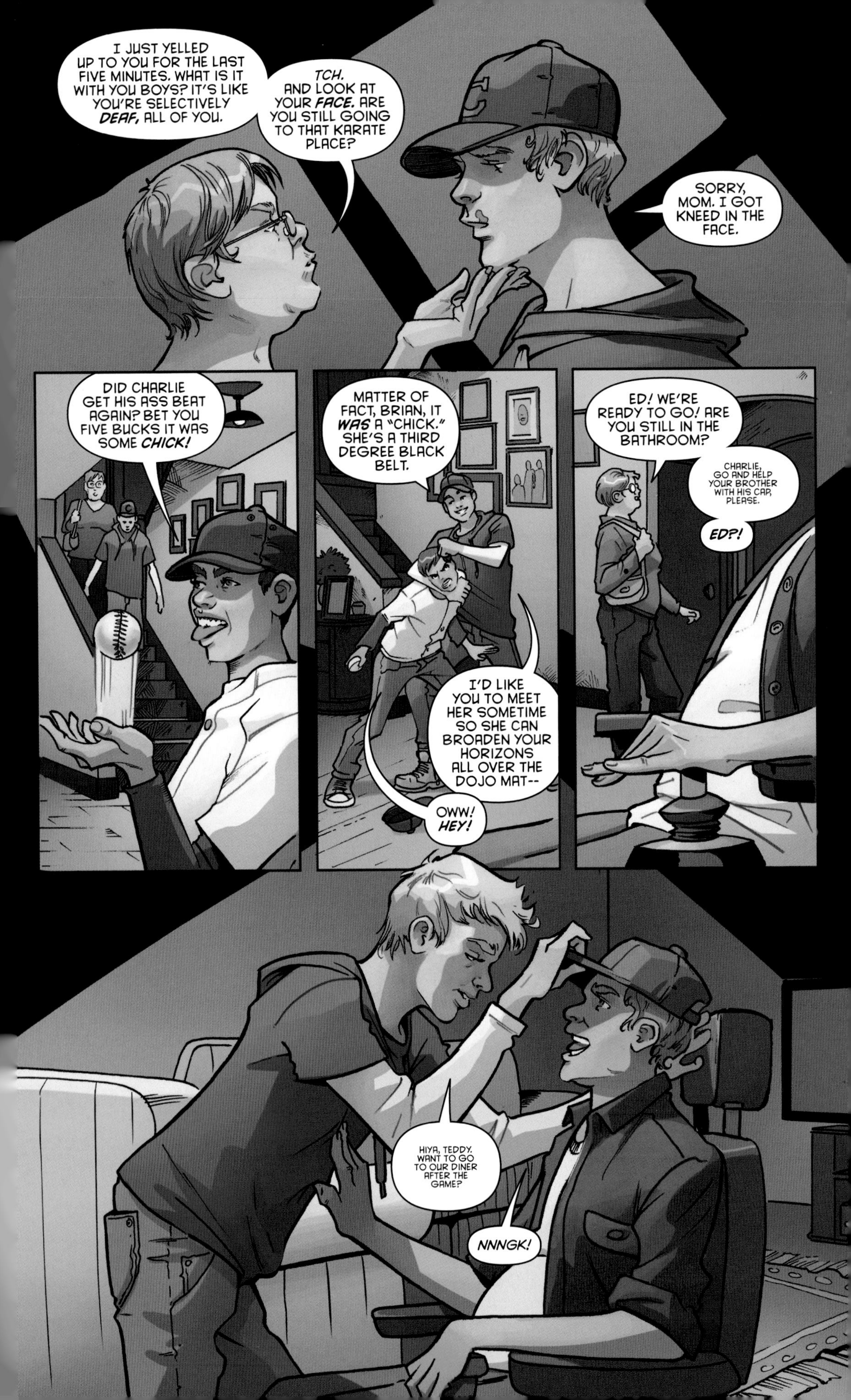
I JUST YELLED UP TO YOU FOR THE LAST FIVE MINUTES. WHAT IS IT WITH YOU BOYS? IT'S LIKE YOU'RE SELECTIVELY DEAF, ALL OF YOU.
TCH. AND LOOK AT YOUR FACE. ARE YOU STILL GOING TO THAT KARATE PLACE?
SORRY, MOM. I GOT KNEED IN THE FACE.
DID CHARLIE GET HIS ASS BEAT AGAIN? BET YOU FIVE BUCKS IT WAS SOME CHICK!
MATTER OF FACT, BRIAN, IT WAS A "CHICK." SHE'S A THIRD DEGREE BLACK BELT.
I'D LIKE YOU TO MEET HER SOMETIME SO SHE CAN BROADEN YOUR HORIZONS ALL OVER THE DOJO MAT--
OWW! HEY!
ED! WE'RE READY TO GO! ARE YOU STILL IN THE BATHROOM?
CHARLIE, GO AND HELP YOUR BROTHER WITH HIS CAP, PLEASE.
ED?!
HIYA, TEDDY. WANT TO GO TO OUR DINER AFTER THE GAME?
NNNGK!

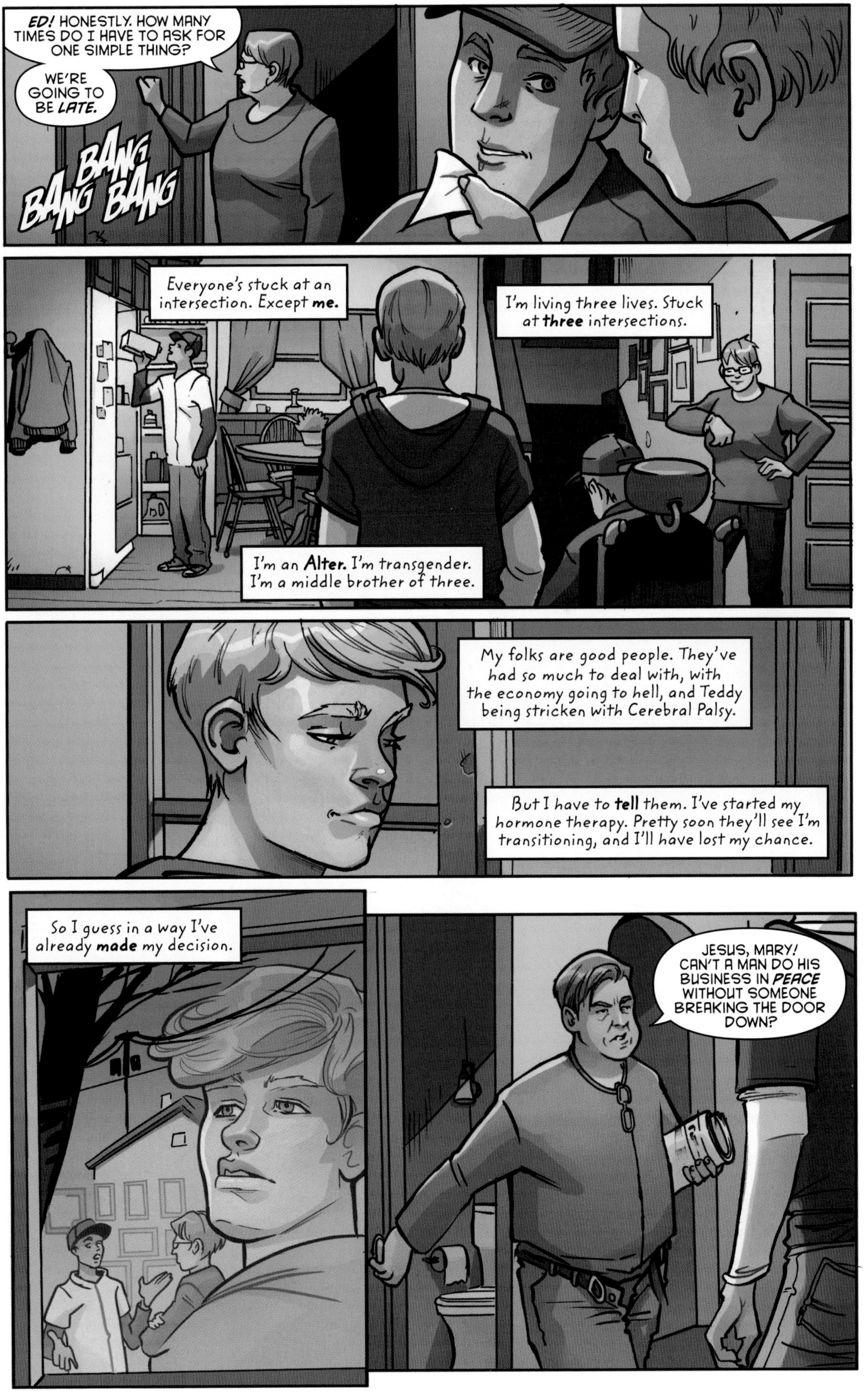

ED! HONESTLY. HOW MANY TIMES DO I HAVE TO ASK FOR ONE SIMPLE THING?
WE'RE GOING TO BE LATE.
BANG BANG BANG BANG
Everyone's stuck at an intersection. Except me.
I'm living three lives. Stuck at three intersections.
I'm an Alter. I'm transgender. I'm a middle brother of three.
My folks are good people. They've had so much to deal with, with the economy going to hell, and Teddy being stricken with Cerebral Palsy.
But I have to tell them. I've started my hormone therapy. Pretty soon they'll see I'm transitioning, and I'll have lost my chance.
So I guess in a way I've already made my decision.
JESUS, MARY! CAN'T A MAN DO HIS BUSINESS IN PEACE WITHOUT SOMEONE BREAKING THE DOOR DOWN?

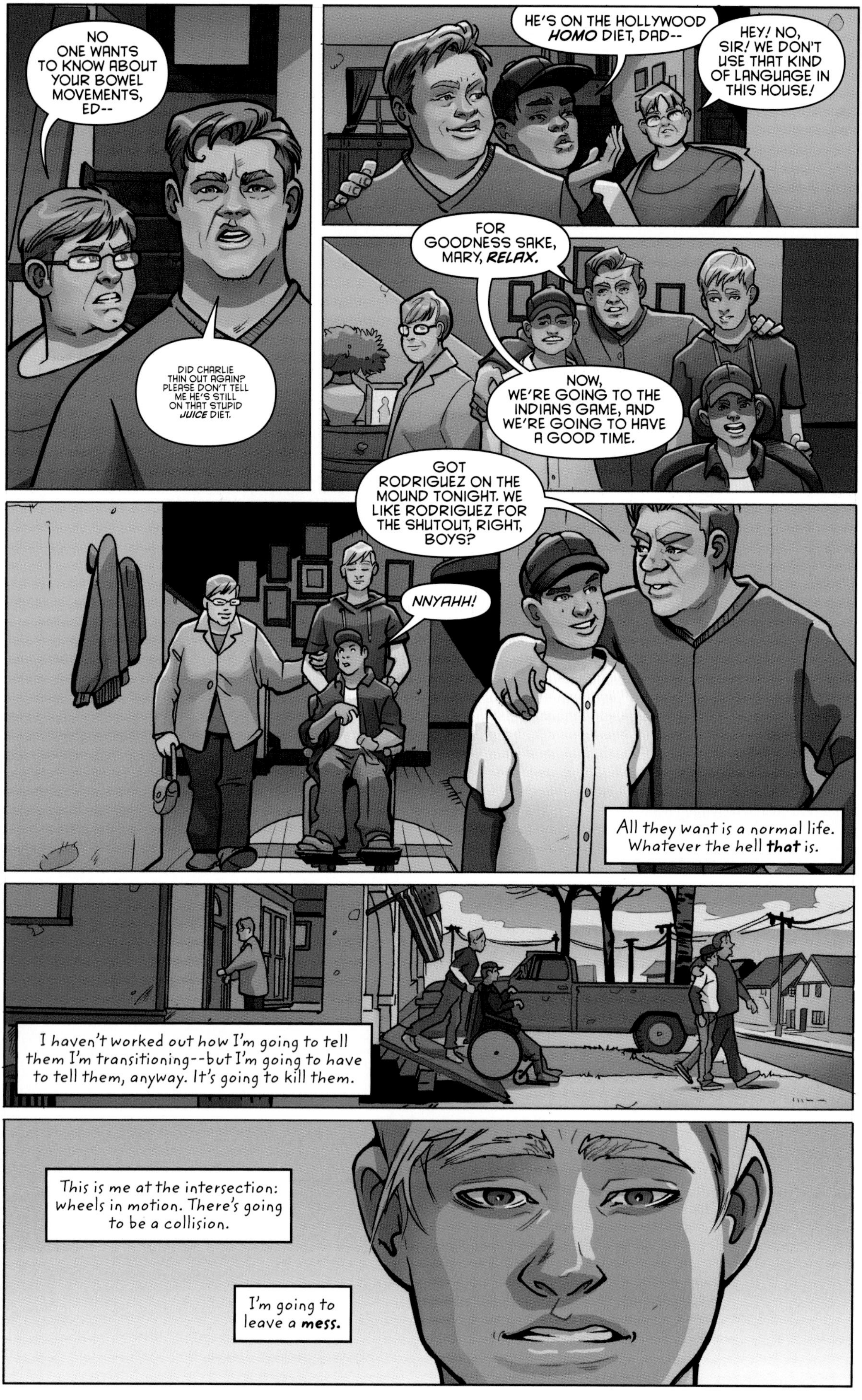
NO ONE WANTS TO KNOW ABOUT YOUR BOWEL MOVEMENTS, ED--
DID CHARLIE THIN OUT AGAIN? PLEASE DON'T TELL ME HE'S STILL ON THAT STUPID JUICE DIET.
HE'S ON THE HOLLYWOOD HOMO DIET, DAD--
HEY! NO, SIR! WE DON'T USE THAT KIND OF LANGUAGE IN THIS HOUSE!
FOR GOODNESS SAKE, MARY, RELAX.
NOW, WE'RE GOING TO THE INDIANS GAME, AND WE'RE GOING TO HAVE A GOOD TIME.
GOT RODRIGUEZ ON THE MOUND TONIGHT. WE LIKE RODRIGUEZ FOR THE SHUTOUT, RIGHT, BOYS?
NNYAHH!
All they want is a normal life. Whatever the hell that is.
I haven't worked out how I'm going to tell them I'm transitioning--but I'm going to have to tell them, anyway. It's going to kill them.
This is me at the intersection: wheels in motion. There's going to be a collision.
I'm going to leave a mess.

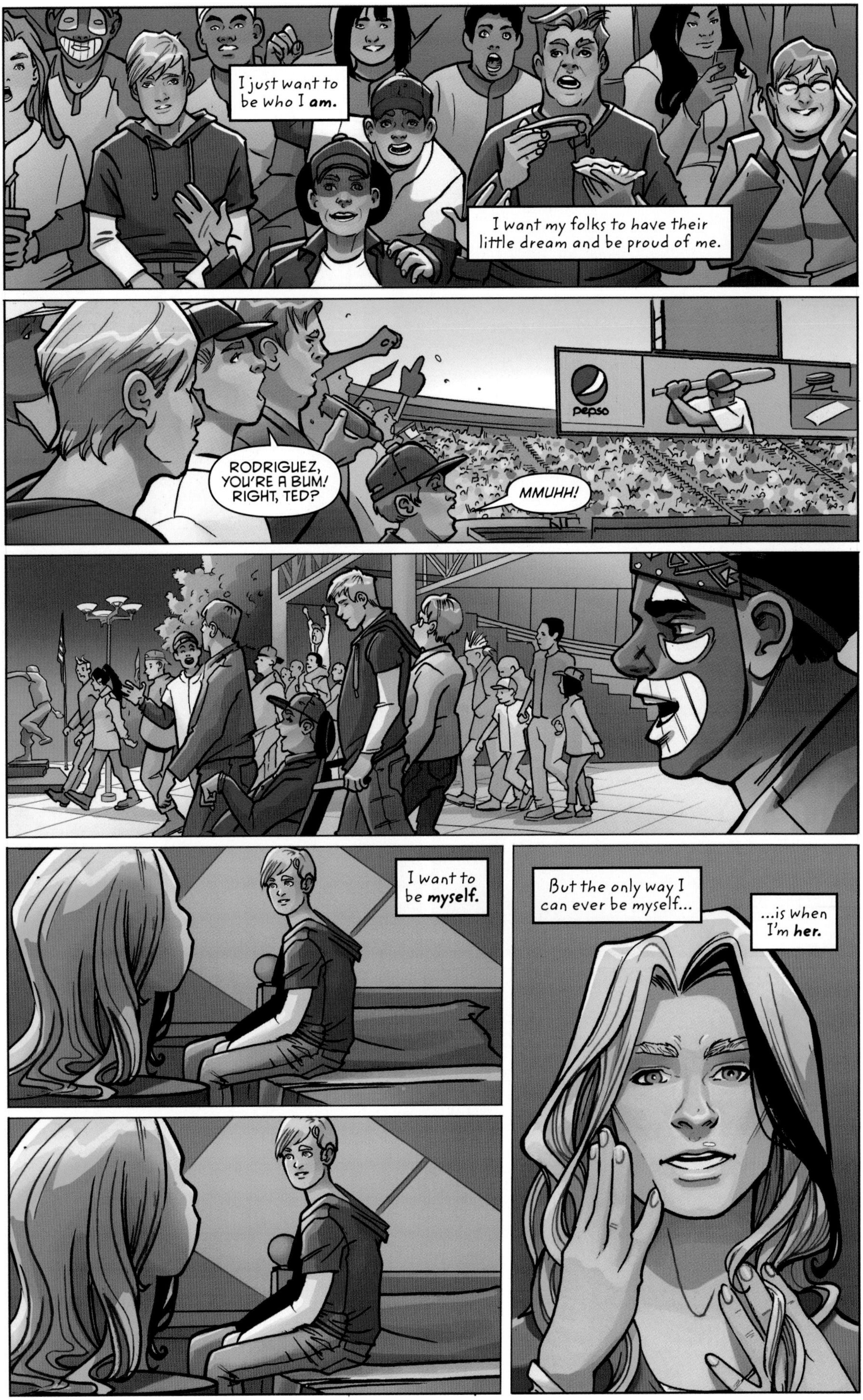
I just want to be who I **am.**
I want my folks to have their little dream and be proud of me.
RODRIGUEZ, YOU'RE A BUM! RIGHT, TED?
MMUHH!
pepsi
I want to be **myself.**
But the only way I can ever be myself...
...is when I'm **her.**

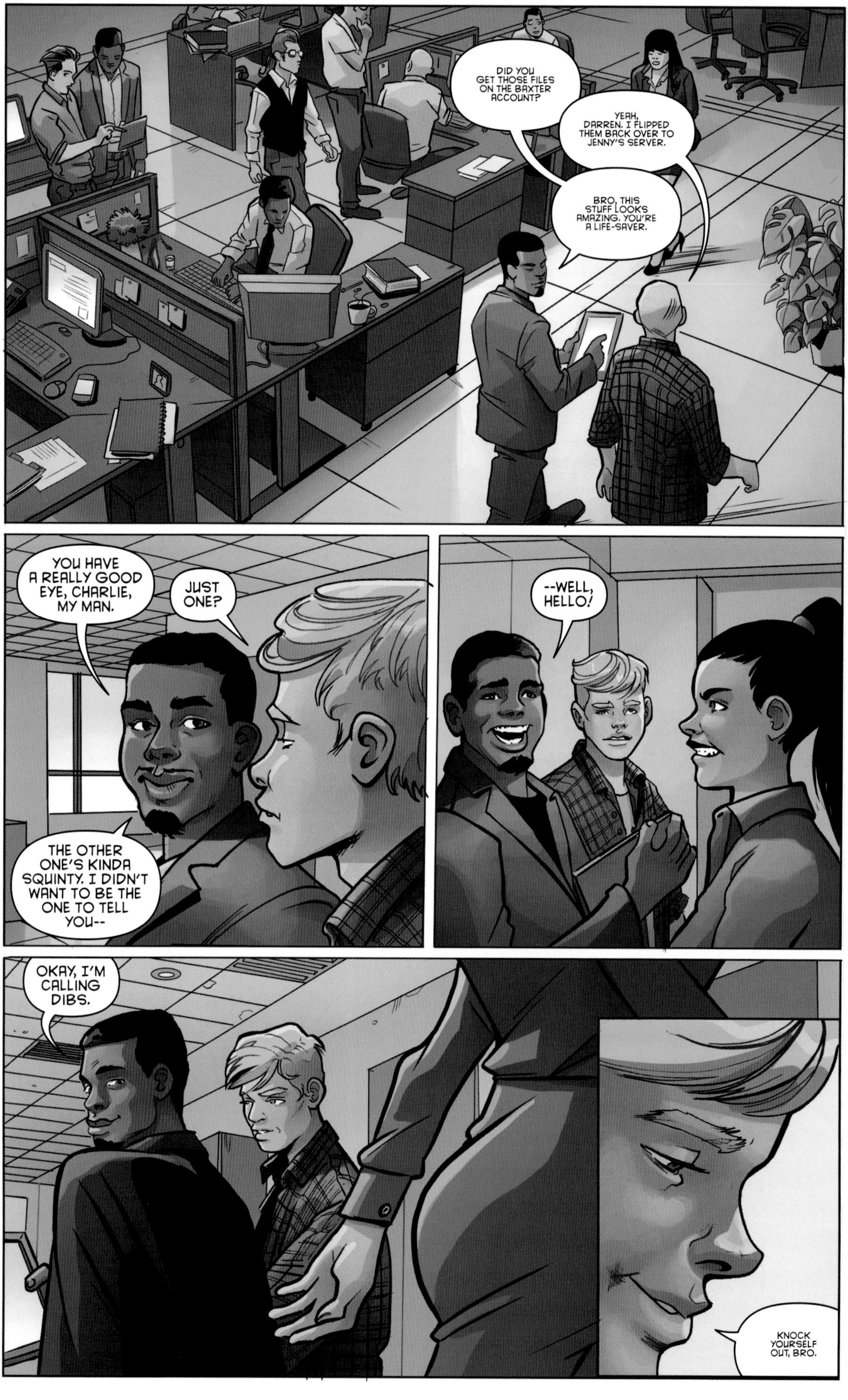
DID YOU GET THOSE FILES ON THE BAXTER ACCOUNT?
YEAH, DARREN. I FLIPPED THEM BACK OVER TO JENNY'S SERVER.
BRO, THIS STUFF LOOKS AMAZING. YOU'RE A LIFE-SAVER.
YOU HAVE A REALLY GOOD EYE, CHARLIE, MY MAN.
JUST ONE?
THE OTHER ONE'S KINDA SQUINTY. I DIDN'T WANT TO BE THE ONE TO TELL YOU--
--WELL, HELLO!
OKAY, I'M CALLING DIBS.
KNOCK YOURSELF OUT, BRO.

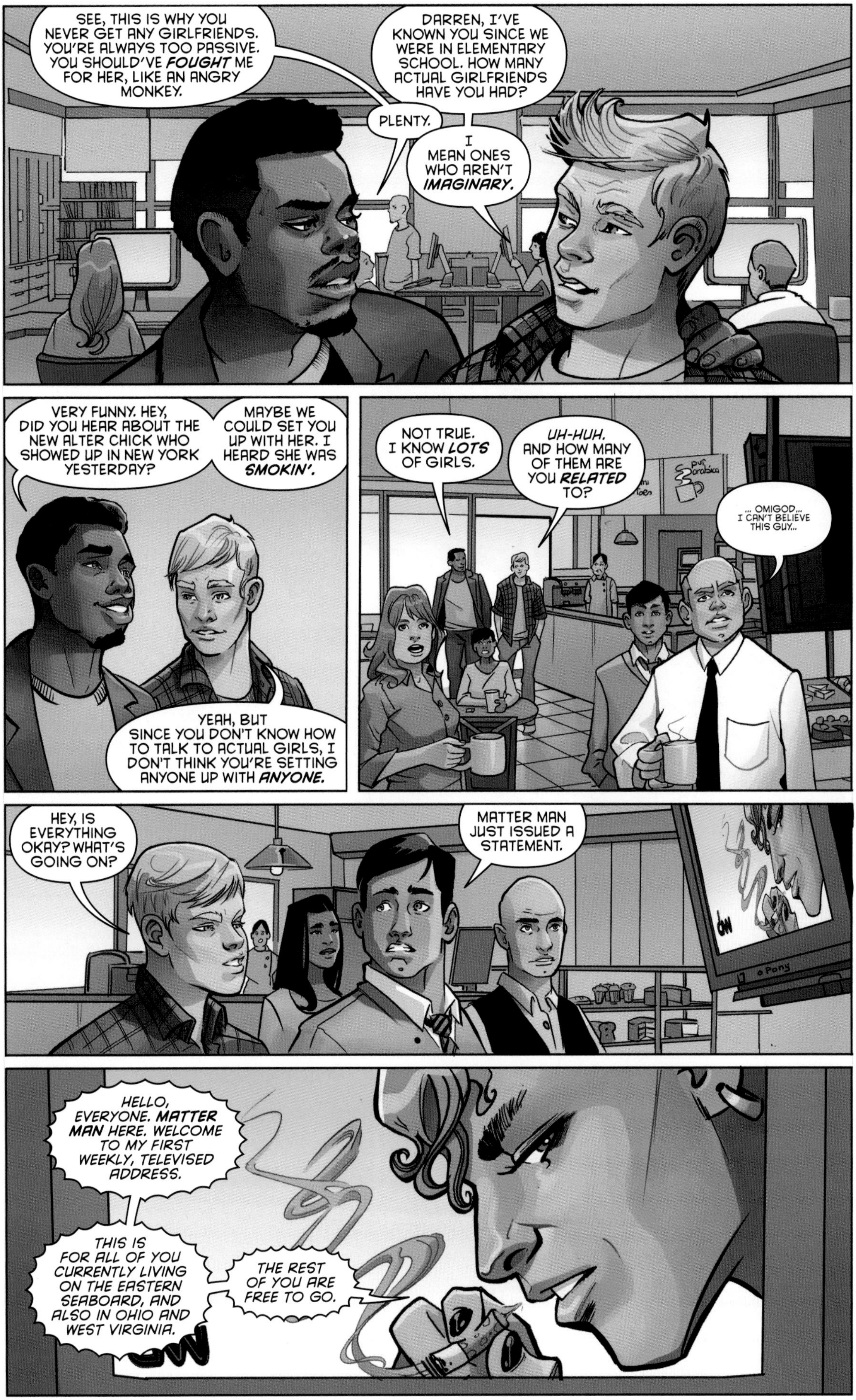

SEE, THIS IS WHY YOU NEVER GET ANY GIRLFRIENDS. YOU'RE ALWAYS TOO PASSIVE. YOU SHOULD'VE *FOUGHT* ME FOR HER, LIKE AN ANGRY MONKEY.
DARREN, I'VE KNOWN YOU SINCE WE WERE IN ELEMENTARY SCHOOL. HOW MANY ACTUAL GIRLFRIENDS HAVE YOU HAD?
PLENTY.
I MEAN ONES WHO AREN'T *IMAGINARY.*
VERY FUNNY. HEY, DID YOU HEAR ABOUT THE NEW ALTER CHICK WHO SHOWED UP IN NEW YORK YESTERDAY?
MAYBE WE COULD SET YOU UP WITH HER. I HEARD SHE WAS *SMOKIN'.*
YEAH, BUT SINCE YOU DON'T KNOW HOW TO TALK TO ACTUAL GIRLS, I DON'T THINK YOU'RE SETTING ANYONE UP WITH *ANYONE.*
NOT TRUE. I KNOW *LOTS* OF GIRLS.
UH-HUH. AND HOW MANY OF THEM ARE YOU *RELATED* TO?
... OMIGOD... I CAN'T BELIEVE THIS GUY...
HEY, IS EVERYTHING OKAY? WHAT'S GOING ON?
MATTER MAN JUST ISSUED A STATEMENT.
*HELLO, EVERYONE. **MATTER MAN** HERE. WELCOME TO MY FIRST WEEKLY, TELEVISED ADDRESS.*
THIS IS FOR ALL OF YOU CURRENTLY LIVING ON THE EASTERN SEABOARD, AND ALSO IN OHIO AND WEST VIRGINIA.
THE REST OF YOU ARE FREE TO GO.

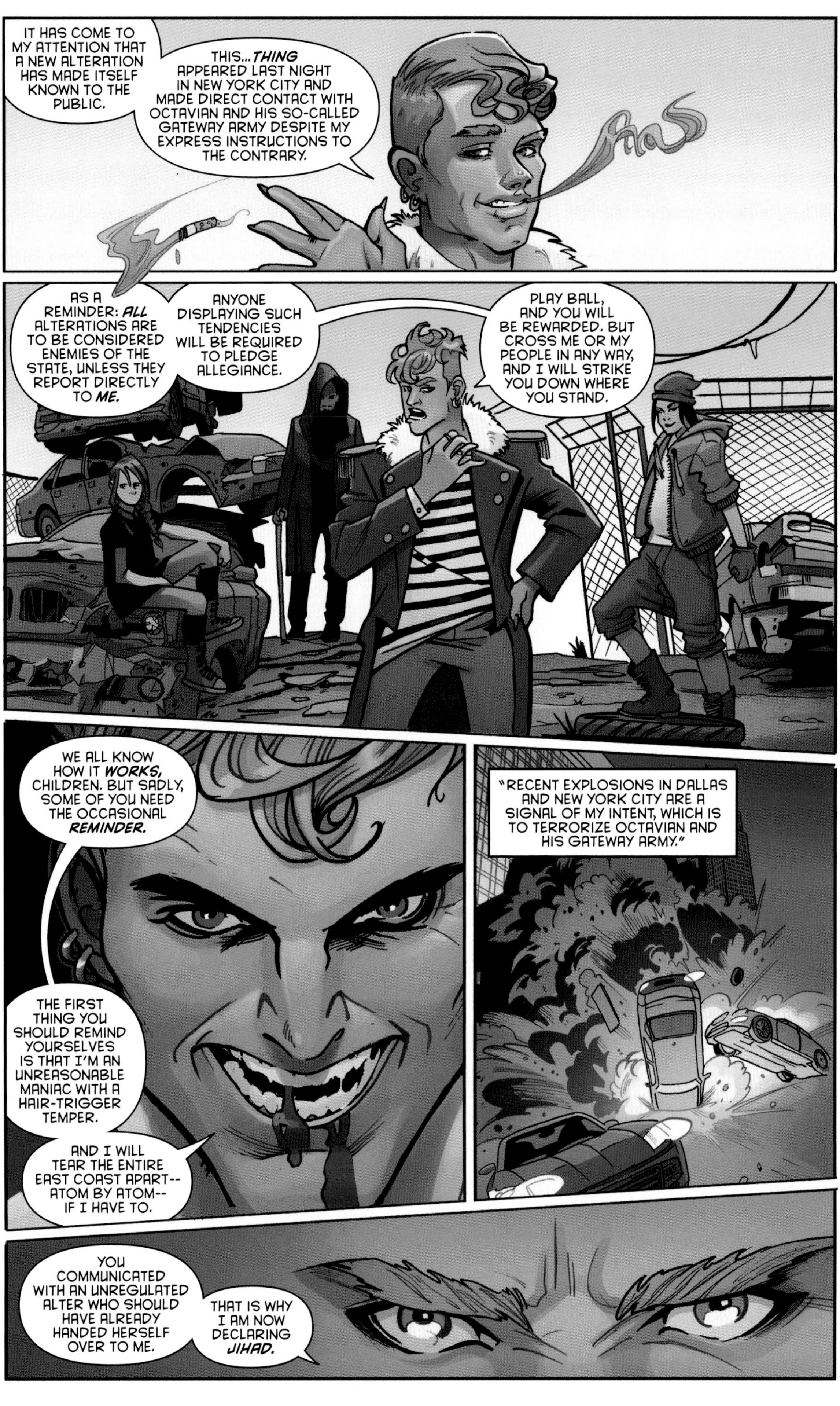
IT HAS COME TO MY ATTENTION THAT A NEW ALTERATION HAS MADE ITSELF KNOWN TO THE PUBLIC.
THIS...THING APPEARED LAST NIGHT IN NEW YORK CITY AND MADE DIRECT CONTACT WITH OCTAVIAN AND HIS SO-CALLED GATEWAY ARMY DESPITE MY EXPRESS INSTRUCTIONS TO THE CONTRARY.
AS A REMINDER: ALL ALTERATIONS ARE TO BE CONSIDERED ENEMIES OF THE STATE, UNLESS THEY REPORT DIRECTLY TO ME.
ANYONE DISPLAYING SUCH TENDENCIES WILL BE REQUIRED TO PLEDGE ALLEGIANCE.
PLAY BALL, AND YOU WILL BE REWARDED. BUT CROSS ME OR MY PEOPLE IN ANY WAY, AND I WILL STRIKE YOU DOWN WHERE YOU STAND.
WE ALL KNOW HOW IT WORKS, CHILDREN. BUT SADLY, SOME OF YOU NEED THE OCCASIONAL REMINDER.
THE FIRST THING YOU SHOULD REMIND YOURSELVES IS THAT I'M AN UNREASONABLE MANIAC WITH A HAIR-TRIGGER TEMPER.
AND I WILL TEAR THE ENTIRE EAST COAST APART--ATOM BY ATOM--IF I HAVE TO.
"RECENT EXPLOSIONS IN DALLAS AND NEW YORK CITY ARE A SIGNAL OF MY INTENT, WHICH IS TO TERRORIZE OCTAVIAN AND HIS GATEWAY ARMY."
YOU COMMUNICATED WITH AN UNREGULATED ALTER WHO SHOULD HAVE ALREADY HANDED HERSELF OVER TO ME.
THAT IS WHY I AM NOW DECLARING JIHAD.

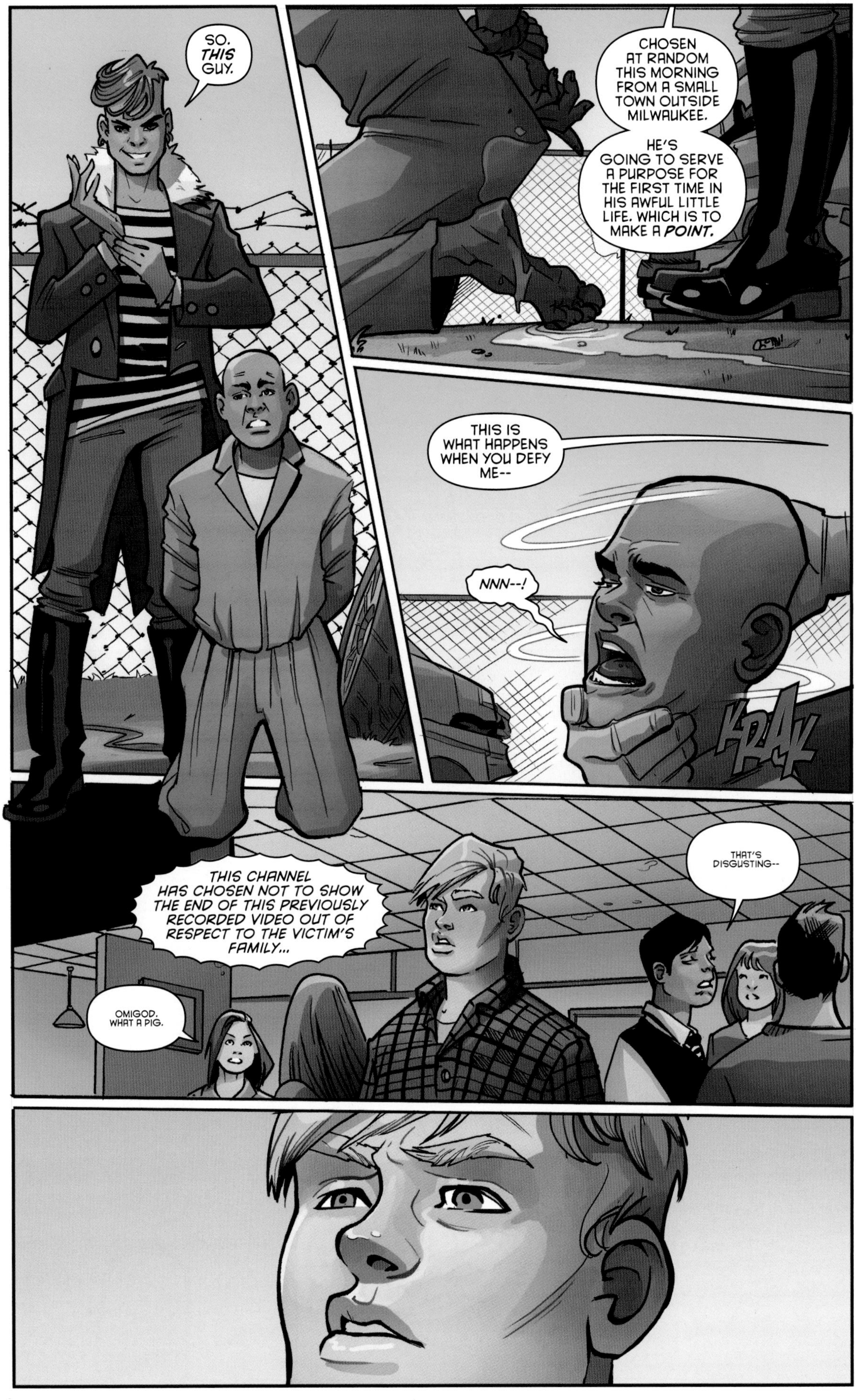
SO. THIS GUY.
CHOSEN AT RANDOM THIS MORNING FROM A SMALL TOWN OUTSIDE MILWAUKEE.
HE'S GOING TO SERVE A PURPOSE FOR THE FIRST TIME IN HIS AWFUL LITTLE LIFE. WHICH IS TO MAKE A POINT.
THIS IS WHAT HAPPENS WHEN YOU DEFY ME--
NNN--!
KRAK
THIS CHANNEL HAS CHOSEN NOT TO SHOW THE END OF THIS PREVIOUSLY RECORDED VIDEO OUT OF RESPECT TO THE VICTIM'S FAMILY...
THAT'S DISGUSTING--
OMIGOD. WHAT A PIG.

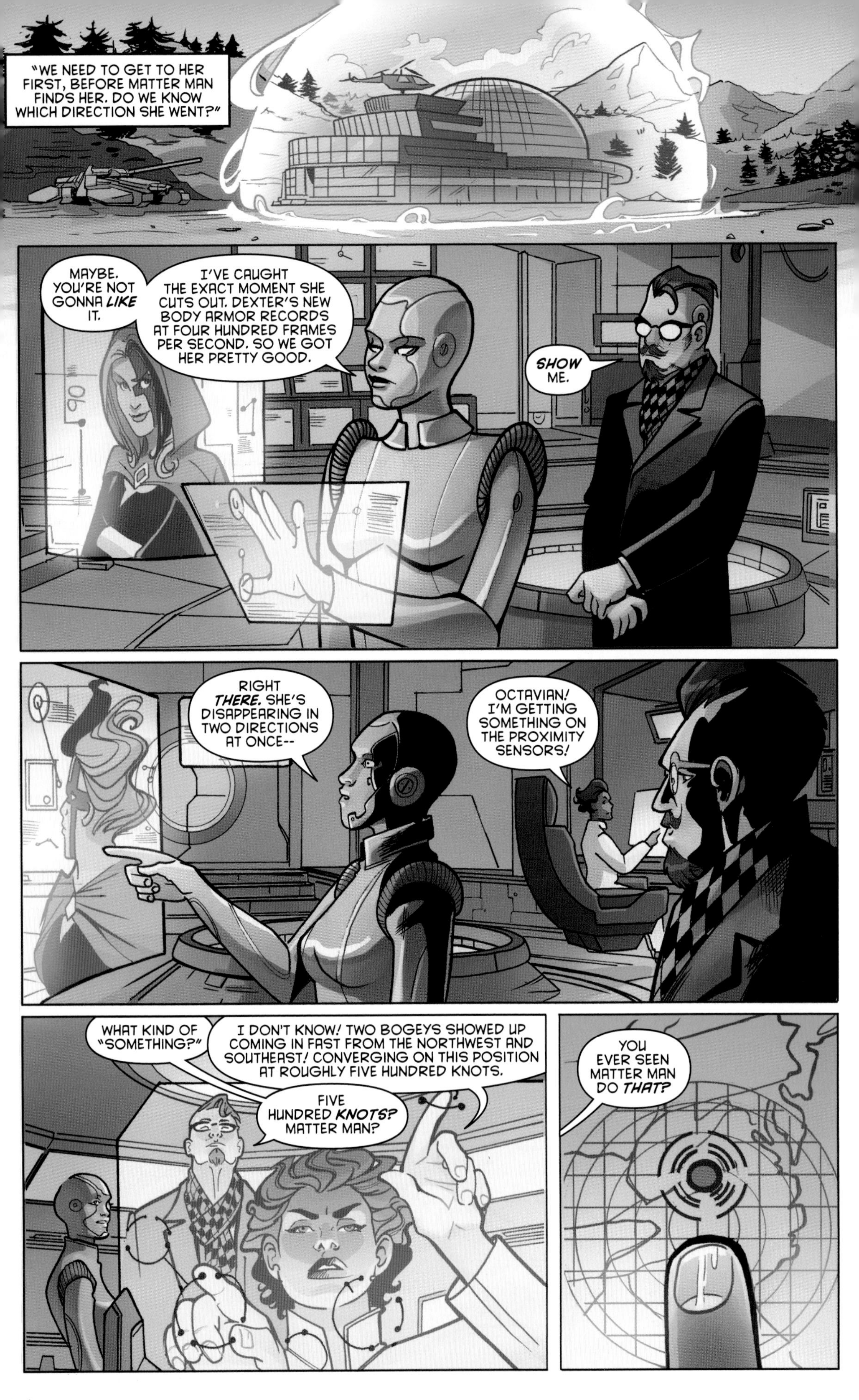
"WE NEED TO GET TO HER FIRST, BEFORE MATTER MAN FINDS HER. DO WE KNOW WHICH DIRECTION SHE WENT?"
MAYBE. YOU'RE NOT GONNA *LIKE* IT.
I'VE CAUGHT THE EXACT MOMENT SHE CUTS OUT. DEXTER'S NEW BODY ARMOR RECORDS AT FOUR HUNDRED FRAMES PER SECOND. SO WE GOT HER PRETTY GOOD.
SHOW ME.
RIGHT *THERE.* SHE'S DISAPPEARING IN TWO DIRECTIONS AT ONCE--
OCTAVIAN! I'M GETTING SOMETHING ON THE PROXIMITY SENSORS!
WHAT KIND OF "SOMETHING?"
I DON'T KNOW! TWO BOGEYS SHOWED UP COMING IN FAST FROM THE NORTHWEST AND SOUTHEAST! CONVERGING ON THIS POSITION AT ROUGHLY FIVE HUNDRED KNOTS.
FIVE HUNDRED *KNOTS?* MATTER MAN?
YOU EVER SEEN MATTER MAN DO *THAT?*

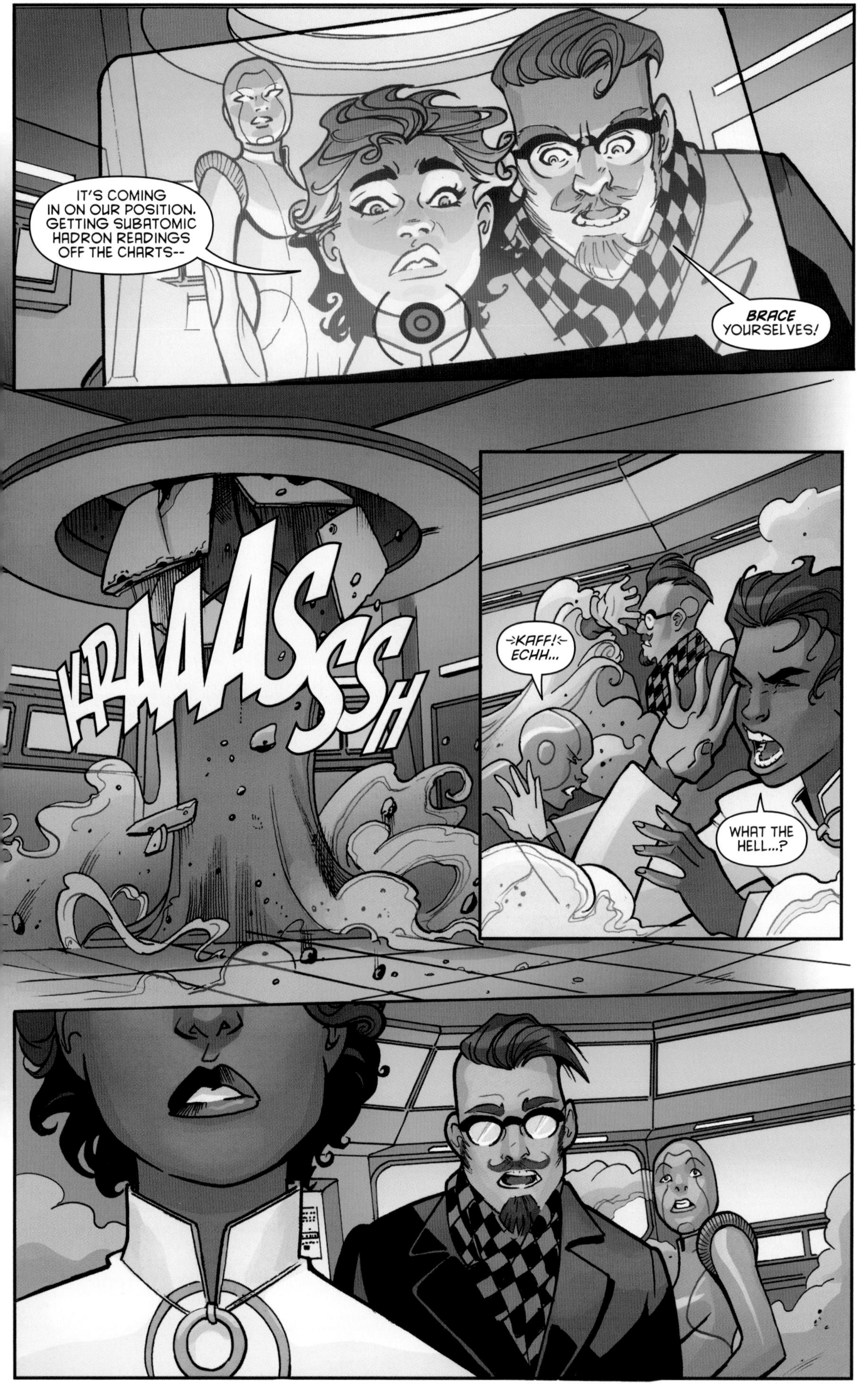

IT'S COMING IN ON OUR POSITION. GETTING SUBATOMIC HADRON READINGS OFF THE CHARTS--
BRACE YOURSELVES!
KRAAASSSH
KAFF! ECHH...
WHAT THE HELL...?

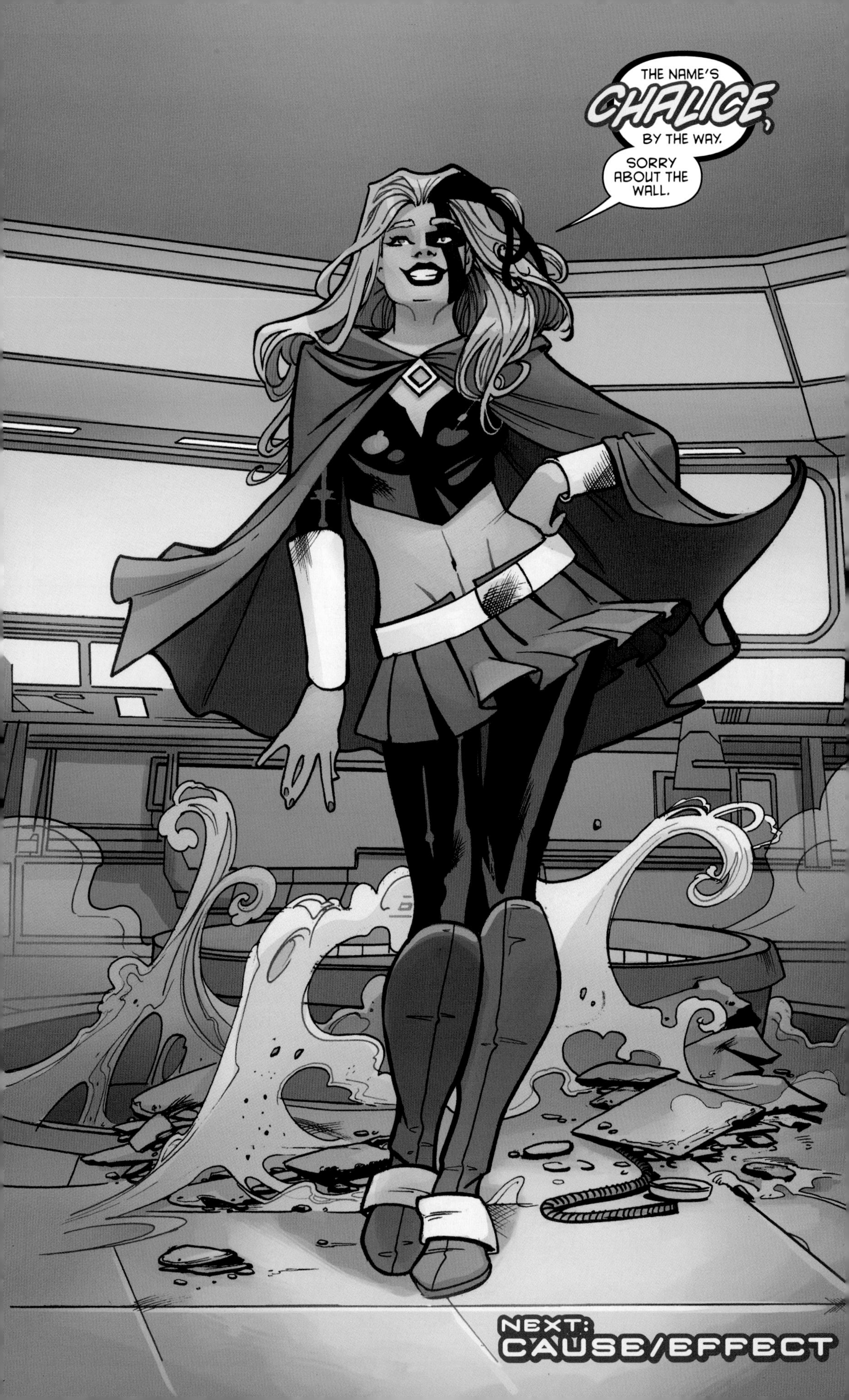
THE NAME'S CHALICE, BY THE WAY.
SORRY ABOUT THE WALL.
NEXT: CAUSE/EFFECT

"EGO SUM"

2

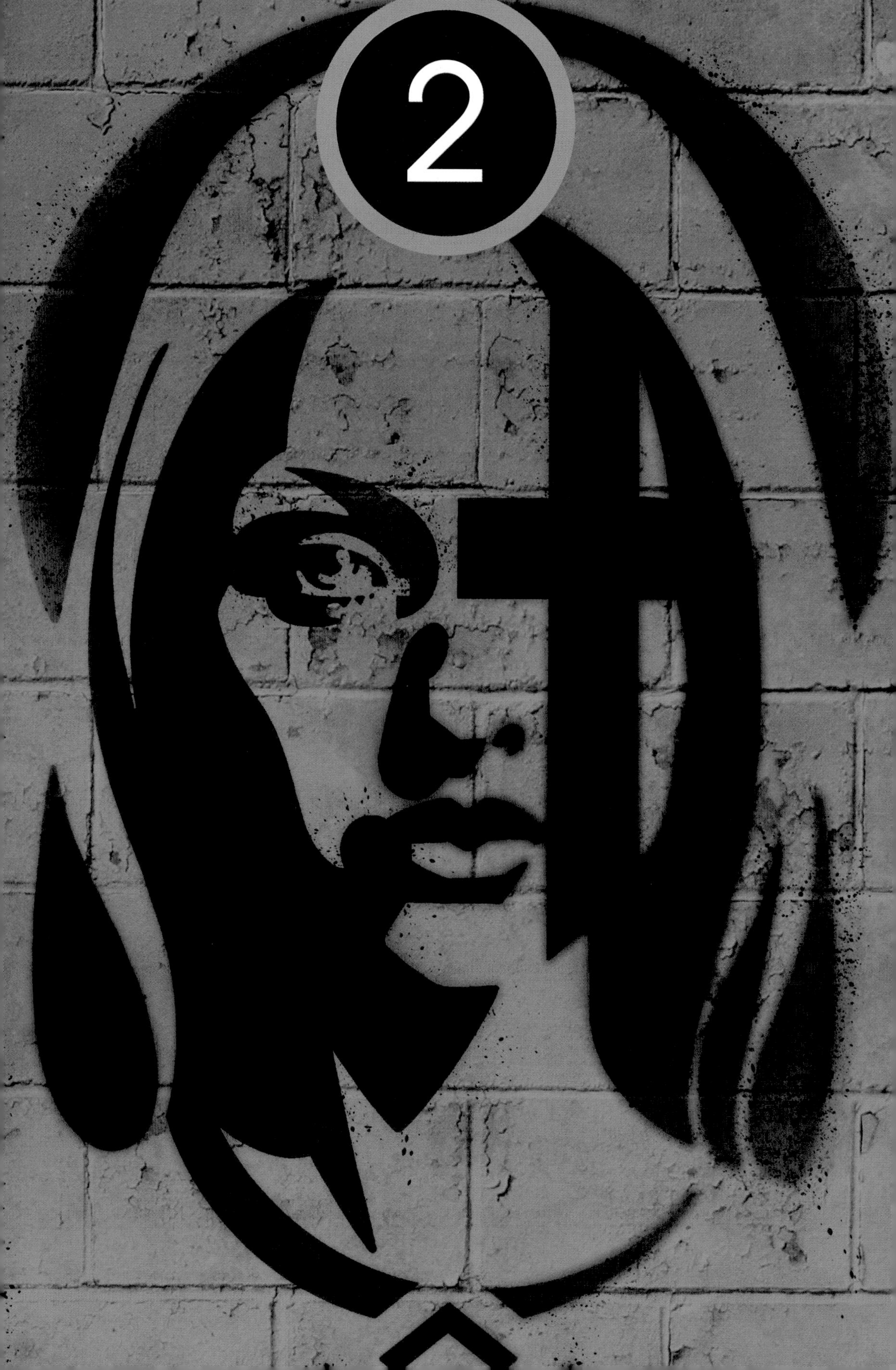

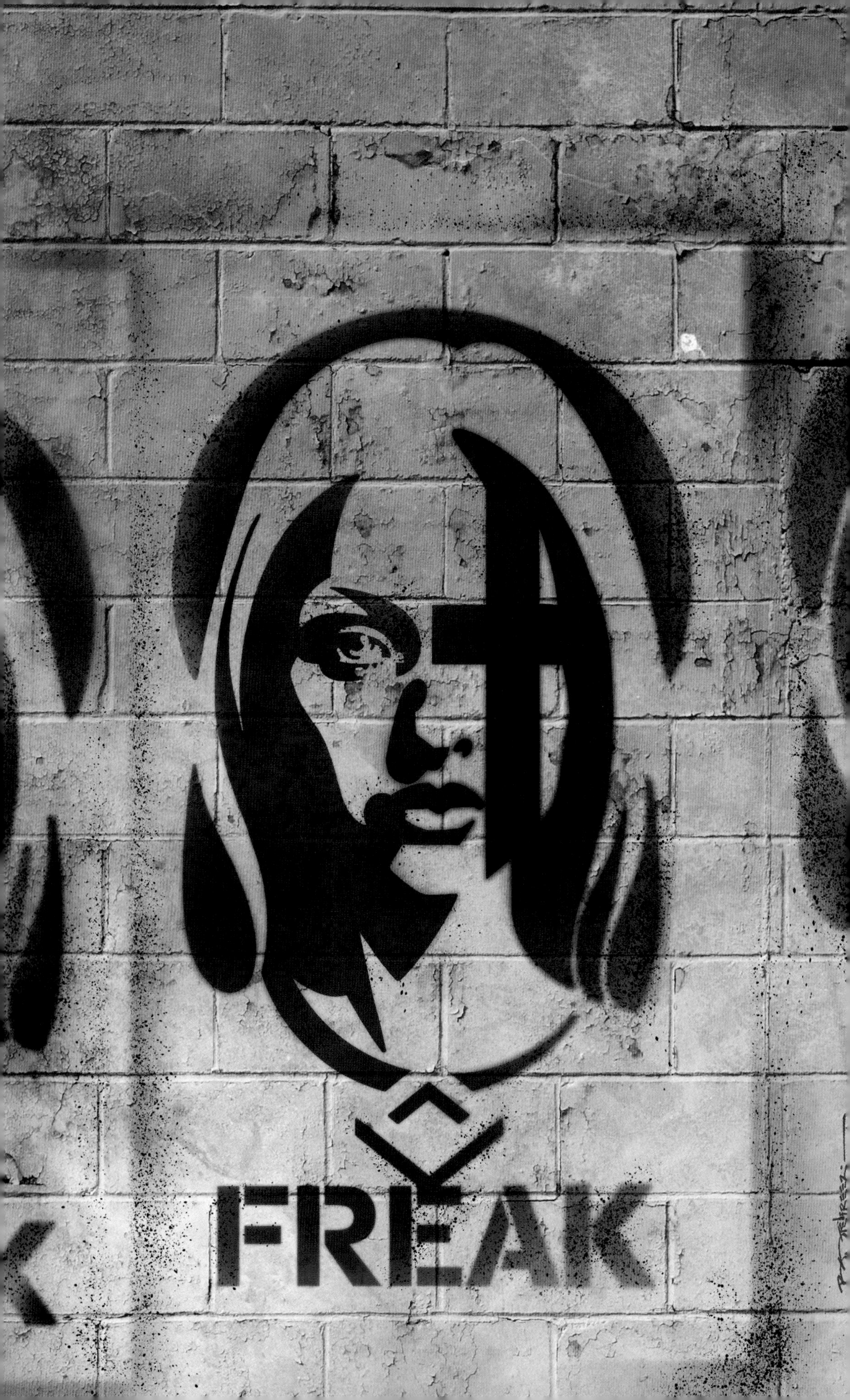
FREAK

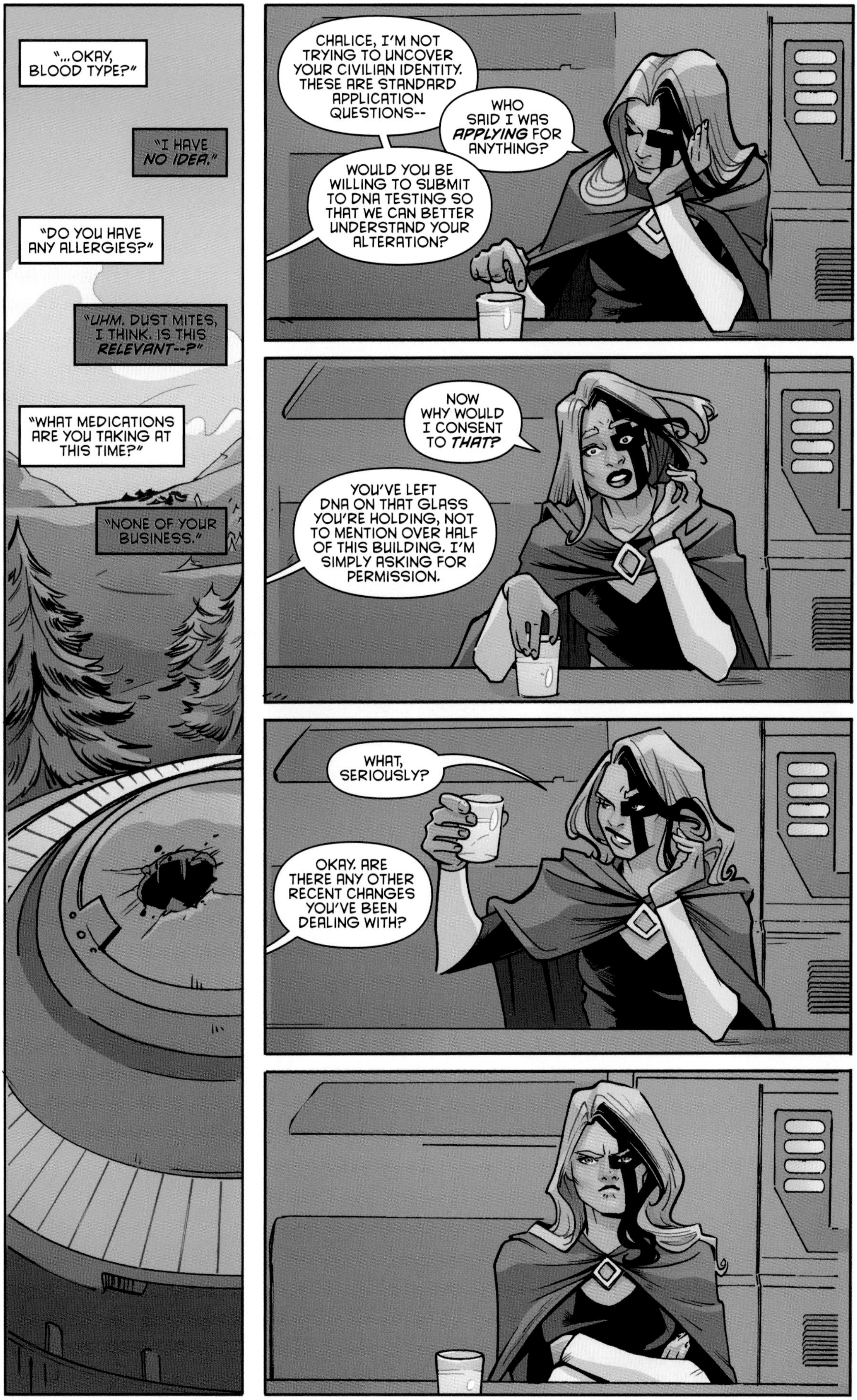
"...OKAY, BLOOD TYPE?"
"I HAVE NO IDEA."
"DO YOU HAVE ANY ALLERGIES?"
"UHM. DUST MITES, I THINK. IS THIS RELEVANT--?"
"WHAT MEDICATIONS ARE YOU TAKING AT THIS TIME?"
"NONE OF YOUR BUSINESS."
CHALICE, I'M NOT TRYING TO UNCOVER YOUR CIVILIAN IDENTITY. THESE ARE STANDARD APPLICATION QUESTIONS--
WHO SAID I WAS APPLYING FOR ANYTHING?
WOULD YOU BE WILLING TO SUBMIT TO DNA TESTING SO THAT WE CAN BETTER UNDERSTAND YOUR ALTERATION?
NOW WHY WOULD I CONSENT TO THAT?
YOU'VE LEFT DNA ON THAT GLASS YOU'RE HOLDING, NOT TO MENTION OVER HALF OF THIS BUILDING. I'M SIMPLY ASKING FOR PERMISSION.
WHAT, SERIOUSLY?
OKAY. ARE THERE ANY OTHER RECENT CHANGES YOU'VE BEEN DEALING WITH?

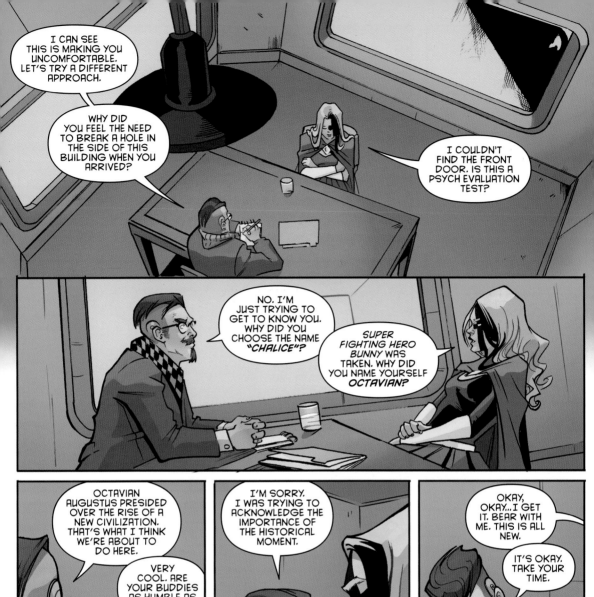

I CAN SEE THIS IS MAKING YOU UNCOMFORTABLE. LET'S TRY A DIFFERENT APPROACH.

WHY DID YOU FEEL THE NEED TO BREAK A HOLE IN THE SIDE OF THIS BUILDING WHEN YOU ARRIVED?

I COULDN'T FIND THE FRONT DOOR. IS THIS A PSYCH EVALUATION TEST?

NO. I'M JUST TRYING TO GET TO KNOW YOU. WHY DID YOU CHOOSE THE NAME "CHALICE"?

SUPER FIGHTING HERO BUNNY WAS TAKEN. WHY DID YOU NAME YOURSELF OCTAVIAN?

OCTAVIAN AUGUSTUS PRESIDED OVER THE RISE OF A NEW CIVILIZATION. THAT'S WHAT I THINK WE'RE ABOUT TO DO HERE.

VERY COOL. ARE YOUR BUDDIES AS HUMBLE AS YOU?

I'M SORRY. I WAS TRYING TO ACKNOWLEDGE THE IMPORTANCE OF THE HISTORICAL MOMENT.

LOOK, CHALICE, I'D LIKE TO BE A FRIEND, IF YOU'LL ALLOW IT. COMING TO TERMS WITH AN ALTERATION CAN BE EXTREMELY COMPLEX--

OKAY, OKAY... I GET IT. BEAR WITH ME. THIS IS ALL NEW.

IT'S OKAY. TAKE YOUR TIME.

TO ANSWER YOUR QUESTION: KNOCKING HOLES IN PEOPLE'S WALLS IS NOT REALLY ME. I MEAN, NOT IN MY DAILY LIFE.

I'M NOT LIKE THAT. BUT SINCE MY ALTERATION, IT'S LIKE I CAN DO ANYTHING. SO THAT'S KIND OF A CONFIDENCE BUILDER. I CAN'T TELL IF I'M MORE MYSELF RIGHT NOW, OR LESS.

BUT I KINDA LIKE IT.

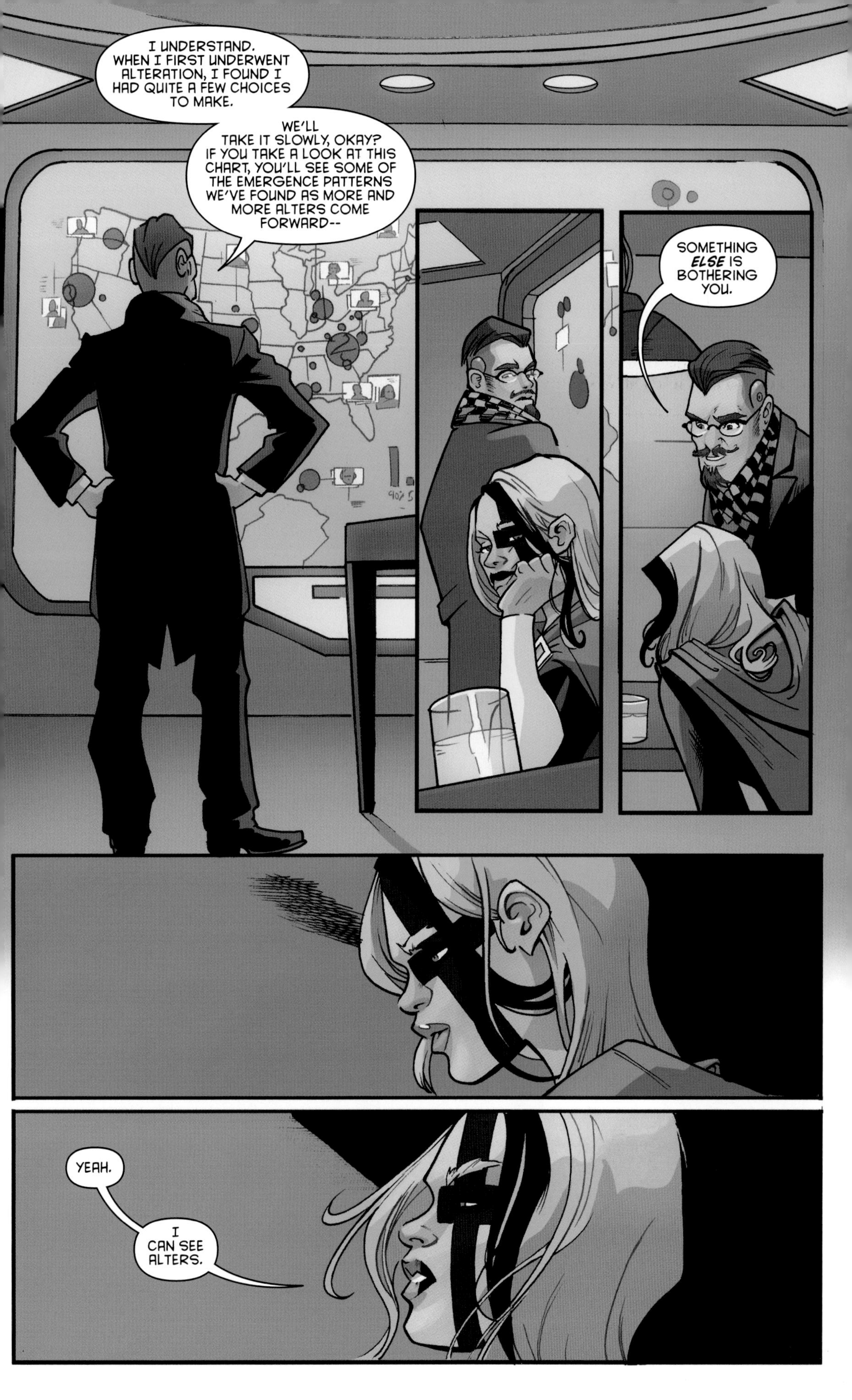
I UNDERSTAND. WHEN I FIRST UNDERWENT ALTERATION, I FOUND I HAD QUITE A FEW CHOICES TO MAKE.
WE'LL TAKE IT SLOWLY, OKAY? IF YOU TAKE A LOOK AT THIS CHART, YOU'LL SEE SOME OF THE EMERGENCE PATTERNS WE'VE FOUND AS MORE AND MORE ALTERS COME FORWARD--
SOMETHING ELSE IS BOTHERING YOU.
YEAH.
I CAN SEE ALTERS.

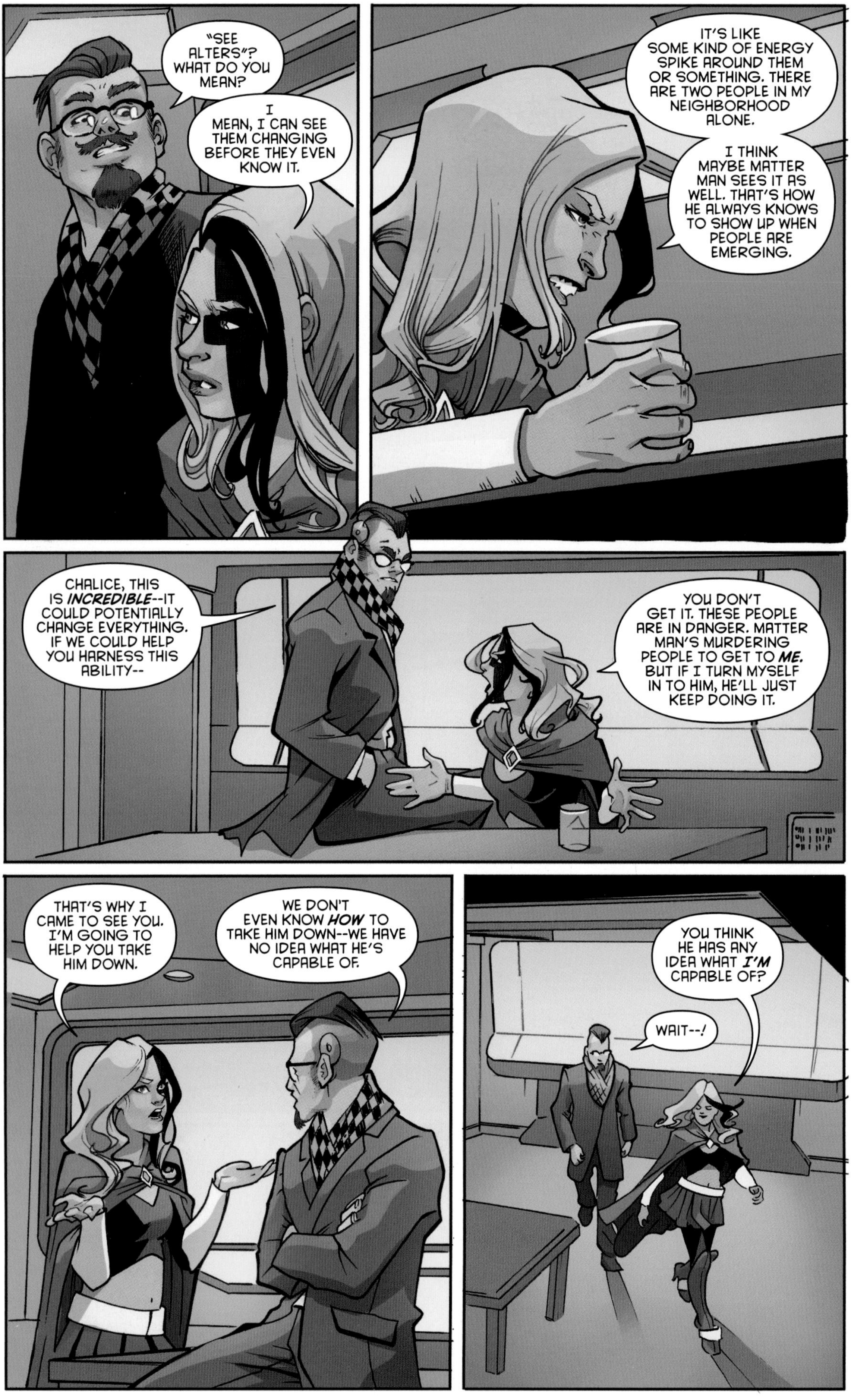
"SEE ALTERS"? WHAT DO YOU MEAN?
I MEAN, I CAN SEE THEM CHANGING BEFORE THEY EVEN KNOW IT.
IT'S LIKE SOME KIND OF ENERGY SPIKE AROUND THEM OR SOMETHING. THERE ARE TWO PEOPLE IN MY NEIGHBORHOOD ALONE.
I THINK MAYBE MATTER MAN SEES IT AS WELL. THAT'S HOW HE ALWAYS KNOWS TO SHOW UP WHEN PEOPLE ARE EMERGING.
CHALICE, THIS IS *INCREDIBLE*--IT COULD POTENTIALLY CHANGE EVERYTHING. IF WE COULD HELP YOU HARNESS THIS ABILITY--
YOU DON'T GET IT. THESE PEOPLE ARE IN DANGER. MATTER MAN'S MURDERING PEOPLE TO GET TO *ME.* BUT IF I TURN MYSELF IN TO HIM, HE'LL JUST KEEP DOING IT.
THAT'S WHY I CAME TO SEE YOU. I'M GOING TO HELP YOU TAKE HIM DOWN.
WE DON'T EVEN KNOW *HOW* TO TAKE HIM DOWN--WE HAVE NO IDEA WHAT HE'S CAPABLE OF.
YOU THINK HE HAS ANY IDEA WHAT *I'M* CAPABLE OF?
WAIT--!

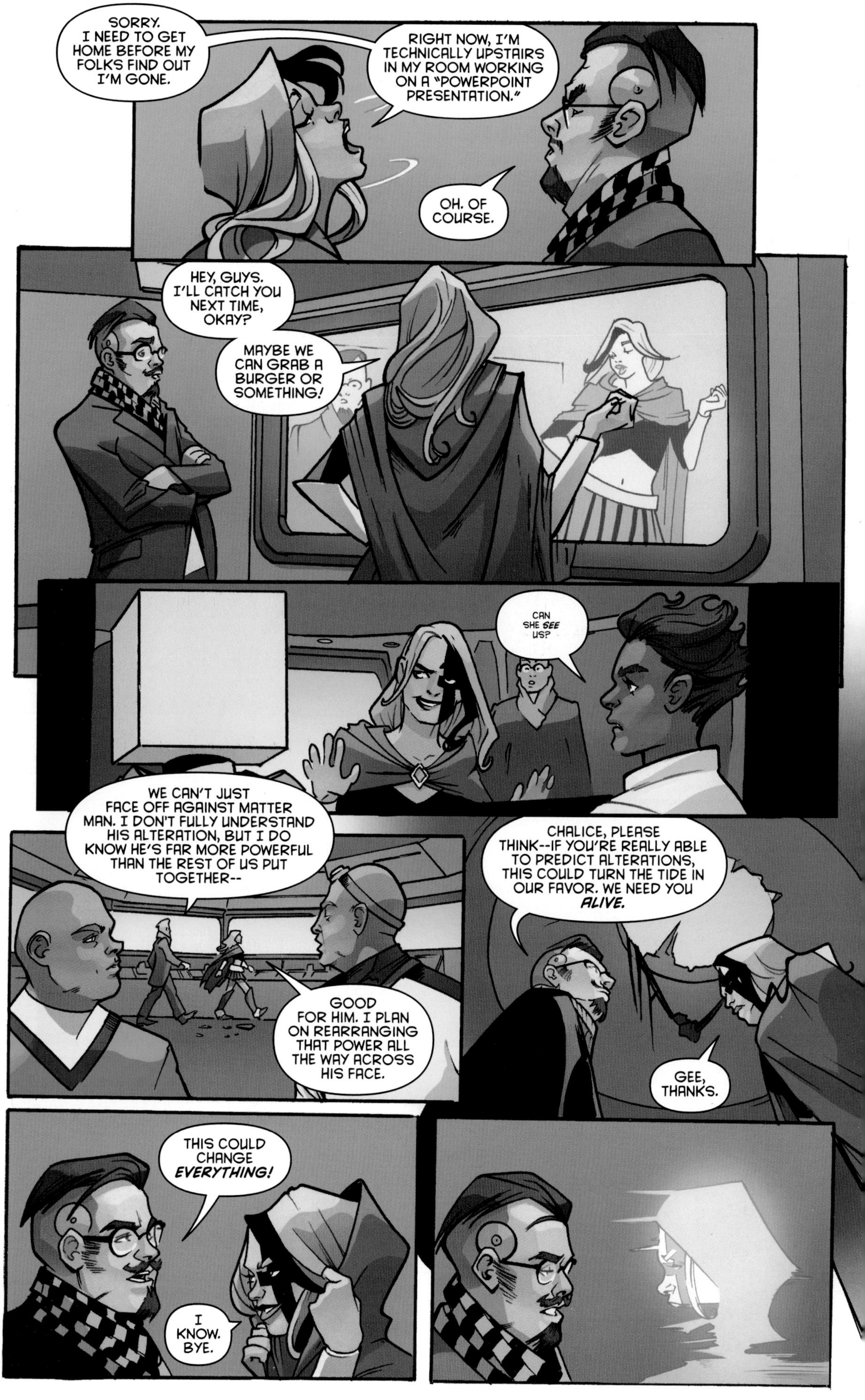
SORRY. I NEED TO GET HOME BEFORE MY FOLKS FIND OUT I'M GONE.
RIGHT NOW, I'M TECHNICALLY UPSTAIRS IN MY ROOM WORKING ON A "POWERPOINT PRESENTATION."
OH. OF COURSE.
HEY, GUYS. I'LL CATCH YOU NEXT TIME, OKAY?
MAYBE WE CAN GRAB A BURGER OR SOMETHING!
CAN SHE *SEE* US?
WE CAN'T JUST FACE OFF AGAINST MATTER MAN. I DON'T FULLY UNDERSTAND HIS ALTERATION, BUT I DO KNOW HE'S FAR MORE POWERFUL THAN THE REST OF US PUT TOGETHER--
GOOD FOR HIM. I PLAN ON REARRANGING THAT POWER ALL THE WAY ACROSS HIS FACE.
CHALICE, PLEASE THINK--IF YOU'RE REALLY ABLE TO PREDICT ALTERATIONS, THIS COULD TURN THE TIDE IN OUR FAVOR. WE NEED YOU *ALIVE.*
GEE, THANKS.
THIS COULD CHANGE *EVERYTHING!*
I KNOW. BYE.

And so this is **me,** dear Diary, stranded in my own personal intersection. The cat's out of the bag. I can see Alters, and I think Matter Man can, as well.

Half of me thinks I should run away, and the other half thinks I should run headfirst at the problem.

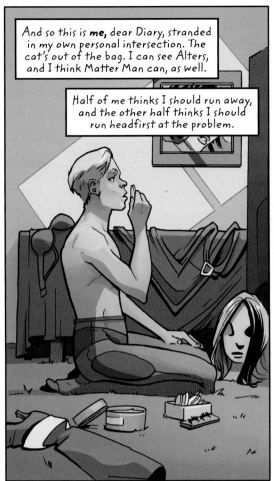

I'm on estrogen now. Means I'm on a **timer.** My family's going to find out, whether I like it or not.

But I'm also transitioning into an Alter. So how much do I tell them?

I feel like I'm just taking off one costume...

...and swapping it for a **different** one.

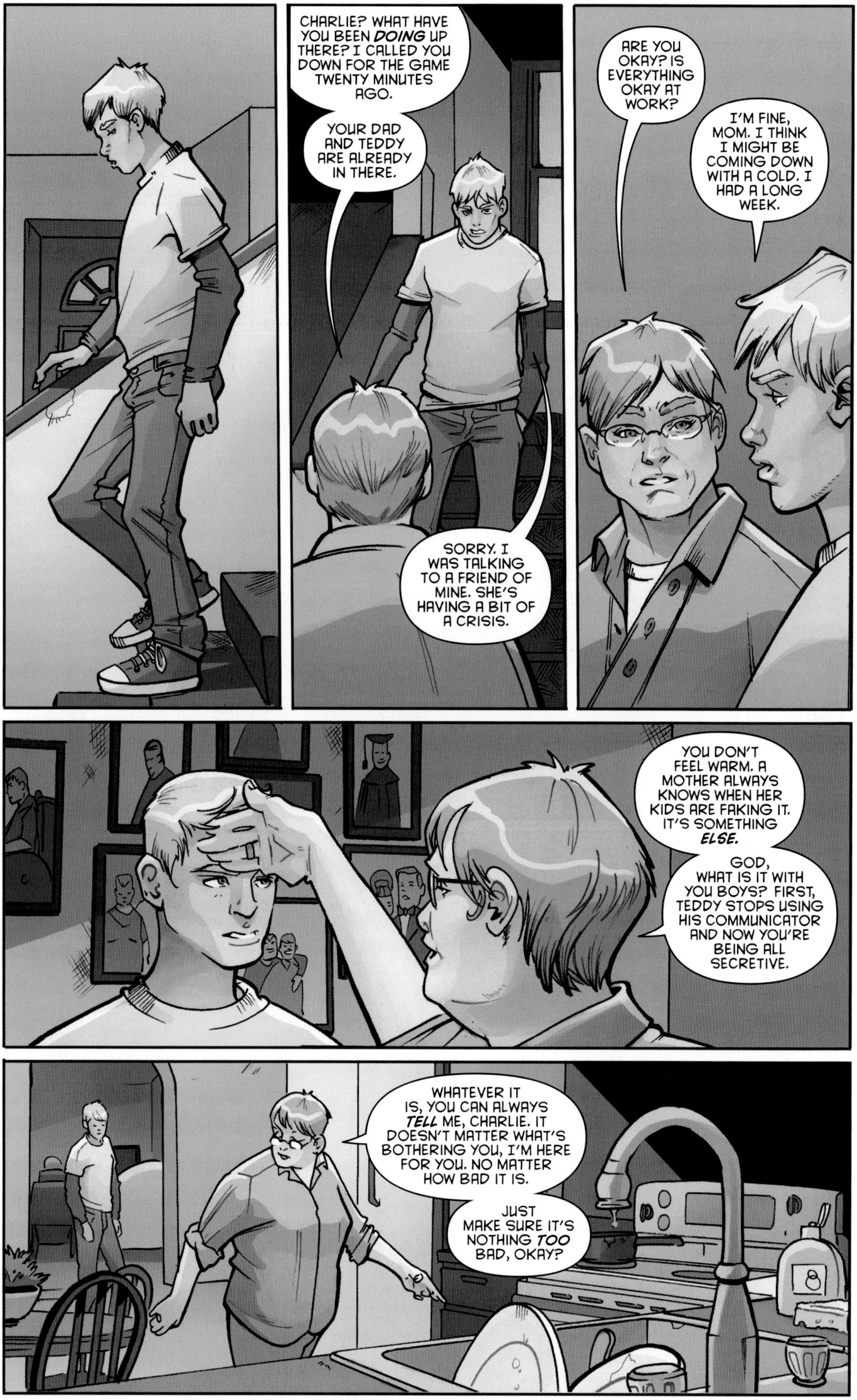
CHARLIE? WHAT HAVE YOU BEEN *DOING* UP THERE? I CALLED YOU DOWN FOR THE GAME TWENTY MINUTES AGO.
YOUR DAD AND TEDDY ARE ALREADY IN THERE.
SORRY. I WAS TALKING TO A FRIEND OF MINE. SHE'S HAVING A BIT OF A CRISIS.
ARE YOU OKAY? IS EVERYTHING OKAY AT WORK?
I'M FINE, MOM. I THINK I MIGHT BE COMING DOWN WITH A COLD. I HAD A LONG WEEK.
YOU DON'T FEEL WARM. A MOTHER ALWAYS KNOWS WHEN HER KIDS ARE FAKING IT. IT'S SOMETHING *ELSE.*
GOD, WHAT IS IT WITH YOU BOYS? FIRST, TEDDY STOPS USING HIS COMMUNICATOR AND NOW YOU'RE BEING ALL SECRETIVE.
WHATEVER IT IS, YOU CAN ALWAYS *TELL* ME, CHARLIE. IT DOESN'T MATTER WHAT'S BOTHERING YOU, I'M HERE FOR YOU. NO MATTER HOW BAD IT IS.
JUST MAKE SURE IT'S NOTHING *TOO* BAD, OKAY?

HIYA, DAD. HI, TEDDY. WHO'S WINNING?

GAME GOT CANNED. SOME KIND OF SPECIAL REPORT ABOUT MATTER MAN.

A POSTING, THEN, ON NUMEROUS SOCIAL AND PUBLIC WEBSITES DEPICTING THE GRUESOME DECAPITATION...

...AND EVISCERATION OF ELEMENTARY SCHOOL-TEACHER IRVING WRIGHT AT THE HANDS OF THE DOMESTIC TERRORIST, MATTER MAN.

THIS NETWORK HAS CHOSEN NOT TO SHOW THE END OF THE VIDEO OUT OF RESPECT TO THE VICTIM'S FAMILY AND COLLEAGUES...

SEE WHAT I'M SAYING? THIS IS WHY WE SHOULD HAVE STAYED OUT OF THE MIDDLE EAST. YOU STIR UP A NEST OF HORNETS, DON'T BE SURPRISED IF YOU GET STUNG. RIGHT, BIG TED?

TEDDY'S NOT AGREEING WITH YOU, DAD. HE'S JUST NOT USING HIS COMMUNICATOR. I HATE IT WHEN YOU DO THAT.

NO ONE AGREES WITH YOU. MATTER MAN'S A *LUNATIC*.

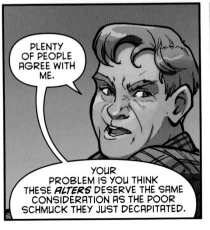

PLENTY OF PEOPLE AGREE WITH ME.

YOUR PROBLEM IS YOU THINK THESE *ALTERS* DESERVE THE SAME CONSIDERATION AS THE POOR SCHMUCK THEY JUST DECAPITATED.

I CAN'T BELIEVE YOU'RE EVEN *SAYING* THAT!

ALTERS ARE PEOPLE! YOU THINK THEY *CHOSE* TO BE DIFFERENT?

WHAT WOULD YOU SAY IF *I* WAS AN ALTER?

I'D SAY GET OUT BEFORE YOUR FAMILY GOT HURT.

THAT'S WHAT ANY REASONABLE PERSON WOULD SAY.

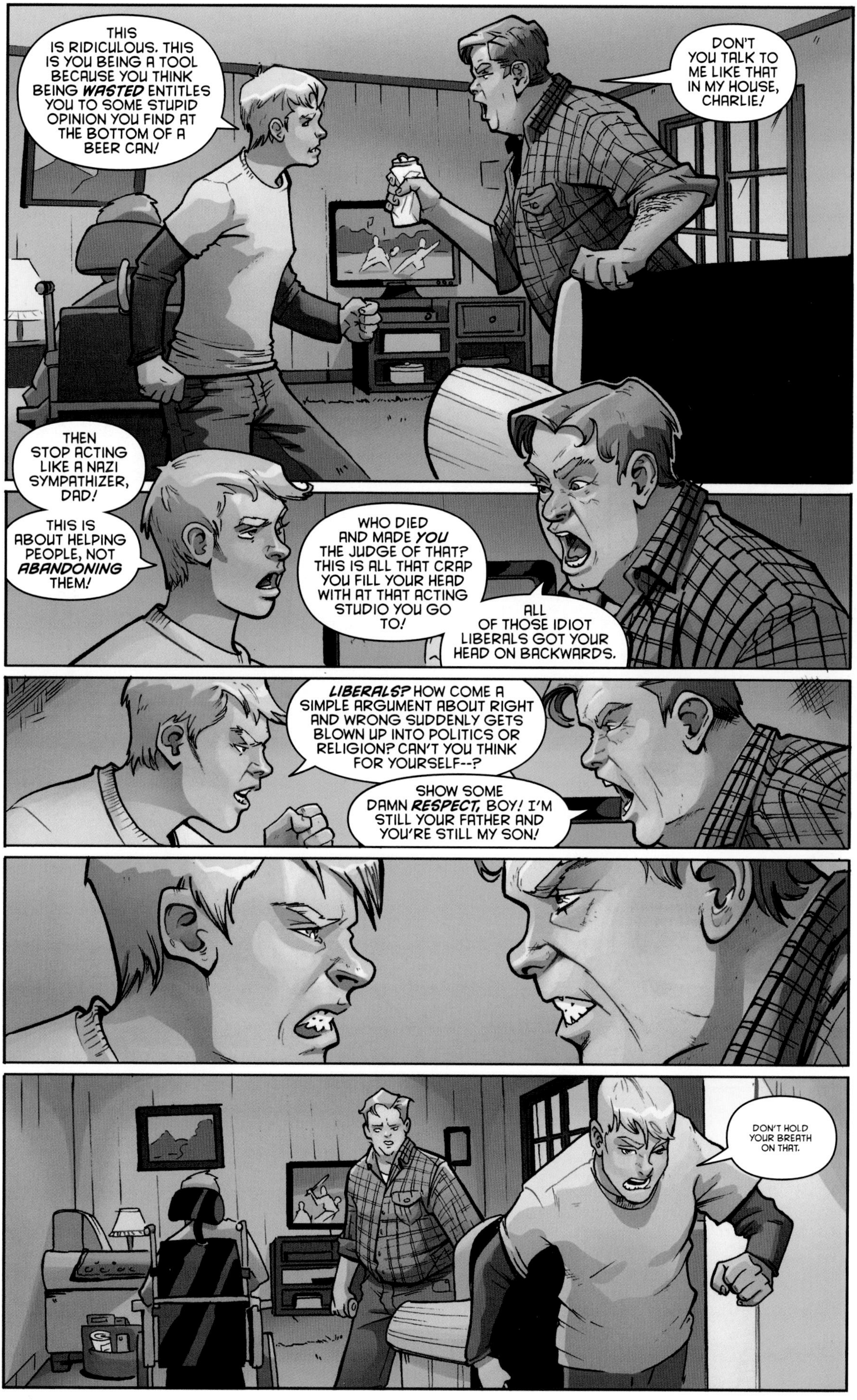
THIS IS RIDICULOUS. THIS IS YOU BEING A TOOL BECAUSE YOU THINK BEING *WASTED* ENTITLES YOU TO SOME STUPID OPINION YOU FIND AT THE BOTTOM OF A BEER CAN!
DON'T YOU TALK TO ME LIKE THAT IN MY HOUSE, CHARLIE!
THEN STOP ACTING LIKE A NAZI SYMPATHIZER, DAD!
THIS IS ABOUT HELPING PEOPLE, NOT *ABANDONING* THEM!
WHO DIED AND MADE *YOU* THE JUDGE OF THAT? THIS IS ALL THAT CRAP YOU FILL YOUR HEAD WITH AT THAT ACTING STUDIO YOU GO TO!
ALL OF THOSE IDIOT LIBERALS GOT YOUR HEAD ON BACKWARDS.
LIBERALS? HOW COME A SIMPLE ARGUMENT ABOUT RIGHT AND WRONG SUDDENLY GETS BLOWN UP INTO POLITICS OR RELIGION? CAN'T YOU THINK FOR YOURSELF--?
SHOW SOME DAMN *RESPECT,* BOY! I'M STILL YOUR FATHER AND YOU'RE STILL MY SON!
DON'T HOLD YOUR BREATH ON THAT.

YOU DON'T EAT.

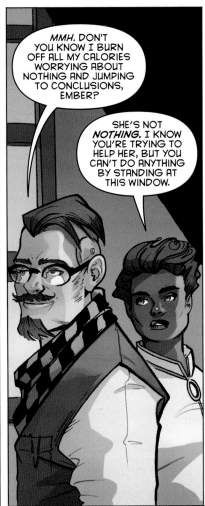

MMH. DON'T YOU KNOW I BURN OFF ALL MY CALORIES WORRYING ABOUT NOTHING AND JUMPING TO CONCLUSIONS, EMBER?

SHE'S NOT *NOTHING.* I KNOW YOU'RE TRYING TO HELP HER, BUT YOU CAN'T DO ANYTHING BY STANDING AT THIS WINDOW.

LET'S GO AND EAT. YOU CAN SOLVE THE WORLD'S PROBLEMS OVER A BURRITO.

IF WE'RE LUCKY, MAYBE SHE'LL DROP BY AGAIN. AND IF WE'RE EVEN LUCKIER, MAYBE SHE WON'T SMASH UP HALF OUR BUILDING.

IF WE'RE LUCKY, MAYBE SHE WON'T GET HERSELF KILLED BEFORE WE HAVE A CHANCE TO *SAVE* HER.

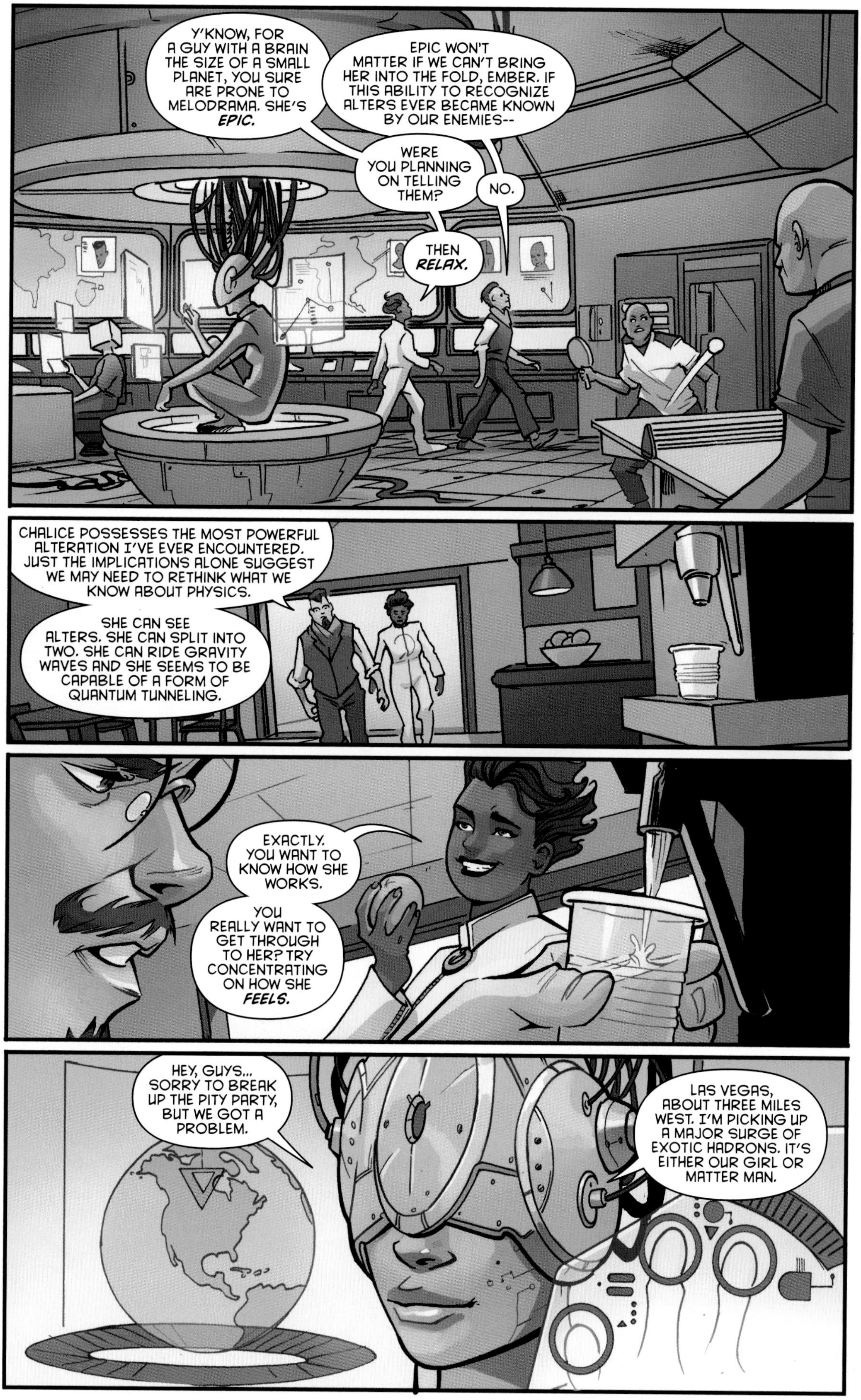
Y'KNOW, FOR A GUY WITH A BRAIN THE SIZE OF A SMALL PLANET, YOU SURE ARE PRONE TO MELODRAMA. SHE'S *EPIC.*
EPIC WON'T MATTER IF WE CAN'T BRING HER INTO THE FOLD, EMBER. IF THIS ABILITY TO RECOGNIZE ALTERS EVER BECAME KNOWN BY OUR ENEMIES--
WERE YOU PLANNING ON TELLING THEM?
NO.
THEN *RELAX.*
CHALICE POSSESSES THE MOST POWERFUL ALTERATION I'VE EVER ENCOUNTERED. JUST THE IMPLICATIONS ALONE SUGGEST WE MAY NEED TO RETHINK WHAT WE KNOW ABOUT PHYSICS.
SHE CAN SEE ALTERS. SHE CAN SPLIT INTO TWO. SHE CAN RIDE GRAVITY WAVES AND SHE SEEMS TO BE CAPABLE OF A FORM OF QUANTUM TUNNELING.
EXACTLY. YOU WANT TO KNOW HOW SHE WORKS.
YOU REALLY WANT TO GET THROUGH TO HER? TRY CONCENTRATING ON HOW SHE *FEELS.*
HEY, GUYS... SORRY TO BREAK UP THE PITY PARTY, BUT WE GOT A PROBLEM.
LAS VEGAS, ABOUT THREE MILES WEST. I'M PICKING UP A MAJOR SURGE OF EXOTIC HADRONS. IT'S EITHER OUR GIRL OR MATTER MAN.

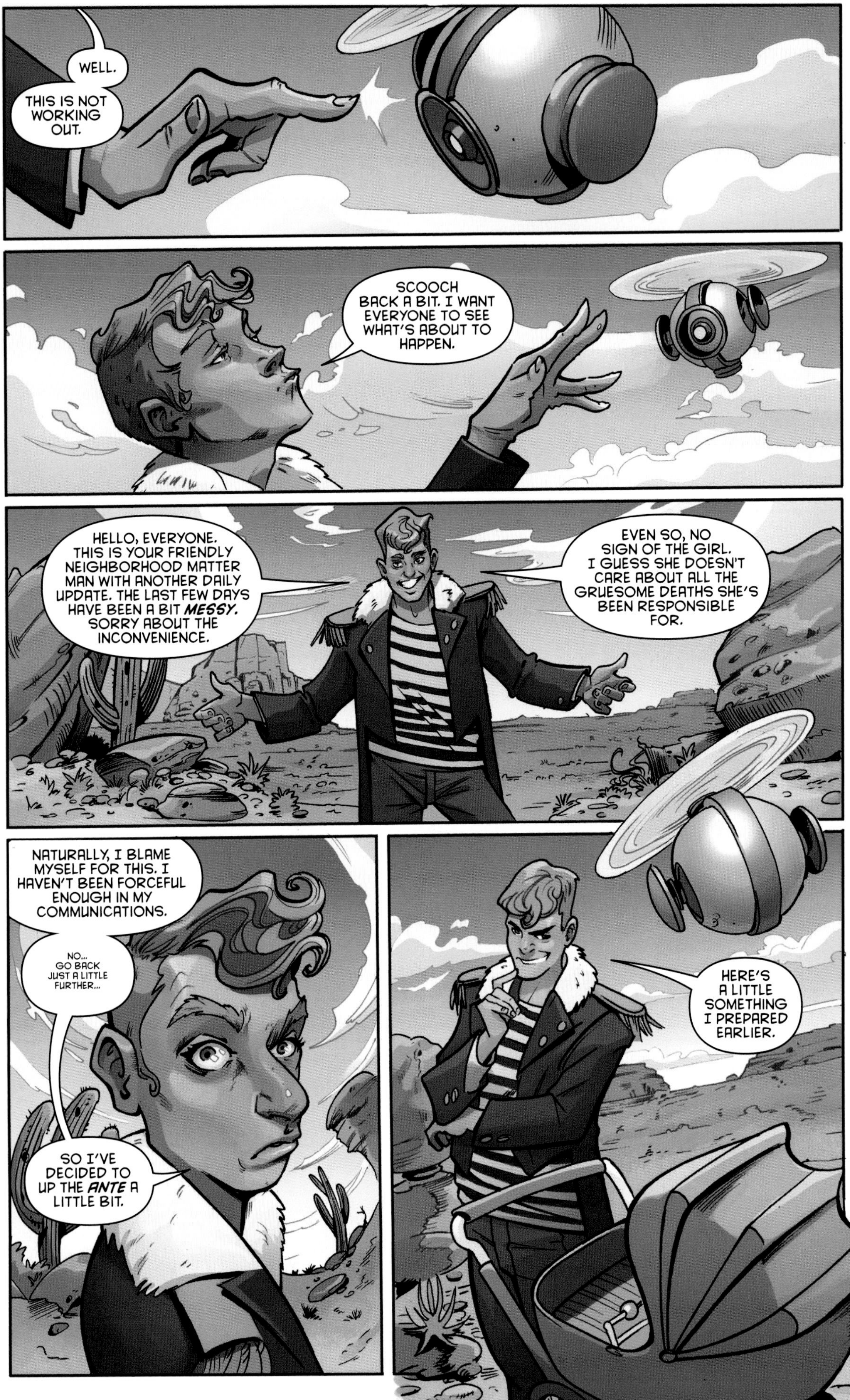
WELL.
THIS IS NOT WORKING OUT.
SCOOCH BACK A BIT. I WANT EVERYONE TO SEE WHAT'S ABOUT TO HAPPEN.
HELLO, EVERYONE. THIS IS YOUR FRIENDLY NEIGHBORHOOD MATTER MAN WITH ANOTHER DAILY UPDATE. THE LAST FEW DAYS HAVE BEEN A BIT *MESSY.* SORRY ABOUT THE INCONVENIENCE.
EVEN SO, NO SIGN OF THE GIRL. I GUESS SHE DOESN'T CARE ABOUT ALL THE GRUESOME DEATHS SHE'S BEEN RESPONSIBLE FOR.
NATURALLY, I BLAME MYSELF FOR THIS. I HAVEN'T BEEN FORCEFUL ENOUGH IN MY COMMUNICATIONS.
NO... GO BACK JUST A LITTLE FURTHER...
SO I'VE DECIDED TO UP THE *ANTE* A LITTLE BIT.
HERE'S A LITTLE SOMETHING I PREPARED EARLIER.

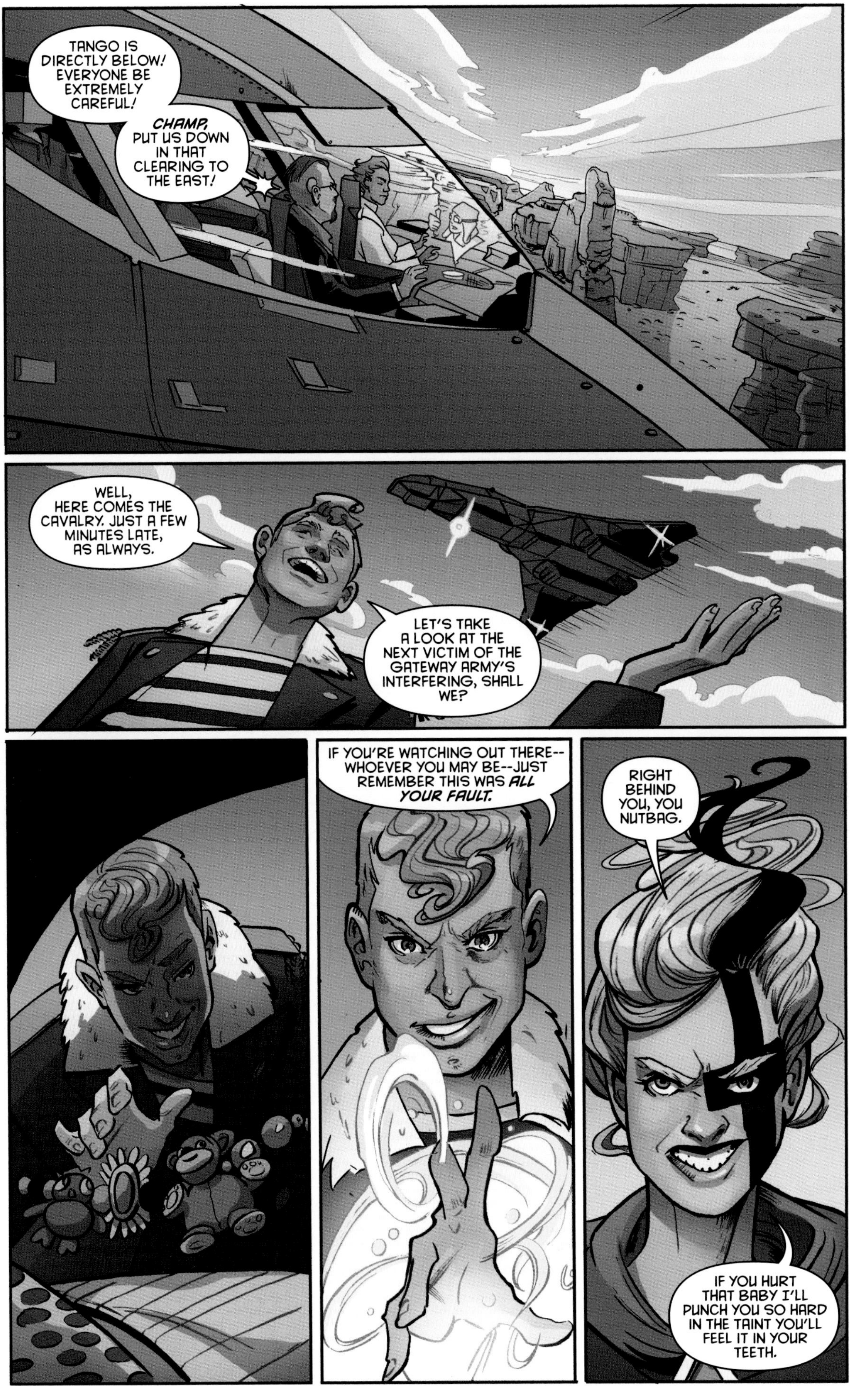
TANGO IS DIRECTLY BELOW! EVERYONE BE EXTREMELY CAREFUL!
CHAMP, PUT US DOWN IN THAT CLEARING TO THE EAST!
WELL, HERE COMES THE CAVALRY. JUST A FEW MINUTES LATE, AS ALWAYS.
LET'S TAKE A LOOK AT THE NEXT VICTIM OF THE GATEWAY ARMY'S INTERFERING, SHALL WE?
IF YOU'RE WATCHING OUT THERE--WHOEVER YOU MAY BE--JUST REMEMBER THIS WAS *ALL YOUR FAULT.*
RIGHT BEHIND YOU, YOU NUTBAG.
IF YOU HURT THAT BABY I'LL PUNCH YOU SO HARD IN THE TAINT YOU'LL FEEL IT IN YOUR TEETH.

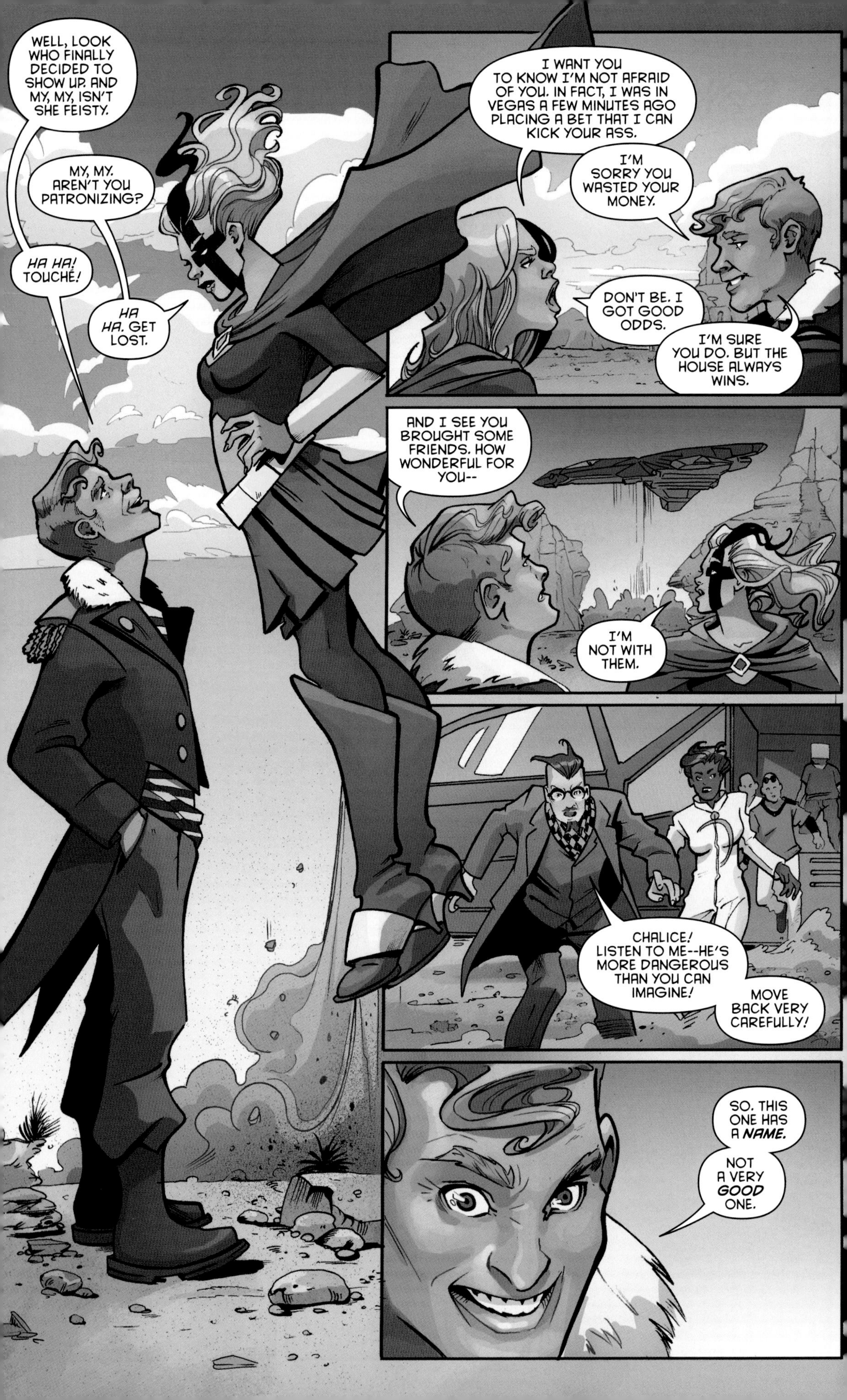
WELL, LOOK WHO FINALLY DECIDED TO SHOW UP. AND MY, MY, ISN'T SHE FEISTY.
MY, MY. AREN'T YOU PATRONIZING?
HA HA! TOUCHÉ!
HA HA. GET LOST.
I WANT YOU TO KNOW I'M NOT AFRAID OF YOU. IN FACT, I WAS IN VEGAS A FEW MINUTES AGO PLACING A BET THAT I CAN KICK YOUR ASS.
I'M SORRY YOU WASTED YOUR MONEY.
DON'T BE. I GOT GOOD ODDS.
I'M SURE YOU DO. BUT THE HOUSE ALWAYS WINS.
AND I SEE YOU BROUGHT SOME FRIENDS. HOW WONDERFUL FOR YOU--
I'M NOT WITH THEM.
CHALICE! LISTEN TO ME--HE'S MORE DANGEROUS THAN YOU CAN IMAGINE!
MOVE BACK VERY CAREFULLY!
SO. THIS ONE HAS A *NAME.*
NOT A VERY *GOOD* ONE.

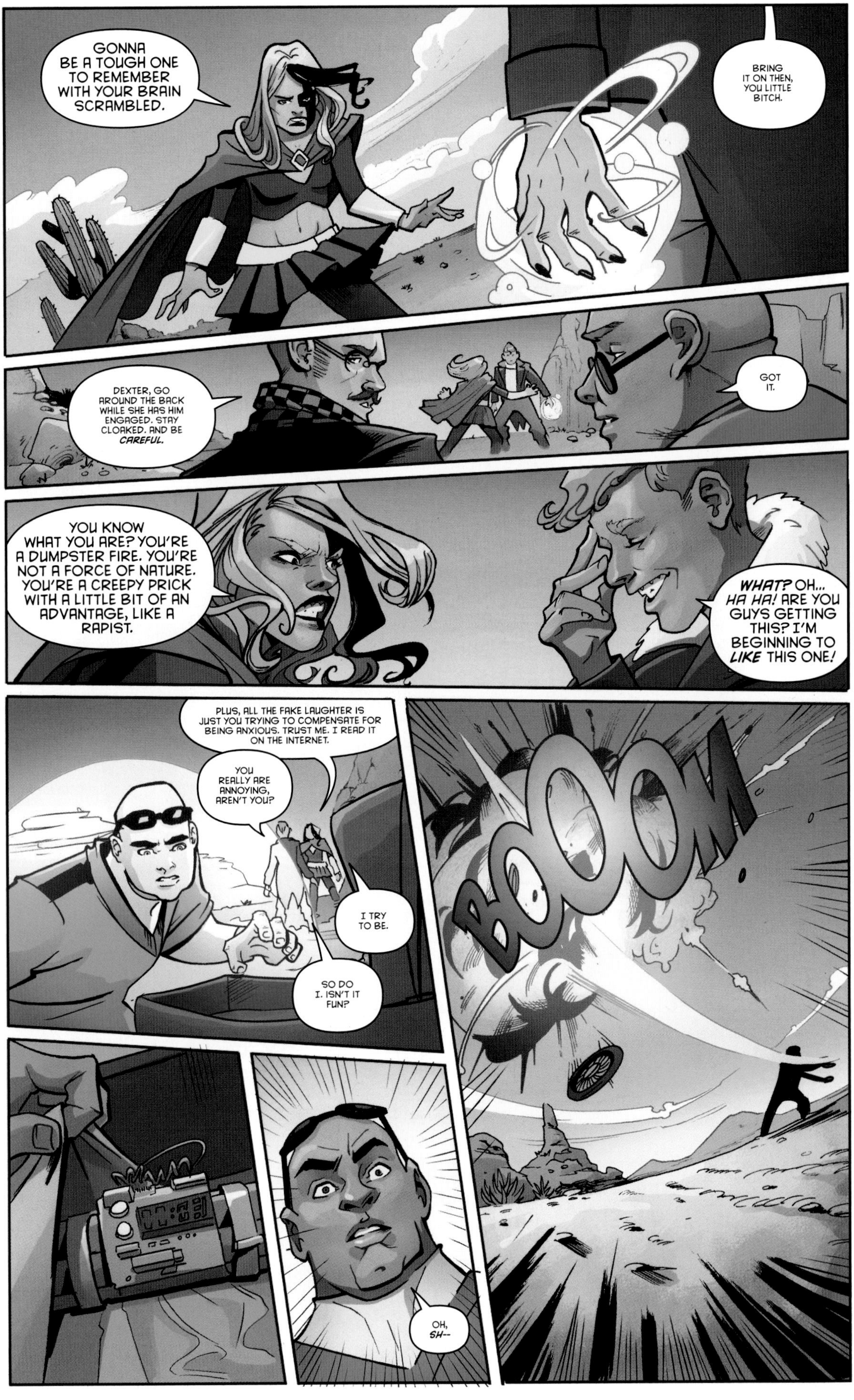
GONNA BE A TOUGH ONE TO REMEMBER WITH YOUR BRAIN SCRAMBLED.
BRING IT ON THEN, YOU LITTLE BITCH.
DEXTER, GO AROUND THE BACK WHILE SHE HAS HIM ENGAGED. STAY CLOAKED. AND BE *CAREFUL.*
GOT IT.
YOU KNOW WHAT YOU ARE? YOU'RE A DUMPSTER FIRE. YOU'RE NOT A FORCE OF NATURE. YOU'RE A CREEPY PRICK WITH A LITTLE BIT OF AN ADVANTAGE, LIKE A RAPIST.
WHAT? OH... *HA HA!* ARE YOU GUYS GETTING THIS? I'M BEGINNING TO ***LIKE*** THIS ONE!
PLUS, ALL THE FAKE LAUGHTER IS JUST YOU TRYING TO COMPENSATE FOR BEING ANXIOUS. TRUST ME. I READ IT ON THE INTERNET.
YOU REALLY ARE ANNOYING, AREN'T YOU?
I TRY TO BE.
SO DO I. ISN'T IT FUN?
BOOOM
OH, *SH--*

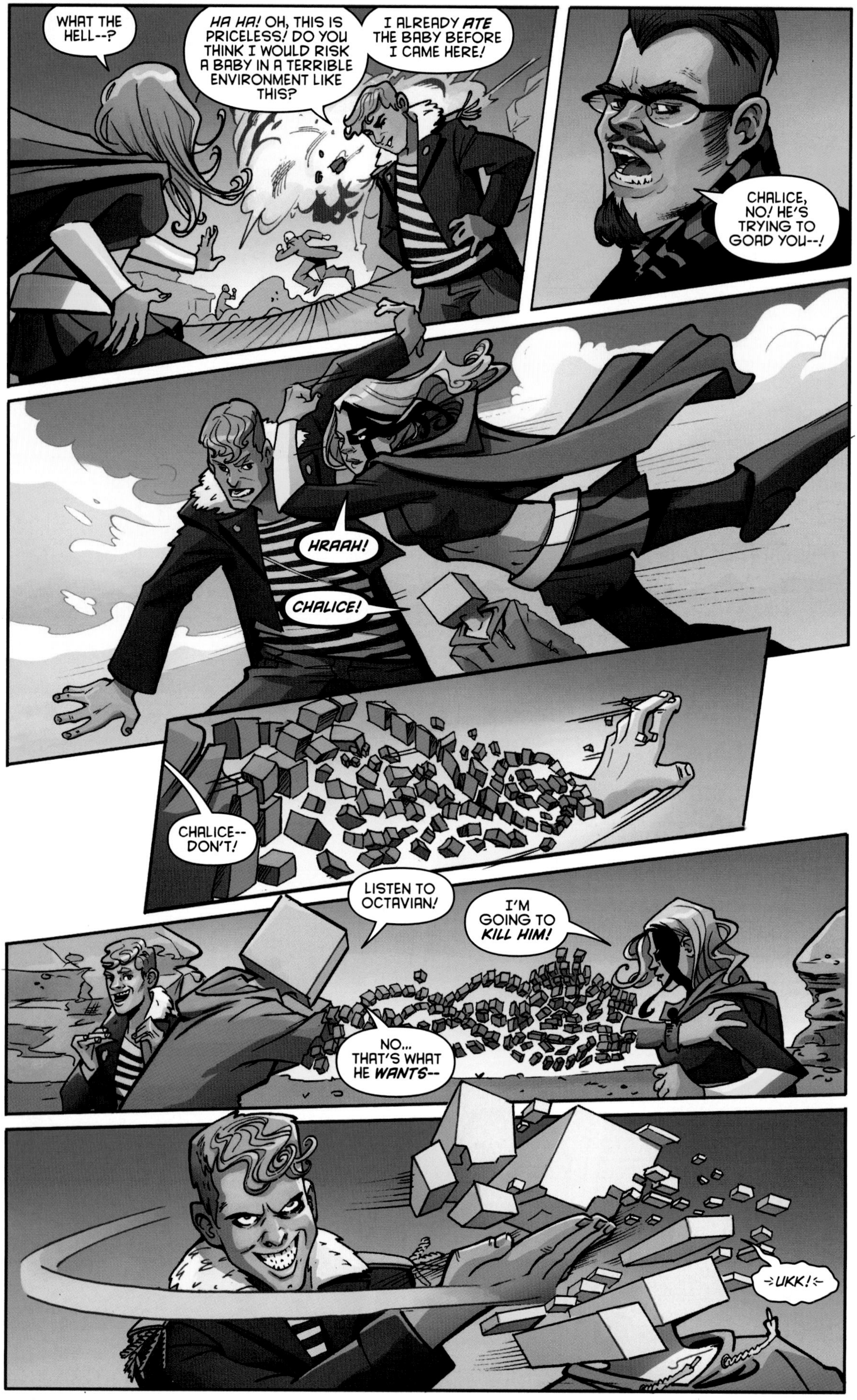
WHAT THE HELL--?
HA HA! OH, THIS IS PRICELESS! DO YOU THINK I WOULD RISK A BABY IN A TERRIBLE ENVIRONMENT LIKE THIS?
I ALREADY ATE THE BABY BEFORE I CAME HERE!
CHALICE, NO! HE'S TRYING TO GOAD YOU--!
HRAAH!
CHALICE!
CHALICE-- DON'T!
LISTEN TO OCTAVIAN!
I'M GOING TO KILL HIM!
NO... THAT'S WHAT HE WANTS--
UKK!

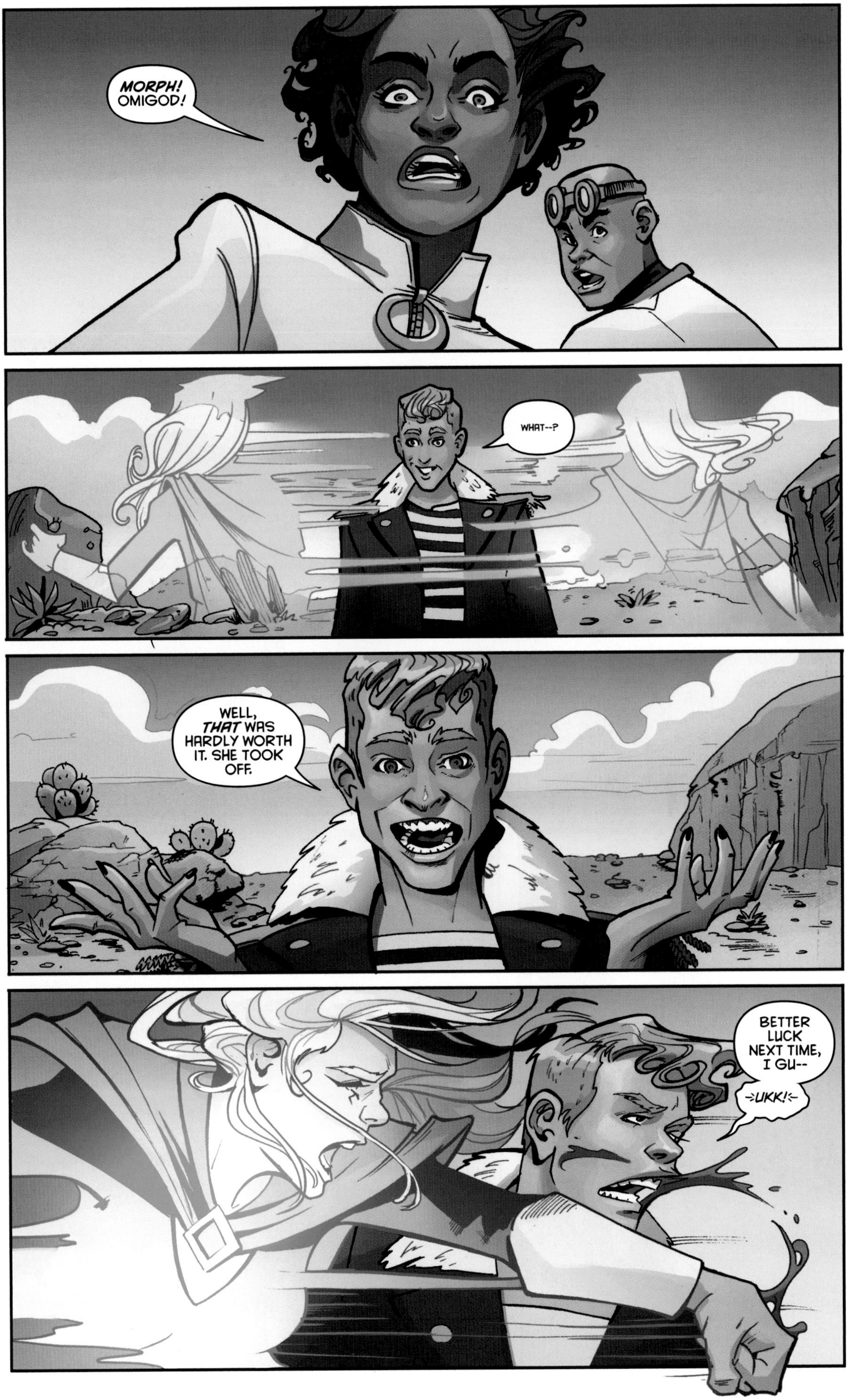
MORPH! OMIGOD!
WHAT--?
WELL, THAT WAS HARDLY WORTH IT. SHE TOOK OFF.
BETTER LUCK NEXT TIME, I GU--
UKK!

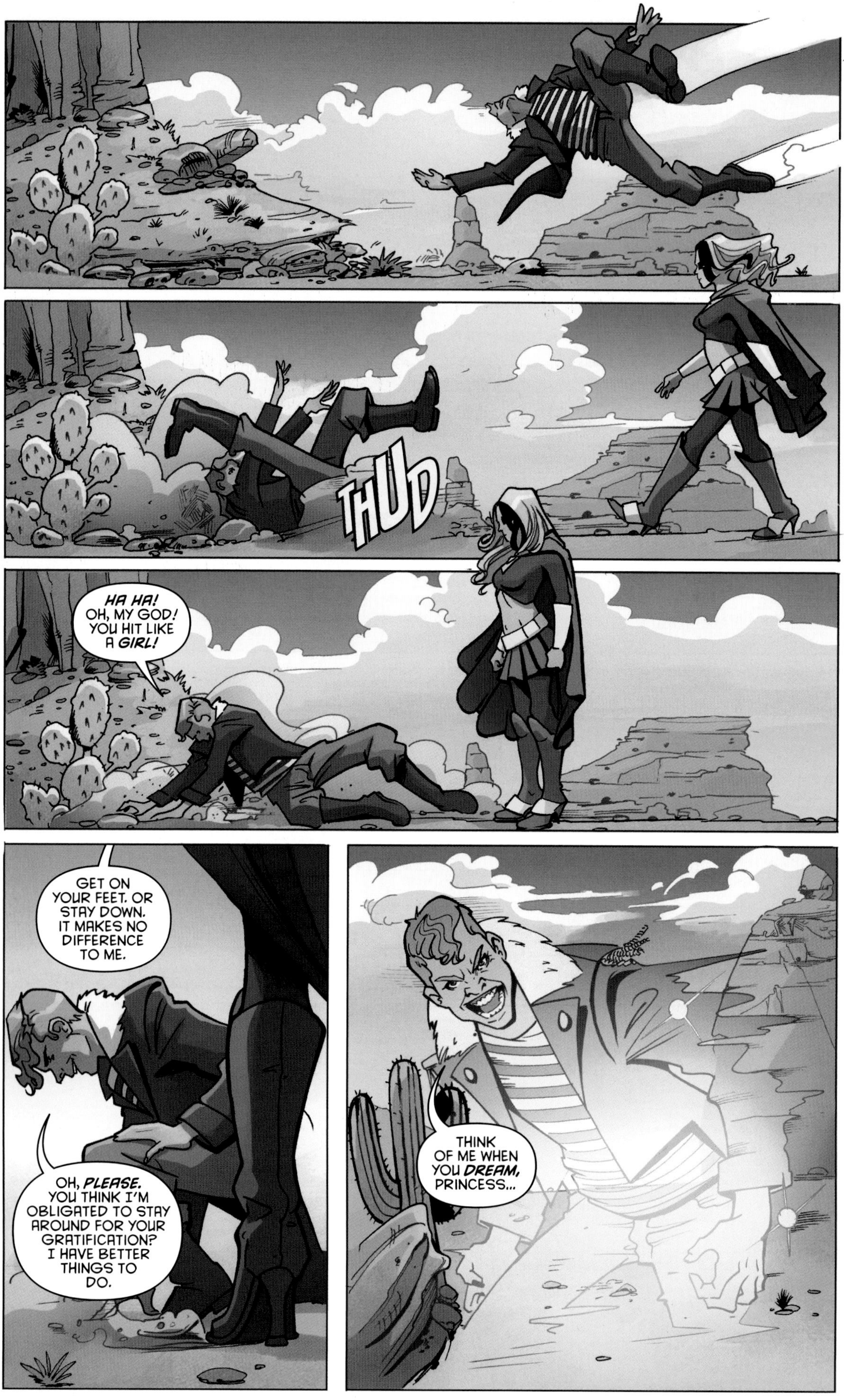
THUD
HA HA! OH, MY GOD! YOU HIT LIKE A GIRL!
GET ON YOUR FEET. OR STAY DOWN. IT MAKES NO DIFFERENCE TO ME.
OH, PLEASE. YOU THINK I'M OBLIGATED TO STAY AROUND FOR YOUR GRATIFICATION? I HAVE BETTER THINGS TO DO.
THINK OF ME WHEN YOU DREAM, PRINCESS...

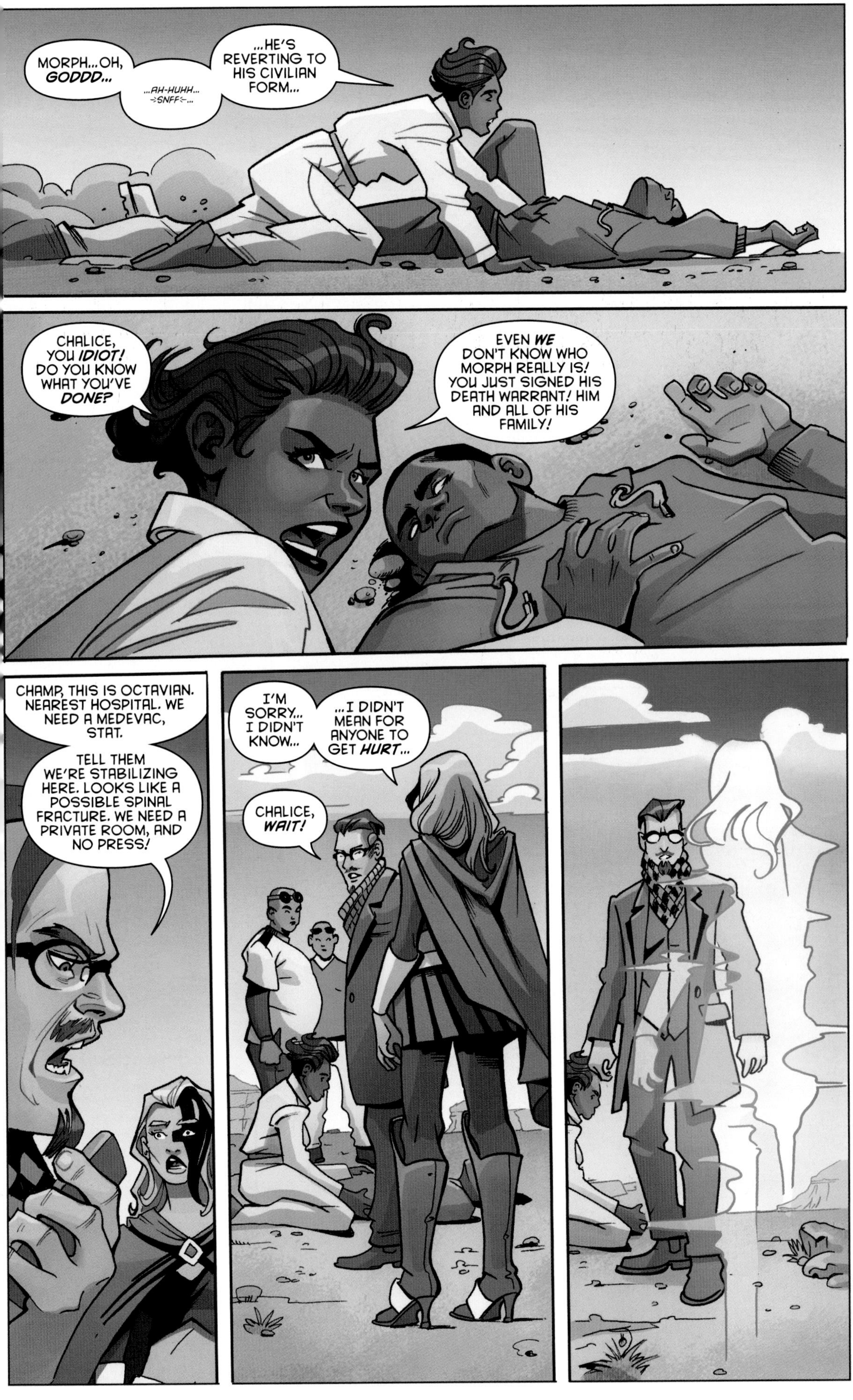
MORPH...OH, GODDD...
...AH-HUHH... SNFF...
...HE'S REVERTING TO HIS CIVILIAN FORM...
CHALICE, YOU IDIOT! DO YOU KNOW WHAT YOU'VE DONE?
EVEN WE DON'T KNOW WHO MORPH REALLY IS! YOU JUST SIGNED HIS DEATH WARRANT! HIM AND ALL OF HIS FAMILY!
CHAMP, THIS IS OCTAVIAN. NEAREST HOSPITAL. WE NEED A MEDEVAC, STAT.
TELL THEM WE'RE STABILIZING HERE. LOOKS LIKE A POSSIBLE SPINAL FRACTURE. WE NEED A PRIVATE ROOM, AND NO PRESS!
I'M SORRY... I DIDN'T KNOW...
...I DIDN'T MEAN FOR ANYONE TO GET HURT...
CHALICE, WAIT!

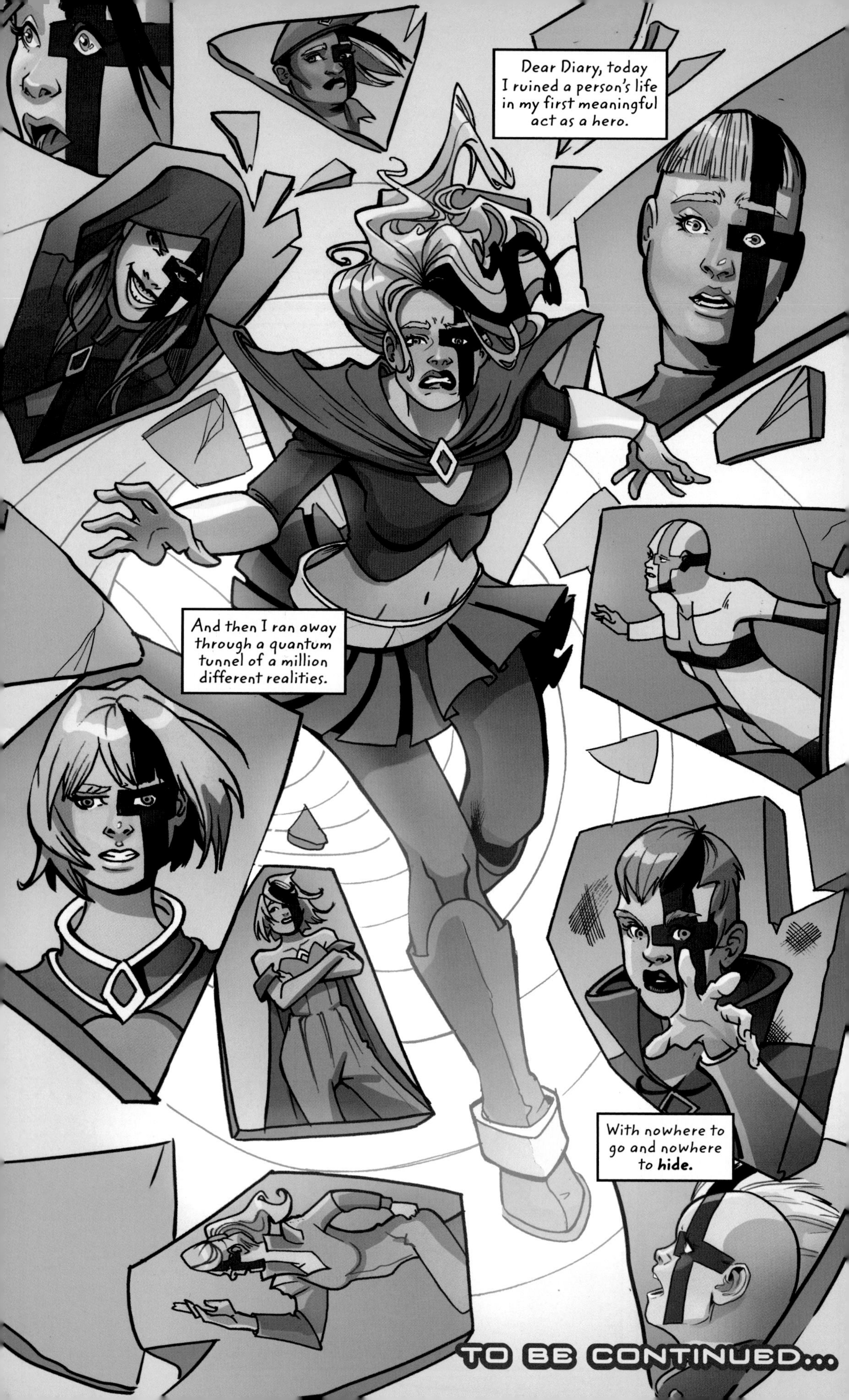
Dear Diary, today I ruined a person's life in my first meaningful act as a hero.
And then I ran away through a quantum tunnel of a million different realities.
With nowhere to go and nowhere to **hide.**
TO BE CONTINUED...

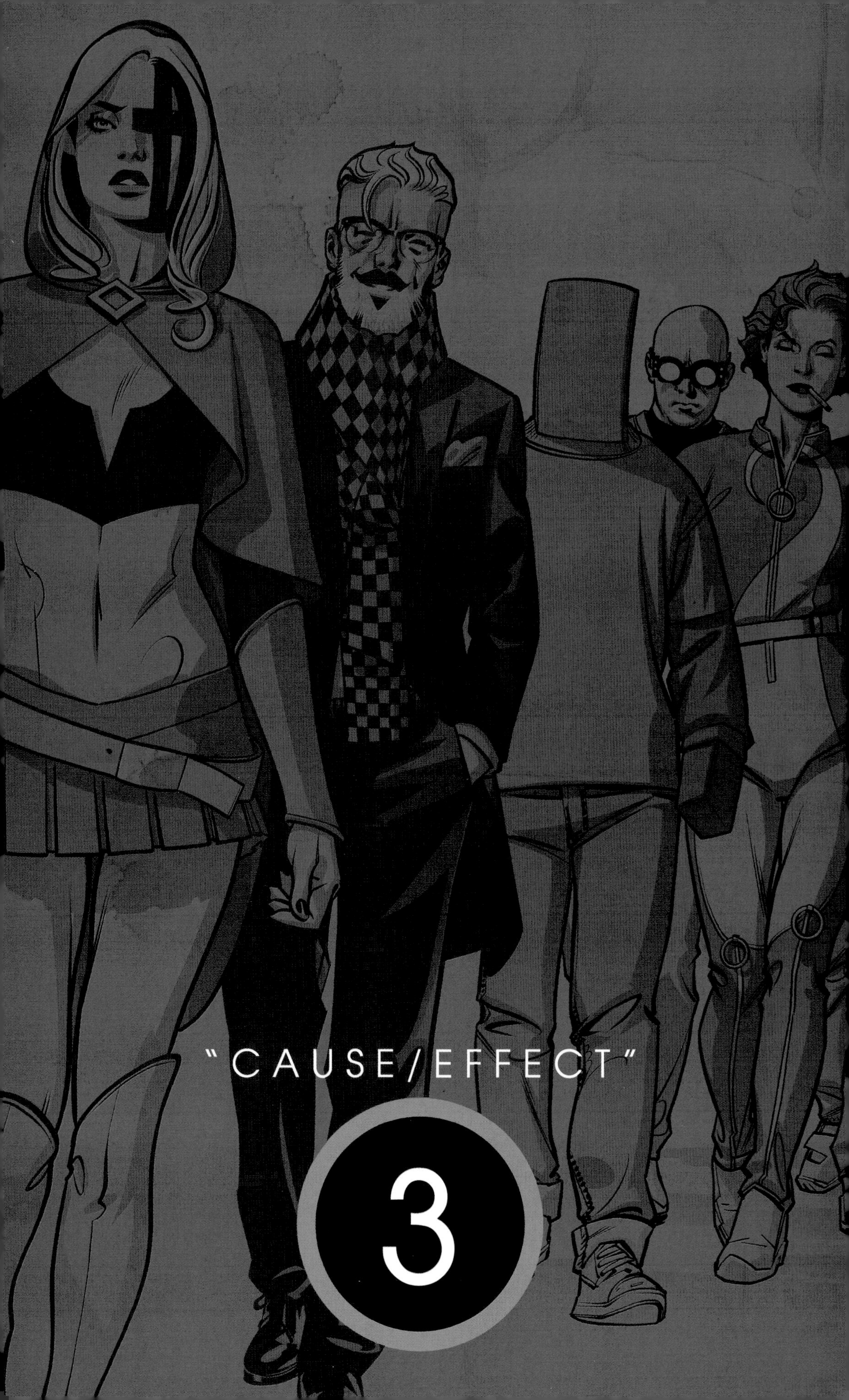
"CAUSE/EFFECT"
3

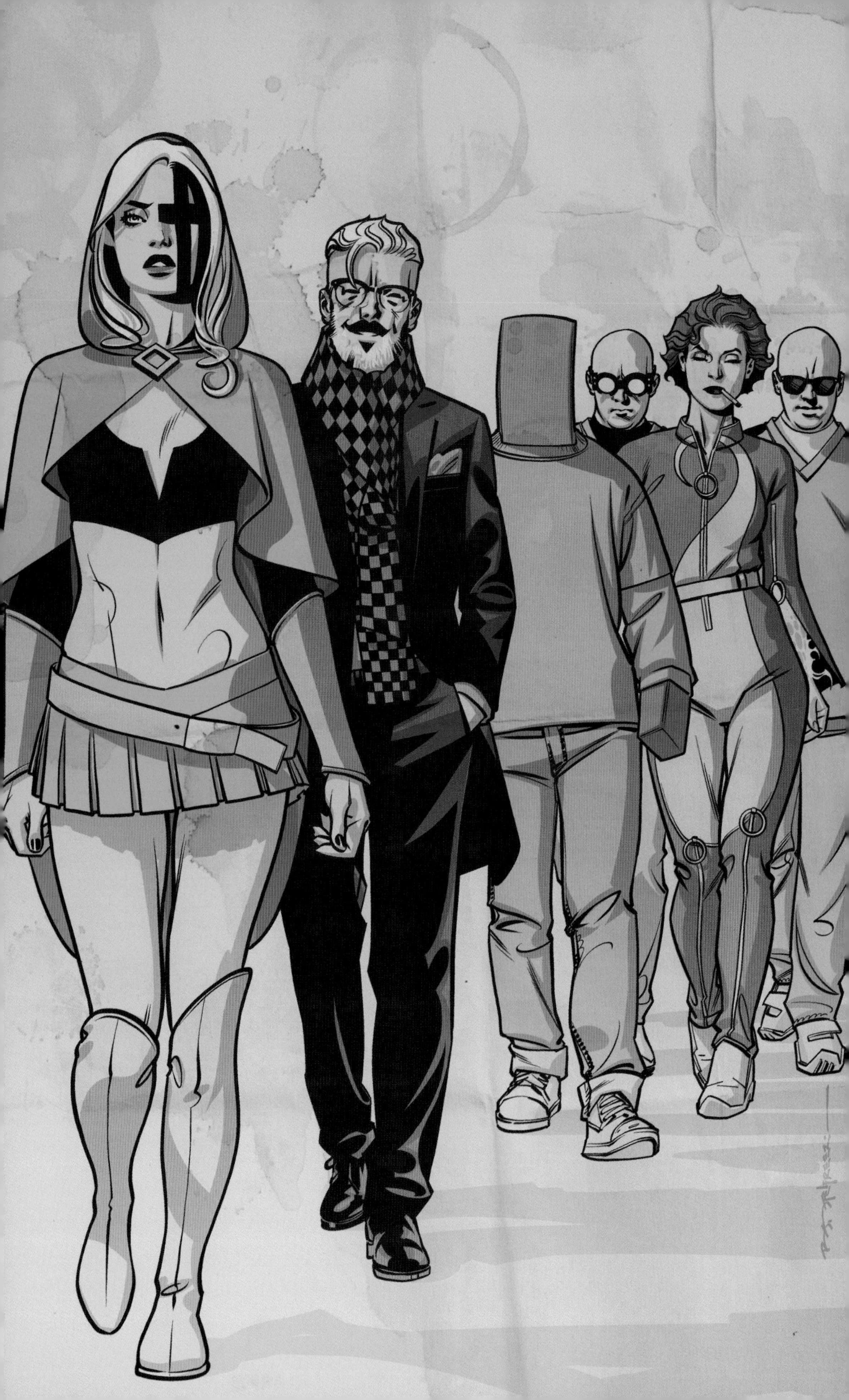

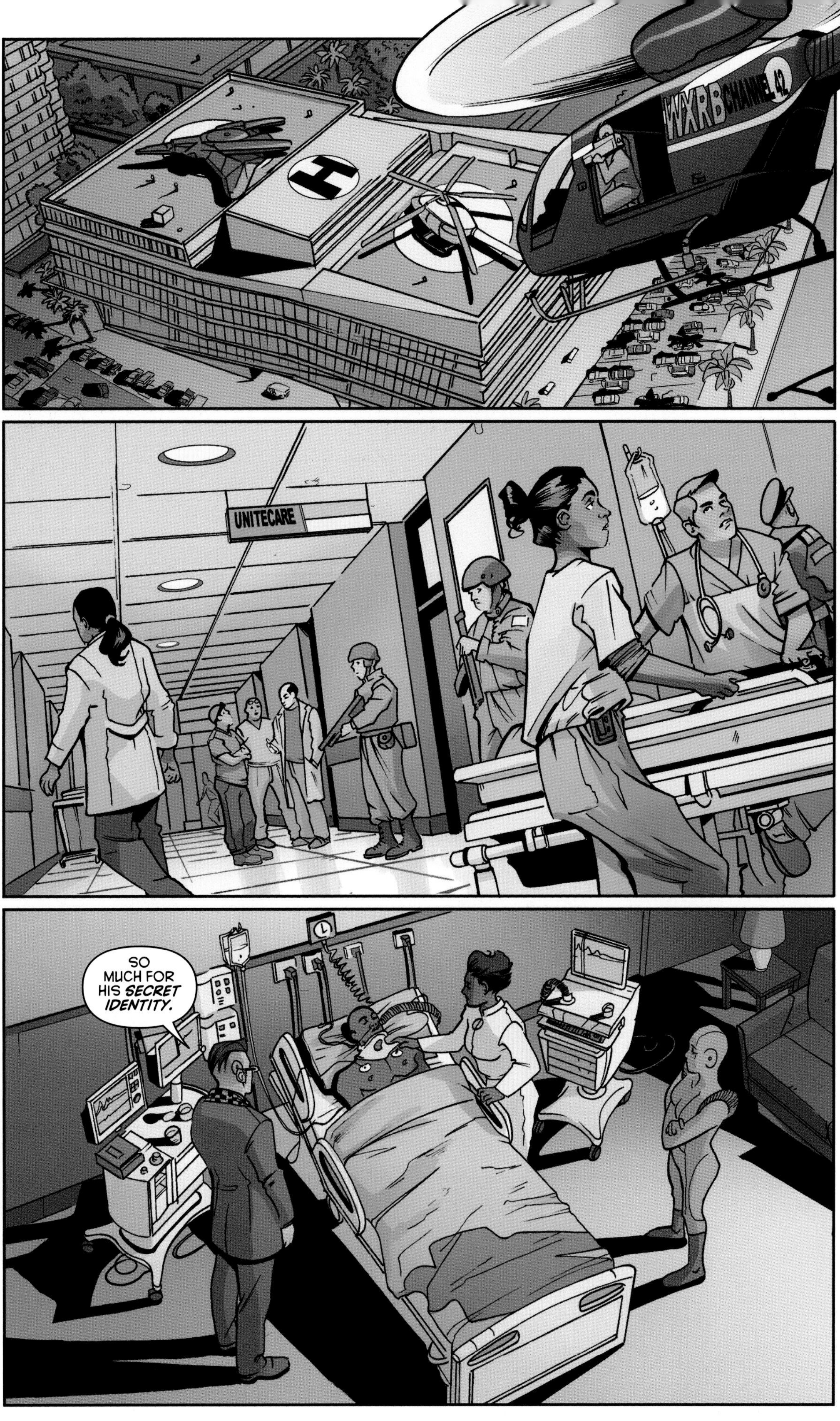
WXRB CHANNEL 42
UNITECARE
SO MUCH FOR HIS *SECRET IDENTITY.*

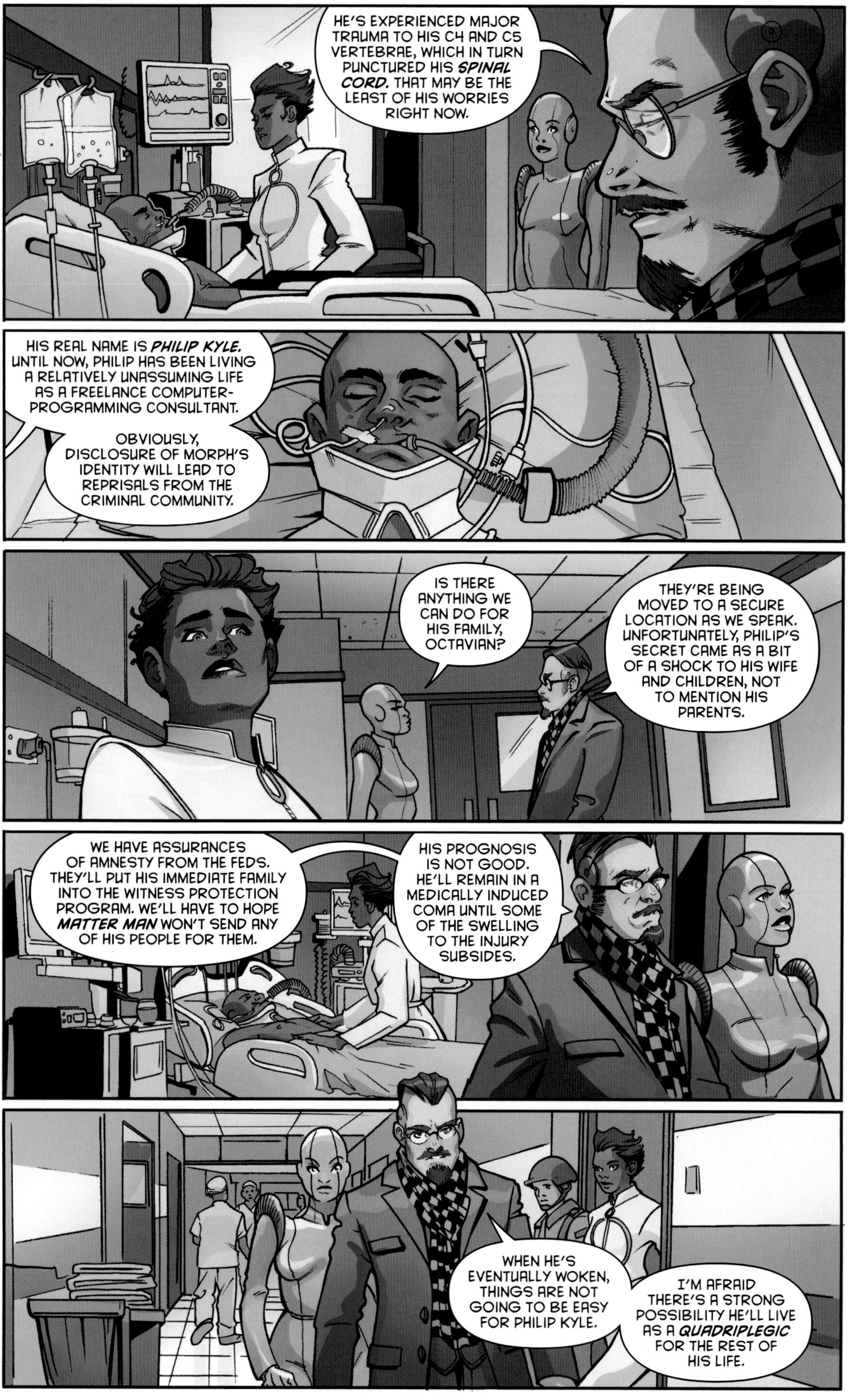
HE'S EXPERIENCED MAJOR TRAUMA TO HIS C4 AND C5 VERTEBRAE, WHICH IN TURN PUNCTURED HIS *SPINAL CORD.* THAT MAY BE THE LEAST OF HIS WORRIES RIGHT NOW.
HIS REAL NAME IS *PHILIP KYLE.* UNTIL NOW, PHILIP HAS BEEN LIVING A RELATIVELY UNASSUMING LIFE AS A FREELANCE COMPUTER-PROGRAMMING CONSULTANT.
OBVIOUSLY, DISCLOSURE OF MORPH'S IDENTITY WILL LEAD TO REPRISALS FROM THE CRIMINAL COMMUNITY.
IS THERE ANYTHING WE CAN DO FOR HIS FAMILY, OCTAVIAN?
THEY'RE BEING MOVED TO A SECURE LOCATION AS WE SPEAK. UNFORTUNATELY, PHILIP'S SECRET CAME AS A BIT OF A SHOCK TO HIS WIFE AND CHILDREN, NOT TO MENTION HIS PARENTS.
WE HAVE ASSURANCES OF AMNESTY FROM THE FEDS. THEY'LL PUT HIS IMMEDIATE FAMILY INTO THE WITNESS PROTECTION PROGRAM. WE'LL HAVE TO HOPE *MATTER MAN* WON'T SEND ANY OF HIS PEOPLE FOR THEM.
HIS PROGNOSIS IS NOT GOOD. HE'LL REMAIN IN A MEDICALLY INDUCED COMA UNTIL SOME OF THE SWELLING TO THE INJURY SUBSIDES.
WHEN HE'S EVENTUALLY WOKEN, THINGS ARE NOT GOING TO BE EASY FOR PHILIP KYLE.
I'M AFRAID THERE'S A STRONG POSSIBILITY HE'LL LIVE AS A *QUADRIPLEGIC* FOR THE REST OF HIS LIFE.

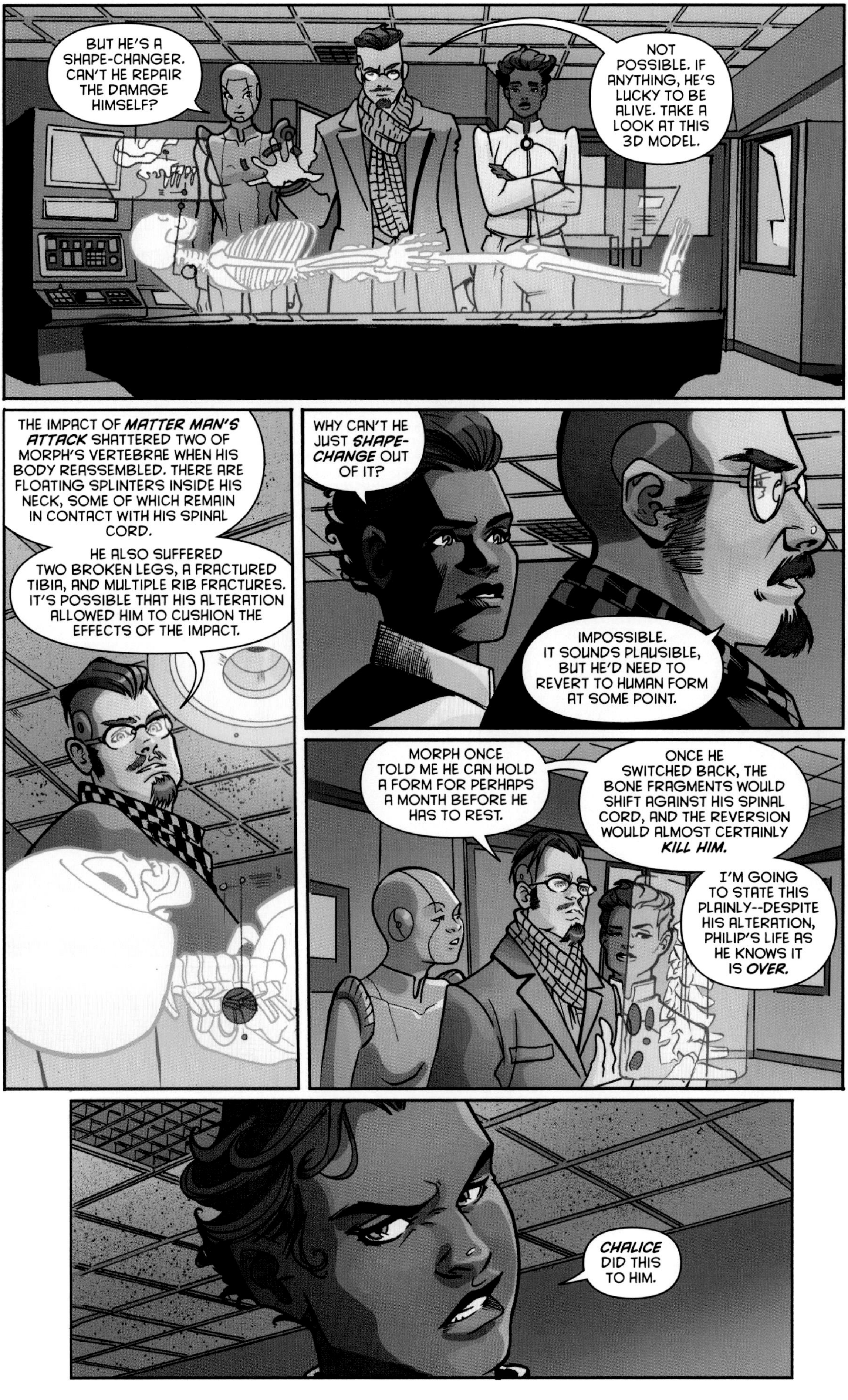
BUT HE'S A SHAPE-CHANGER. CAN'T HE REPAIR THE DAMAGE HIMSELF?
NOT POSSIBLE. IF ANYTHING, HE'S LUCKY TO BE ALIVE. TAKE A LOOK AT THIS 3D MODEL.
THE IMPACT OF MATTER MAN'S ATTACK SHATTERED TWO OF MORPH'S VERTEBRAE WHEN HIS BODY REASSEMBLED. THERE ARE FLOATING SPLINTERS INSIDE HIS NECK, SOME OF WHICH REMAIN IN CONTACT WITH HIS SPINAL CORD.
HE ALSO SUFFERED TWO BROKEN LEGS, A FRACTURED TIBIA, AND MULTIPLE RIB FRACTURES. IT'S POSSIBLE THAT HIS ALTERATION ALLOWED HIM TO CUSHION THE EFFECTS OF THE IMPACT.
WHY CAN'T HE JUST SHAPE-CHANGE OUT OF IT?
IMPOSSIBLE. IT SOUNDS PLAUSIBLE, BUT HE'D NEED TO REVERT TO HUMAN FORM AT SOME POINT.
MORPH ONCE TOLD ME HE CAN HOLD A FORM FOR PERHAPS A MONTH BEFORE HE HAS TO REST.
ONCE HE SWITCHED BACK, THE BONE FRAGMENTS WOULD SHIFT AGAINST HIS SPINAL CORD, AND THE REVERSION WOULD ALMOST CERTAINLY KILL HIM.
I'M GOING TO STATE THIS PLAINLY--DESPITE HIS ALTERATION, PHILIP'S LIFE AS HE KNOWS IT IS OVER.
CHALICE DID THIS TO HIM.

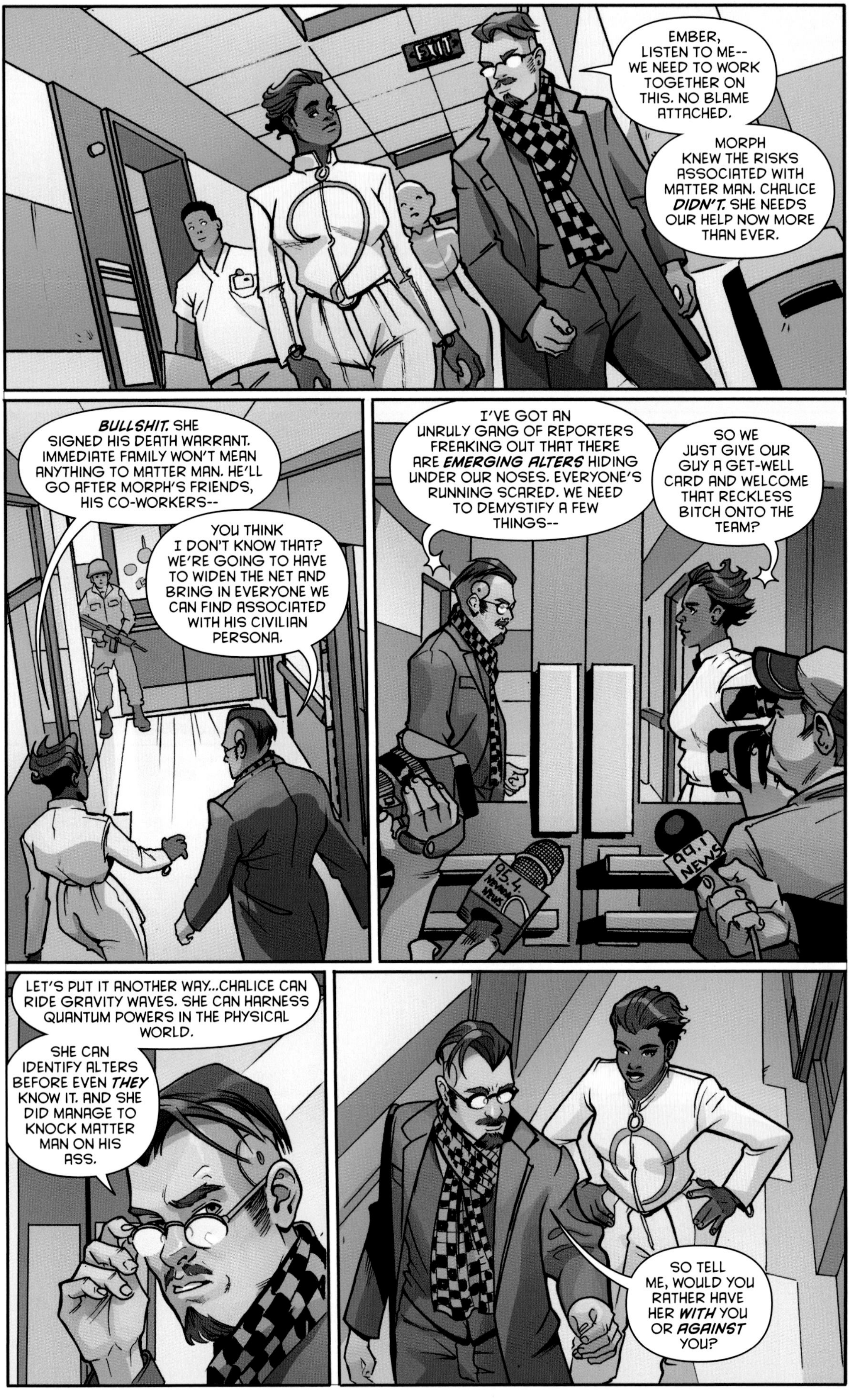
EXIT
EMBER, LISTEN TO ME-- WE NEED TO WORK TOGETHER ON THIS. NO BLAME ATTACHED.
MORPH KNEW THE RISKS ASSOCIATED WITH MATTER MAN. CHALICE *DIDN'T.* SHE NEEDS OUR HELP NOW MORE THAN EVER.
BULLSHIT. SHE SIGNED HIS DEATH WARRANT. IMMEDIATE FAMILY WON'T MEAN ANYTHING TO MATTER MAN. HE'LL GO AFTER MORPH'S FRIENDS, HIS CO-WORKERS--
YOU THINK I DON'T KNOW THAT? WE'RE GOING TO HAVE TO WIDEN THE NET AND BRING IN EVERYONE WE CAN FIND ASSOCIATED WITH HIS CIVILIAN PERSONA.
I'VE GOT AN UNRULY GANG OF REPORTERS FREAKING OUT THAT THERE ARE ***EMERGING ALTERS*** HIDING UNDER OUR NOSES. EVERYONE'S RUNNING SCARED. WE NEED TO DEMYSTIFY A FEW THINGS--
SO WE JUST GIVE OUR GUY A GET-WELL CARD AND WELCOME THAT RECKLESS BITCH ONTO THE TEAM?
95.4 NEVADA NEWS
99.1 NEWS
LET'S PUT IT ANOTHER WAY...CHALICE CAN RIDE GRAVITY WAVES. SHE CAN HARNESS QUANTUM POWERS IN THE PHYSICAL WORLD.
SHE CAN IDENTIFY ALTERS BEFORE EVEN ***THEY*** KNOW IT. AND SHE DID MANAGE TO KNOCK MATTER MAN ON HIS ASS.
SO TELL ME, WOULD YOU RATHER HAVE HER ***WITH*** YOU OR ***AGAINST*** YOU?

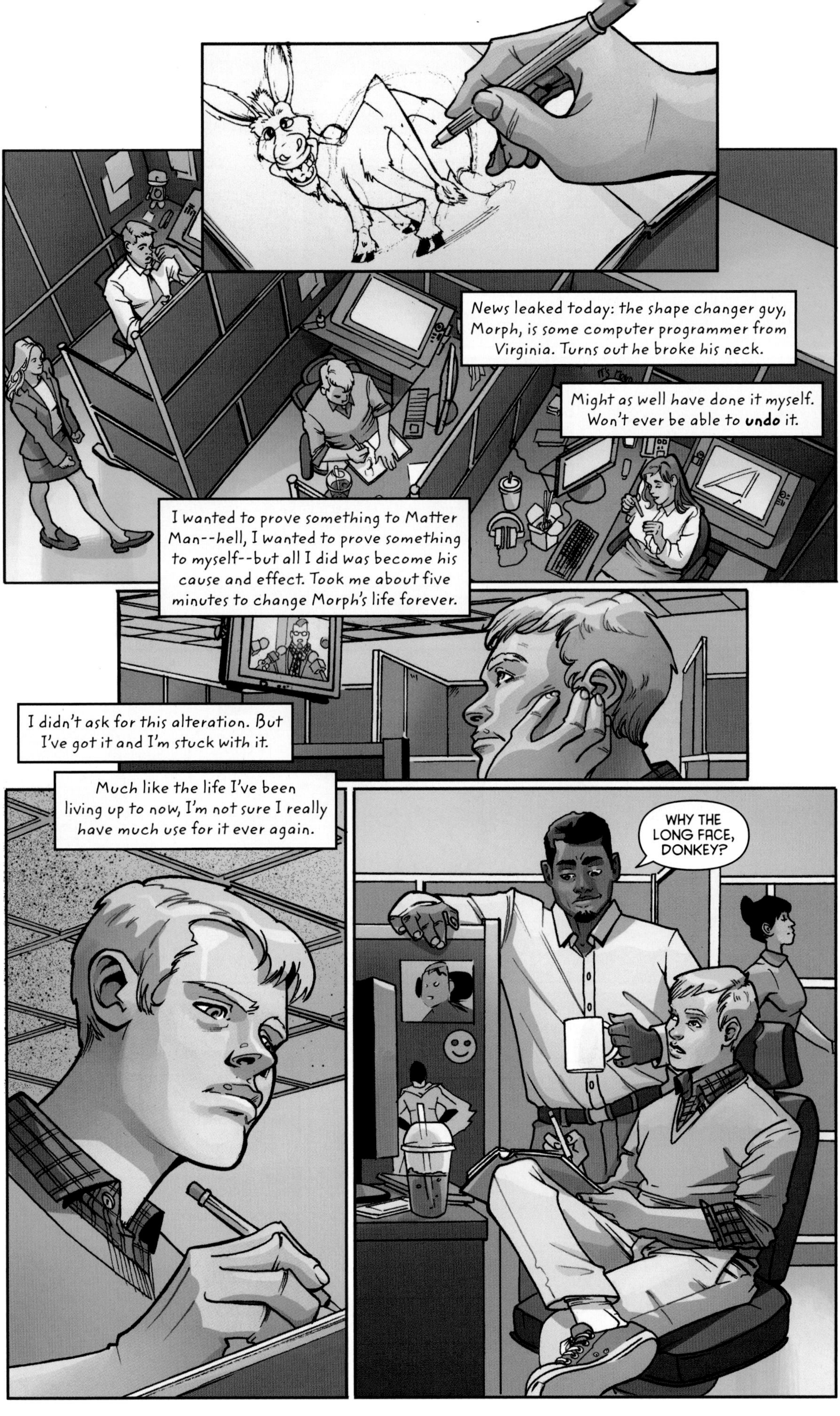
News leaked today: the shape changer guy, Morph, is some computer programmer from Virginia. Turns out he broke his neck.
Might as well have done it myself. Won't ever be able to **undo** it.
I wanted to prove something to Matter Man--hell, I wanted to prove something to myself--but all I did was become his cause and effect. Took me about five minutes to change Morph's life forever.
I didn't ask for this alteration. But I've got it and I'm stuck with it.
Much like the life I've been living up to now, I'm not sure I really have much use for it ever again.
WHY THE LONG FACE, DONKEY?

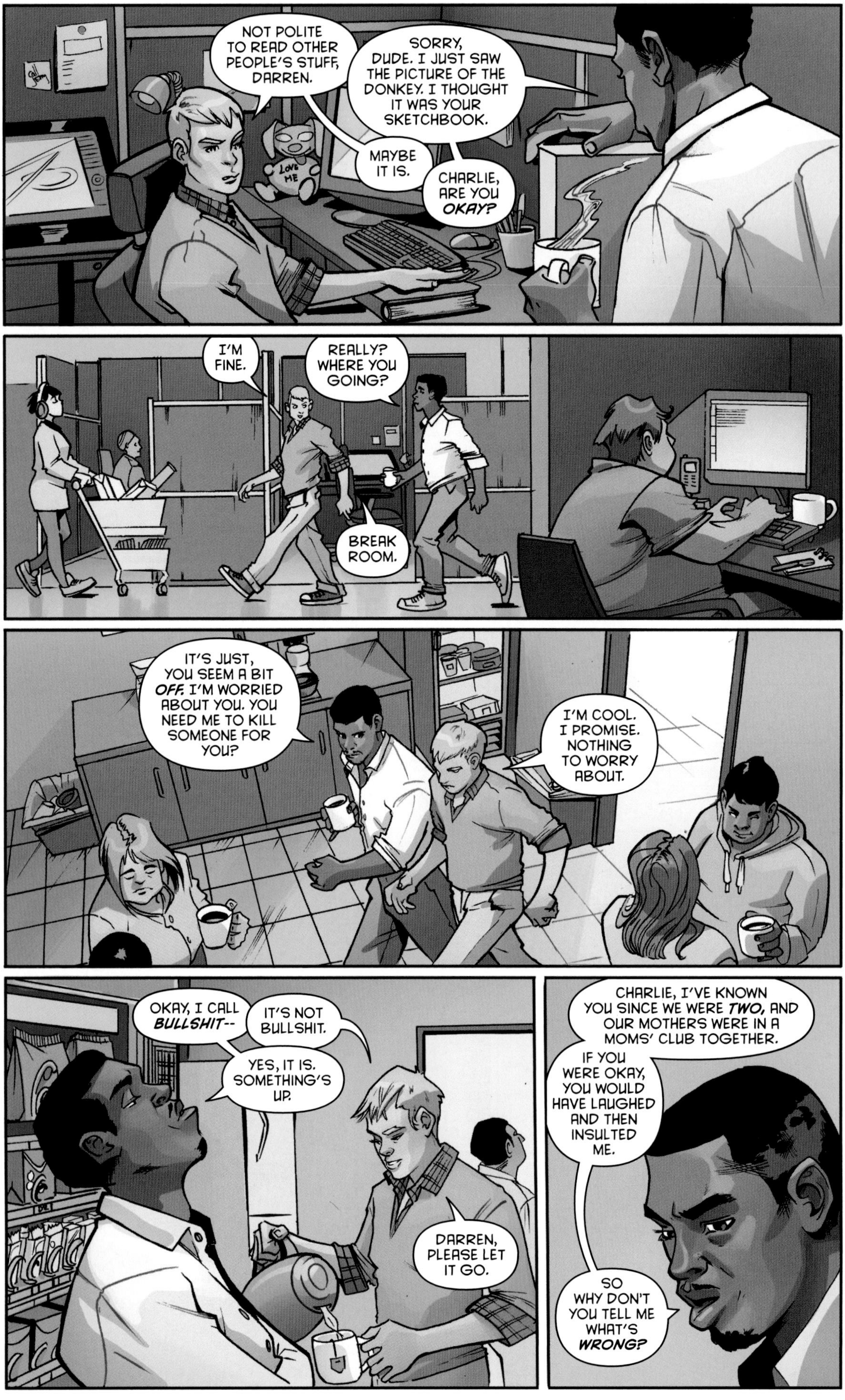
NOT POLITE TO READ OTHER PEOPLE'S STUFF, DARREN.
SORRY, DUDE. I JUST SAW THE PICTURE OF THE DONKEY. I THOUGHT IT WAS YOUR SKETCHBOOK.
MAYBE IT IS.
CHARLIE, ARE YOU *OKAY?*
LOVE ME
I'M FINE.
REALLY? WHERE YOU GOING?
BREAK ROOM.
IT'S JUST, YOU SEEM A BIT *OFF.* I'M WORRIED ABOUT YOU. YOU NEED ME TO KILL SOMEONE FOR YOU?
I'M COOL. I PROMISE. NOTHING TO WORRY ABOUT.
OKAY, I CALL *BULLSHIT*--
IT'S NOT BULLSHIT.
YES, IT IS. SOMETHING'S UP.
DARREN, PLEASE LET IT GO.
CHARLIE, I'VE KNOWN YOU SINCE WE WERE *TWO,* AND OUR MOTHERS WERE IN A MOMS' CLUB TOGETHER.
IF YOU WERE OKAY, YOU WOULD HAVE LAUGHED AND THEN INSULTED ME.
SO WHY DON'T YOU TELL ME WHAT'S *WRONG?*

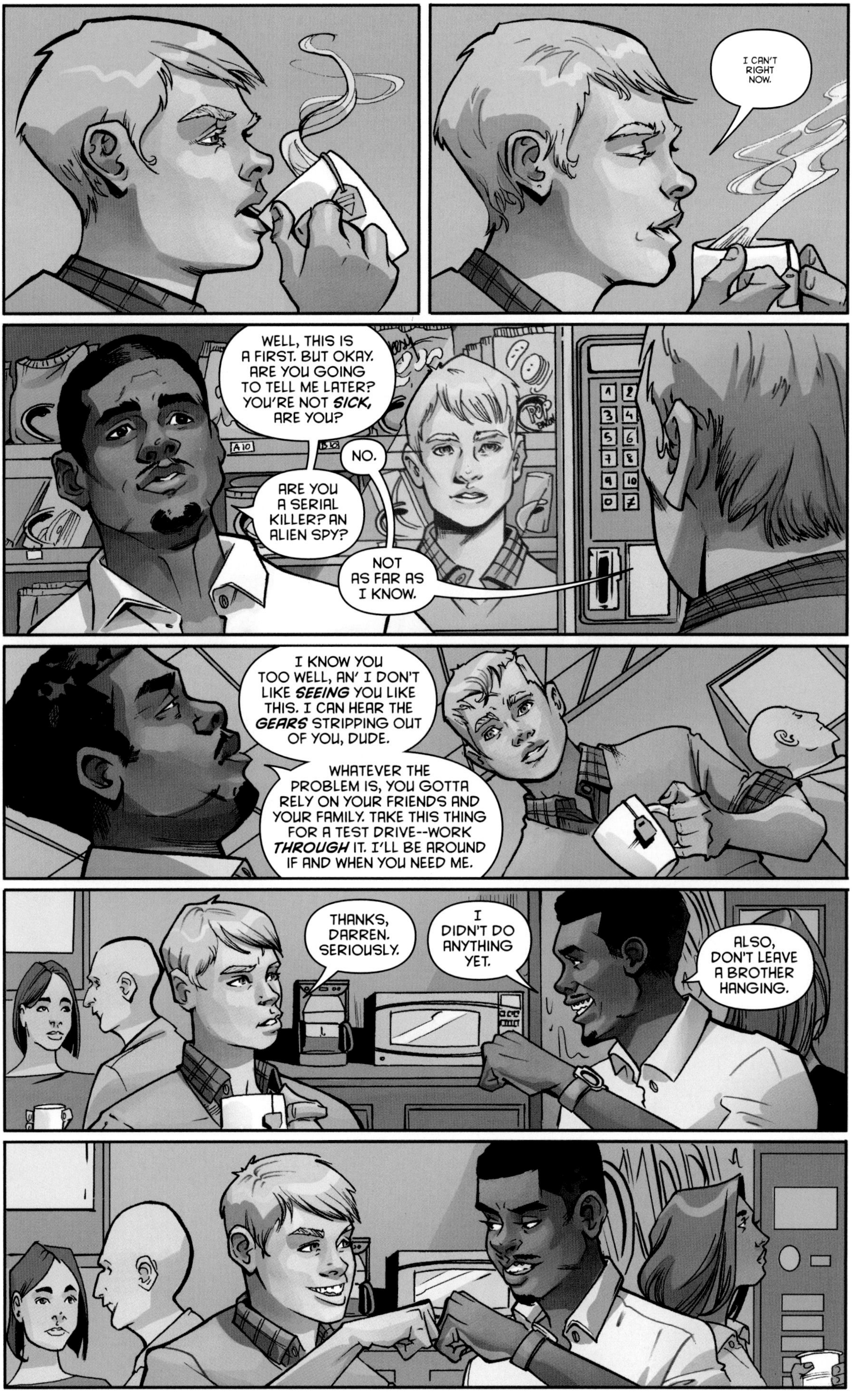
I CAN'T RIGHT NOW.
WELL, THIS IS A FIRST. BUT OKAY. ARE YOU GOING TO TELL ME LATER? YOU'RE NOT SICK, ARE YOU?
NO.
ARE YOU A SERIAL KILLER? AN ALIEN SPY?
NOT AS FAR AS I KNOW.
I KNOW YOU TOO WELL, AN' I DON'T LIKE SEEING YOU LIKE THIS. I CAN HEAR THE GEARS STRIPPING OUT OF YOU, DUDE.
WHATEVER THE PROBLEM IS, YOU GOTTA RELY ON YOUR FRIENDS AND YOUR FAMILY. TAKE THIS THING FOR A TEST DRIVE--WORK THROUGH IT. I'LL BE AROUND IF AND WHEN YOU NEED ME.
THANKS, DARREN. SERIOUSLY.
I DIDN'T DO ANYTHING YET.
ALSO, DON'T LEAVE A BROTHER HANGING.

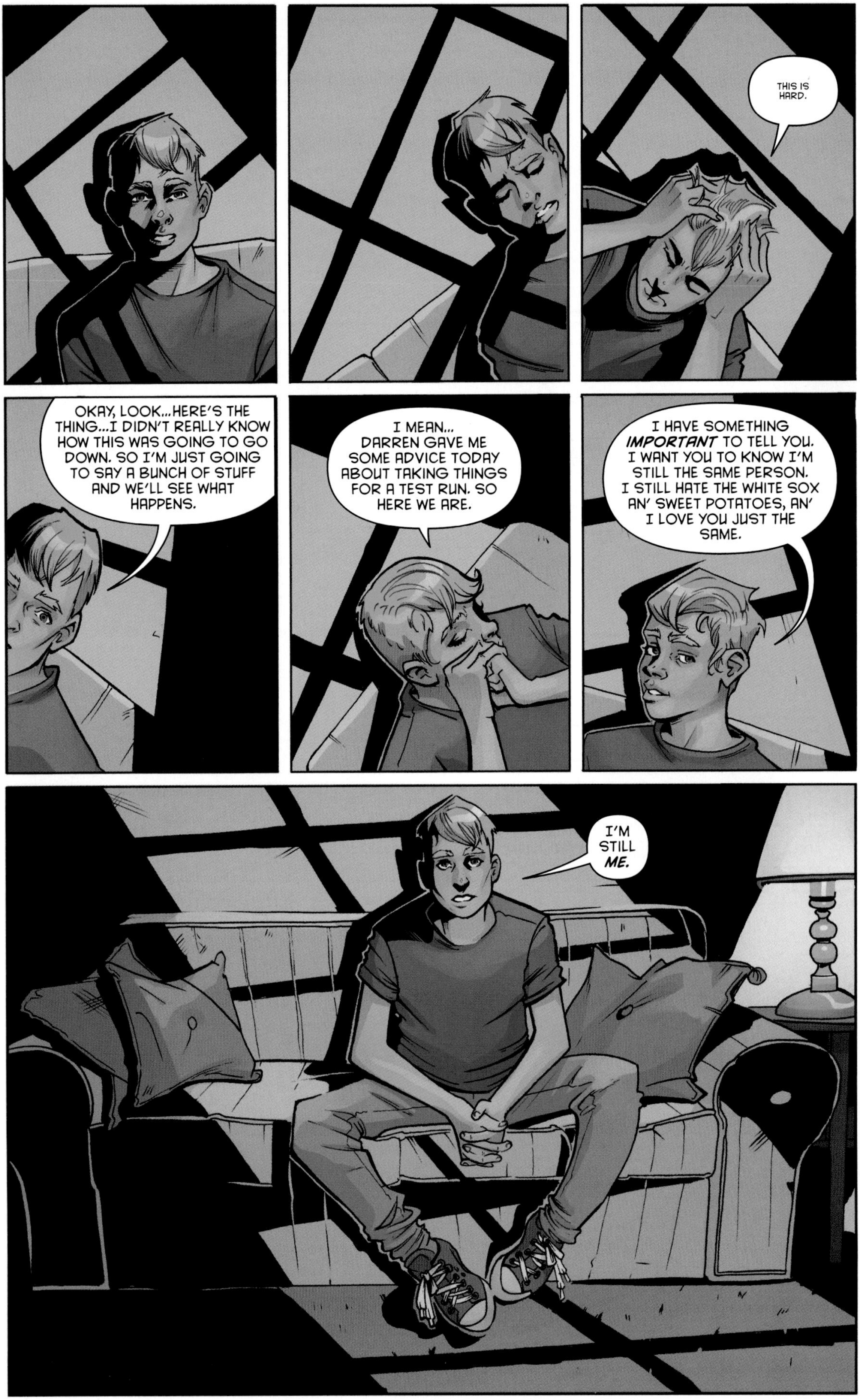

THIS IS HARD.
OKAY, LOOK...HERE'S THE THING...I DIDN'T REALLY KNOW HOW THIS WAS GOING TO GO DOWN. SO I'M JUST GOING TO SAY A BUNCH OF STUFF AND WE'LL SEE WHAT HAPPENS.
I MEAN... DARREN GAVE ME SOME ADVICE TODAY ABOUT TAKING THINGS FOR A TEST RUN. SO HERE WE ARE.
I HAVE SOMETHING ***IMPORTANT*** TO TELL YOU. I WANT YOU TO KNOW I'M STILL THE SAME PERSON. I STILL HATE THE WHITE SOX AN' SWEET POTATOES, AN' I LOVE YOU JUST THE SAME.
I'M STILL ***ME.***

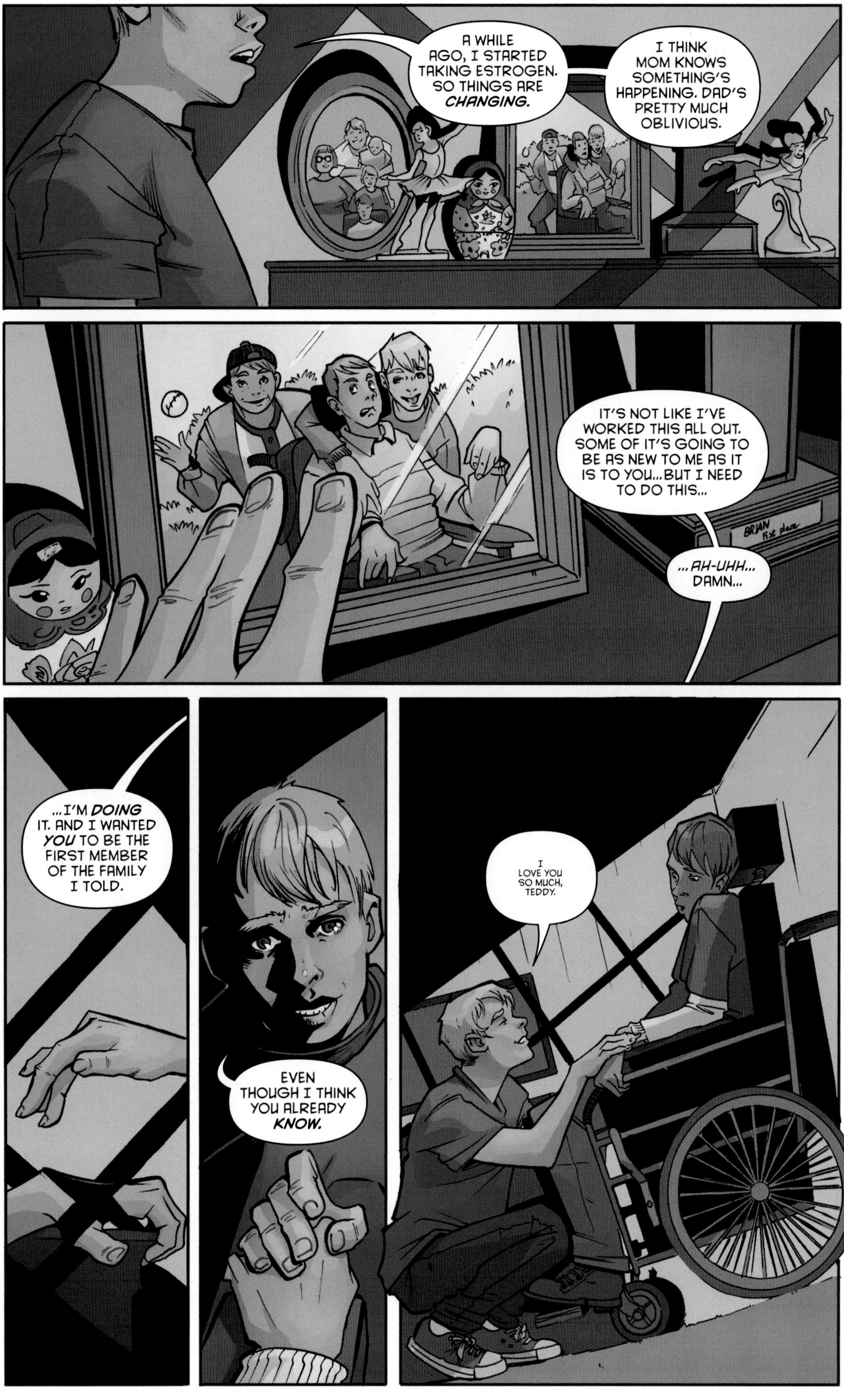
A WHILE AGO, I STARTED TAKING ESTROGEN. SO THINGS ARE *CHANGING.*
I THINK MOM KNOWS SOMETHING'S HAPPENING. DAD'S PRETTY MUCH OBLIVIOUS.
IT'S NOT LIKE I'VE WORKED THIS ALL OUT. SOME OF IT'S GOING TO BE AS NEW TO ME AS IT IS TO YOU...BUT I NEED TO DO THIS...
...*AH-UHH...* DAMN...
...I'M *DOING* IT. AND I WANTED *YOU* TO BE THE FIRST MEMBER OF THE FAMILY I TOLD.
EVEN THOUGH I THINK YOU ALREADY *KNOW.*
I LOVE YOU SO MUCH, TEDDY.

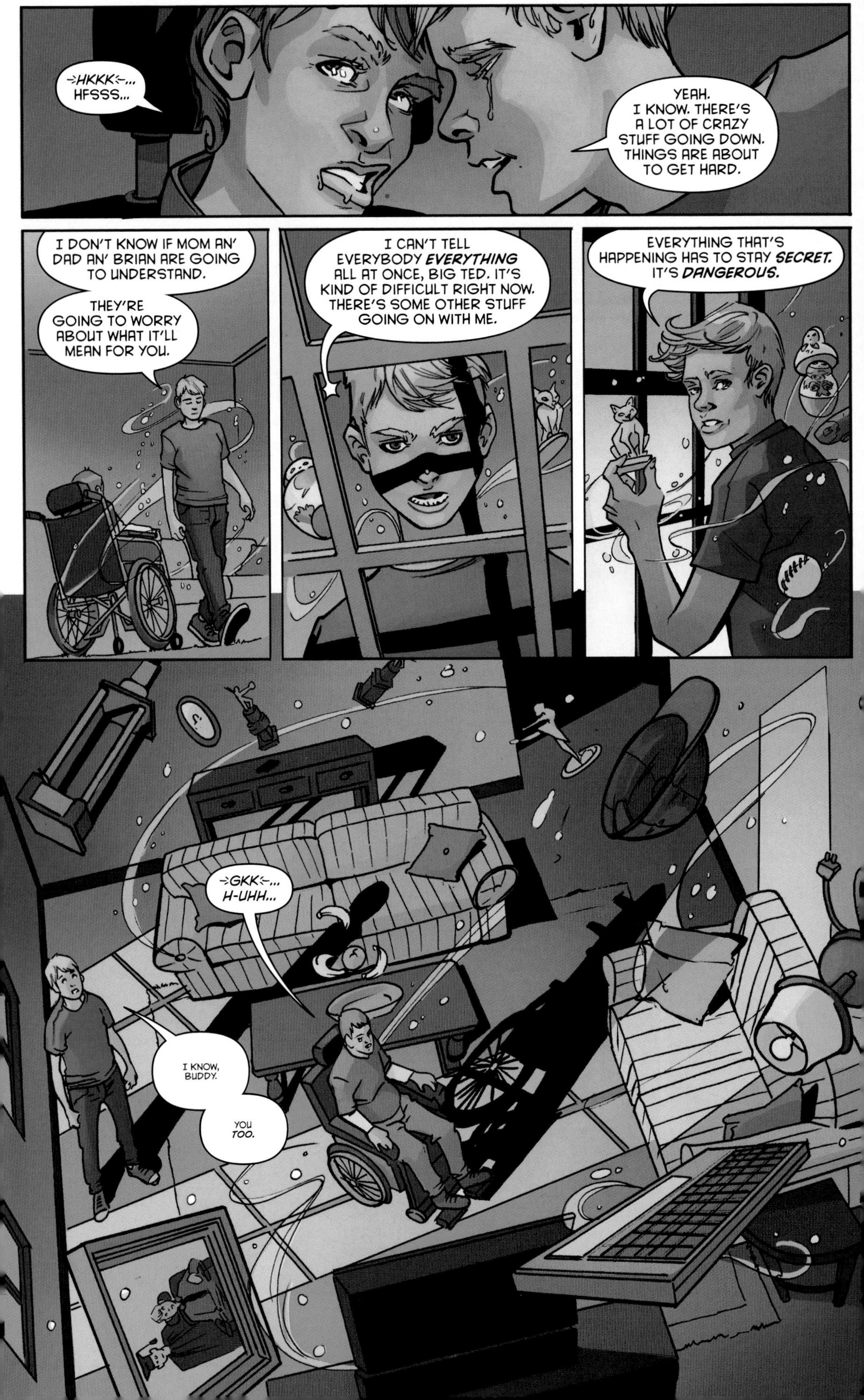
⇛HKKK⇚...
HFSSS...
YEAH.
I KNOW. THERE'S
A LOT OF CRAZY
STUFF GOING DOWN.
THINGS ARE ABOUT
TO GET HARD.
I DON'T KNOW IF MOM AN'
DAD AN' BRIAN ARE GOING
TO UNDERSTAND.
THEY'RE
GOING TO WORRY
ABOUT WHAT IT'LL
MEAN FOR YOU.
I CAN'T TELL
EVERYBODY *EVERYTHING*
ALL AT ONCE, BIG TED. IT'S
KIND OF DIFFICULT RIGHT NOW.
THERE'S SOME OTHER STUFF
GOING ON WITH ME.
EVERYTHING THAT'S
HAPPENING HAS TO STAY *SECRET.*
IT'S *DANGEROUS.*
⇛GKK⇚...
H-UHH...
I KNOW,
BUDDY.
YOU
TOO.

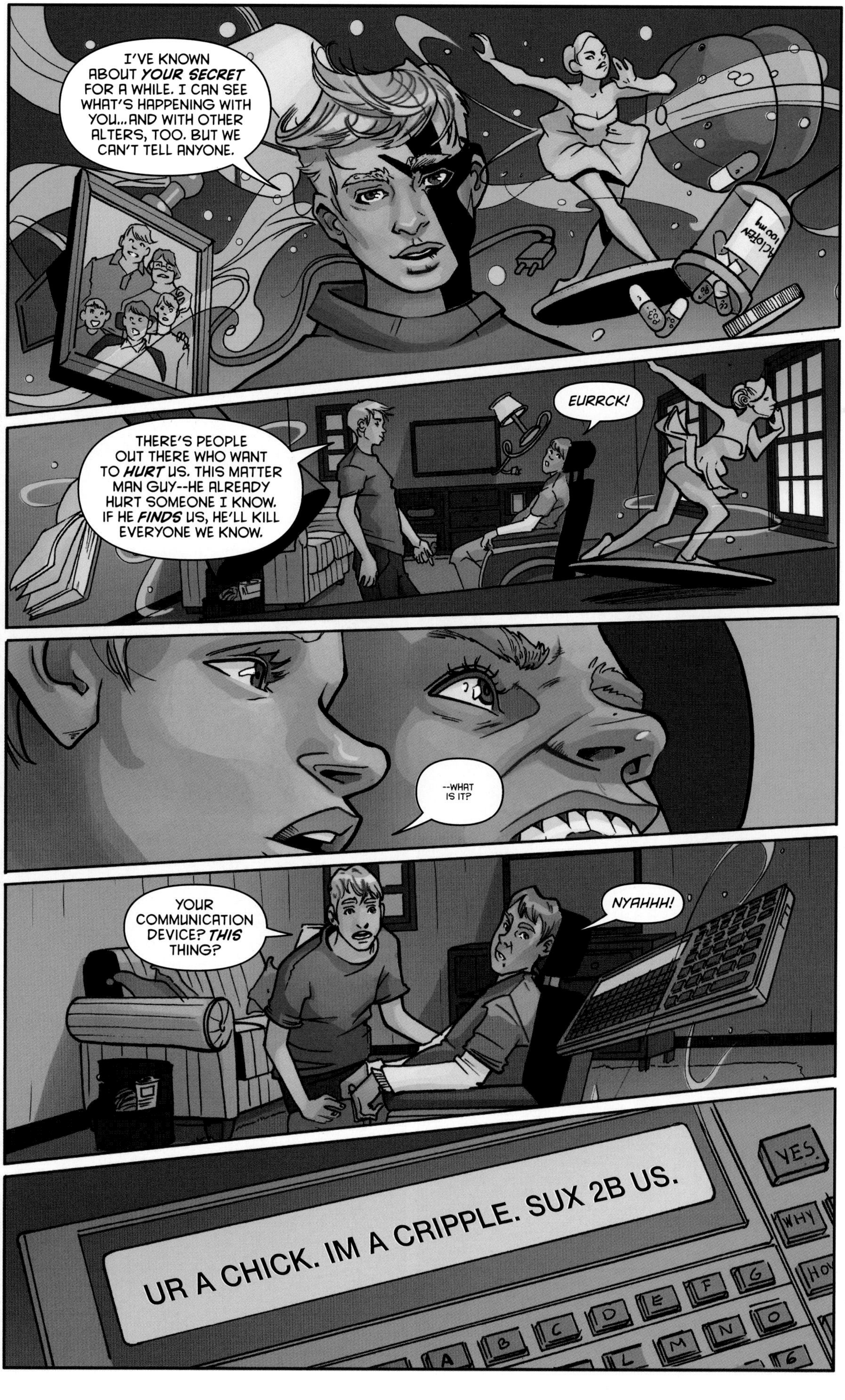
I'VE KNOWN ABOUT *YOUR SECRET* FOR A WHILE. I CAN SEE WHAT'S HAPPENING WITH YOU...AND WITH OTHER ALTERS, TOO. BUT WE CAN'T TELL ANYONE.
THERE'S PEOPLE OUT THERE WHO WANT TO *HURT* US. THIS MATTER MAN GUY--HE ALREADY HURT SOMEONE I KNOW. IF HE *FINDS* US, HE'LL KILL EVERYONE WE KNOW.
EURRCK!
--WHAT IS IT?
YOUR COMMUNICATION DEVICE? *THIS* THING?
NYAHHH!
UR A CHICK. IM A CRIPPLE. SUX 2B US.
YES.
WHY

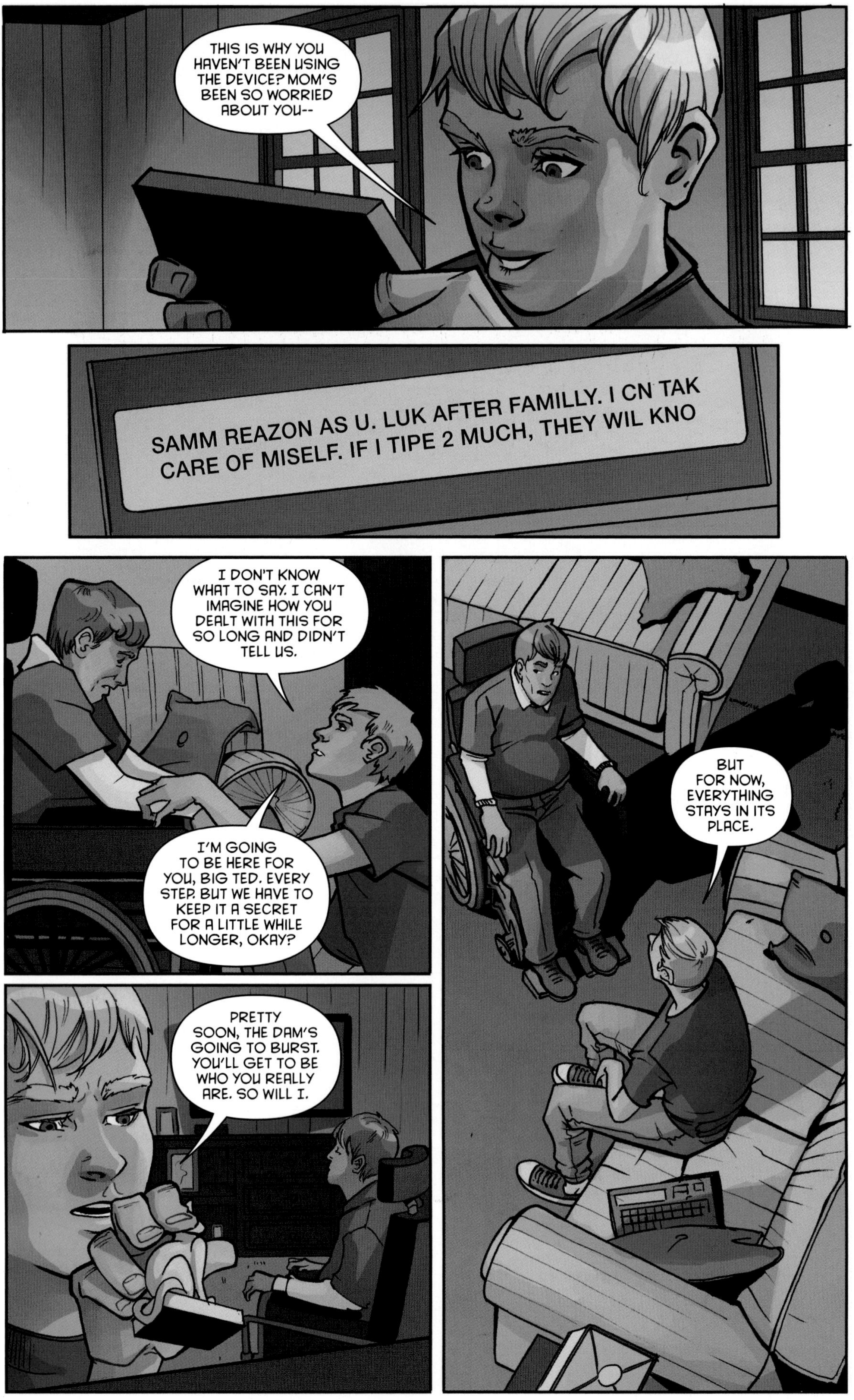
THIS IS WHY YOU HAVEN'T BEEN USING THE DEVICE? MOM'S BEEN SO WORRIED ABOUT YOU--
SAMM REAZON AS U. LUK AFTER FAMILLY. I CN TAK CARE OF MISELF. IF I TIPE 2 MUCH, THEY WIL KNO
I DON'T KNOW WHAT TO SAY. I CAN'T IMAGINE HOW YOU DEALT WITH THIS FOR SO LONG AND DIDN'T TELL US.
I'M GOING TO BE HERE FOR YOU, BIG TED. EVERY STEP. BUT WE HAVE TO KEEP IT A SECRET FOR A LITTLE WHILE LONGER, OKAY?
PRETTY SOON, THE DAM'S GOING TO BURST. YOU'LL GET TO BE WHO YOU REALLY ARE. SO WILL I.
BUT FOR NOW, EVERYTHING STAYS IN ITS PLACE.

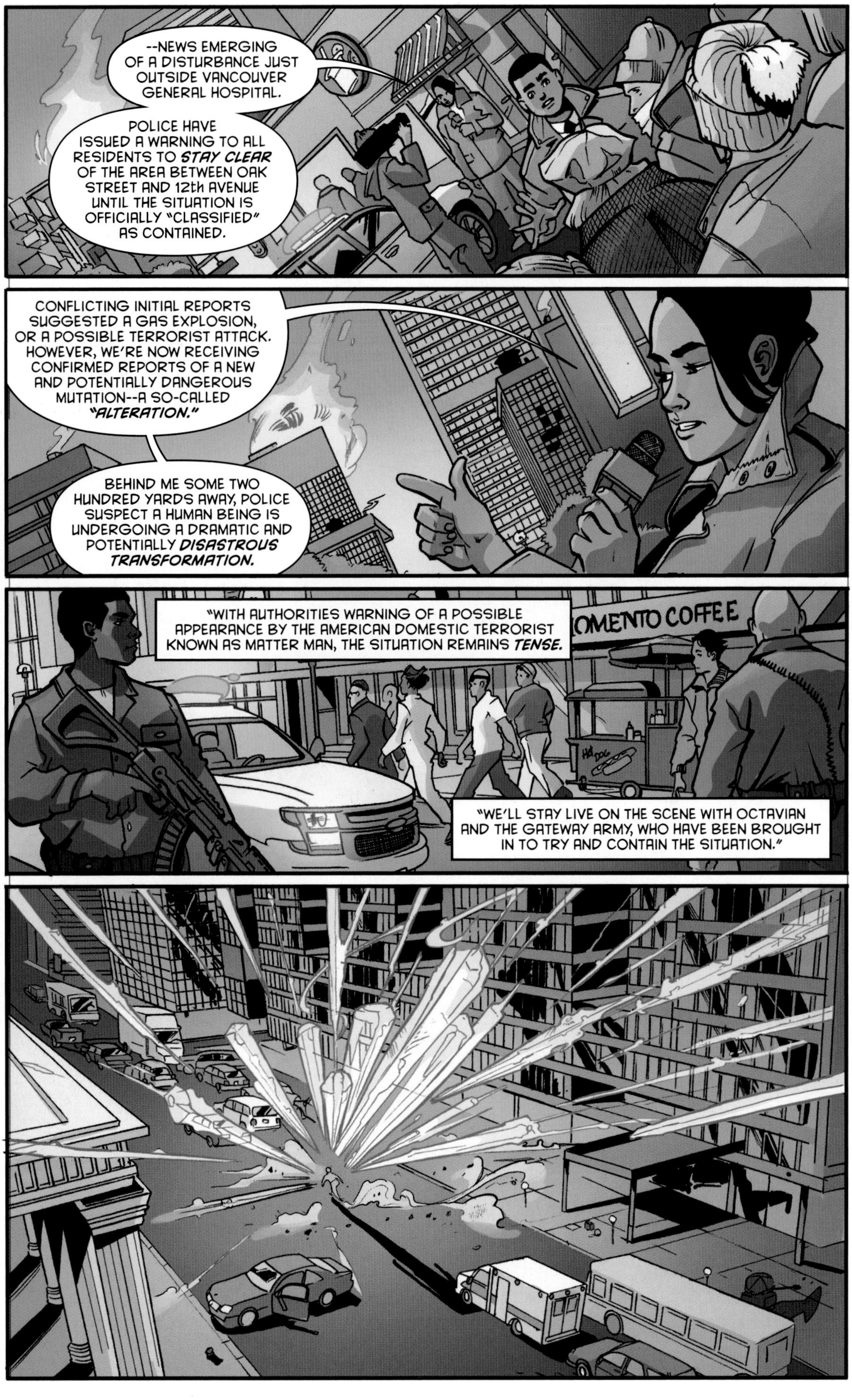
--NEWS EMERGING OF A DISTURBANCE JUST OUTSIDE VANCOUVER GENERAL HOSPITAL.
POLICE HAVE ISSUED A WARNING TO ALL RESIDENTS TO *STAY CLEAR* OF THE AREA BETWEEN OAK STREET AND 12th AVENUE UNTIL THE SITUATION IS OFFICIALLY "CLASSIFIED" AS CONTAINED.
CONFLICTING INITIAL REPORTS SUGGESTED A GAS EXPLOSION, OR A POSSIBLE TERRORIST ATTACK. HOWEVER, WE'RE NOW RECEIVING CONFIRMED REPORTS OF A NEW AND POTENTIALLY DANGEROUS MUTATION--A SO-CALLED *"ALTERATION."*
BEHIND ME SOME TWO HUNDRED YARDS AWAY, POLICE SUSPECT A HUMAN BEING IS UNDERGOING A DRAMATIC AND POTENTIALLY *DISASTROUS TRANSFORMATION.*
"WITH AUTHORITIES WARNING OF A POSSIBLE APPEARANCE BY THE AMERICAN DOMESTIC TERRORIST KNOWN AS MATTER MAN, THE SITUATION REMAINS *TENSE.*
OMENTO COFFEE
"WE'LL STAY LIVE ON THE SCENE WITH OCTAVIAN AND THE GATEWAY ARMY, WHO HAVE BEEN BROUGHT IN TO TRY AND CONTAIN THE SITUATION."

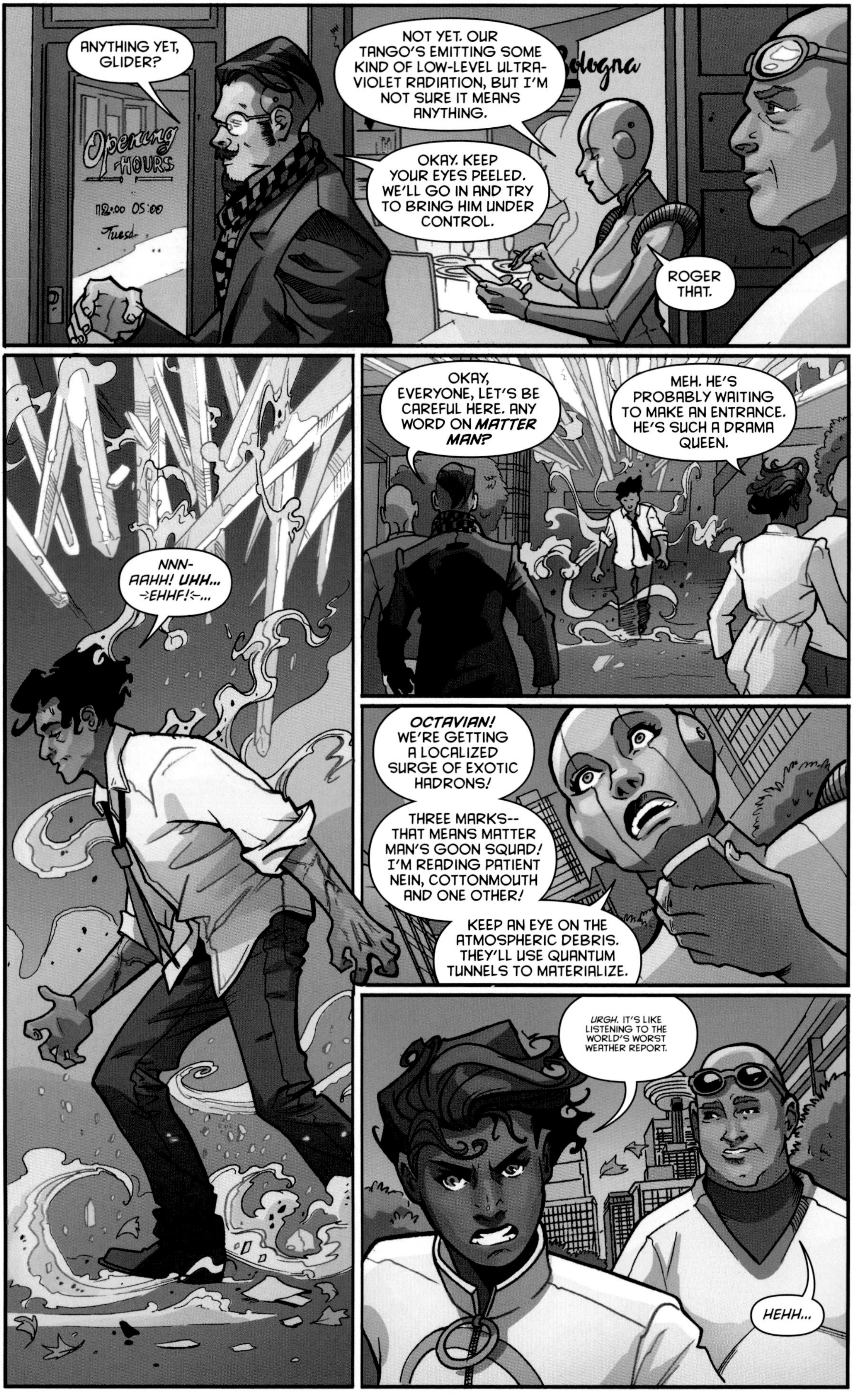
ANYTHING YET, GLIDER?
NOT YET. OUR TANGO'S EMITTING SOME KIND OF LOW-LEVEL ULTRA-VIOLET RADIATION, BUT I'M NOT SURE IT MEANS ANYTHING.
OKAY. KEEP YOUR EYES PEELED. WE'LL GO IN AND TRY TO BRING HIM UNDER CONTROL.
ROGER THAT.
NNN-AAHH! UHH... EHHF!...
OKAY, EVERYONE, LET'S BE CAREFUL HERE. ANY WORD ON MATTER MAN?
MEH. HE'S PROBABLY WAITING TO MAKE AN ENTRANCE. HE'S SUCH A DRAMA QUEEN.
OCTAVIAN! WE'RE GETTING A LOCALIZED SURGE OF EXOTIC HADRONS!
THREE MARKS-- THAT MEANS MATTER MAN'S GOON SQUAD! I'M READING PATIENT NEIN, COTTONMOUTH AND ONE OTHER!
KEEP AN EYE ON THE ATMOSPHERIC DEBRIS. THEY'LL USE QUANTUM TUNNELS TO MATERIALIZE.
URGH. IT'S LIKE LISTENING TO THE WORLD'S WORST WEATHER REPORT.
HEHH...

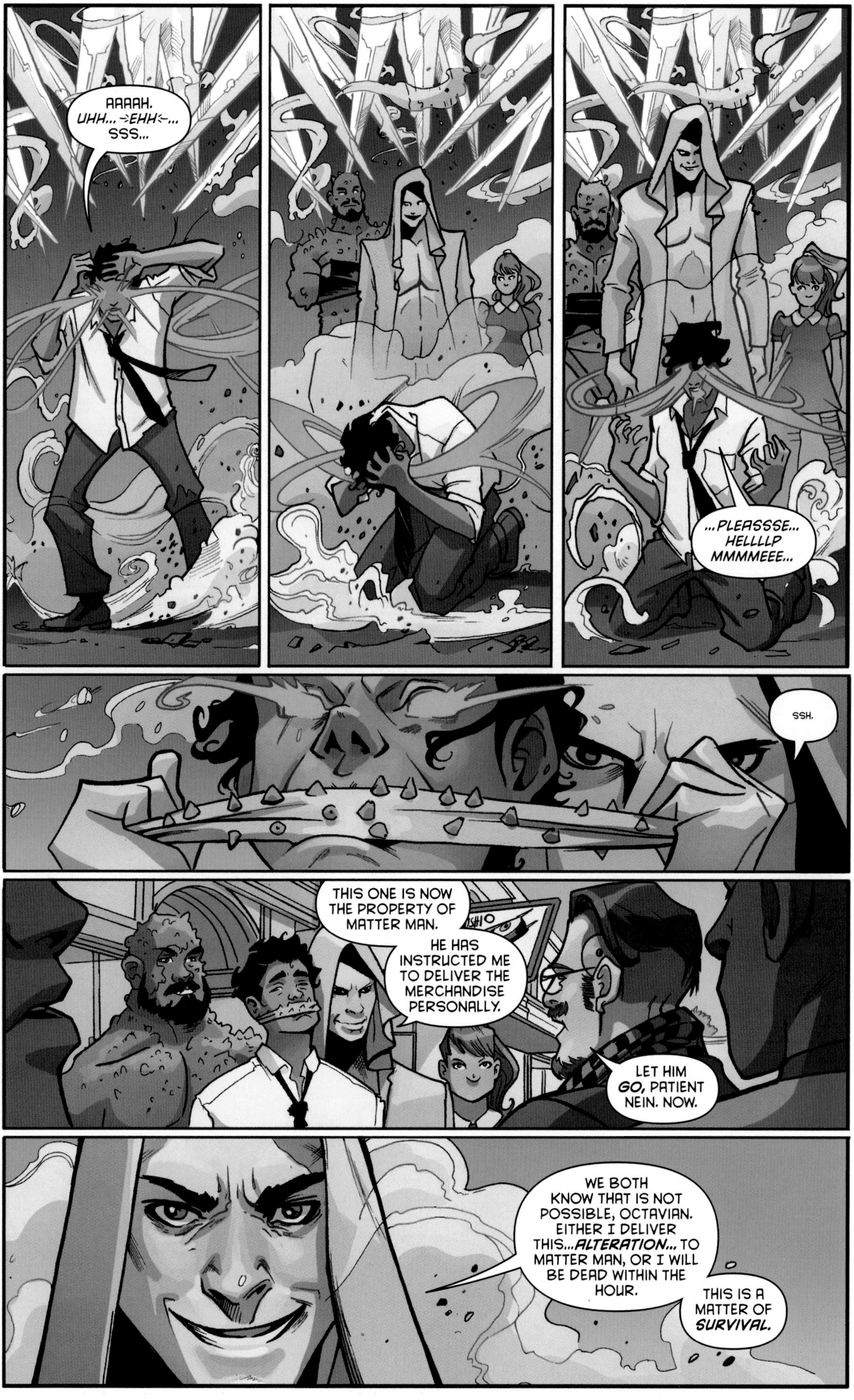
AAAAH. UHH... EHH... SSS...
...PLEASSSE... HELLLLP MMMMEEE...
SSH.
THIS ONE IS NOW THE PROPERTY OF MATTER MAN.
HE HAS INSTRUCTED ME TO DELIVER THE MERCHANDISE PERSONALLY.
LET HIM GO, PATIENT NEIN. NOW.
WE BOTH KNOW THAT IS NOT POSSIBLE, OCTAVIAN. EITHER I DELIVER THIS...ALTERATION... TO MATTER MAN, OR I WILL BE DEAD WITHIN THE HOUR.
THIS IS A MATTER OF SURVIVAL.

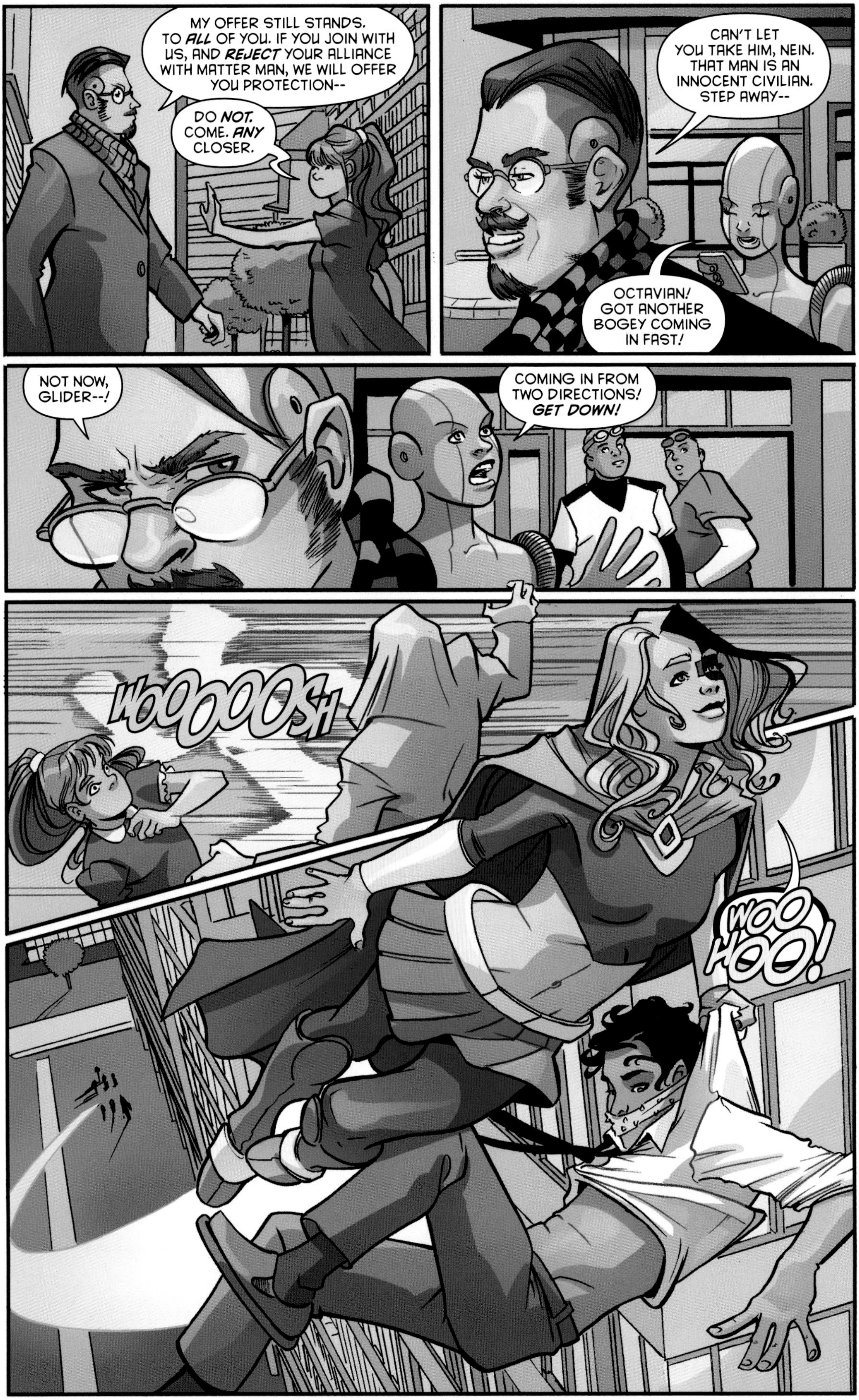
MY OFFER STILL STANDS. TO ALL OF YOU. IF YOU JOIN WITH US, AND REJECT YOUR ALLIANCE WITH MATTER MAN, WE WILL OFFER YOU PROTECTION--
DO NOT. COME. ANY CLOSER.
CAN'T LET YOU TAKE HIM, NEIN. THAT MAN IS AN INNOCENT CIVILIAN. STEP AWAY--
OCTAVIAN! GOT ANOTHER BOGEY COMING IN FAST!
NOT NOW, GLIDER--!
COMING IN FROM TWO DIRECTIONS! GET DOWN!
WOOOOOOSH
WOO HOO!

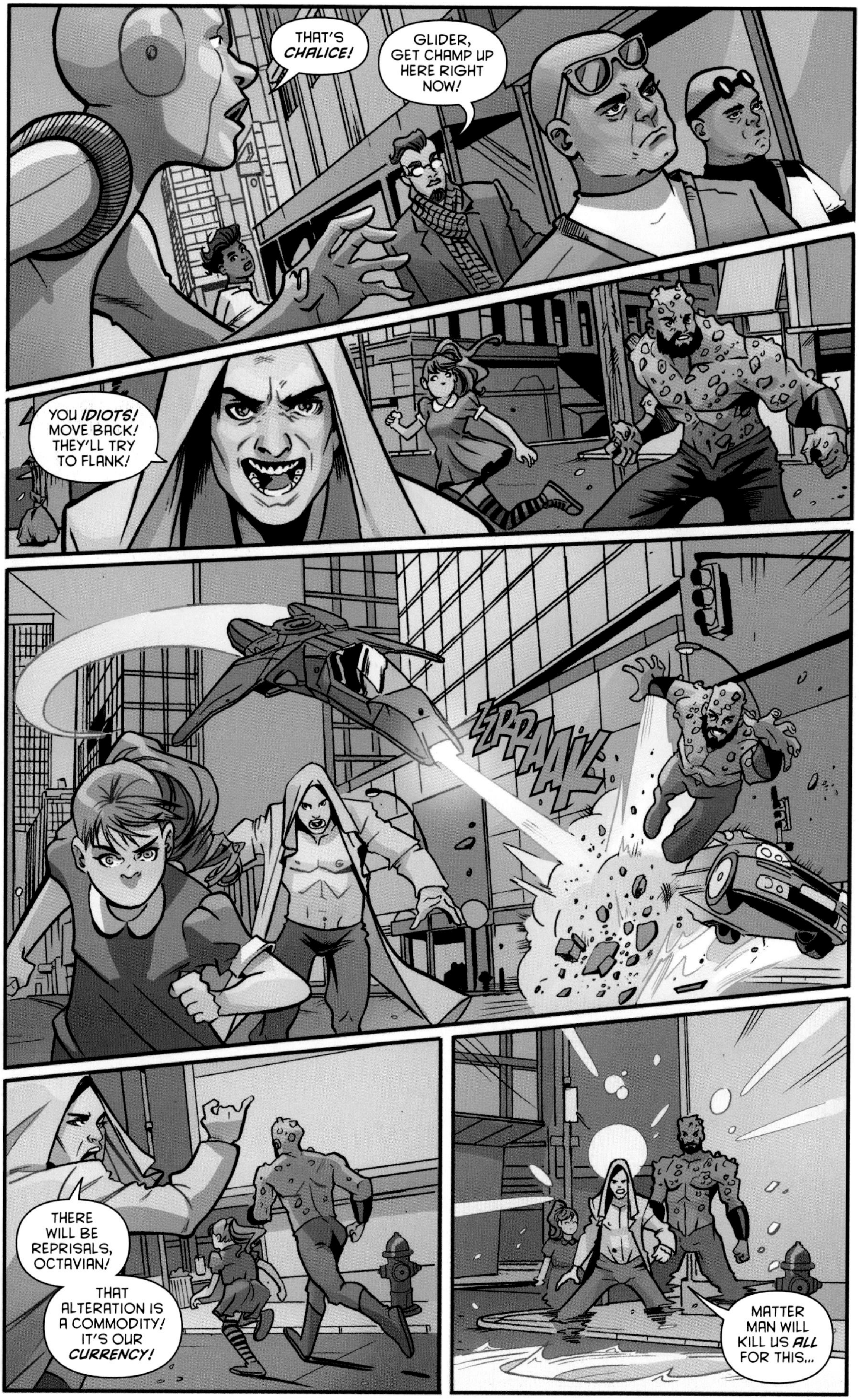
THAT'S *CHALICE!*
GLIDER, GET CHAMP UP HERE RIGHT NOW!
YOU *IDIOTS!* MOVE BACK! THEY'LL TRY TO FLANK!
ZZRAAK
THERE WILL BE REPRISALS, OCTAVIAN!
THAT ALTERATION IS A COMMODITY! IT'S OUR *CURRENCY!*
MATTER MAN WILL KILL US *ALL* FOR THIS...

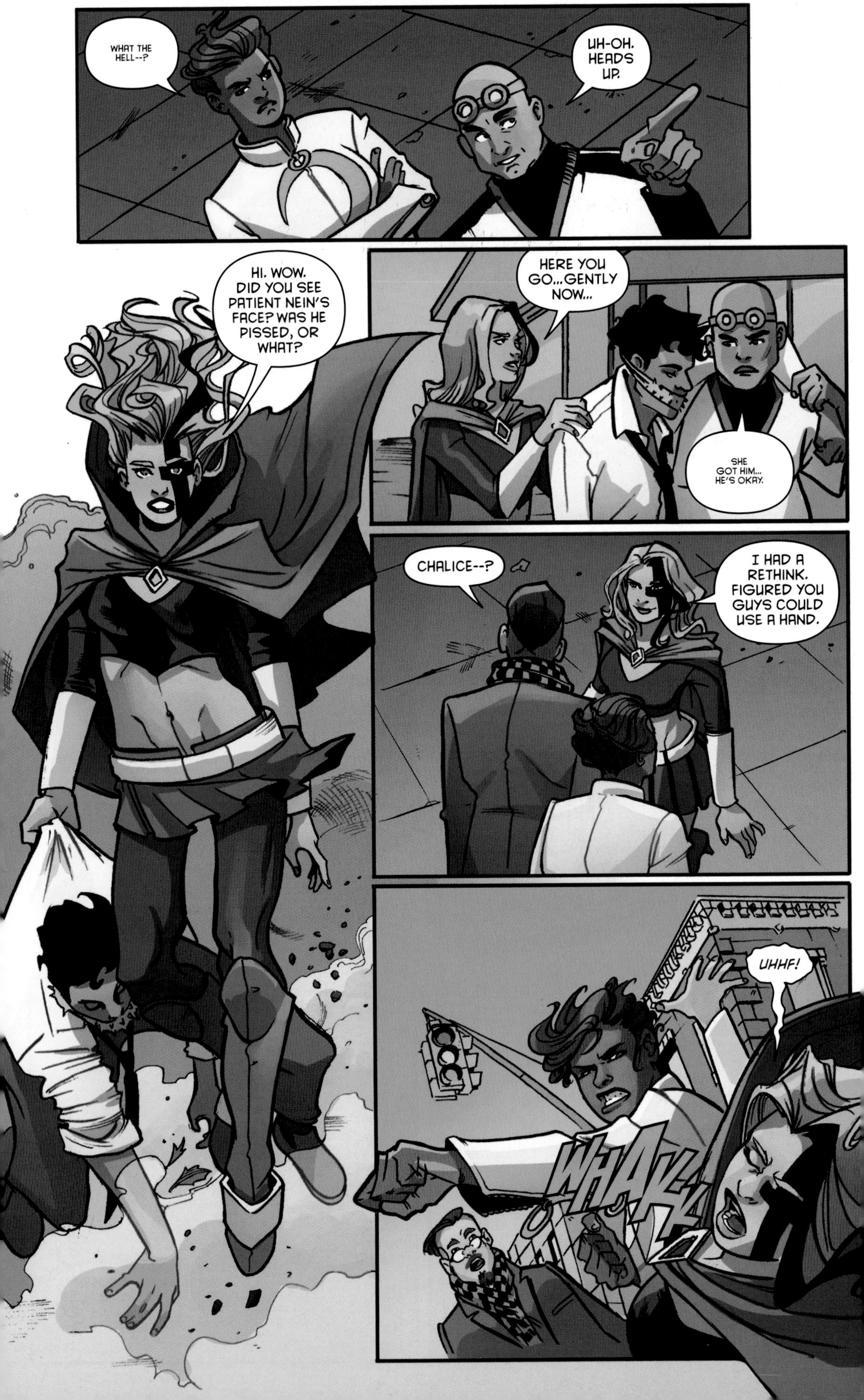
WHAT THE HELL--?
UH-OH. HEADS UP.
HI. WOW. DID YOU SEE PATIENT NEIN'S FACE? WAS HE PISSED, OR WHAT?
HERE YOU GO...GENTLY NOW...
SHE GOT HIM... HE'S OKAY.
CHALICE--?
I HAD A RETHINK. FIGURED YOU GUYS COULD USE A HAND.
UHHF!
WHAK!

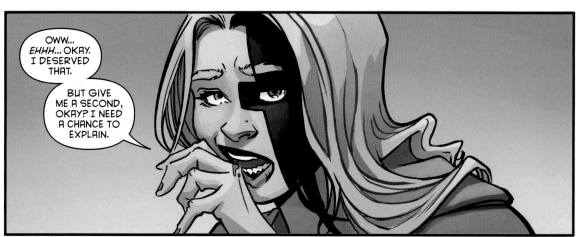

OWW... *EHHH...* OKAY. I DESERVED THAT.

BUT GIVE ME A SECOND, OKAY? I NEED A CHANCE TO EXPLAIN.

REALLY? WHAT CHANCE DID YOU GIVE *MORPH?*

HE'S IN A HOSPITAL BED RIGHT NOW, AND HE'S GONNA WAKE UP WITH A *CEILING* AS HIS BEST FRIEND!

BECAUSE OF *YOU,* OUR GUY IS IN A *COMA,* AND HIS LIFE IS UPSIDE-DOWN!

EMBER--

NO, THIS HAS TO BE SAID RIGHT NOW! I'M NOT ABOUT TO LET SOME HOTHEAD RUN IN ON EVERYTHING WE TRY TO ACHIEVE JUST BECAUSE SHE WOKE UP AND FOUND OUT SHE COULD FLY THROUGH SPACE!

YOU'RE RIGHT. EVERYTHING YOU'VE SAID. BUT I'VE NEVER DONE THIS BEFORE, AN' I'M WORKING THROUGH A LOT OF STUFF RIGHT NOW.

I DIDN'T MEAN TO PUT MORPH IN HARM'S WAY. I DIDN'T UNDERSTAND WHAT KIND OF MISTAKE I WAS MAKING. BUT IT'S NOT LIKE I *PLANNED* FOR ANY OF THIS.

SO *PLEASE.* I CAN'T GO BACK. I CAN ONLY GO FORWARD.

PLEASE LET ME *HELP.*

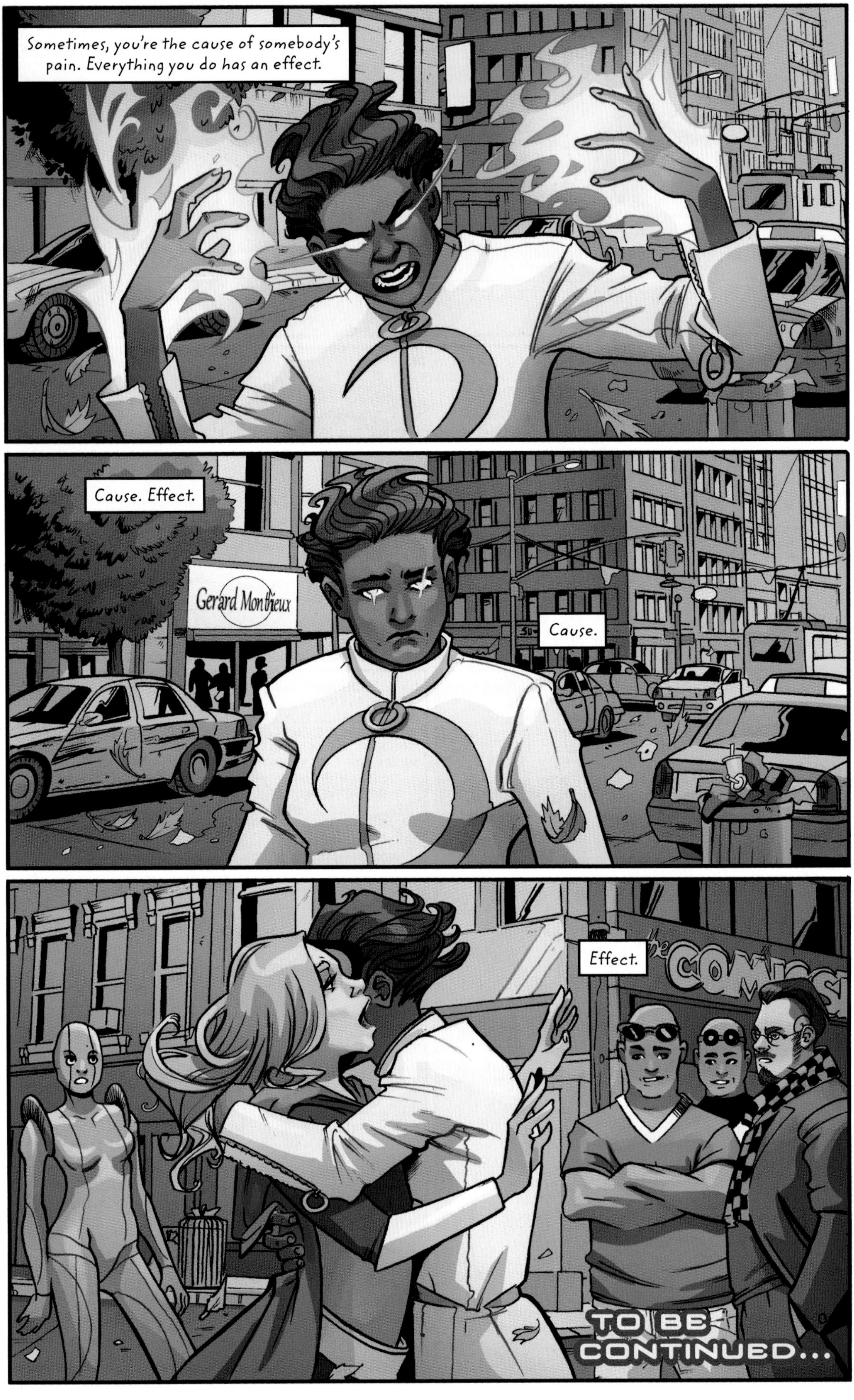
Sometimes, you're the cause of somebody's pain. Everything you do has an effect.
Cause. Effect.
Gerard Montfieux
Cause.
Effect.
TO BE CONTINUED...

4

"THE RISING TIDE"

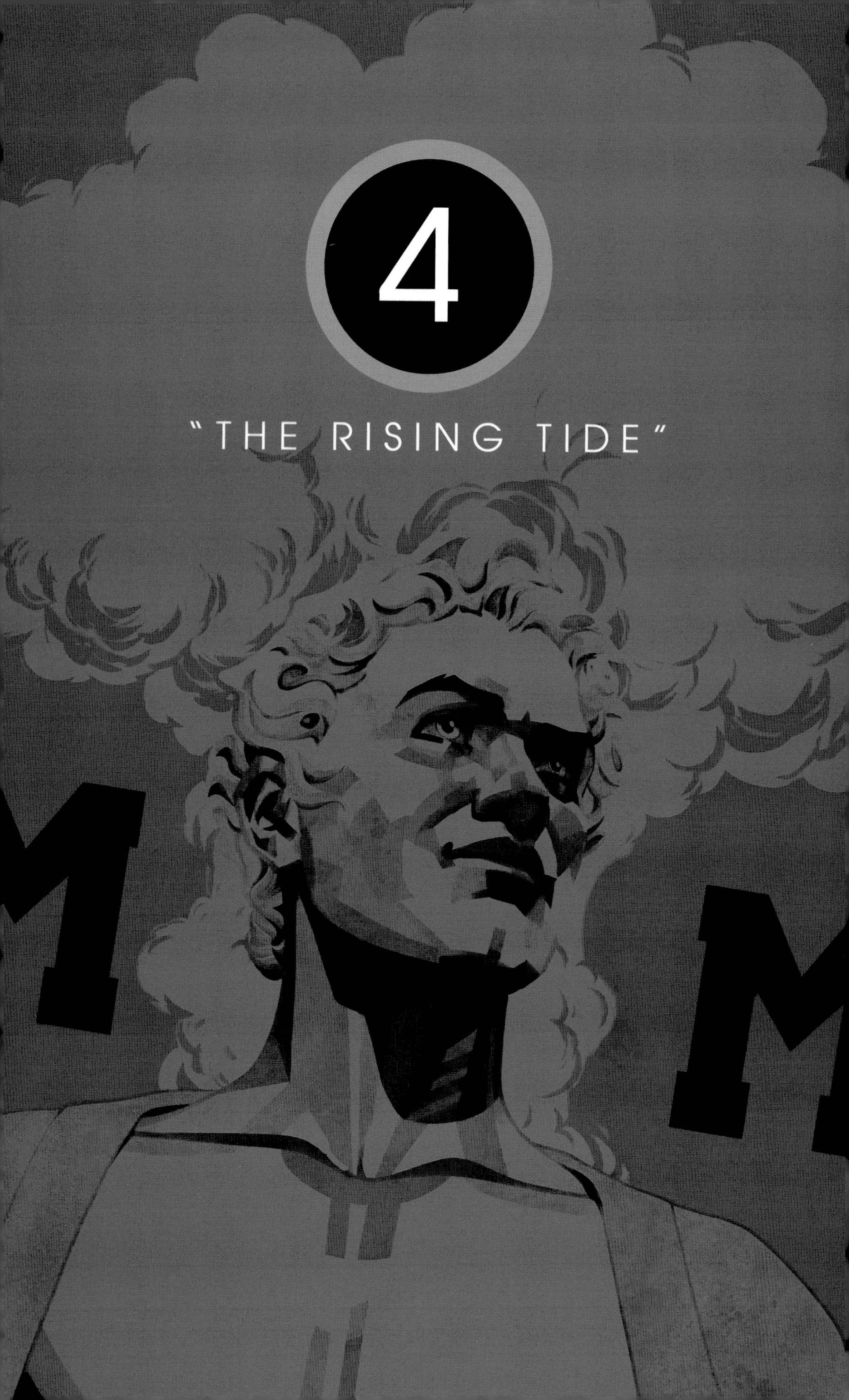

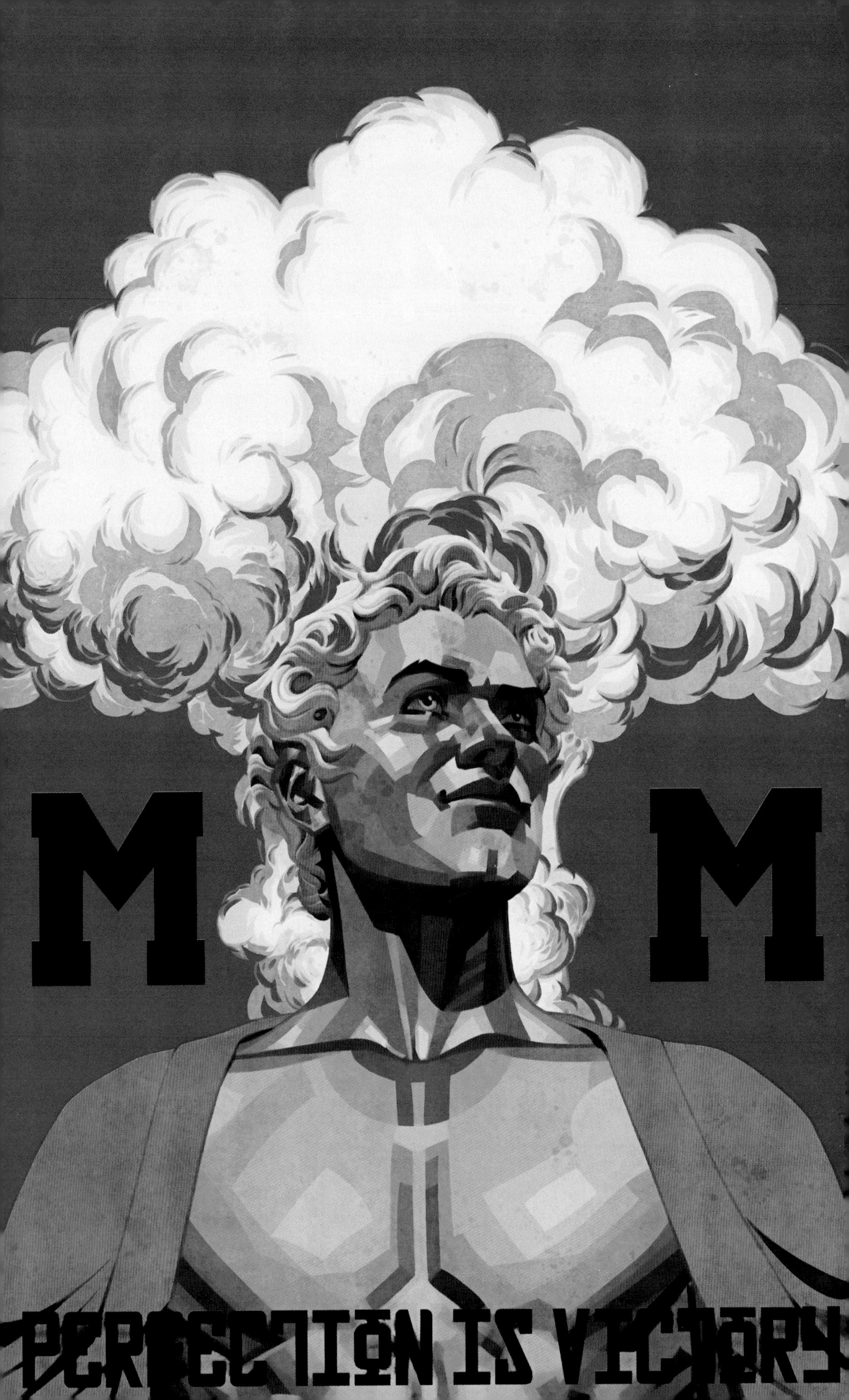
M
M
PERFECTION IS VICTORY

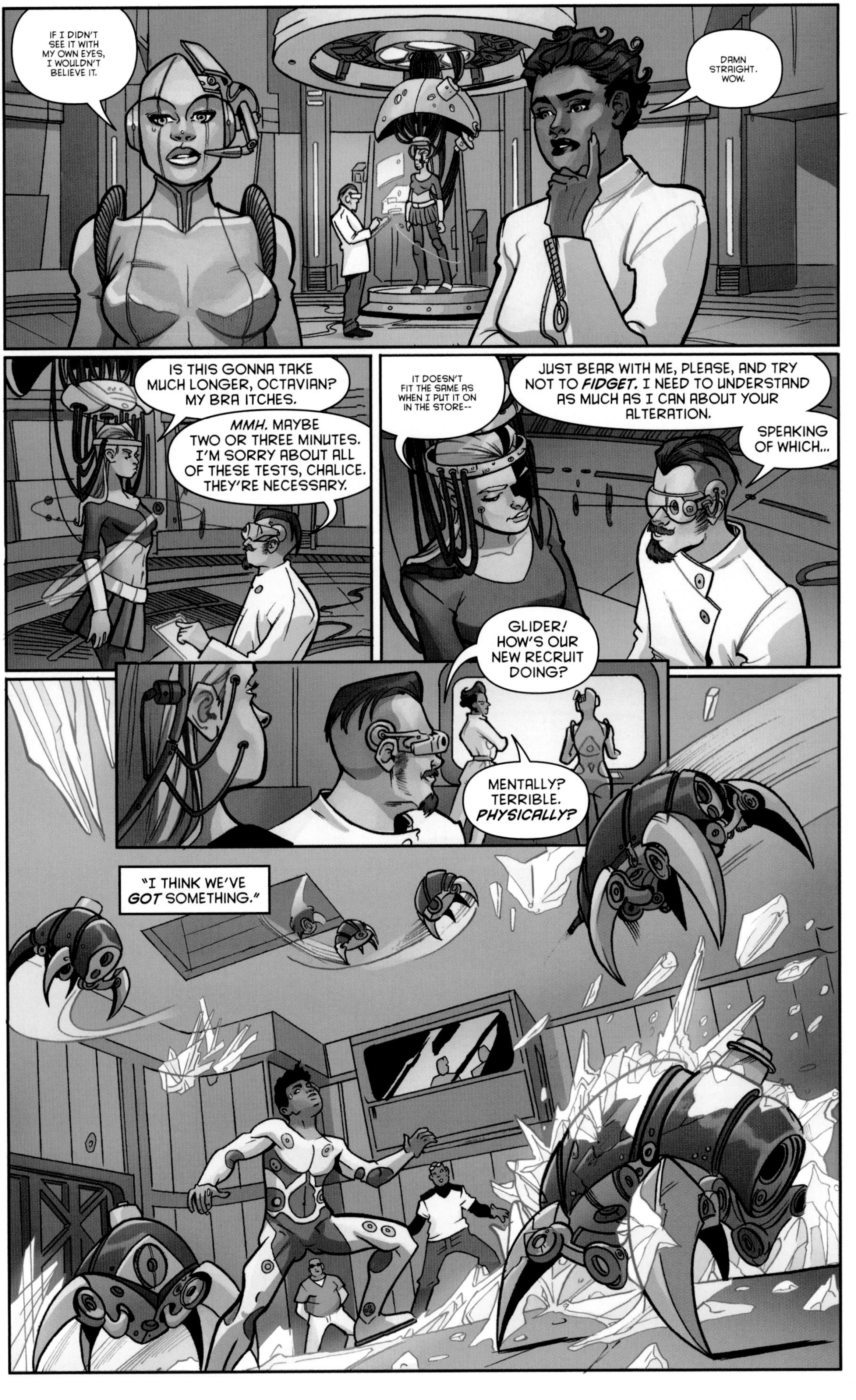
IF I DIDN'T SEE IT WITH MY OWN EYES, I WOULDN'T BELIEVE IT.
DAMN STRAIGHT. WOW.
IS THIS GONNA TAKE MUCH LONGER, OCTAVIAN? MY BRA ITCHES.
MMH. MAYBE TWO OR THREE MINUTES. I'M SORRY ABOUT ALL OF THESE TESTS, CHALICE. THEY'RE NECESSARY.
IT DOESN'T FIT THE SAME AS WHEN I PUT IT ON IN THE STORE--
JUST BEAR WITH ME, PLEASE, AND TRY NOT TO FIDGET. I NEED TO UNDERSTAND AS MUCH AS I CAN ABOUT YOUR ALTERATION.
SPEAKING OF WHICH...
GLIDER! HOW'S OUR NEW RECRUIT DOING?
MENTALLY? TERRIBLE. PHYSICALLY?
"I THINK WE'VE GOT SOMETHING."

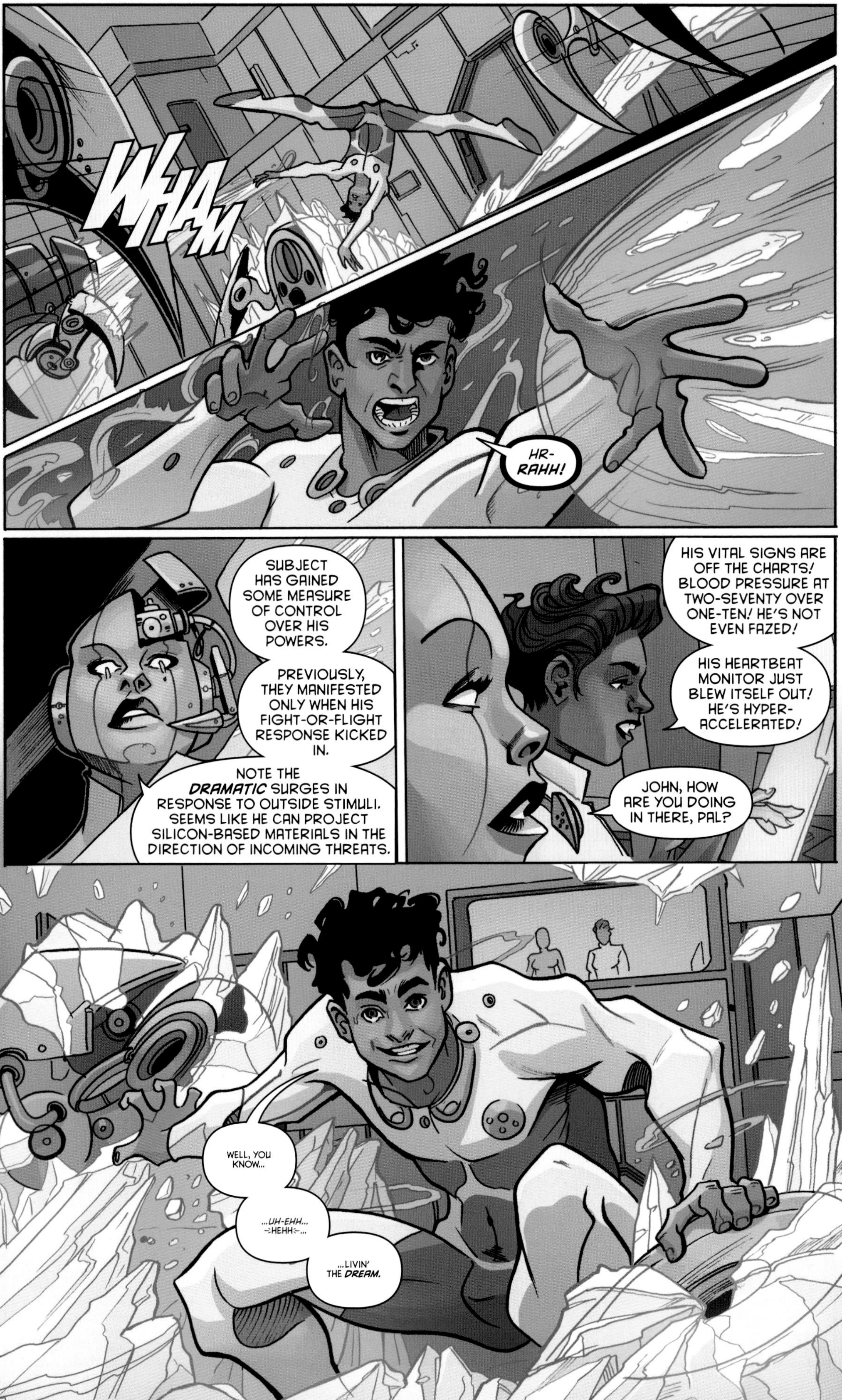
WHAM
HR-RAHH!
SUBJECT HAS GAINED SOME MEASURE OF CONTROL OVER HIS POWERS.
PREVIOUSLY, THEY MANIFESTED ONLY WHEN HIS FIGHT-OR-FLIGHT RESPONSE KICKED IN.
NOTE THE DRAMATIC SURGES IN RESPONSE TO OUTSIDE STIMULI. SEEMS LIKE HE CAN PROJECT SILICON-BASED MATERIALS IN THE DIRECTION OF INCOMING THREATS.
HIS VITAL SIGNS ARE OFF THE CHARTS! BLOOD PRESSURE AT TWO-SEVENTY OVER ONE-TEN! HE'S NOT EVEN FAZED!
HIS HEARTBEAT MONITOR JUST BLEW ITSELF OUT! HE'S HYPER-ACCELERATED!
JOHN, HOW ARE YOU DOING IN THERE, PAL?
WELL, YOU KNOW...
...UH-EHH... HEHH...
...LIVIN' THE DREAM.

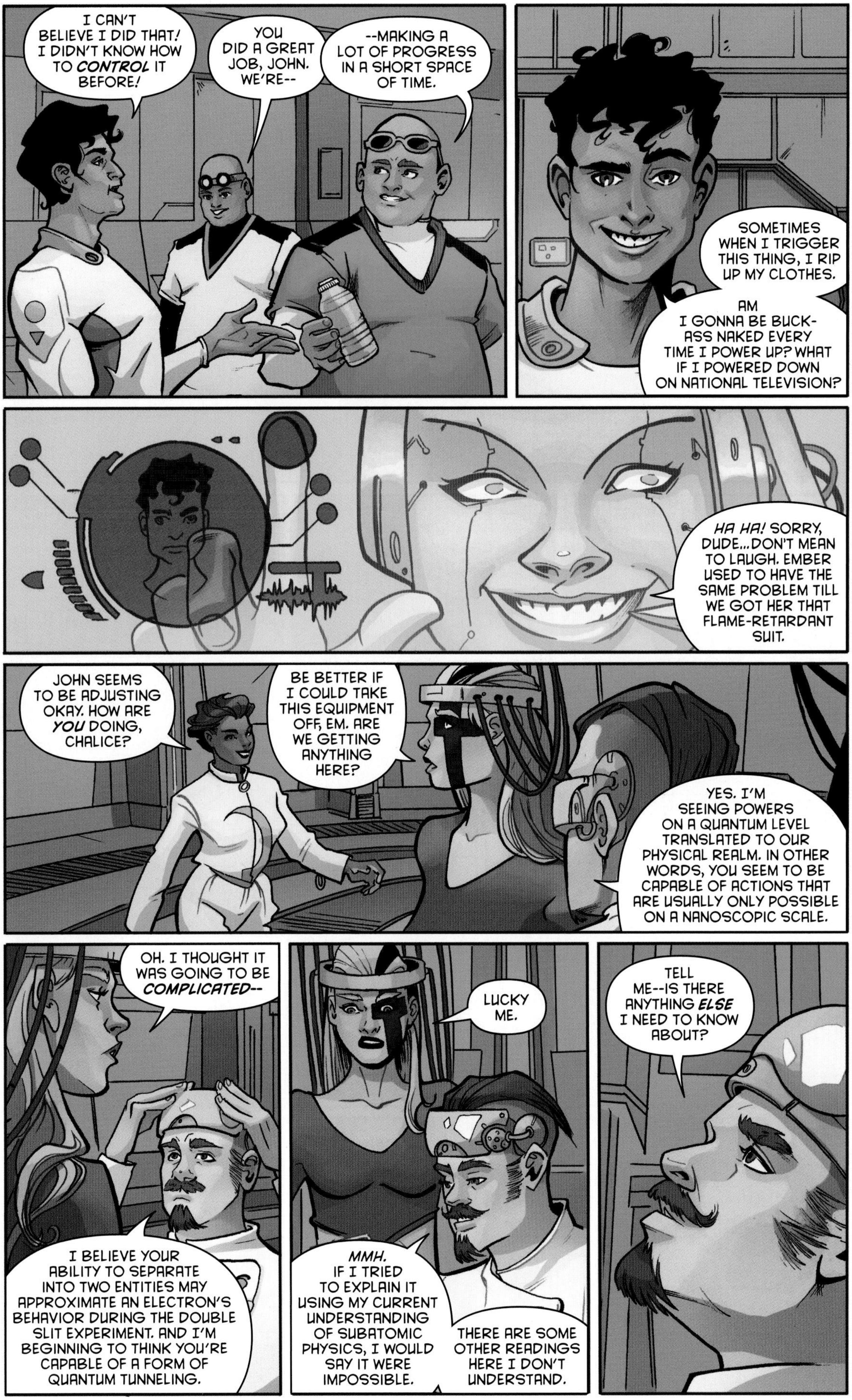
I CAN'T BELIEVE I DID THAT! I DIDN'T KNOW HOW TO *CONTROL* IT BEFORE!
YOU DID A GREAT JOB, JOHN. WE'RE--
--MAKING A LOT OF PROGRESS IN A SHORT SPACE OF TIME.
SOMETIMES WHEN I TRIGGER THIS THING, I RIP UP MY CLOTHES.
AM I GONNA BE BUCK-ASS NAKED EVERY TIME I POWER UP? WHAT IF I POWERED DOWN ON NATIONAL TELEVISION?
HA HA! SORRY, DUDE...DON'T MEAN TO LAUGH. EMBER USED TO HAVE THE SAME PROBLEM TILL WE GOT HER THAT FLAME-RETARDANT SUIT.
JOHN SEEMS TO BE ADJUSTING OKAY. HOW ARE *YOU* DOING, CHALICE?
BE BETTER IF I COULD TAKE THIS EQUIPMENT OFF, EM. ARE WE GETTING ANYTHING HERE?
YES. I'M SEEING POWERS ON A QUANTUM LEVEL TRANSLATED TO OUR PHYSICAL REALM. IN OTHER WORDS, YOU SEEM TO BE CAPABLE OF ACTIONS THAT ARE USUALLY ONLY POSSIBLE ON A NANOSCOPIC SCALE.
OH. I THOUGHT IT WAS GOING TO BE *COMPLICATED*--
I BELIEVE YOUR ABILITY TO SEPARATE INTO TWO ENTITIES MAY APPROXIMATE AN ELECTRON'S BEHAVIOR DURING THE DOUBLE SLIT EXPERIMENT. AND I'M BEGINNING TO THINK YOU'RE CAPABLE OF A FORM OF QUANTUM TUNNELING.
LUCKY ME.
MMH. IF I TRIED TO EXPLAIN IT USING MY CURRENT UNDERSTANDING OF SUBATOMIC PHYSICS, I WOULD SAY IT WERE IMPOSSIBLE.
THERE ARE SOME OTHER READINGS HERE I DON'T UNDERSTAND.
TELL ME--IS THERE ANYTHING *ELSE* I NEED TO KNOW ABOUT?

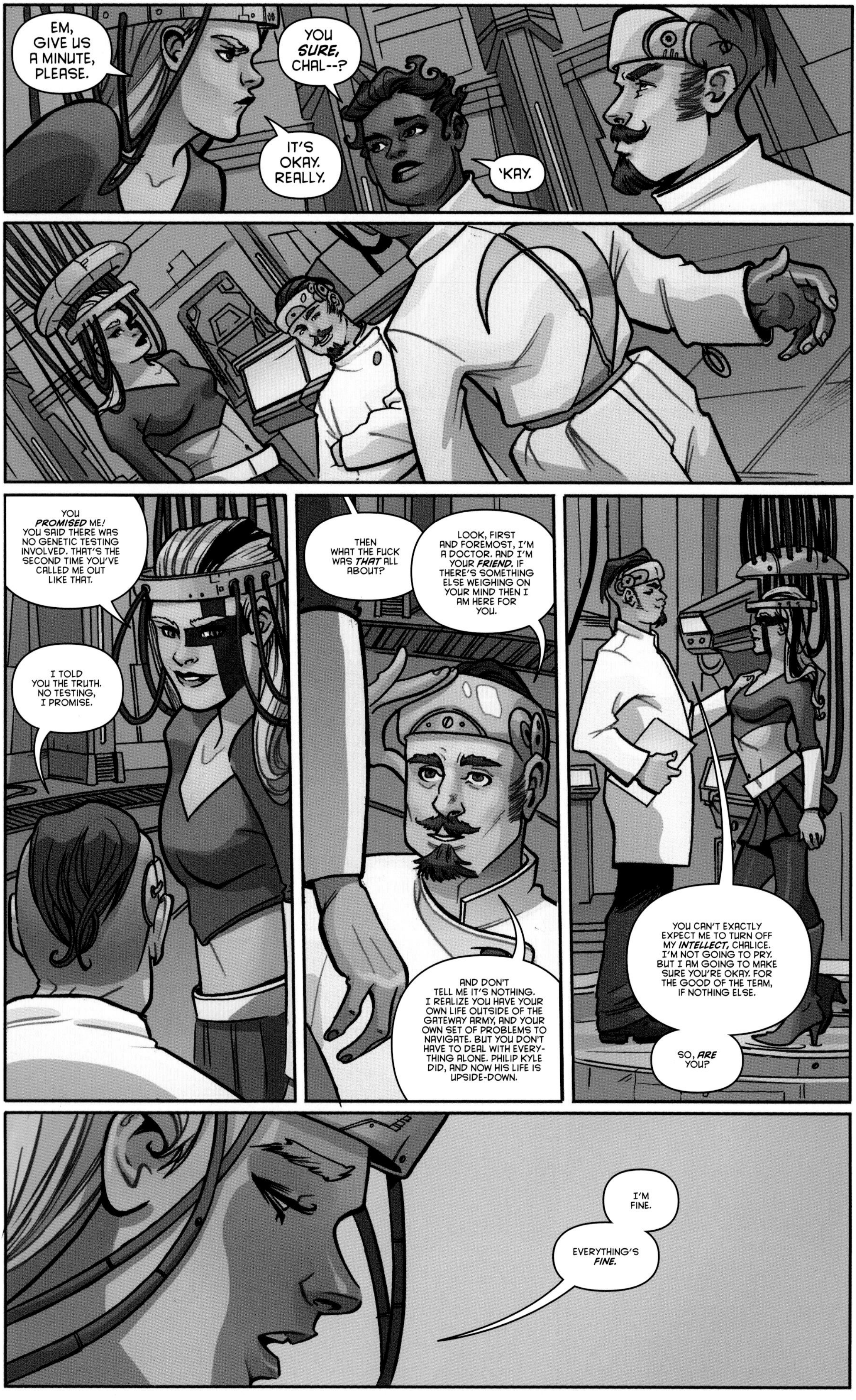
EM, GIVE US A MINUTE, PLEASE.
YOU *SURE,* CHAL--?
IT'S OKAY. REALLY.
'KAY.
YOU *PROMISED* ME! YOU SAID THERE WAS NO GENETIC TESTING INVOLVED. THAT'S THE SECOND TIME YOU'VE CALLED ME OUT LIKE THAT.
I TOLD YOU THE TRUTH. NO TESTING, I PROMISE.
THEN WHAT THE FUCK WAS *THAT* ALL ABOUT?
LOOK, FIRST AND FOREMOST, I'M A DOCTOR. AND I'M YOUR *FRIEND.* IF THERE'S SOMETHING ELSE WEIGHING ON YOUR MIND THEN I AM HERE FOR YOU.
AND DON'T TELL ME IT'S NOTHING. I REALIZE YOU HAVE YOUR OWN LIFE OUTSIDE OF THE GATEWAY ARMY, AND YOUR OWN SET OF PROBLEMS TO NAVIGATE. BUT YOU DON'T HAVE TO DEAL WITH EVERY-THING ALONE. PHILIP KYLE DID, AND NOW HIS LIFE IS UPSIDE-DOWN.
YOU CAN'T EXACTLY EXPECT ME TO TURN OFF MY *INTELLECT,* CHALICE. I'M NOT GOING TO PRY. BUT I AM GOING TO MAKE SURE YOU'RE OKAY. FOR THE GOOD OF THE TEAM, IF NOTHING ELSE.
SO, *ARE* YOU?
I'M FINE.
EVERYTHING'S *FINE.*

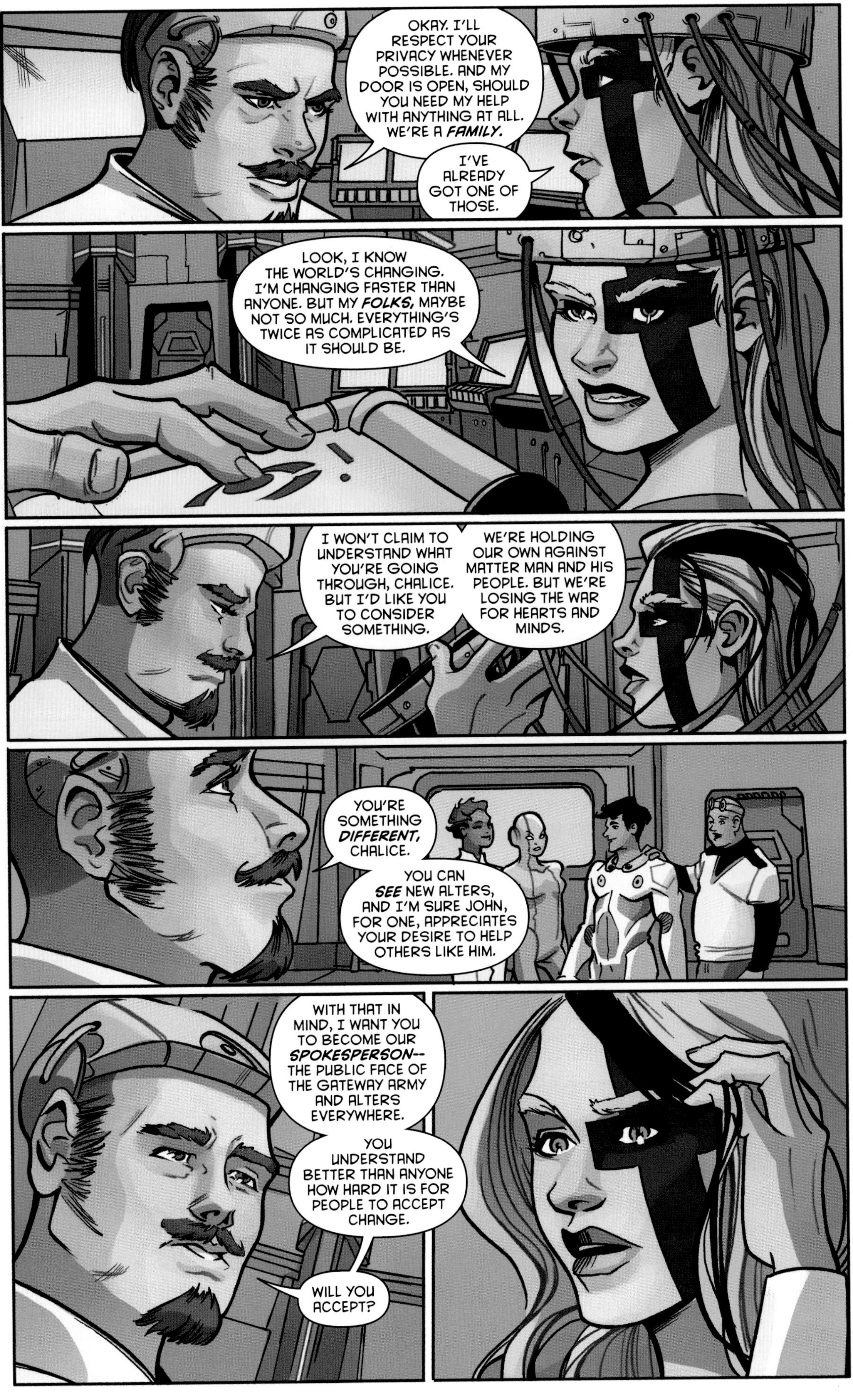

OKAY. I'LL RESPECT YOUR PRIVACY WHENEVER POSSIBLE. AND MY DOOR IS OPEN, SHOULD YOU NEED MY HELP WITH ANYTHING AT ALL. WE'RE A *FAMILY.*
I'VE ALREADY GOT ONE OF THOSE.
LOOK, I KNOW THE WORLD'S CHANGING. I'M CHANGING FASTER THAN ANYONE. BUT MY *FOLKS,* MAYBE NOT SO MUCH. EVERYTHING'S TWICE AS COMPLICATED AS IT SHOULD BE.
I WON'T CLAIM TO UNDERSTAND WHAT YOU'RE GOING THROUGH, CHALICE. BUT I'D LIKE YOU TO CONSIDER SOMETHING.
WE'RE HOLDING OUR OWN AGAINST MATTER MAN AND HIS PEOPLE. BUT WE'RE LOSING THE WAR FOR HEARTS AND MINDS.
YOU'RE SOMETHING *DIFFERENT,* CHALICE.
YOU CAN *SEE* NEW ALTERS, AND I'M SURE JOHN, FOR ONE, APPRECIATES YOUR DESIRE TO HELP OTHERS LIKE HIM.
WITH THAT IN MIND, I WANT YOU TO BECOME OUR *SPOKESPERSON--* THE PUBLIC FACE OF THE GATEWAY ARMY AND ALTERS EVERYWHERE.
YOU UNDERSTAND BETTER THAN ANYONE HOW HARD IT IS FOR PEOPLE TO ACCEPT CHANGE.
WILL YOU ACCEPT?

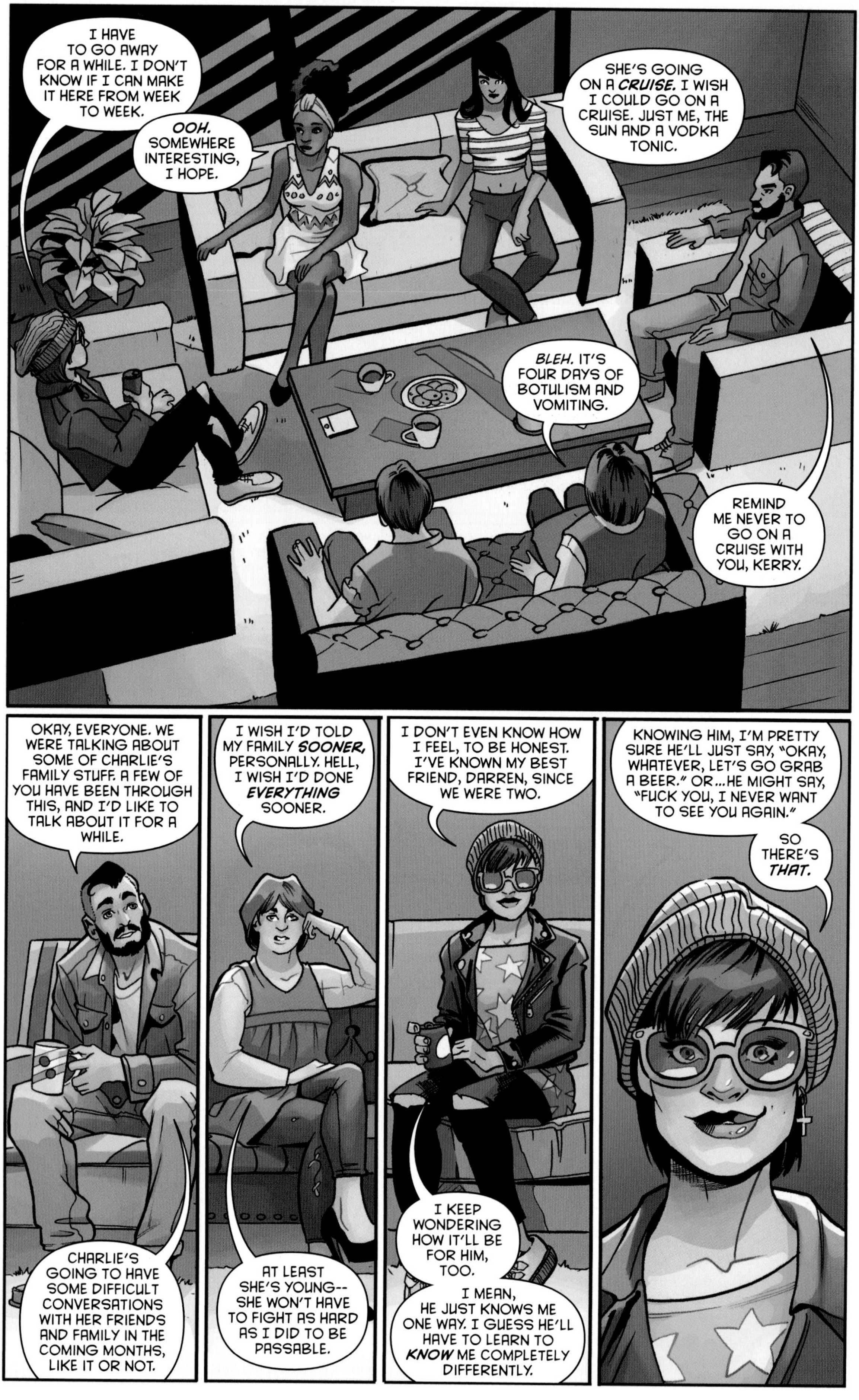
I HAVE TO GO AWAY FOR A WHILE. I DON'T KNOW IF I CAN MAKE IT HERE FROM WEEK TO WEEK.
OOH. SOMEWHERE INTERESTING, I HOPE.
SHE'S GOING ON A ***CRUISE.*** I WISH I COULD GO ON A CRUISE. JUST ME, THE SUN AND A VODKA TONIC.
BLEH. IT'S FOUR DAYS OF BOTULISM AND VOMITING.
REMIND ME NEVER TO GO ON A CRUISE WITH YOU, KERRY.
OKAY, EVERYONE. WE WERE TALKING ABOUT SOME OF CHARLIE'S FAMILY STUFF. A FEW OF YOU HAVE BEEN THROUGH THIS, AND I'D LIKE TO TALK ABOUT IT FOR A WHILE.
CHARLIE'S GOING TO HAVE SOME DIFFICULT CONVERSATIONS WITH HER FRIENDS AND FAMILY IN THE COMING MONTHS, LIKE IT OR NOT.
I WISH I'D TOLD MY FAMILY ***SOONER,*** PERSONALLY. HELL, I WISH I'D DONE ***EVERYTHING*** SOONER.
AT LEAST SHE'S YOUNG-- SHE WON'T HAVE TO FIGHT AS HARD AS I DID TO BE PASSABLE.
I DON'T EVEN KNOW HOW I FEEL, TO BE HONEST. I'VE KNOWN MY BEST FRIEND, DARREN, SINCE WE WERE TWO.
I KEEP WONDERING HOW IT'LL BE FOR HIM, TOO.
I MEAN, HE JUST KNOWS ME ONE WAY. I GUESS HE'LL HAVE TO LEARN TO ***KNOW*** ME COMPLETELY DIFFERENTLY.
KNOWING HIM, I'M PRETTY SURE HE'LL JUST SAY, "OKAY, WHATEVER, LET'S GO GRAB A BEER." OR...HE MIGHT SAY, "FUCK YOU, I NEVER WANT TO SEE YOU AGAIN."
SO THERE'S ***THAT.***

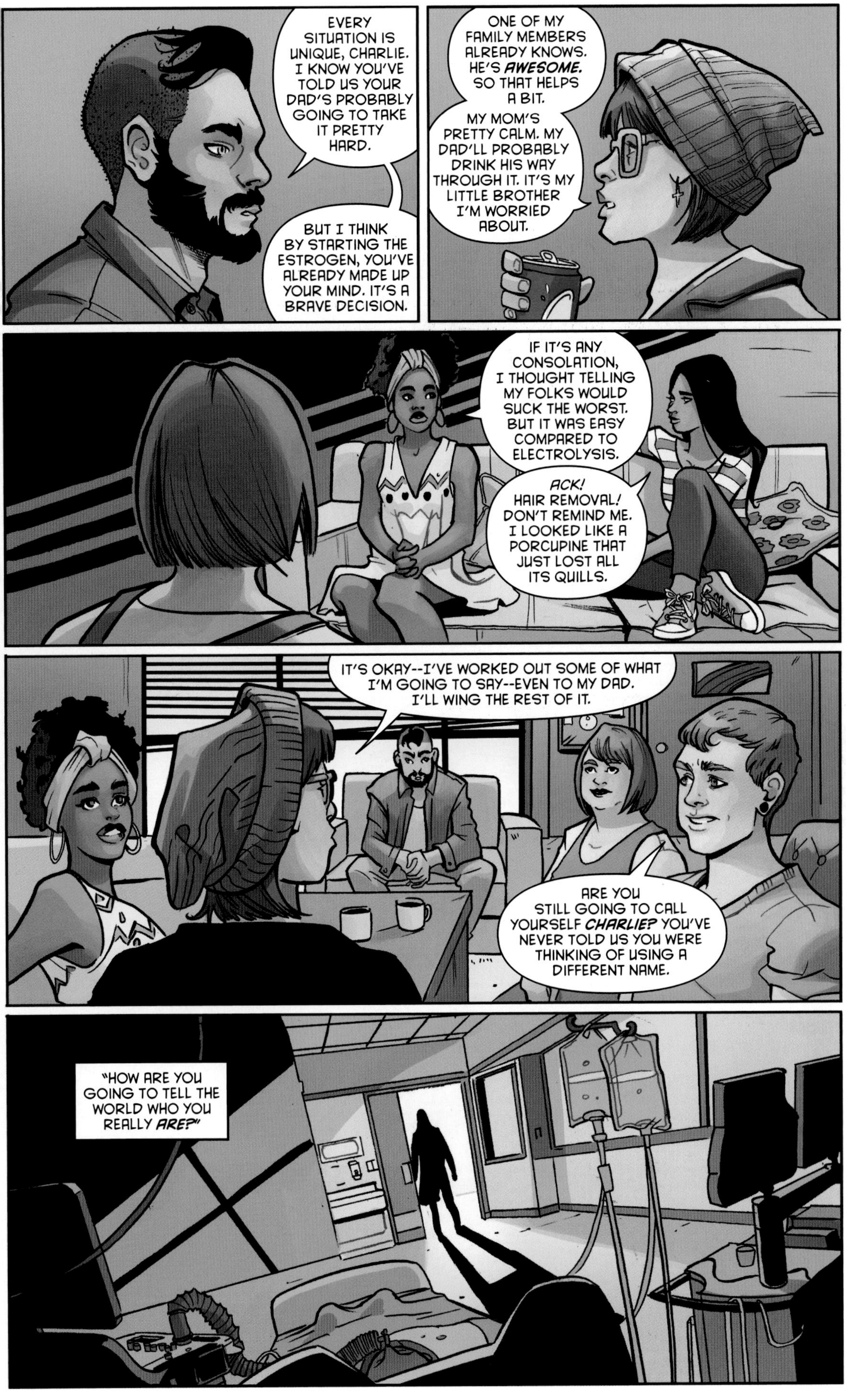
EVERY SITUATION IS UNIQUE, CHARLIE. I KNOW YOU'VE TOLD US YOUR DAD'S PROBABLY GOING TO TAKE IT PRETTY HARD.
BUT I THINK BY STARTING THE ESTROGEN, YOU'VE ALREADY MADE UP YOUR MIND. IT'S A BRAVE DECISION.
ONE OF MY FAMILY MEMBERS ALREADY KNOWS. HE'S AWESOME. SO THAT HELPS A BIT.
MY MOM'S PRETTY CALM. MY DAD'LL PROBABLY DRINK HIS WAY THROUGH IT. IT'S MY LITTLE BROTHER I'M WORRIED ABOUT.
IF IT'S ANY CONSOLATION, I THOUGHT TELLING MY FOLKS WOULD SUCK THE WORST. BUT IT WAS EASY COMPARED TO ELECTROLYSIS.
ACK! HAIR REMOVAL! DON'T REMIND ME. I LOOKED LIKE A PORCUPINE THAT JUST LOST ALL ITS QUILLS.
IT'S OKAY--I'VE WORKED OUT SOME OF WHAT I'M GOING TO SAY--EVEN TO MY DAD. I'LL WING THE REST OF IT.
ARE YOU STILL GOING TO CALL YOURSELF CHARLIE? YOU'VE NEVER TOLD US YOU WERE THINKING OF USING A DIFFERENT NAME.
"HOW ARE YOU GOING TO TELL THE WORLD WHO YOU REALLY ARE?"

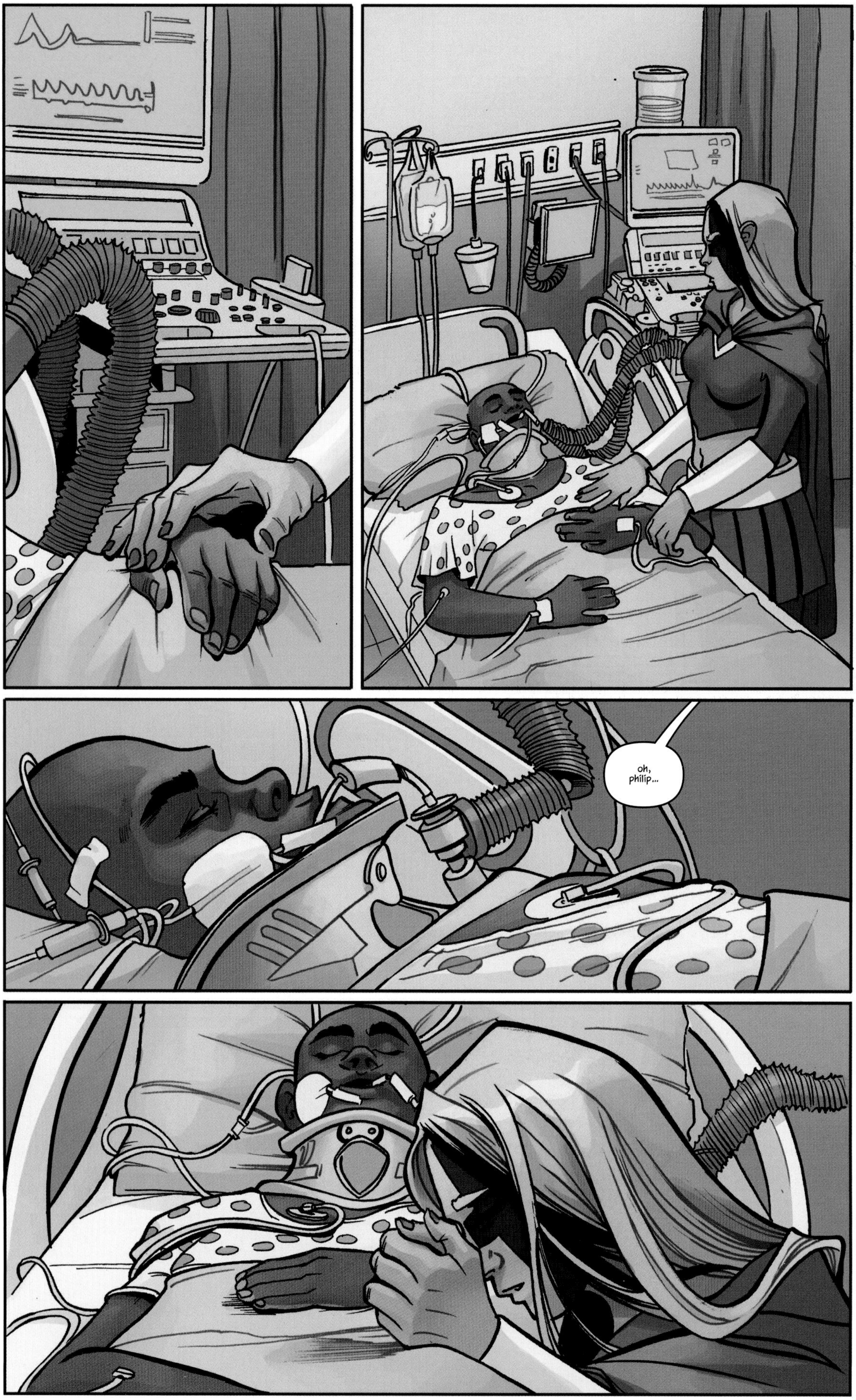
oh, philip...

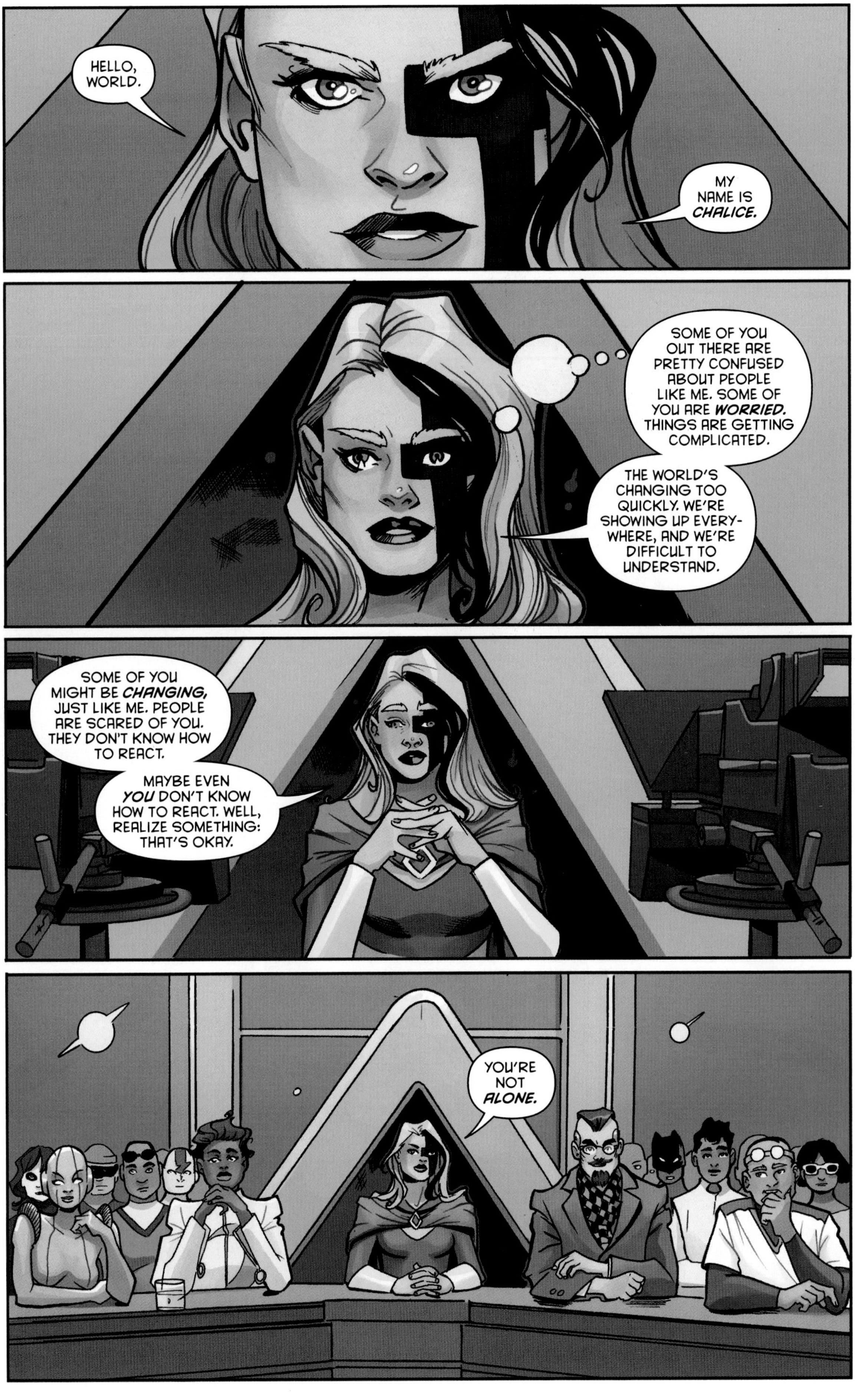
HELLO, WORLD.
MY NAME IS *CHALICE.*
SOME OF YOU OUT THERE ARE PRETTY CONFUSED ABOUT PEOPLE LIKE ME. SOME OF YOU ARE *WORRIED.* THINGS ARE GETTING COMPLICATED.
THE WORLD'S CHANGING TOO QUICKLY. WE'RE SHOWING UP EVERY-WHERE, AND WE'RE DIFFICULT TO UNDERSTAND.
SOME OF YOU MIGHT BE *CHANGING,* JUST LIKE ME. PEOPLE ARE SCARED OF YOU. THEY DON'T KNOW HOW TO REACT.
MAYBE EVEN *YOU* DON'T KNOW HOW TO REACT. WELL, REALIZE SOMETHING: THAT'S OKAY.
YOU'RE NOT *ALONE.*

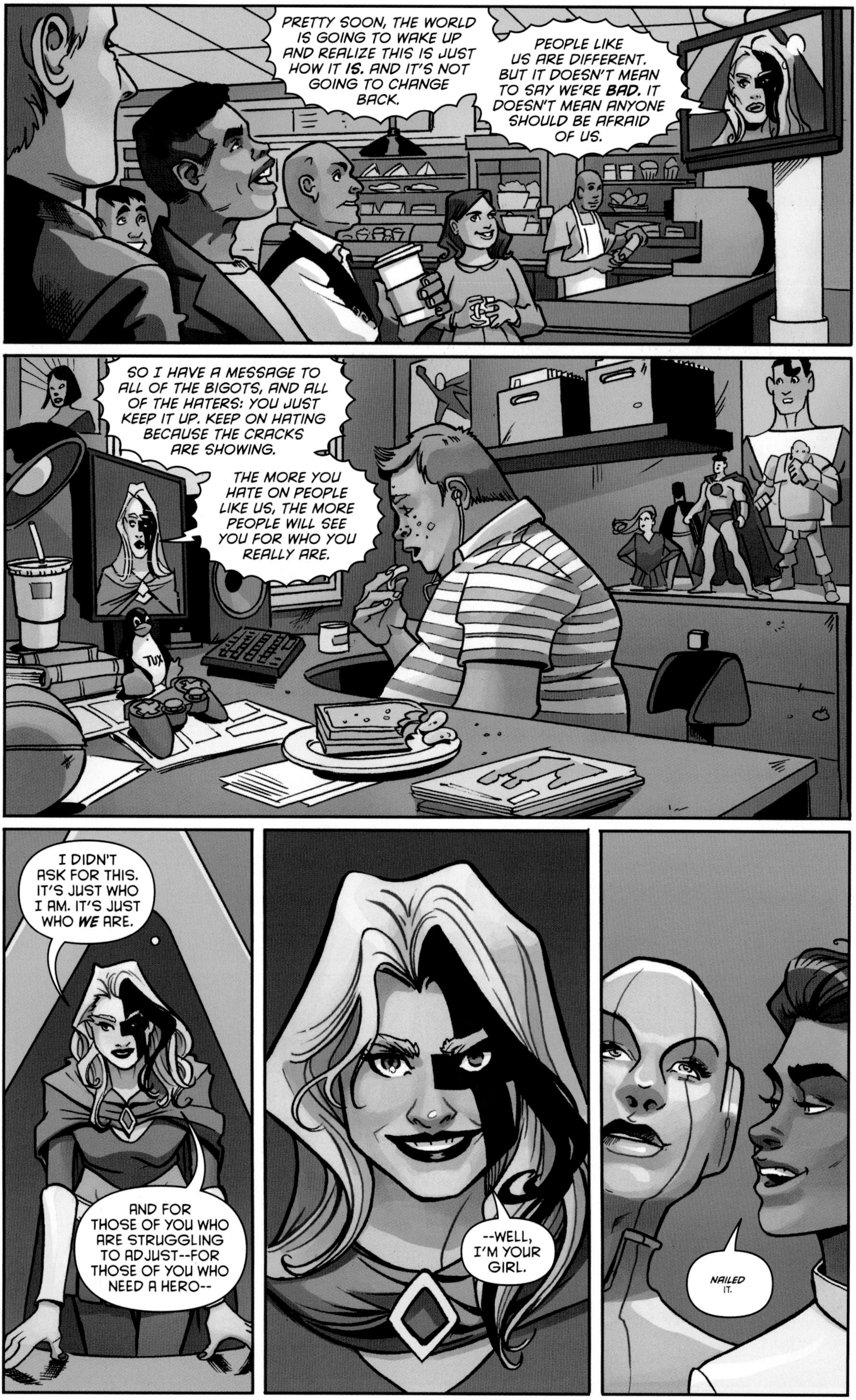
PRETTY SOON, THE WORLD IS GOING TO WAKE UP AND REALIZE THIS IS JUST HOW IT IS. AND IT'S NOT GOING TO CHANGE BACK.
PEOPLE LIKE US ARE DIFFERENT. BUT IT DOESN'T MEAN TO SAY WE'RE BAD. IT DOESN'T MEAN ANYONE SHOULD BE AFRAID OF US.
SO I HAVE A MESSAGE TO ALL OF THE BIGOTS, AND ALL OF THE HATERS: YOU JUST KEEP IT UP. KEEP ON HATING BECAUSE THE CRACKS ARE SHOWING.
THE MORE YOU HATE ON PEOPLE LIKE US, THE MORE PEOPLE WILL SEE YOU FOR WHO YOU REALLY ARE.
TUX
I DIDN'T ASK FOR THIS. IT'S JUST WHO I AM. IT'S JUST WHO WE ARE.
AND FOR THOSE OF YOU WHO ARE STRUGGLING TO ADJUST--FOR THOSE OF YOU WHO NEED A HERO--
--WELL, I'M YOUR GIRL.
NAILED IT.

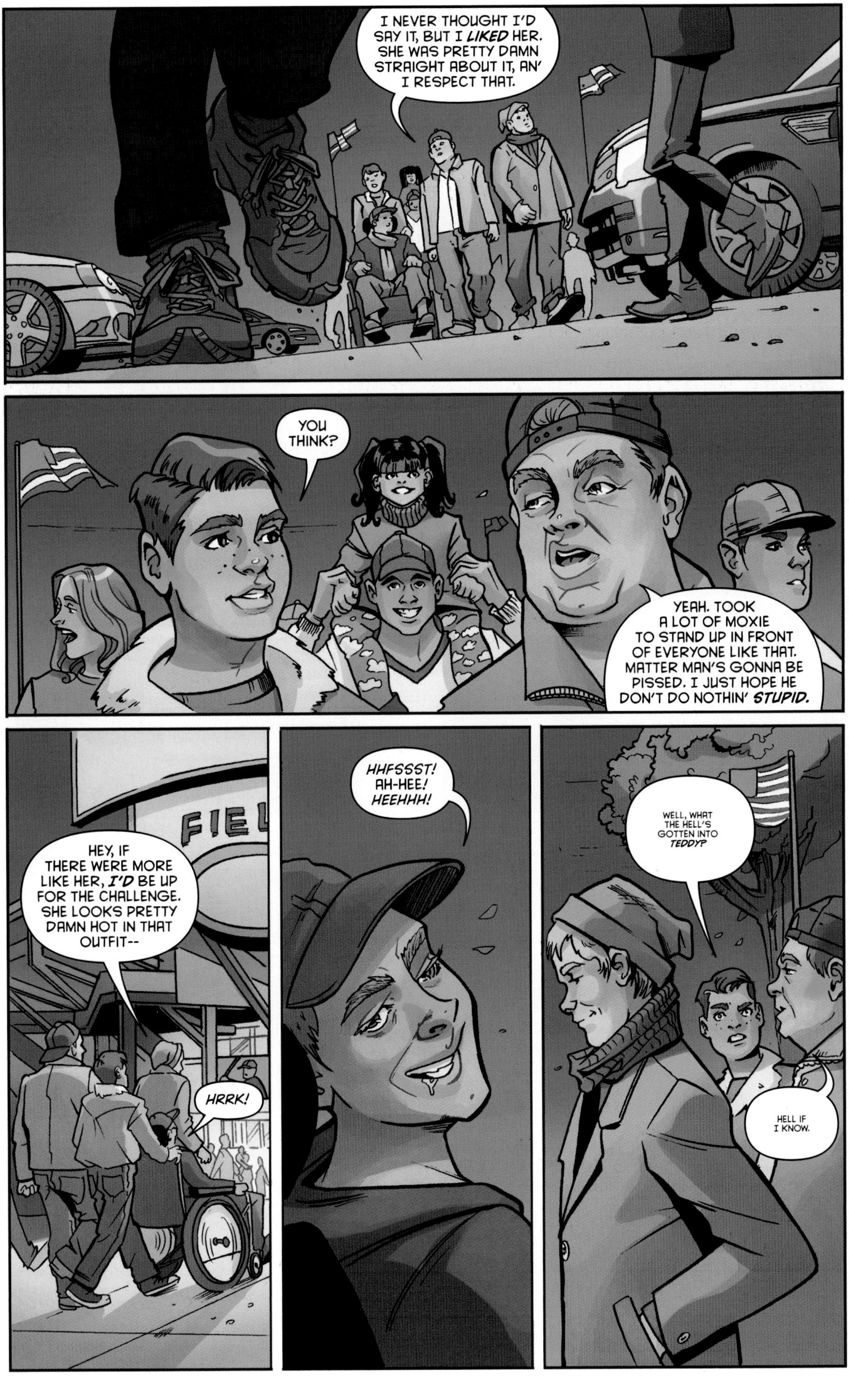
I NEVER THOUGHT I'D SAY IT, BUT I LIKED HER. SHE WAS PRETTY DAMN STRAIGHT ABOUT IT, AN' I RESPECT THAT.
YOU THINK?
YEAH. TOOK A LOT OF MOXIE TO STAND UP IN FRONT OF EVERYONE LIKE THAT. MATTER MAN'S GONNA BE PISSED. I JUST HOPE HE DON'T DO NOTHIN' STUPID.
FIEL
HEY, IF THERE WERE MORE LIKE HER, I'D BE UP FOR THE CHALLENGE. SHE LOOKS PRETTY DAMN HOT IN THAT OUTFIT--
HRRK!
HHFSSST! AH-HEE! HEEHHH!
WELL, WHAT THE HELL'S GOTTEN INTO TEDDY?
HELL IF I KNOW.

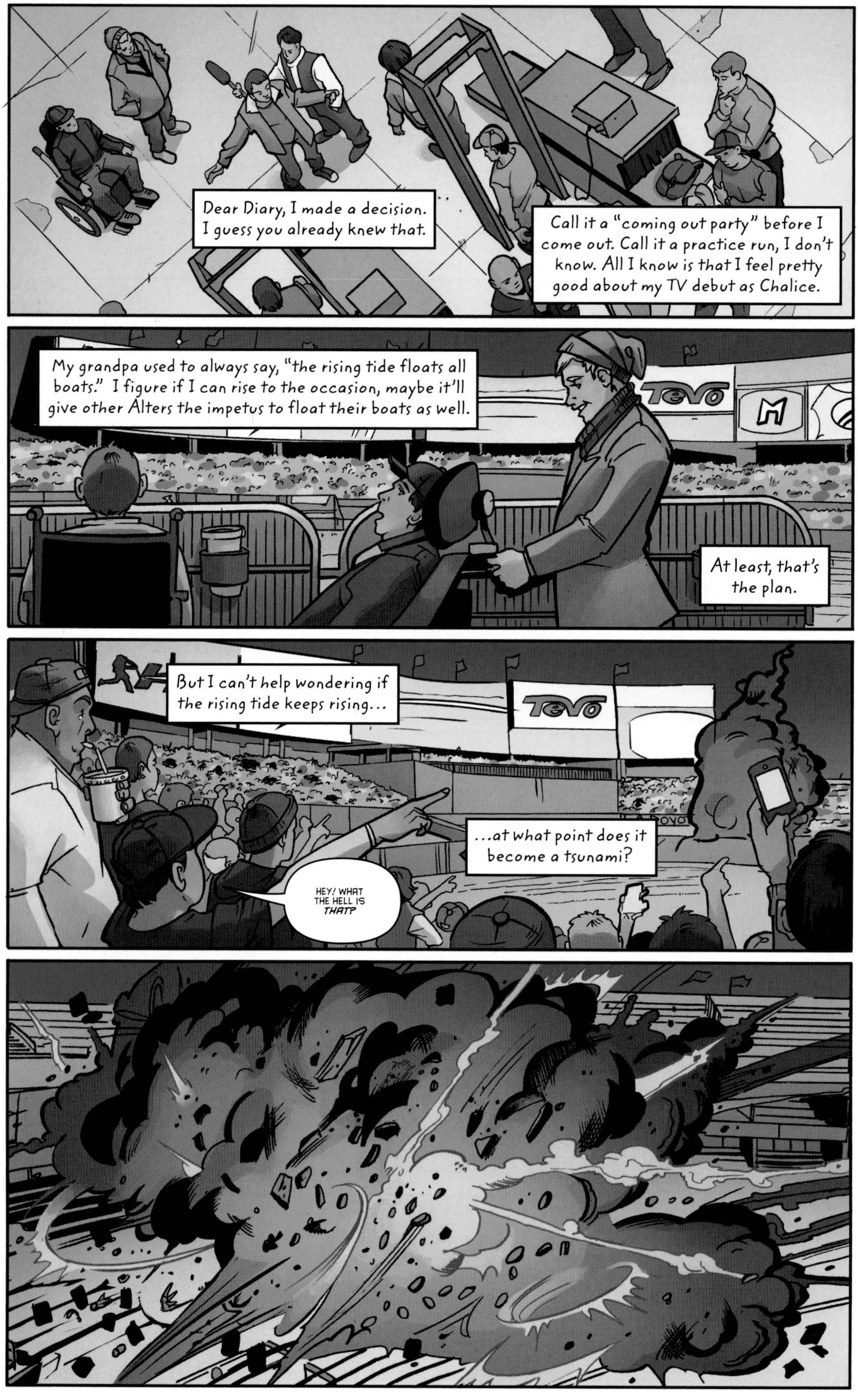
Dear Diary, I made a decision. I guess you already knew that.
Call it a "coming out party" before I come out. Call it a practice run, I don't know. All I know is that I feel pretty good about my TV debut as Chalice.
My grandpa used to always say, "the rising tide floats all boats." I figure if I can rise to the occasion, maybe it'll give other Alters the impetus to float their boats as well.
At least, that's the plan.
But I can't help wondering if the rising tide keeps rising...
...at what point does it become a tsunami?
HEY! WHAT THE HELL IS *THAT?*

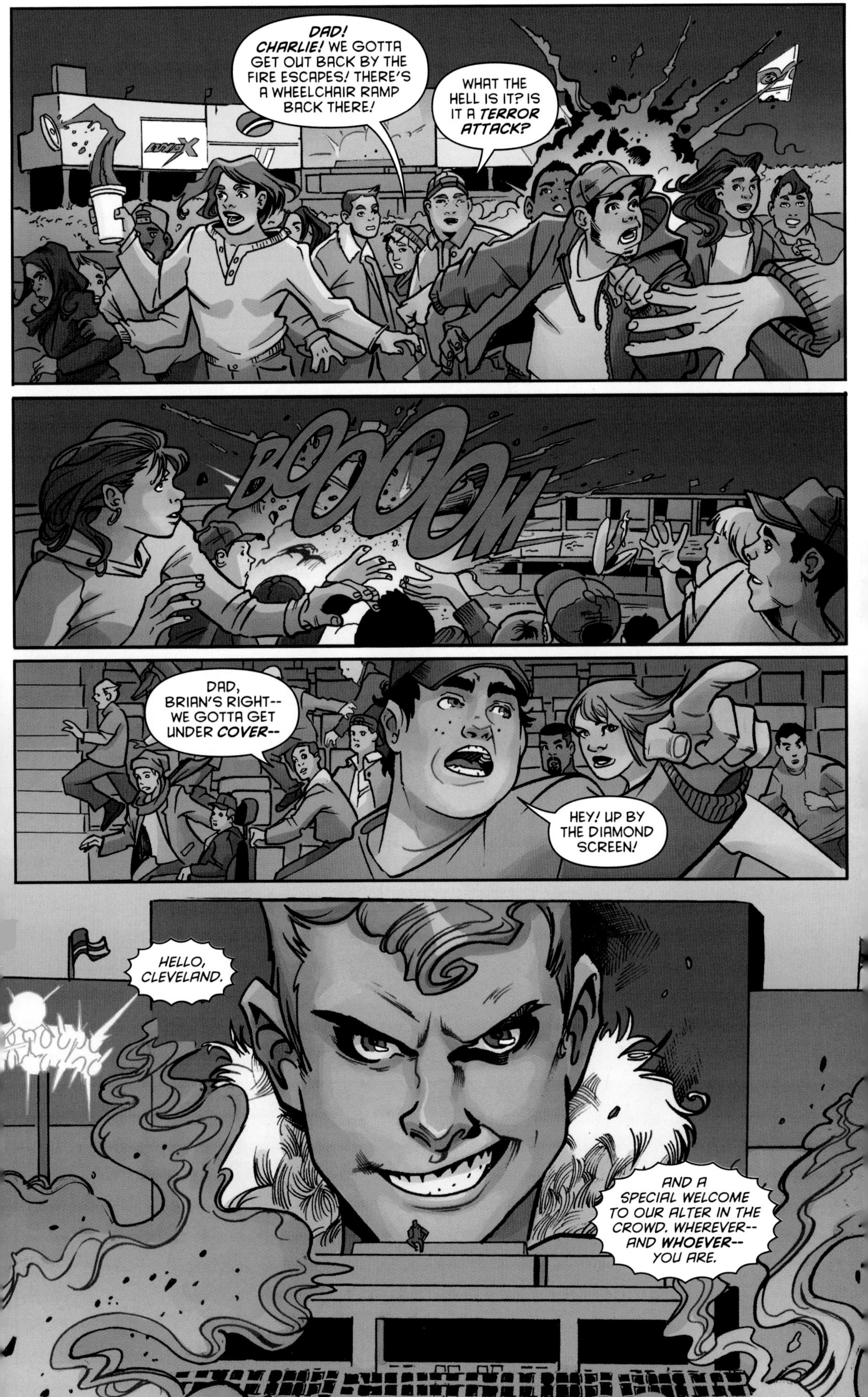
DAD! CHARLIE! WE GOTTA GET OUT BACK BY THE FIRE ESCAPES! THERE'S A WHEELCHAIR RAMP BACK THERE!
WHAT THE HELL IS IT? IS IT A TERROR ATTACK?
BOOOOM
DAD, BRIAN'S RIGHT-- WE GOTTA GET UNDER COVER--
HEY! UP BY THE DIAMOND SCREEN!
HELLO, CLEVELAND.
AND A SPECIAL WELCOME TO OUR ALTER IN THE CROWD. WHEREVER-- AND WHOEVER-- YOU ARE.

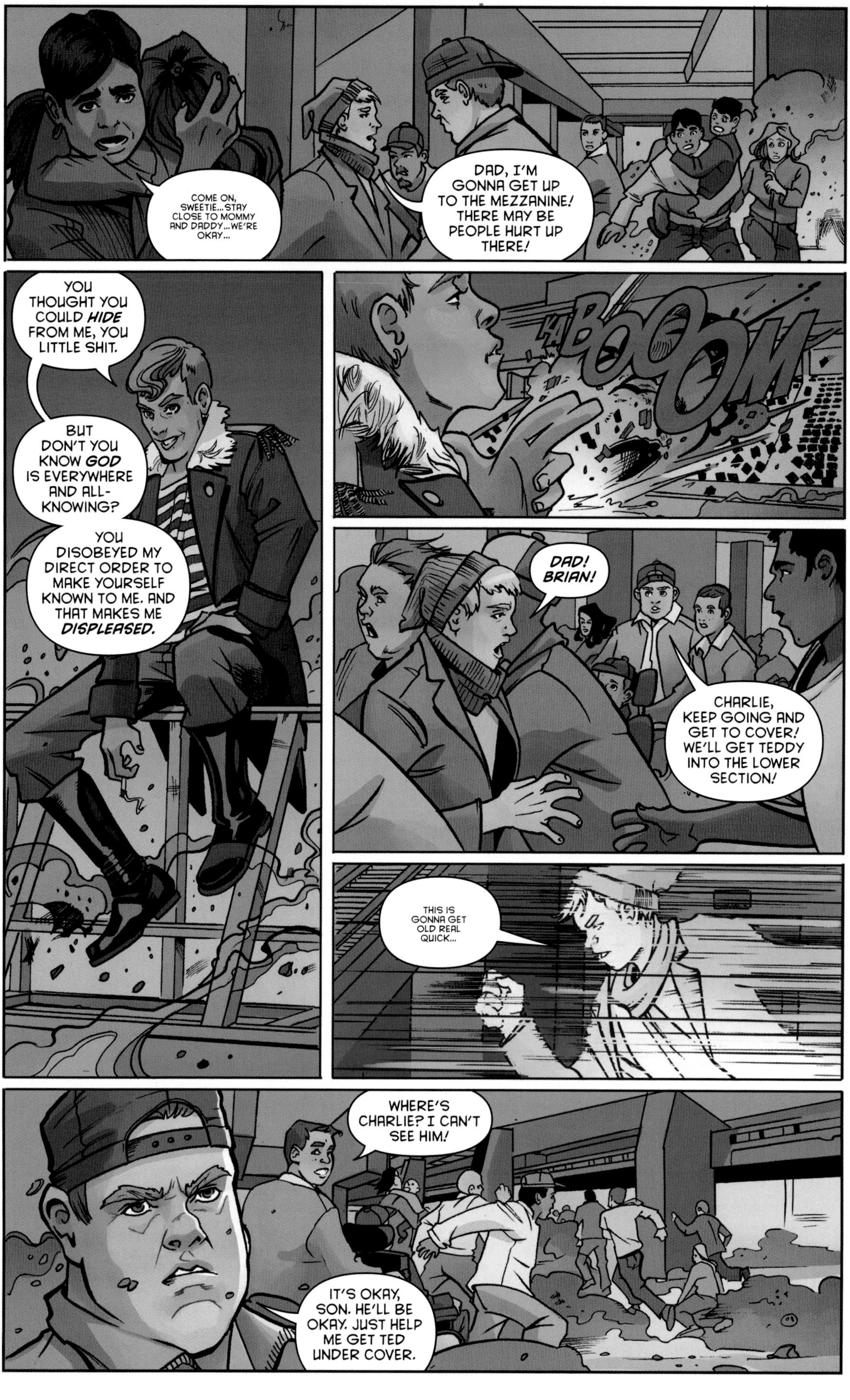
COME ON, SWEETIE...STAY CLOSE TO MOMMY AND DADDY...WE'RE OKAY...
DAD, I'M GONNA GET UP TO THE MEZZANINE! THERE MAY BE PEOPLE HURT UP THERE!
YOU THOUGHT YOU COULD *HIDE* FROM ME, YOU LITTLE SHIT.
BUT DON'T YOU KNOW *GOD* IS EVERYWHERE AND ALL-KNOWING?
YOU DISOBEYED MY DIRECT ORDER TO MAKE YOURSELF KNOWN TO ME. AND THAT MAKES ME *DISPLEASED.*
KA BOOOOM
DAD! BRIAN!
CHARLIE, KEEP GOING AND GET TO COVER! WE'LL GET TEDDY INTO THE LOWER SECTION!
THIS IS GONNA GET OLD REAL QUICK...
WHERE'S CHARLIE? I CAN'T SEE HIM!
IT'S OKAY, SON. HE'LL BE OKAY. JUST HELP ME GET TED UNDER COVER.

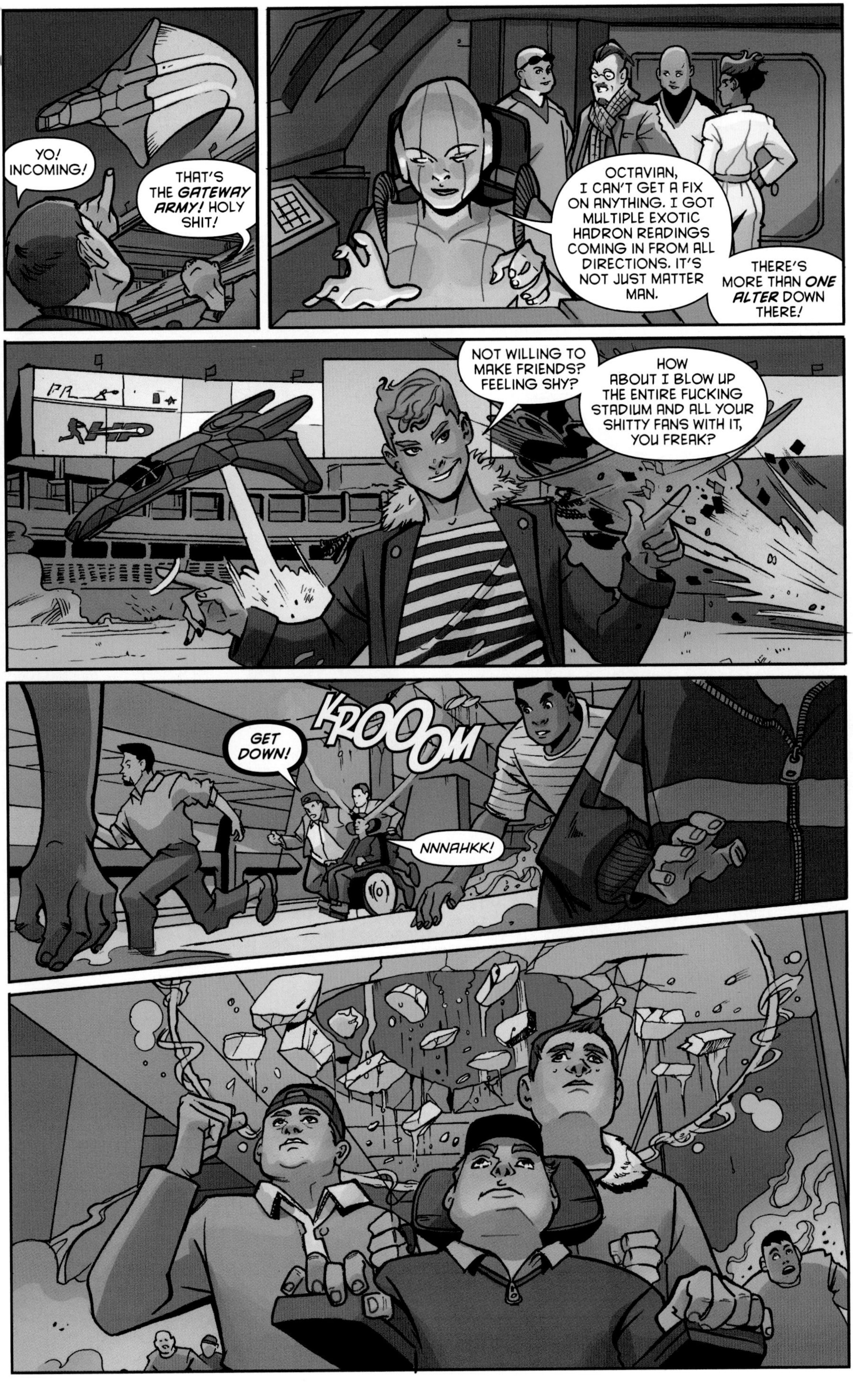
YO! INCOMING!
THAT'S THE GATEWAY ARMY! HOLY SHIT!
OCTAVIAN, I CAN'T GET A FIX ON ANYTHING. I GOT MULTIPLE EXOTIC HADRON READINGS COMING IN FROM ALL DIRECTIONS. IT'S NOT JUST MATTER MAN.
THERE'S MORE THAN ONE ALTER DOWN THERE!
NOT WILLING TO MAKE FRIENDS? FEELING SHY?
HOW ABOUT I BLOW UP THE ENTIRE FUCKING STADIUM AND ALL YOUR SHITTY FANS WITH IT, YOU FREAK?
KROOOOM
GET DOWN!
NNNAHKK!

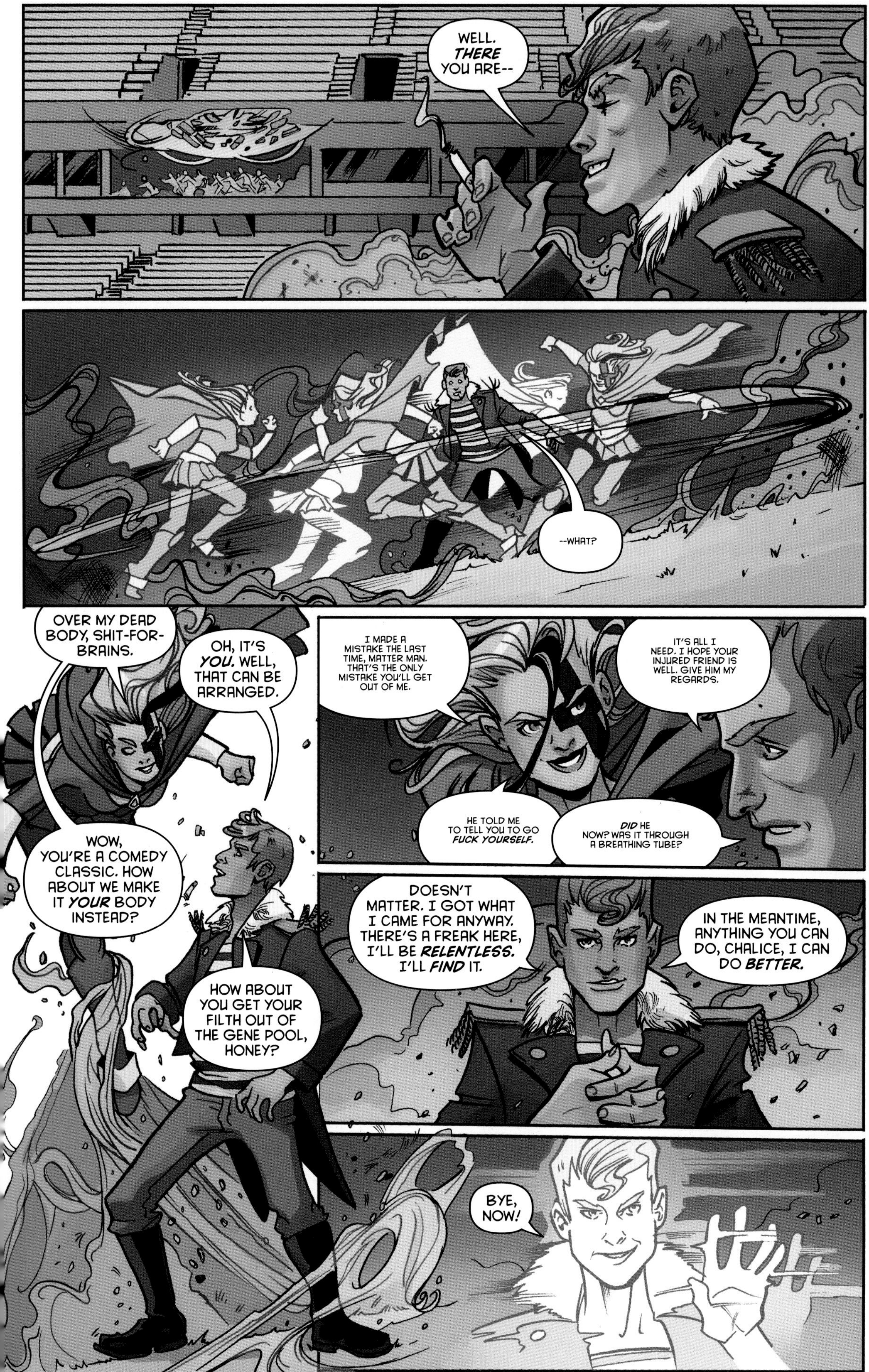

WELL. THERE YOU ARE--
--WHAT?
OVER MY DEAD BODY, SHIT-FOR-BRAINS.
OH, IT'S YOU. WELL, THAT CAN BE ARRANGED.
WOW, YOU'RE A COMEDY CLASSIC. HOW ABOUT WE MAKE IT YOUR BODY INSTEAD?
HOW ABOUT YOU GET YOUR FILTH OUT OF THE GENE POOL, HONEY?
I MADE A MISTAKE THE LAST TIME, MATTER MAN. THAT'S THE ONLY MISTAKE YOU'LL GET OUT OF ME.
IT'S ALL I NEED. I HOPE YOUR INJURED FRIEND IS WELL. GIVE HIM MY REGARDS.
HE TOLD ME TO TELL YOU TO GO FUCK YOURSELF.
DID HE NOW? WAS IT THROUGH A BREATHING TUBE?
DOESN'T MATTER. I GOT WHAT I CAME FOR ANYWAY. THERE'S A FREAK HERE, I'LL BE RELENTLESS. I'LL FIND IT.
IN THE MEANTIME, ANYTHING YOU CAN DO, CHALICE, I CAN DO BETTER.
BYE, NOW!

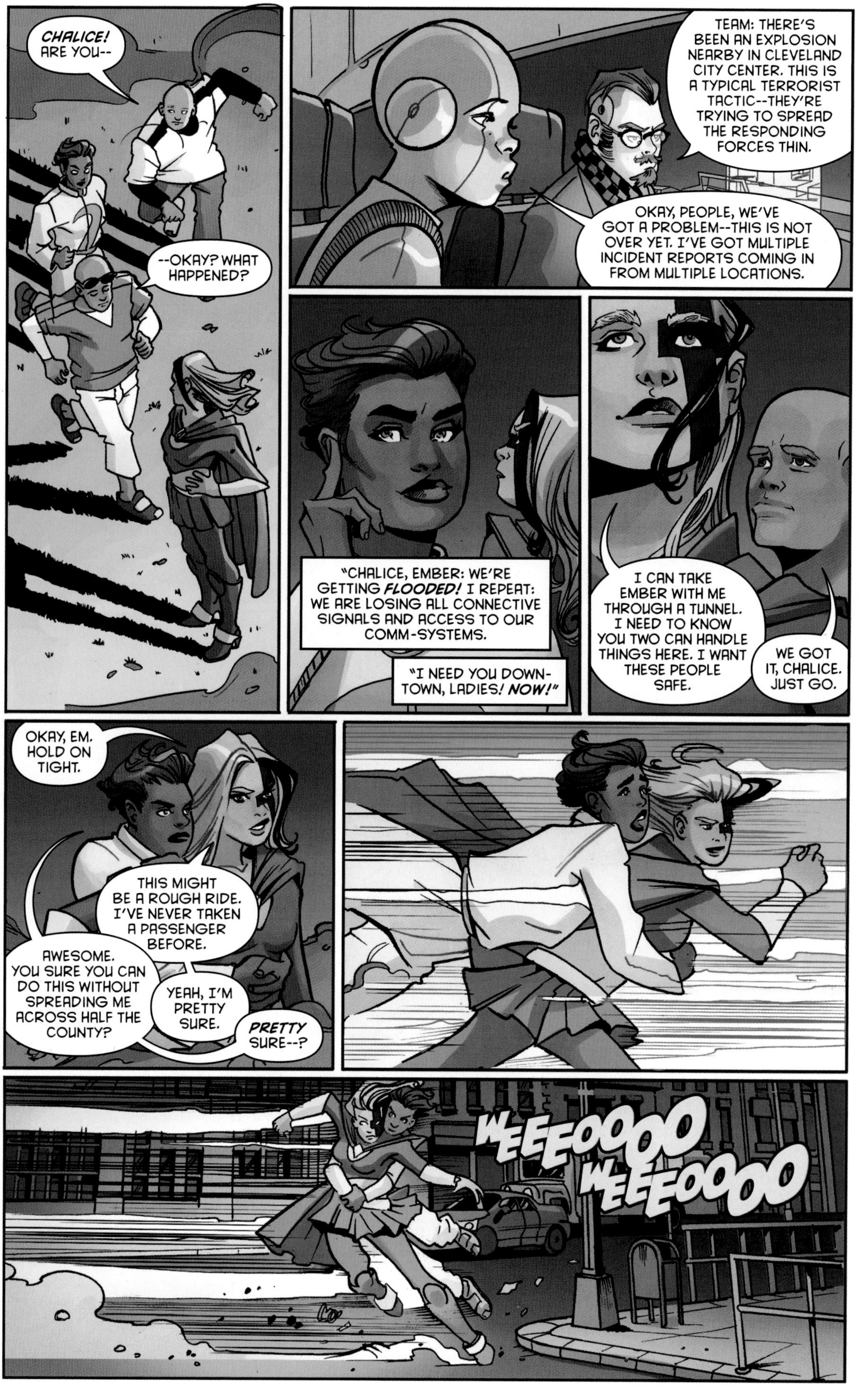
CHALICE! ARE YOU--
--OKAY? WHAT HAPPENED?
TEAM: THERE'S BEEN AN EXPLOSION NEARBY IN CLEVELAND CITY CENTER. THIS IS A TYPICAL TERRORIST TACTIC--THEY'RE TRYING TO SPREAD THE RESPONDING FORCES THIN.
OKAY, PEOPLE, WE'VE GOT A PROBLEM--THIS IS NOT OVER YET. I'VE GOT MULTIPLE INCIDENT REPORTS COMING IN FROM MULTIPLE LOCATIONS.
"CHALICE, EMBER: WE'RE GETTING FLOODED! I REPEAT: WE ARE LOSING ALL CONNECTIVE SIGNALS AND ACCESS TO OUR COMM-SYSTEMS.
"I NEED YOU DOWN-TOWN, LADIES! NOW!"
I CAN TAKE EMBER WITH ME THROUGH A TUNNEL. I NEED TO KNOW YOU TWO CAN HANDLE THINGS HERE. I WANT THESE PEOPLE SAFE.
WE GOT IT, CHALICE. JUST GO.
OKAY, EM. HOLD ON TIGHT.
THIS MIGHT BE A ROUGH RIDE. I'VE NEVER TAKEN A PASSENGER BEFORE.
AWESOME. YOU SURE YOU CAN DO THIS WITHOUT SPREADING ME ACROSS HALF THE COUNTY?
YEAH, I'M PRETTY SURE.
PRETTY SURE--?
WEEEOOOO
WEEEOOOO

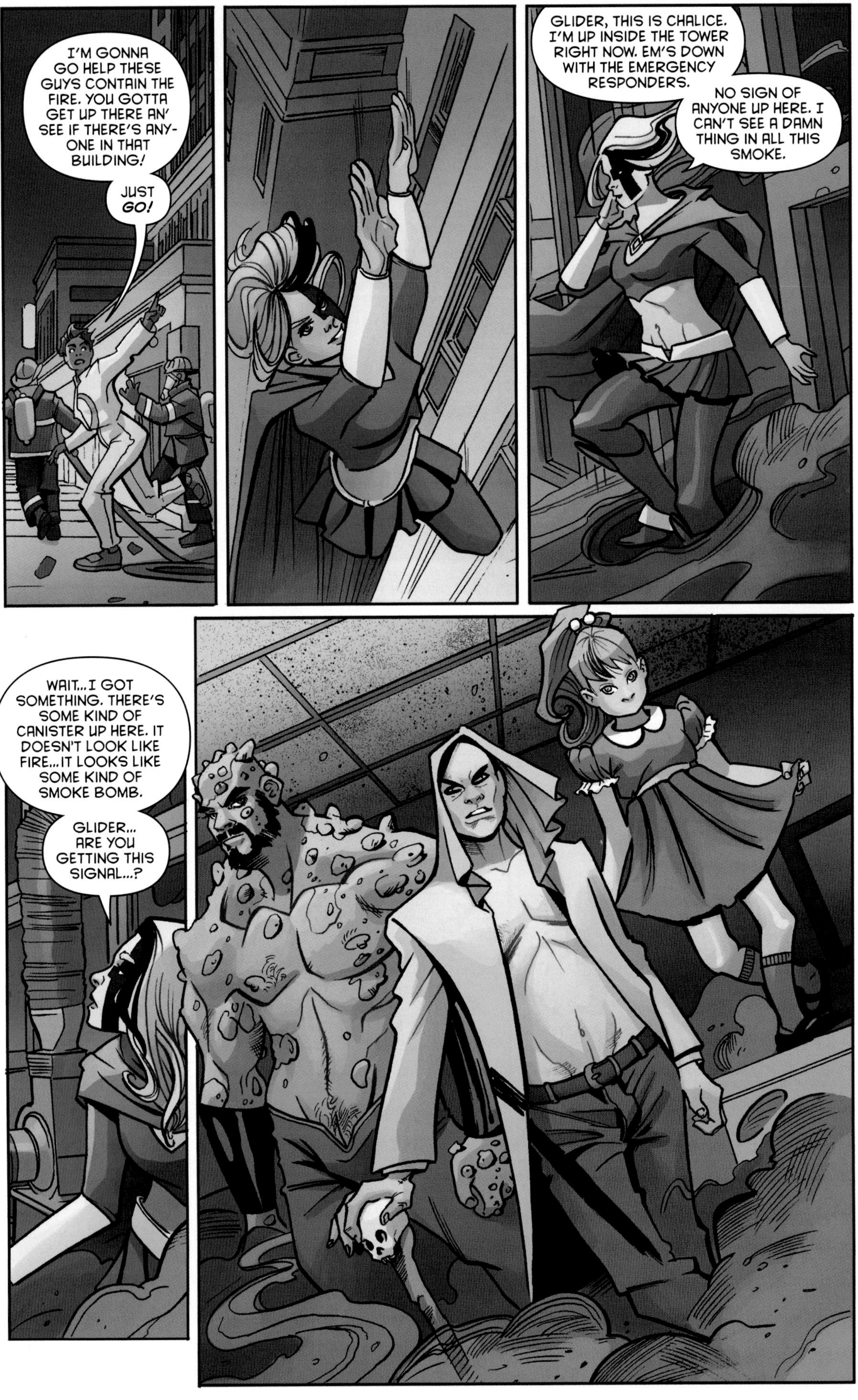
I'M GONNA GO HELP THESE GUYS CONTAIN THE FIRE. YOU GOTTA GET UP THERE AN' SEE IF THERE'S ANY-ONE IN THAT BUILDING!
JUST GO!
GLIDER, THIS IS CHALICE. I'M UP INSIDE THE TOWER RIGHT NOW. EM'S DOWN WITH THE EMERGENCY RESPONDERS.
NO SIGN OF ANYONE UP HERE. I CAN'T SEE A DAMN THING IN ALL THIS SMOKE.
WAIT...I GOT SOMETHING. THERE'S SOME KIND OF CANISTER UP HERE. IT DOESN'T LOOK LIKE FIRE...IT LOOKS LIKE SOME KIND OF SMOKE BOMB.
GLIDER... ARE YOU GETTING THIS SIGNAL...?

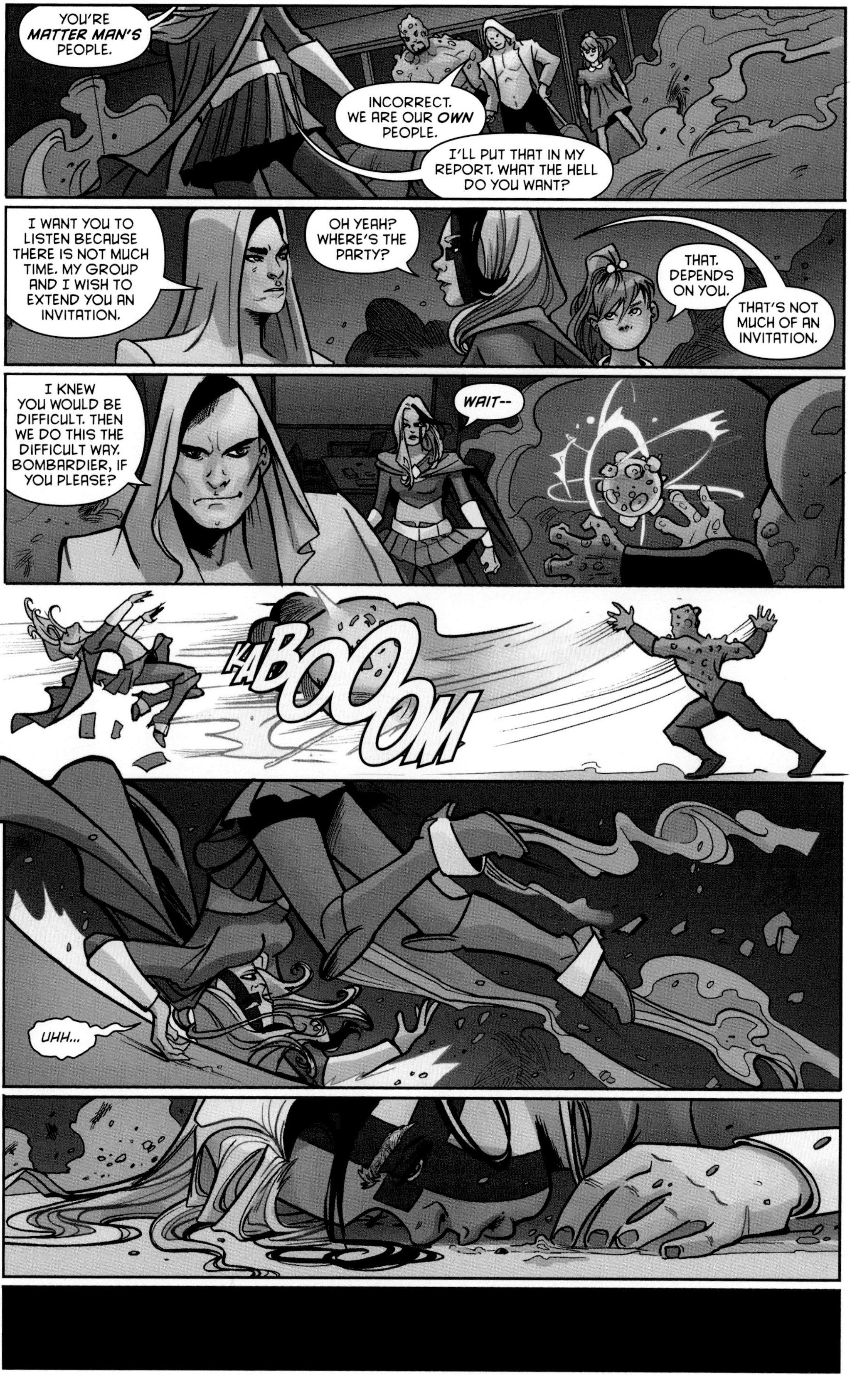
YOU'RE MATTER MAN'S PEOPLE.
INCORRECT. WE ARE OUR OWN PEOPLE.
I'LL PUT THAT IN MY REPORT. WHAT THE HELL DO YOU WANT?
I WANT YOU TO LISTEN BECAUSE THERE IS NOT MUCH TIME. MY GROUP AND I WISH TO EXTEND YOU AN INVITATION.
OH YEAH? WHERE'S THE PARTY?
THAT. DEPENDS ON YOU.
THAT'S NOT MUCH OF AN INVITATION.
I KNEW YOU WOULD BE DIFFICULT. THEN WE DO THIS THE DIFFICULT WAY. BOMBARDIER, IF YOU PLEASE?
WAIT--
KABOOOM
UHH...

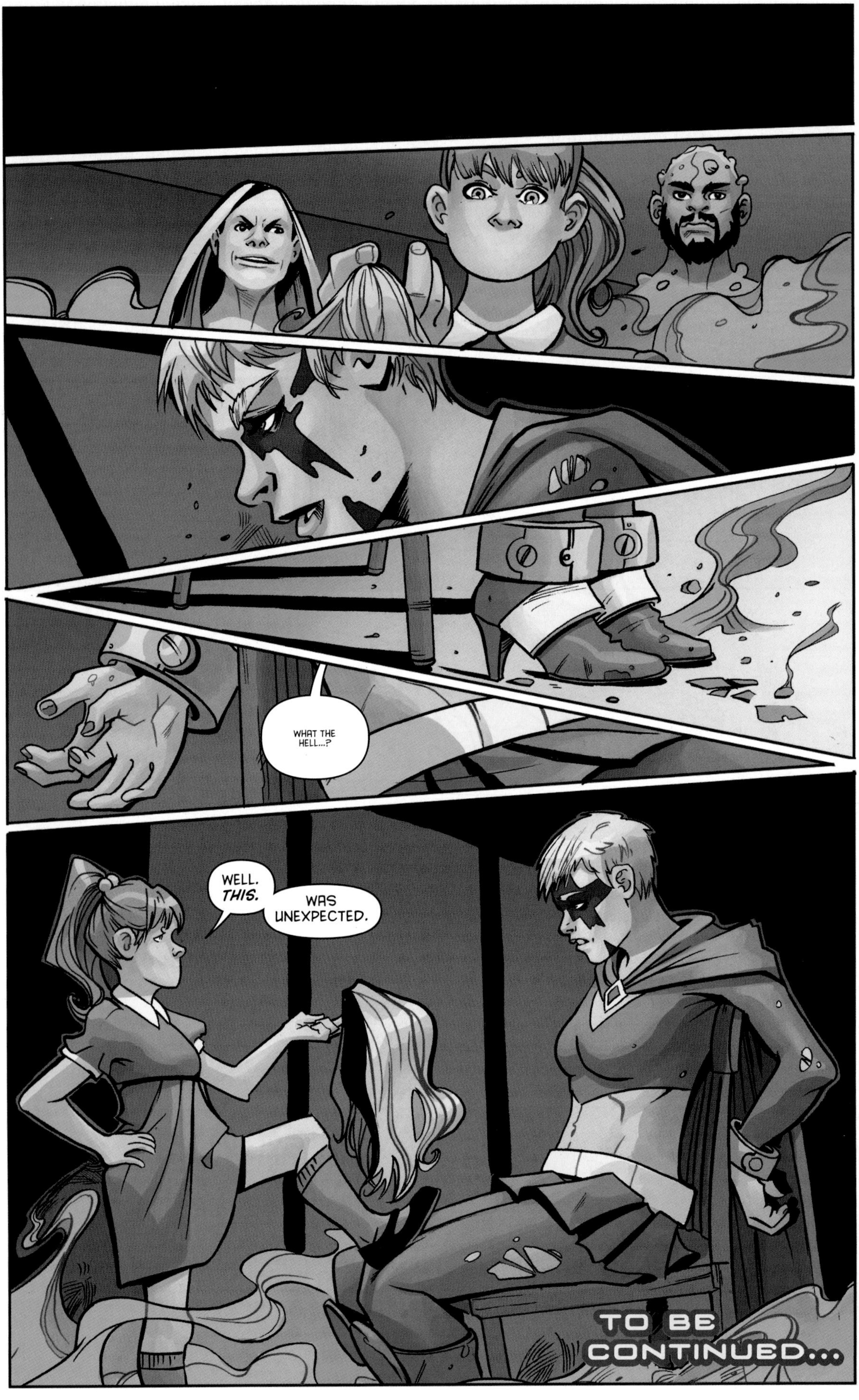
WHAT THE HELL...?
WELL. *THIS.*
WAS UNEXPECTED.
TO BE CONTINUED...

5

"SIXTY-ONE SECONDS"

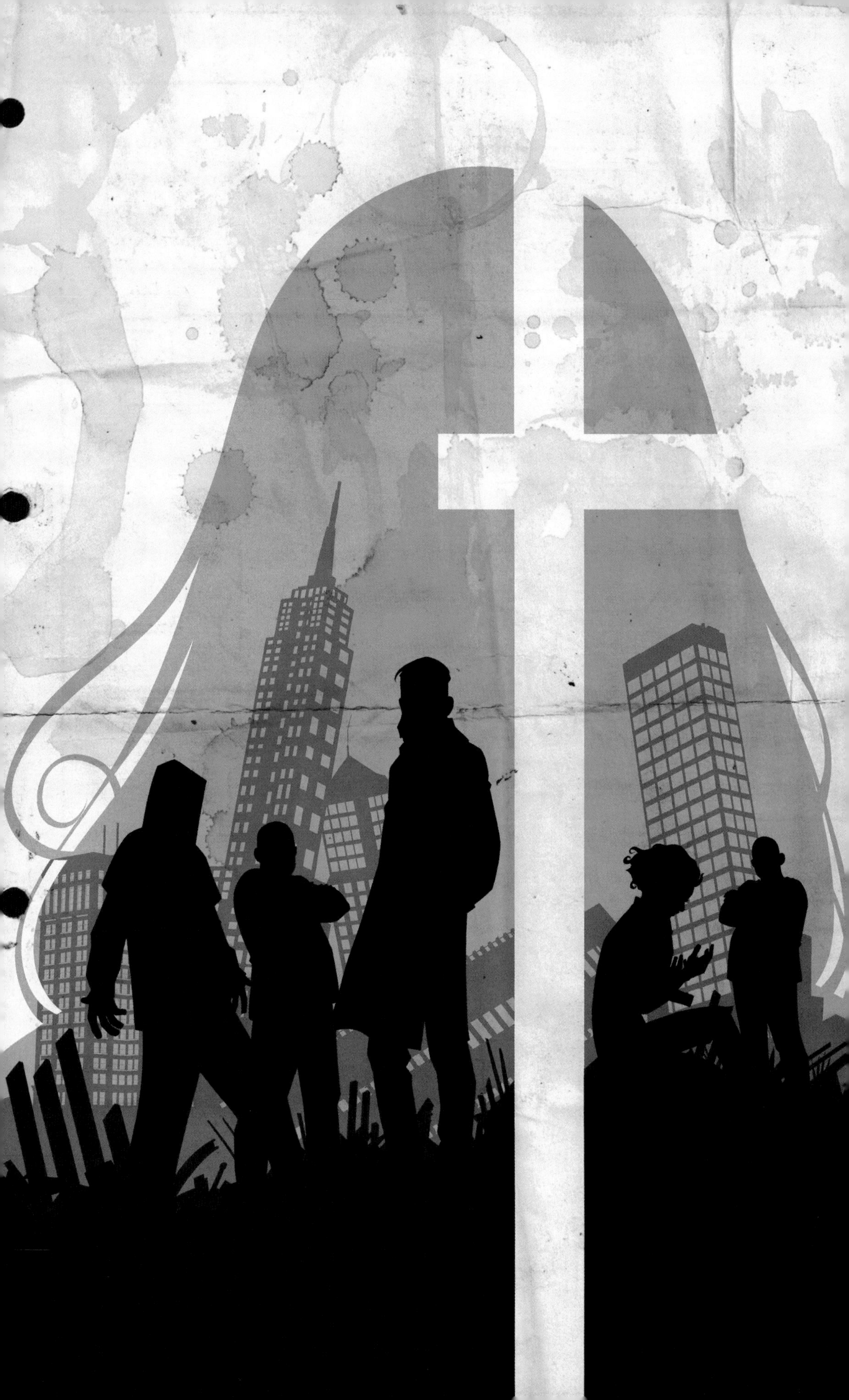

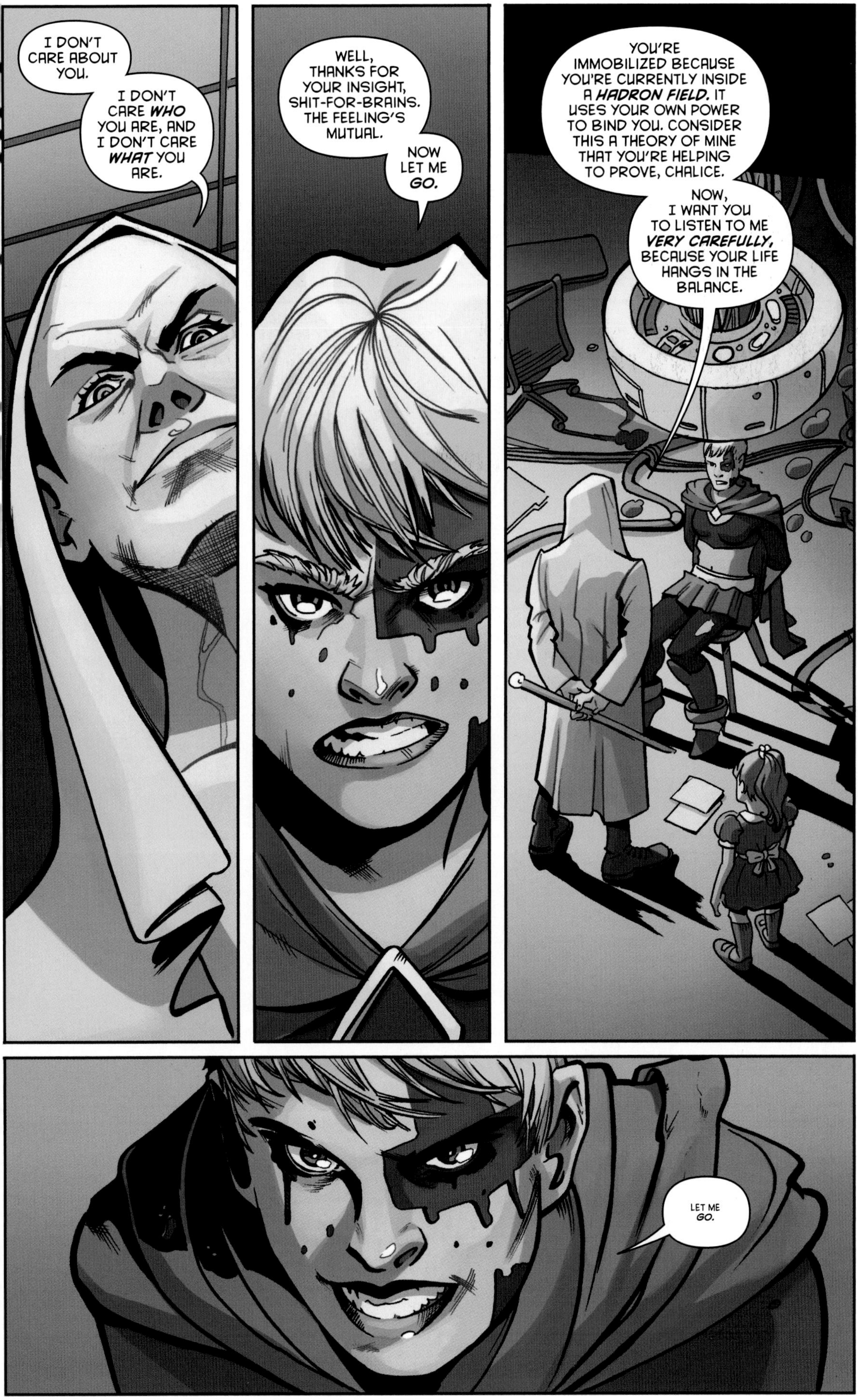
I DON'T CARE ABOUT YOU.
I DON'T CARE *WHO* YOU ARE, AND I DON'T CARE *WHAT* YOU ARE.
WELL, THANKS FOR YOUR INSIGHT, SHIT-FOR-BRAINS. THE FEELING'S MUTUAL.
NOW LET ME *GO.*
YOU'RE IMMOBILIZED BECAUSE YOU'RE CURRENTLY INSIDE A *HADRON FIELD.* IT USES YOUR OWN POWER TO BIND YOU. CONSIDER THIS A THEORY OF MINE THAT YOU'RE HELPING TO PROVE, CHALICE.
NOW, I WANT YOU TO LISTEN TO ME *VERY CAREFULLY,* BECAUSE YOUR LIFE HANGS IN THE BALANCE.
LET ME *GO.*

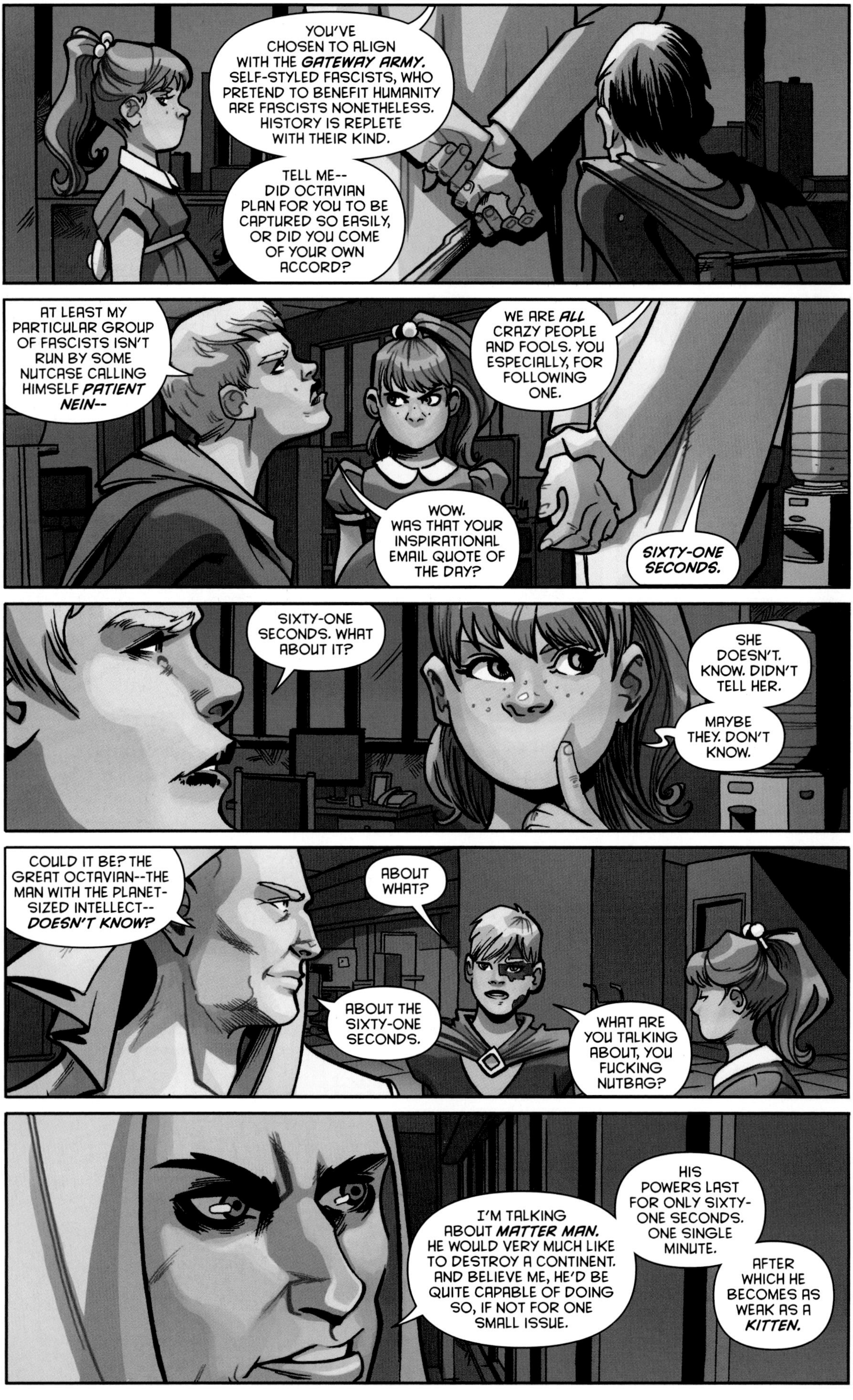

YOU'VE CHOSEN TO ALIGN WITH THE GATEWAY ARMY. SELF-STYLED FASCISTS, WHO PRETEND TO BENEFIT HUMANITY ARE FASCISTS NONETHELESS. HISTORY IS REPLETE WITH THEIR KIND.
TELL ME-- DID OCTAVIAN PLAN FOR YOU TO BE CAPTURED SO EASILY, OR DID YOU COME OF YOUR OWN ACCORD?
AT LEAST MY PARTICULAR GROUP OF FASCISTS ISN'T RUN BY SOME NUTCASE CALLING HIMSELF PATIENT NEIN--
WE ARE ALL CRAZY PEOPLE AND FOOLS. YOU ESPECIALLY, FOR FOLLOWING ONE.
WOW. WAS THAT YOUR INSPIRATIONAL EMAIL QUOTE OF THE DAY?
SIXTY-ONE SECONDS.
SIXTY-ONE SECONDS. WHAT ABOUT IT?
SHE DOESN'T. KNOW. DIDN'T TELL HER.
MAYBE THEY. DON'T KNOW.
COULD IT BE? THE GREAT OCTAVIAN--THE MAN WITH THE PLANET-SIZED INTELLECT-- DOESN'T KNOW?
ABOUT WHAT?
ABOUT THE SIXTY-ONE SECONDS.
WHAT ARE YOU TALKING ABOUT, YOU FUCKING NUTBAG?
I'M TALKING ABOUT MATTER MAN. HE WOULD VERY MUCH LIKE TO DESTROY A CONTINENT. AND BELIEVE ME, HE'D BE QUITE CAPABLE OF DOING SO, IF NOT FOR ONE SMALL ISSUE.
HIS POWERS LAST FOR ONLY SIXTY-ONE SECONDS. ONE SINGLE MINUTE.
AFTER WHICH HE BECOMES AS WEAK AS A KITTEN.

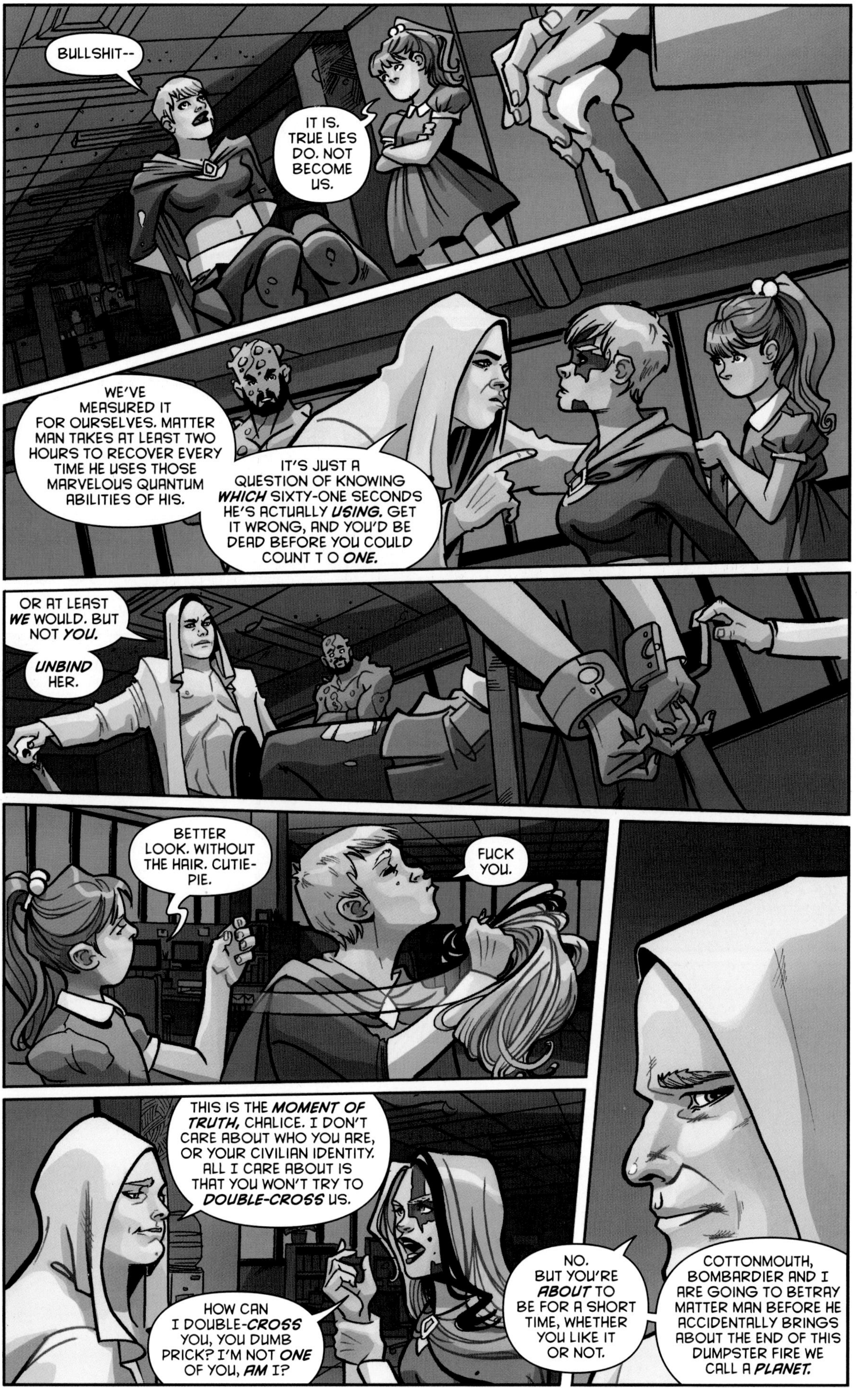
BULLSHIT--
IT IS. TRUE LIES DO. NOT BECOME US.
WE'VE MEASURED IT FOR OURSELVES. MATTER MAN TAKES AT LEAST TWO HOURS TO RECOVER EVERY TIME HE USES THOSE MARVELOUS QUANTUM ABILITIES OF HIS.
IT'S JUST A QUESTION OF KNOWING WHICH SIXTY-ONE SECONDS HE'S ACTUALLY USING. GET IT WRONG, AND YOU'D BE DEAD BEFORE YOU COULD COUNT T O ONE.
OR AT LEAST WE WOULD. BUT NOT YOU.
UNBIND HER.
BETTER LOOK. WITHOUT THE HAIR. CUTIE-PIE.
FUCK YOU.
THIS IS THE MOMENT OF TRUTH, CHALICE. I DON'T CARE ABOUT WHO YOU ARE, OR YOUR CIVILIAN IDENTITY. ALL I CARE ABOUT IS THAT YOU WON'T TRY TO DOUBLE-CROSS US.
HOW CAN I DOUBLE-CROSS YOU, YOU DUMB PRICK? I'M NOT ONE OF YOU, AM I?
NO. BUT YOU'RE ABOUT TO BE FOR A SHORT TIME, WHETHER YOU LIKE IT OR NOT.
COTTONMOUTH, BOMBARDIER AND I ARE GOING TO BETRAY MATTER MAN BEFORE HE ACCIDENTALLY BRINGS ABOUT THE END OF THIS DUMPSTER FIRE WE CALL A PLANET.

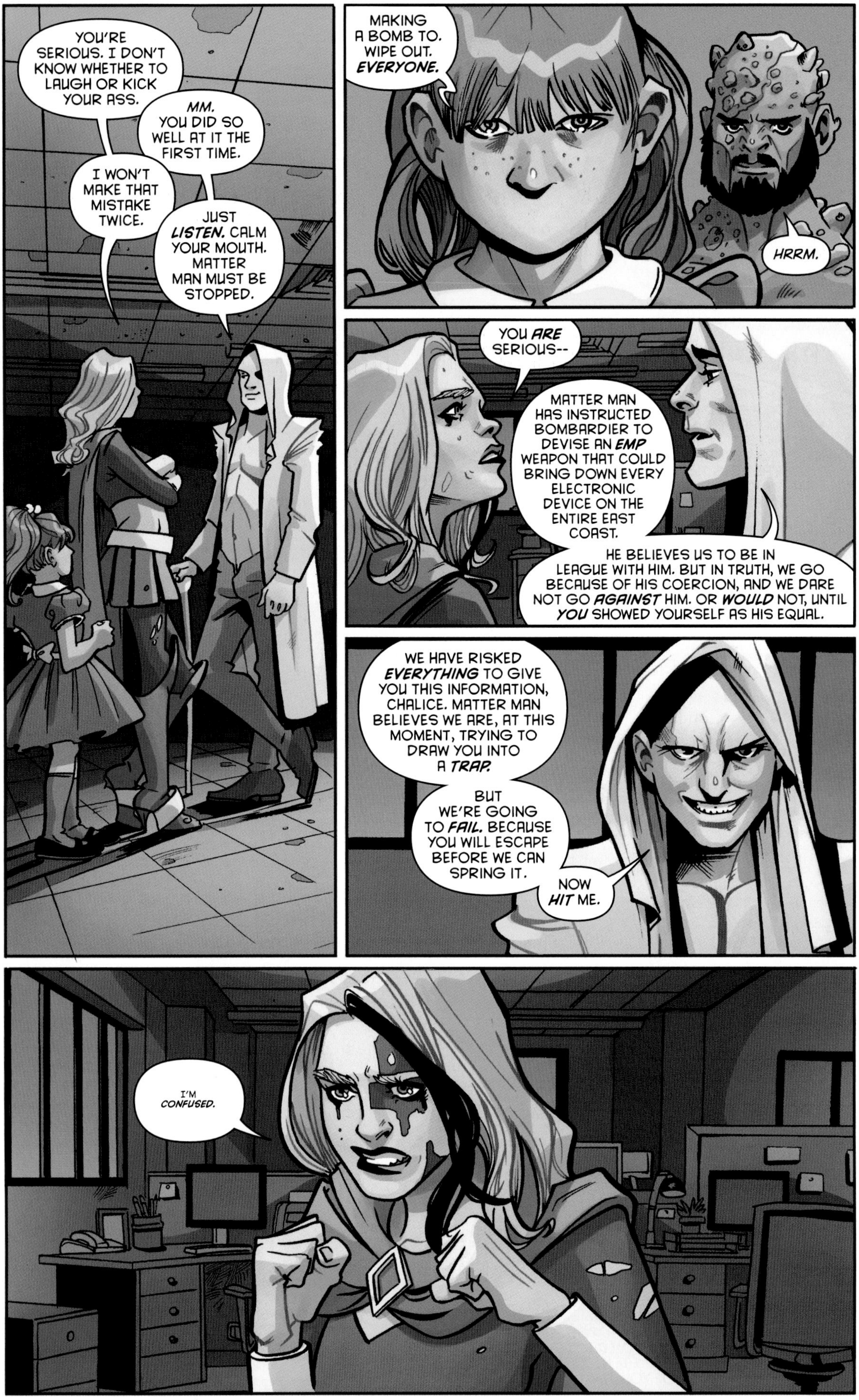
YOU'RE SERIOUS. I DON'T KNOW WHETHER TO LAUGH OR KICK YOUR ASS.
MM. YOU DID SO WELL AT IT THE FIRST TIME.
I WON'T MAKE THAT MISTAKE TWICE.
JUST LISTEN. CALM YOUR MOUTH. MATTER MAN MUST BE STOPPED.
MAKING A BOMB TO. WIPE OUT. EVERYONE.
HRRM.
YOU ARE SERIOUS--
MATTER MAN HAS INSTRUCTED BOMBARDIER TO DEVISE AN EMP WEAPON THAT COULD BRING DOWN EVERY ELECTRONIC DEVICE ON THE ENTIRE EAST COAST.
HE BELIEVES US TO BE IN LEAGUE WITH HIM. BUT IN TRUTH, WE GO BECAUSE OF HIS COERCION, AND WE DARE NOT GO AGAINST HIM. OR WOULD NOT, UNTIL YOU SHOWED YOURSELF AS HIS EQUAL.
WE HAVE RISKED EVERYTHING TO GIVE YOU THIS INFORMATION, CHALICE. MATTER MAN BELIEVES WE ARE, AT THIS MOMENT, TRYING TO DRAW YOU INTO A TRAP.
BUT WE'RE GOING TO FAIL. BECAUSE YOU WILL ESCAPE BEFORE WE CAN SPRING IT.
NOW HIT ME.
I'M CONFUSED.

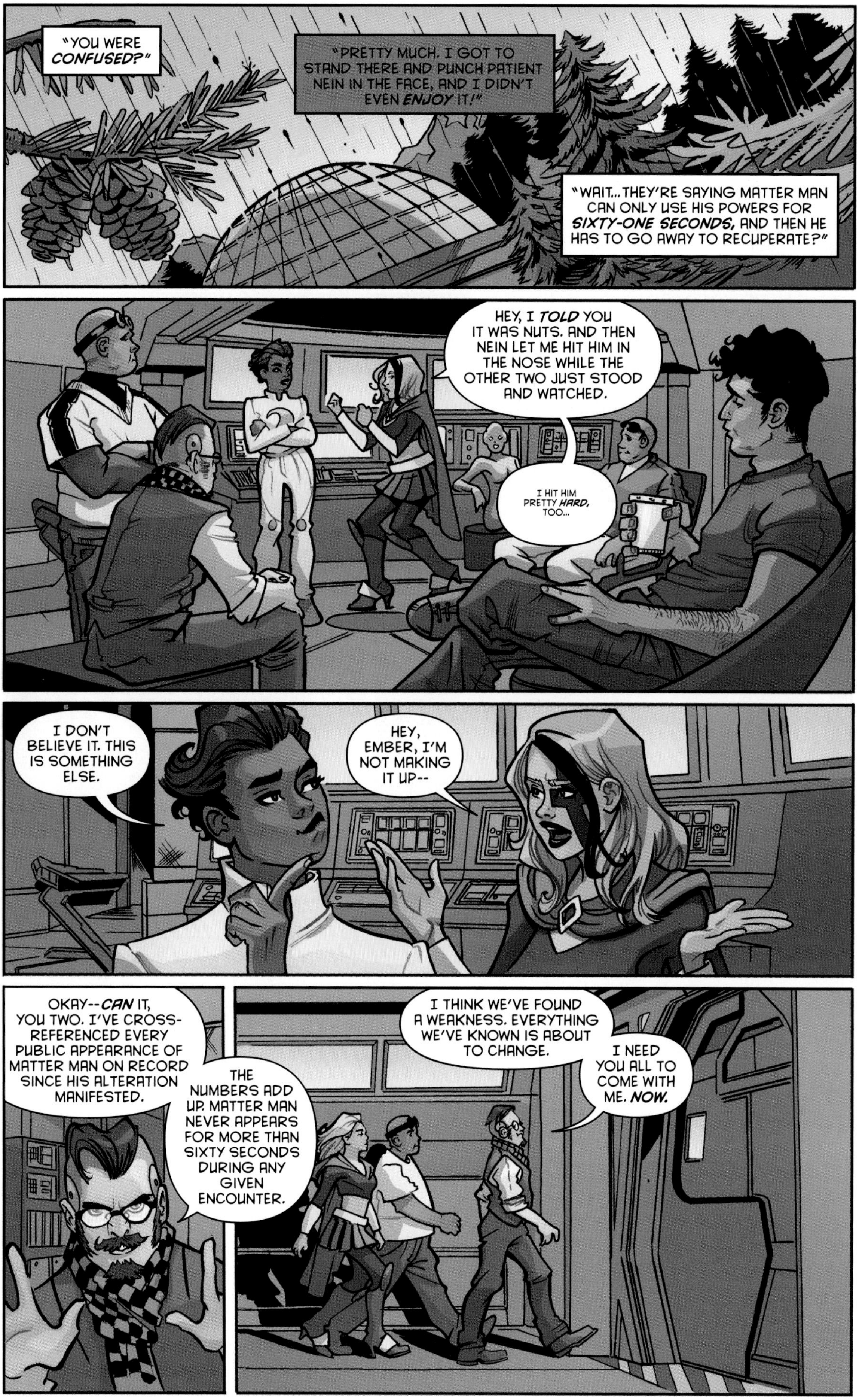

"YOU WERE CONFUSED?"
"PRETTY MUCH. I GOT TO STAND THERE AND PUNCH PATIENT NEIN IN THE FACE, AND I DIDN'T EVEN ENJOY IT!"
"WAIT... THEY'RE SAYING MATTER MAN CAN ONLY USE HIS POWERS FOR SIXTY-ONE SECONDS, AND THEN HE HAS TO GO AWAY TO RECUPERATE?"
HEY, I TOLD YOU IT WAS NUTS. AND THEN NEIN LET ME HIT HIM IN THE NOSE WHILE THE OTHER TWO JUST STOOD AND WATCHED.
I HIT HIM PRETTY HARD, TOO...
I DON'T BELIEVE IT. THIS IS SOMETHING ELSE.
HEY, EMBER, I'M NOT MAKING IT UP--
OKAY--CAN IT, YOU TWO. I'VE CROSS-REFERENCED EVERY PUBLIC APPEARANCE OF MATTER MAN ON RECORD SINCE HIS ALTERATION MANIFESTED.
THE NUMBERS ADD UP. MATTER MAN NEVER APPEARS FOR MORE THAN SIXTY SECONDS DURING ANY GIVEN ENCOUNTER.
I THINK WE'VE FOUND A WEAKNESS. EVERYTHING WE'VE KNOWN IS ABOUT TO CHANGE.
I NEED YOU ALL TO COME WITH ME. NOW.

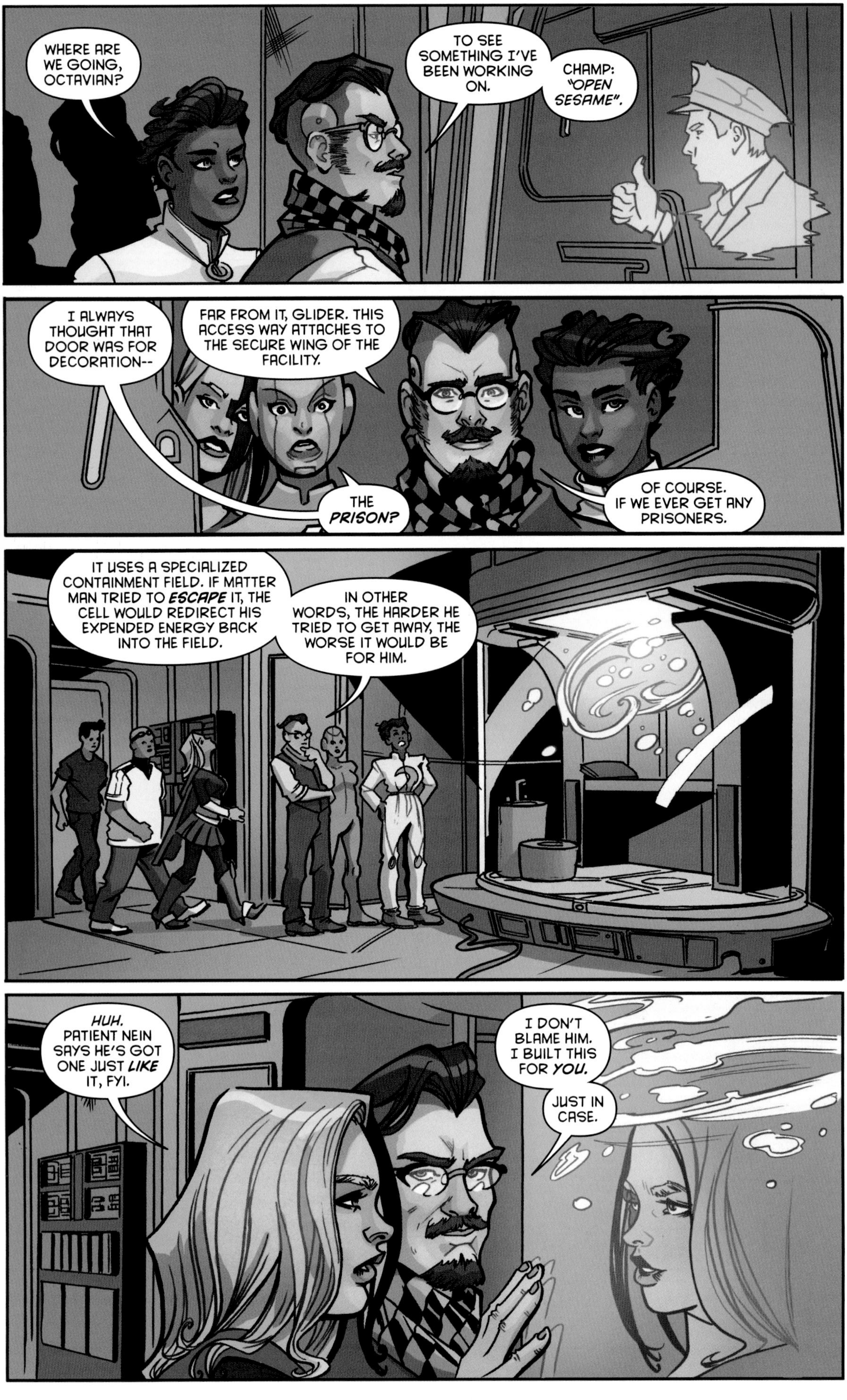
WHERE ARE WE GOING, OCTAVIAN?
TO SEE SOMETHING I'VE BEEN WORKING ON.
CHAMP: "OPEN SESAME".
I ALWAYS THOUGHT THAT DOOR WAS FOR DECORATION--
FAR FROM IT, GLIDER. THIS ACCESS WAY ATTACHES TO THE SECURE WING OF THE FACILITY.
THE PRISON?
OF COURSE. IF WE EVER GET ANY PRISONERS.
IT USES A SPECIALIZED CONTAINMENT FIELD. IF MATTER MAN TRIED TO ESCAPE IT, THE CELL WOULD REDIRECT HIS EXPENDED ENERGY BACK INTO THE FIELD.
IN OTHER WORDS, THE HARDER HE TRIED TO GET AWAY, THE WORSE IT WOULD BE FOR HIM.
HUH. PATIENT NEIN SAYS HE'S GOT ONE JUST LIKE IT, FYI.
I DON'T BLAME HIM. I BUILT THIS FOR YOU.
JUST IN CASE.

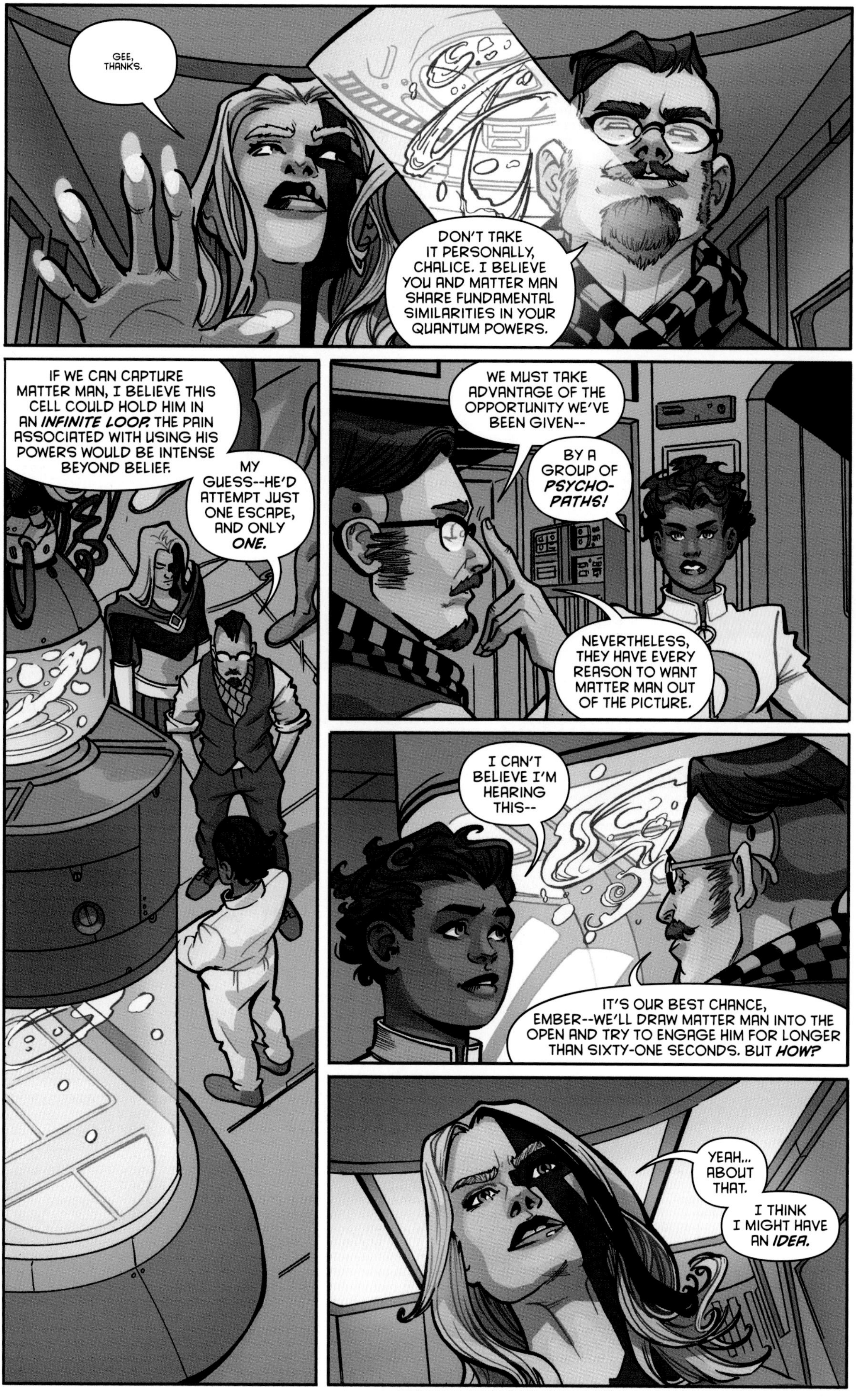
GEE, THANKS.
DON'T TAKE IT PERSONALLY, CHALICE. I BELIEVE YOU AND MATTER MAN SHARE FUNDAMENTAL SIMILARITIES IN YOUR QUANTUM POWERS.
IF WE CAN CAPTURE MATTER MAN, I BELIEVE THIS CELL COULD HOLD HIM IN AN *INFINITE LOOP.* THE PAIN ASSOCIATED WITH USING HIS POWERS WOULD BE INTENSE BEYOND BELIEF.
MY GUESS--HE'D ATTEMPT JUST ONE ESCAPE, AND ONLY *ONE.*
WE MUST TAKE ADVANTAGE OF THE OPPORTUNITY WE'VE BEEN GIVEN--
BY A GROUP OF *PSYCHO-PATHS!*
NEVERTHELESS, THEY HAVE EVERY REASON TO WANT MATTER MAN OUT OF THE PICTURE.
I CAN'T BELIEVE I'M HEARING THIS--
IT'S OUR BEST CHANCE, EMBER--WE'LL DRAW MATTER MAN INTO THE OPEN AND TRY TO ENGAGE HIM FOR LONGER THAN SIXTY-ONE SECONDS. BUT *HOW?*
YEAH... ABOUT THAT.
I THINK I MIGHT HAVE AN *IDEA.*

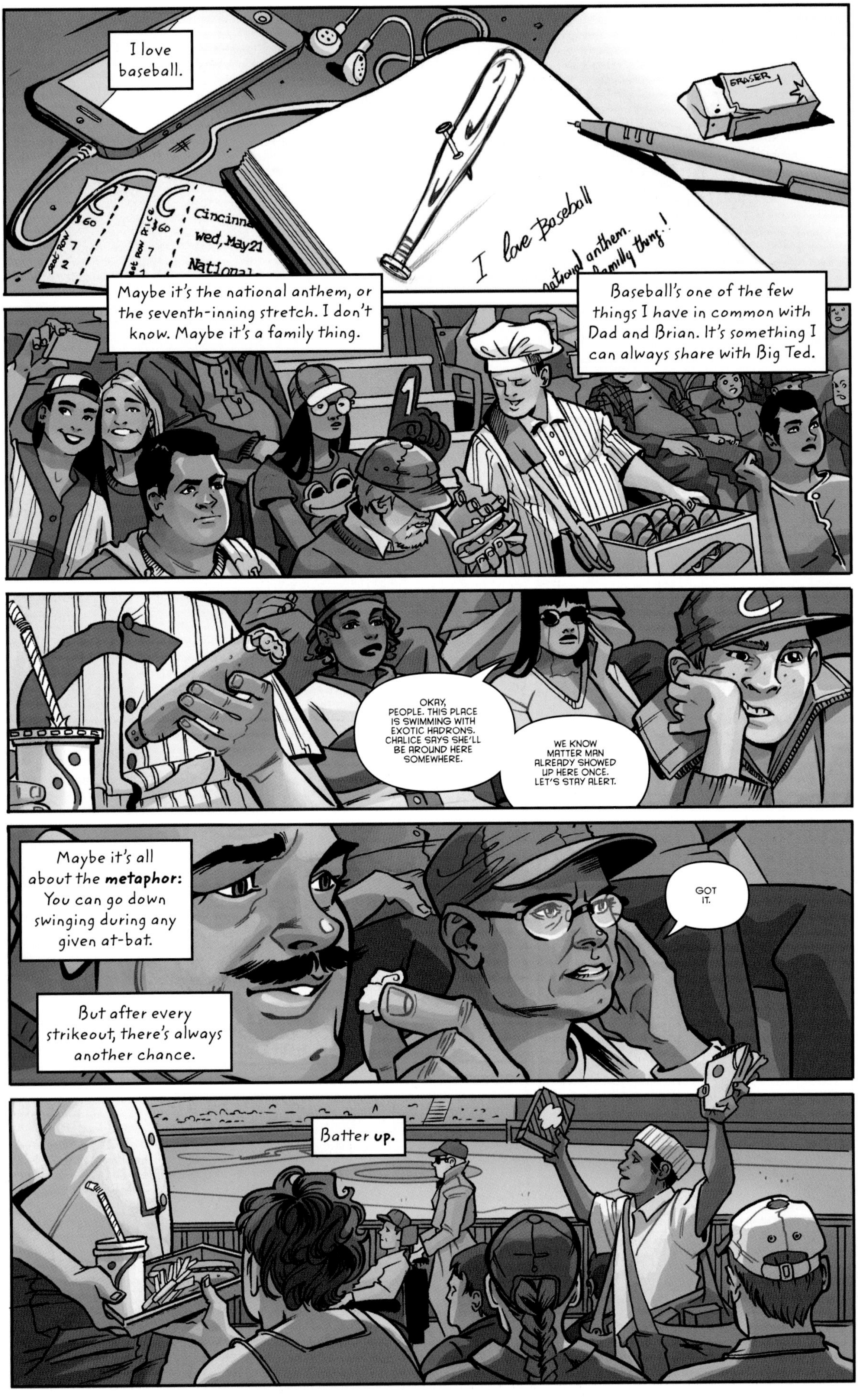
I love baseball.
ERASER
I love Baseball
wed, May21
Maybe it's the national anthem, or the seventh-inning stretch. I don't know. Maybe it's a family thing.
Baseball's one of the few things I have in common with Dad and Brian. It's something I can always share with Big Ted.
OKAY, PEOPLE. THIS PLACE IS SWIMMING WITH EXOTIC HADRONS. CHALICE SAYS SHE'LL BE AROUND HERE SOMEWHERE.
WE KNOW MATTER MAN ALREADY SHOWED UP HERE ONCE. LET'S STAY ALERT.
Maybe it's all about the **metaphor:** You can go down swinging during any given at-bat.
GOT IT.
But after every strikeout, there's always another chance.
Batter **up.**

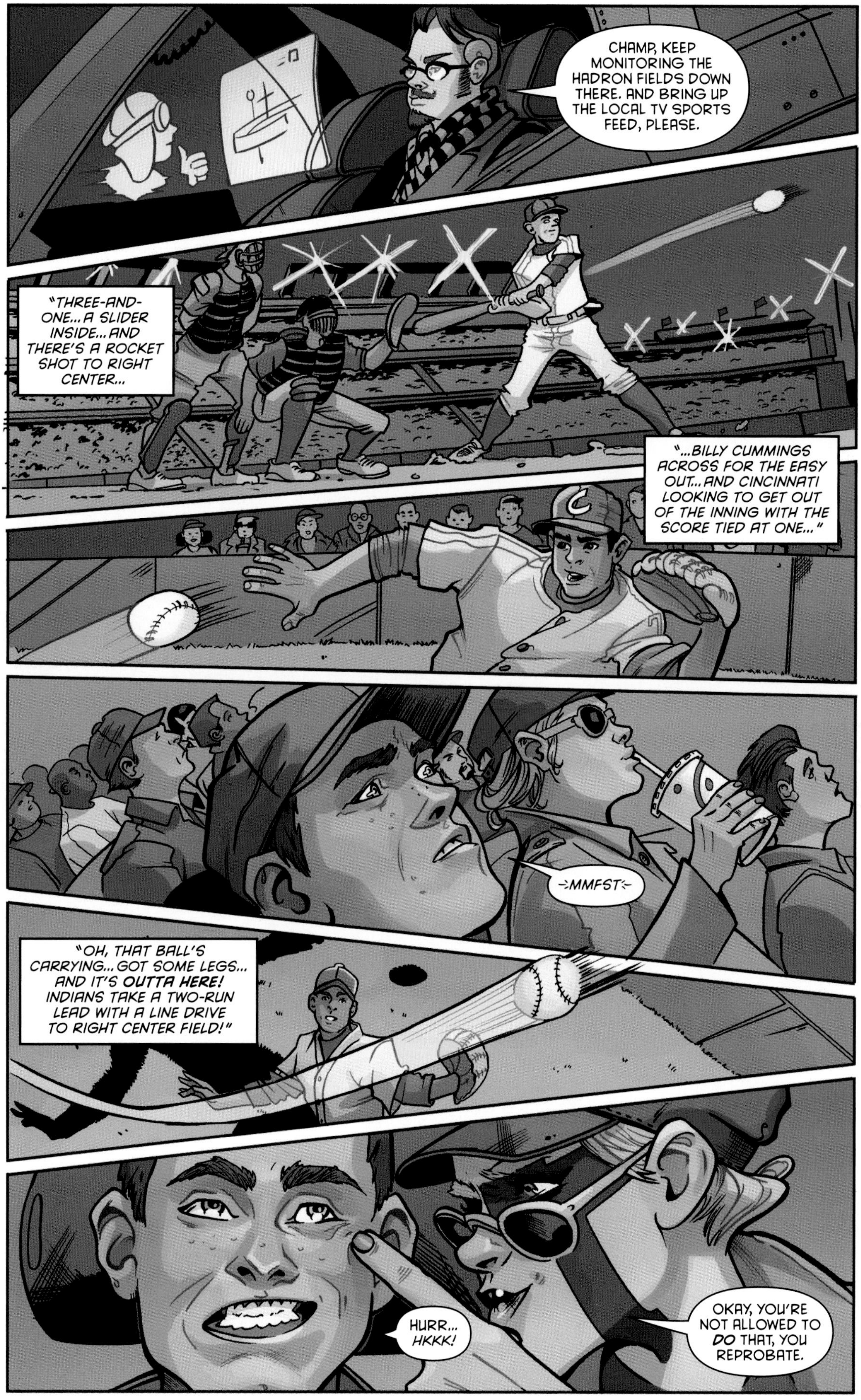
CHAMP, KEEP MONITORING THE HADRON FIELDS DOWN THERE. AND BRING UP THE LOCAL TV SPORTS FEED, PLEASE.
"THREE-AND-ONE... A SLIDER INSIDE... AND THERE'S A ROCKET SHOT TO RIGHT CENTER...
"...BILLY CUMMINGS ACROSS FOR THE EASY OUT... AND CINCINNATI LOOKING TO GET OUT OF THE INNING WITH THE SCORE TIED AT ONE..."
-MMFST-
"OH, THAT BALL'S CARRYING... GOT SOME LEGS... AND IT'S ***OUTTA HERE!*** INDIANS TAKE A TWO-RUN LEAD WITH A LINE DRIVE TO RIGHT CENTER FIELD!"
HURR... HKKK!
OKAY, YOU'RE NOT ALLOWED TO ***DO*** THAT, YOU REPROBATE.

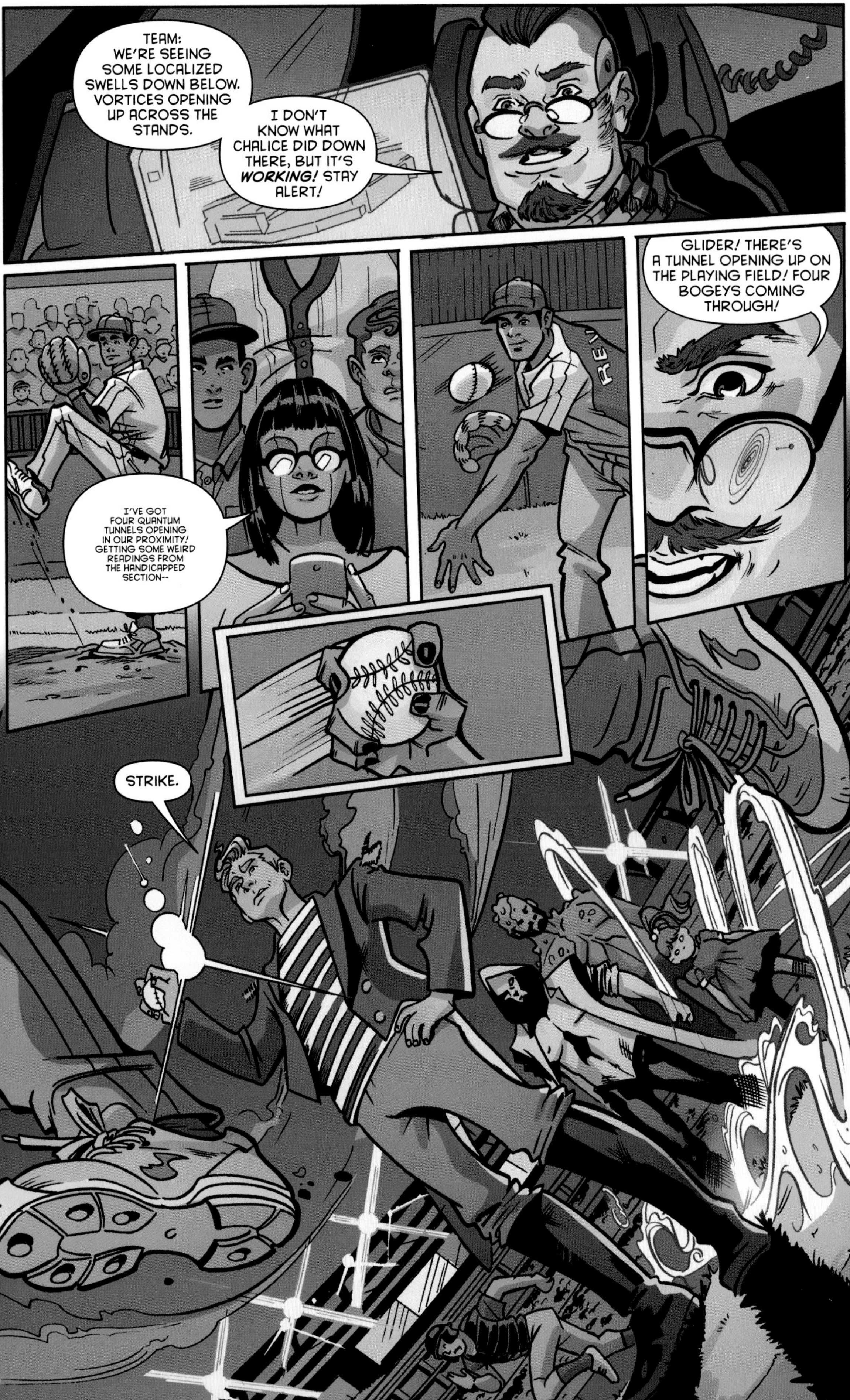
TEAM: WE'RE SEEING SOME LOCALIZED SWELLS DOWN BELOW. VORTICES OPENING UP ACROSS THE STANDS.
I DON'T KNOW WHAT CHALICE DID DOWN THERE, BUT IT'S *WORKING!* STAY ALERT!
I'VE GOT FOUR QUANTUM TUNNELS OPENING IN OUR PROXIMITY! GETTING SOME WEIRD READINGS FROM THE HANDICAPPED SECTION--
GLIDER! THERE'S A TUNNEL OPENING UP ON THE PLAYING FIELD! FOUR BOGEYS COMING THROUGH!
STRIKE.

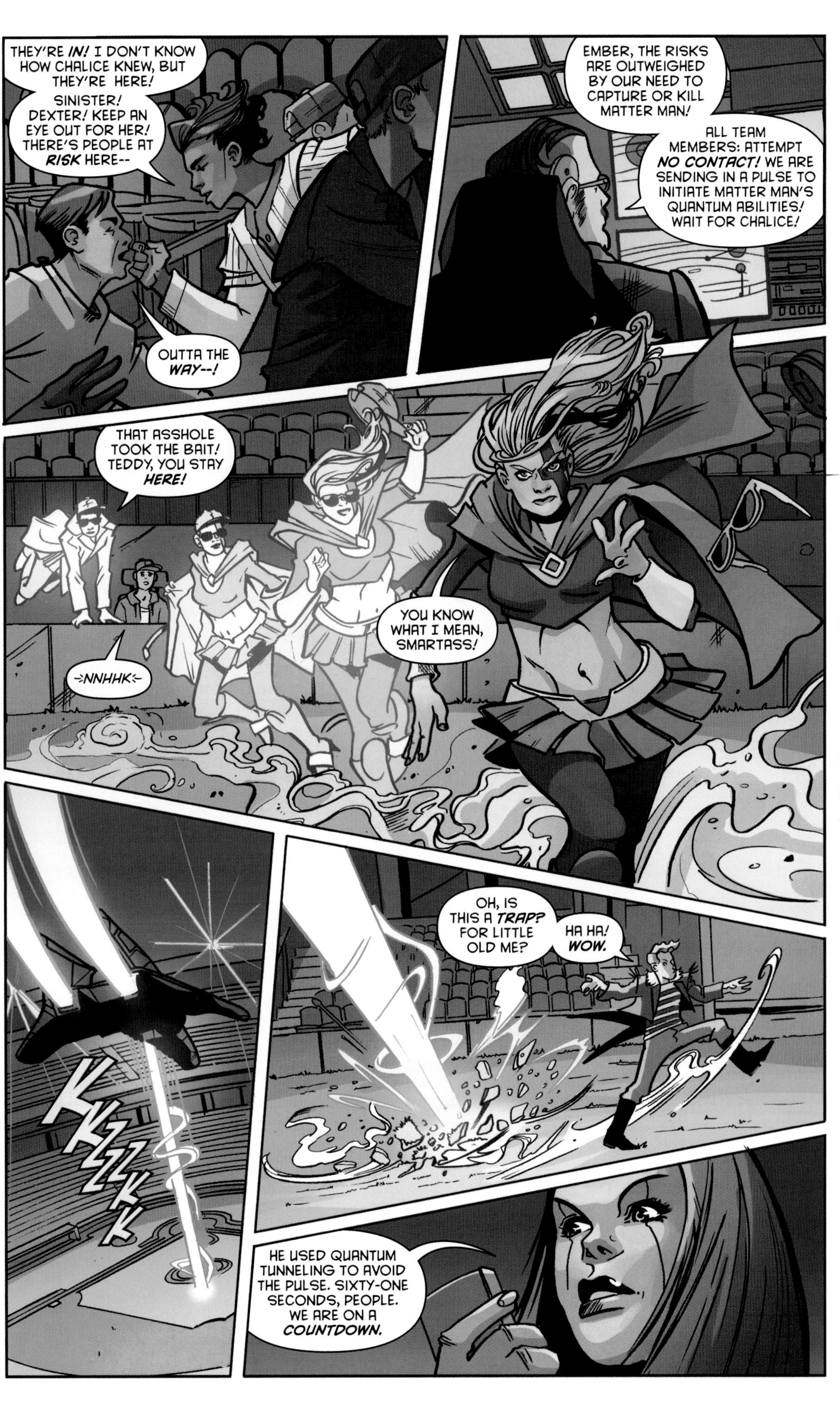
THEY'RE *IN!* I DON'T KNOW HOW CHALICE KNEW, BUT THEY'RE HERE!
SINISTER! DEXTER! KEEP AN EYE OUT FOR HER! THERE'S PEOPLE AT *RISK* HERE--
OUTTA THE *WAY--!*
EMBER, THE RISKS ARE OUTWEIGHED BY OUR NEED TO CAPTURE OR KILL MATTER MAN!
ALL TEAM MEMBERS: ATTEMPT *NO CONTACT!* WE ARE SENDING IN A PULSE TO INITIATE MATTER MAN'S QUANTUM ABILITIES! WAIT FOR CHALICE!
THAT ASSHOLE TOOK THE BAIT! TEDDY, YOU STAY *HERE!*
YOU KNOW WHAT I MEAN, SMARTASS!
NNHHK
KKZZZKK
OH, IS THIS A *TRAP?* FOR LITTLE OLD ME?
HA HA! *WOW.*
HE USED QUANTUM TUNNELING TO AVOID THE PULSE. SIXTY-ONE SECONDS, PEOPLE. WE ARE ON A *COUNTDOWN.*

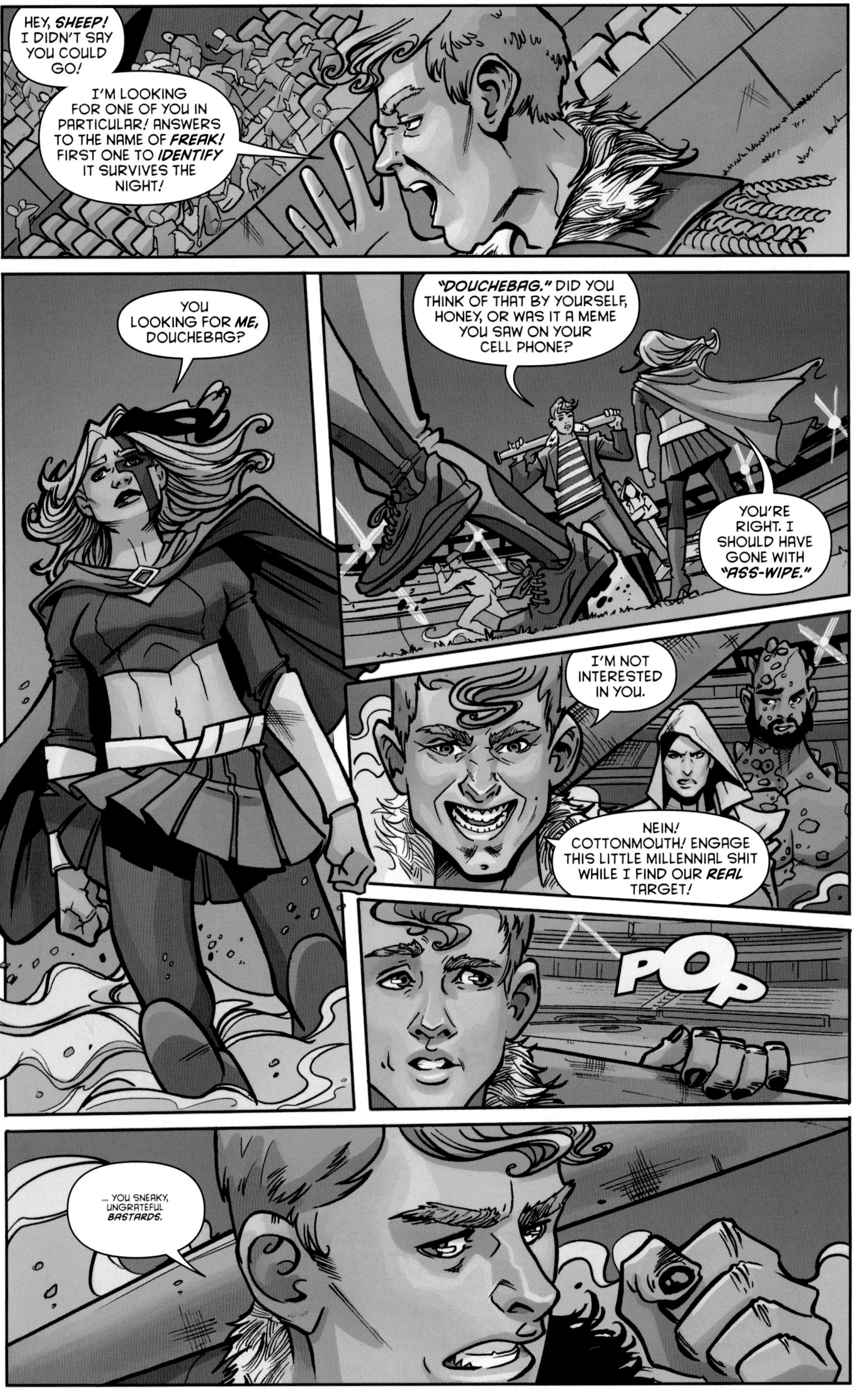
HEY, SHEEP! I DIDN'T SAY YOU COULD GO!
I'M LOOKING FOR ONE OF YOU IN PARTICULAR! ANSWERS TO THE NAME OF FREAK! FIRST ONE TO IDENTIFY IT SURVIVES THE NIGHT!
YOU LOOKING FOR ME, DOUCHEBAG?
"DOUCHEBAG." DID YOU THINK OF THAT BY YOURSELF, HONEY, OR WAS IT A MEME YOU SAW ON YOUR CELL PHONE?
YOU'RE RIGHT. I SHOULD HAVE GONE WITH "ASS-WIPE."
I'M NOT INTERESTED IN YOU.
NEIN! COTTONMOUTH! ENGAGE THIS LITTLE MILLENNIAL SHIT WHILE I FIND OUR REAL TARGET!
POP
... YOU SNEAKY, UNGRATEFUL BASTARDS.

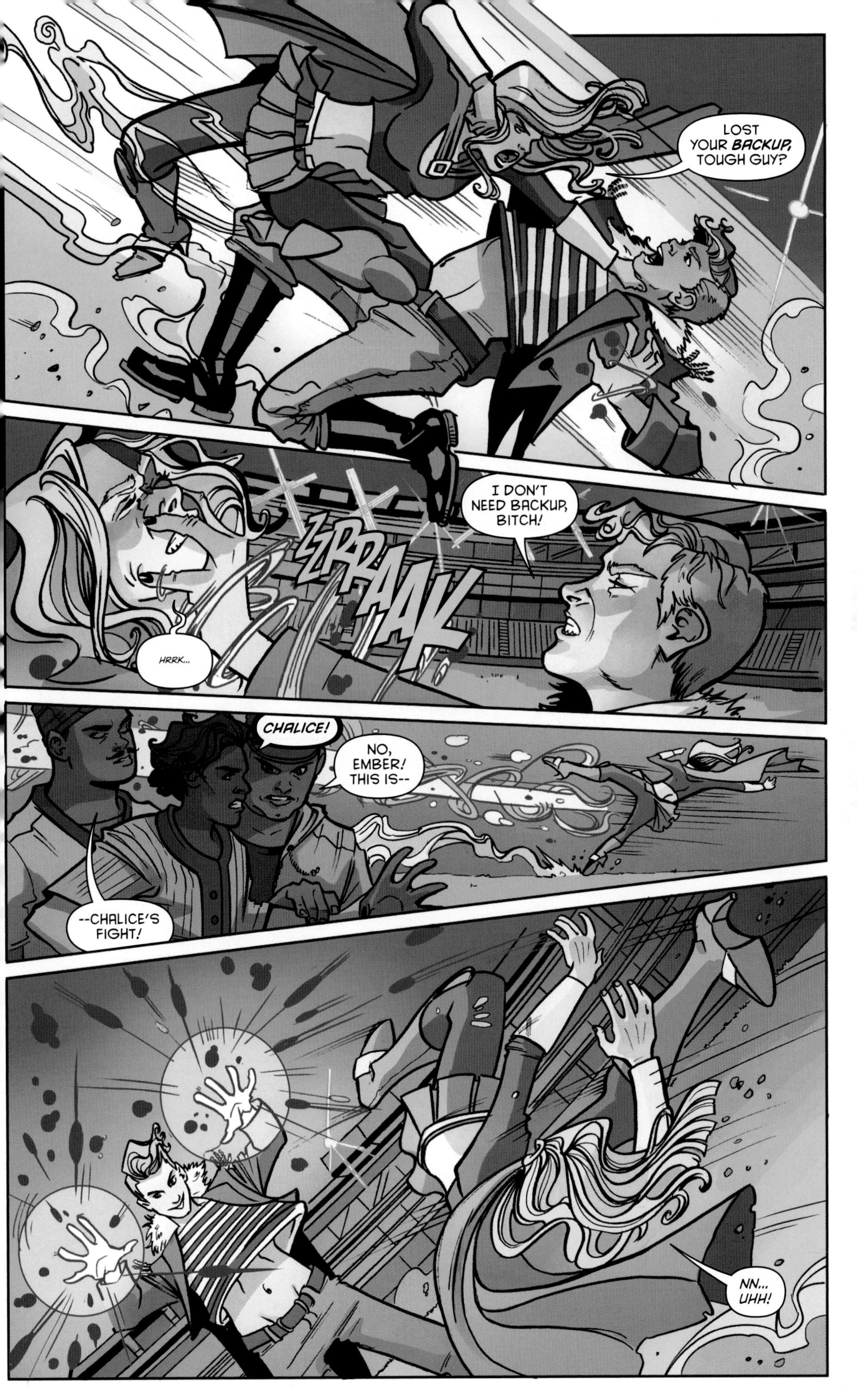
LOST YOUR BACKUP, TOUGH GUY?
I DON'T NEED BACKUP, BITCH!
ZZRRAAK
HRRK...
CHALICE!
NO, EMBER! THIS IS--
--CHALICE'S FIGHT!
NN... UHH!

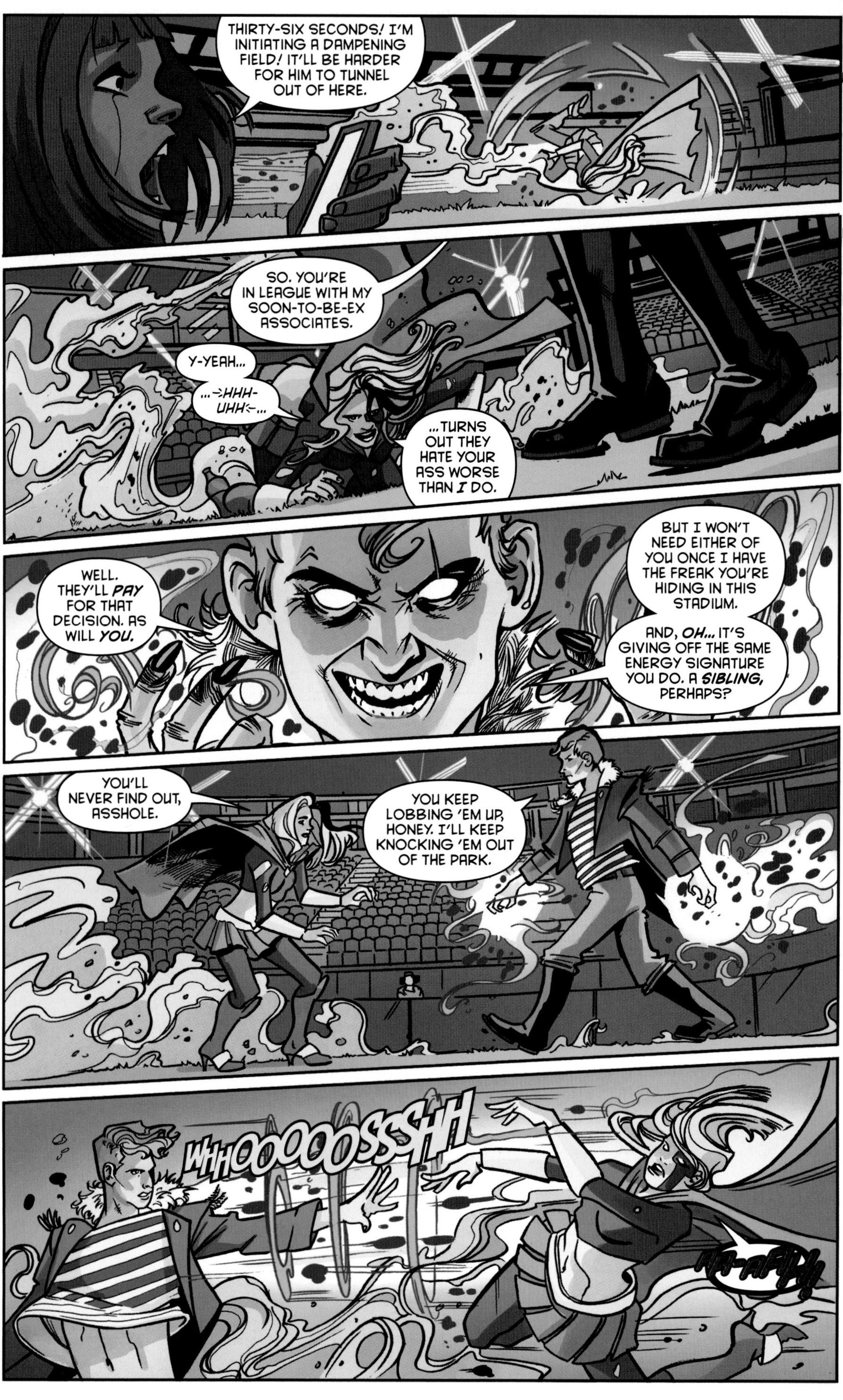
THIRTY-SIX SECONDS! I'M INITIATING A DAMPENING FIELD! IT'LL BE HARDER FOR HIM TO TUNNEL OUT OF HERE.
SO. YOU'RE IN LEAGUE WITH MY SOON-TO-BE-EX ASSOCIATES.
Y-YEAH...
...HHH-UHH...
...TURNS OUT THEY HATE YOUR ASS WORSE THAN *I* DO.
WELL. THEY'LL *PAY* FOR THAT DECISION. AS WILL *YOU.*
BUT I WON'T NEED EITHER OF YOU ONCE I HAVE THE FREAK YOU'RE HIDING IN THIS STADIUM.
AND, *OH...* IT'S GIVING OFF THE SAME ENERGY SIGNATURE YOU DO. A *SIBLING,* PERHAPS?
YOU'LL NEVER FIND OUT, ASSHOLE.
YOU KEEP LOBBING 'EM UP, HONEY. I'LL KEEP KNOCKING 'EM OUT OF THE PARK.
WHHOOOOOOSSSHH

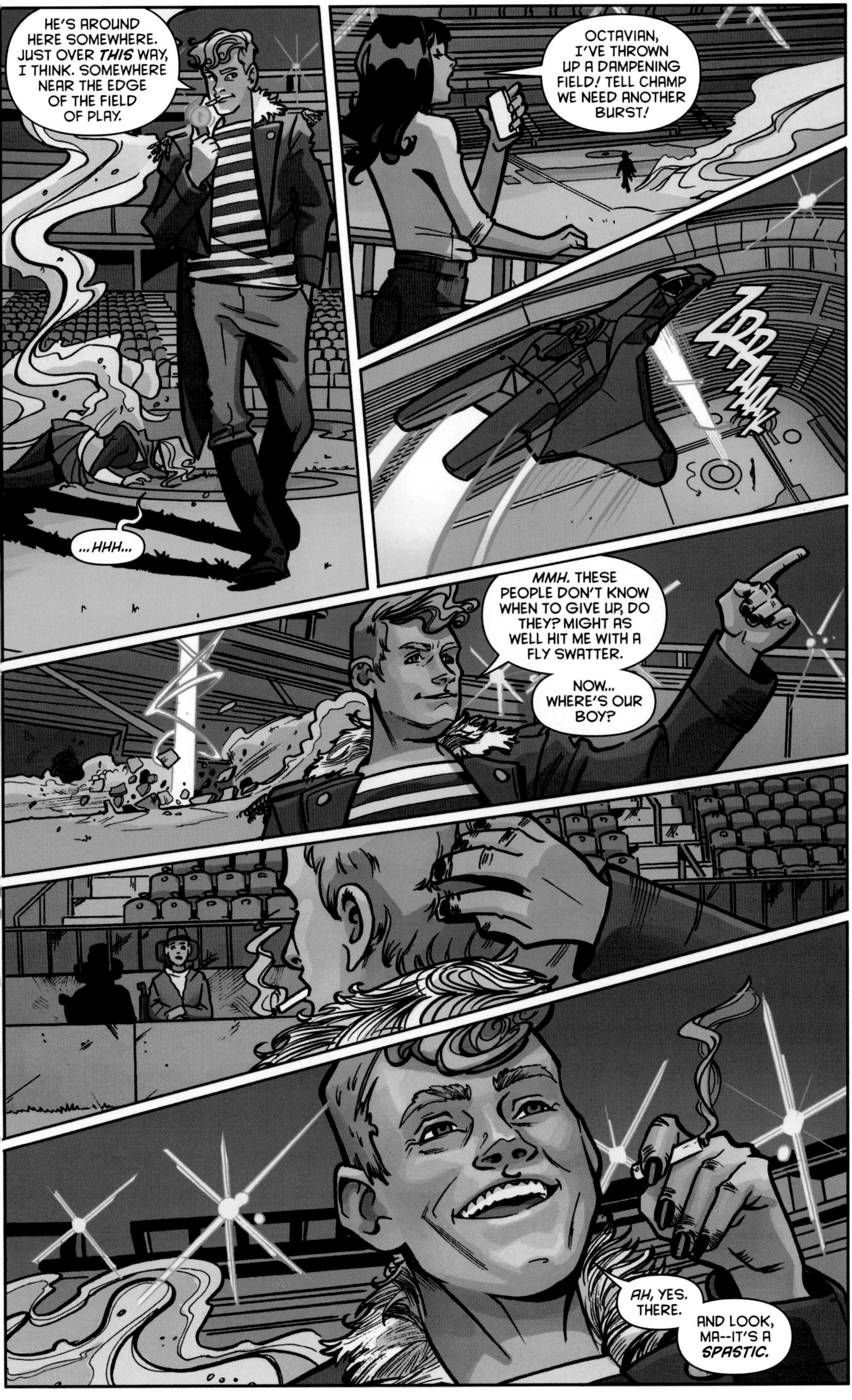
HE'S AROUND HERE SOMEWHERE. JUST OVER *THIS* WAY, I THINK. SOMEWHERE NEAR THE EDGE OF THE FIELD OF PLAY.
...HHH...
OCTAVIAN, I'VE THROWN UP A DAMPENING FIELD! TELL CHAMP WE NEED ANOTHER BURST!
ZRRAAAK
MMH. THESE PEOPLE DON'T KNOW WHEN TO GIVE UP, DO THEY? MIGHT AS WELL HIT ME WITH A FLY SWATTER.
NOW... WHERE'S OUR BOY?
AH, YES. THERE.
AND LOOK, MA--IT'S A *SPASTIC.*

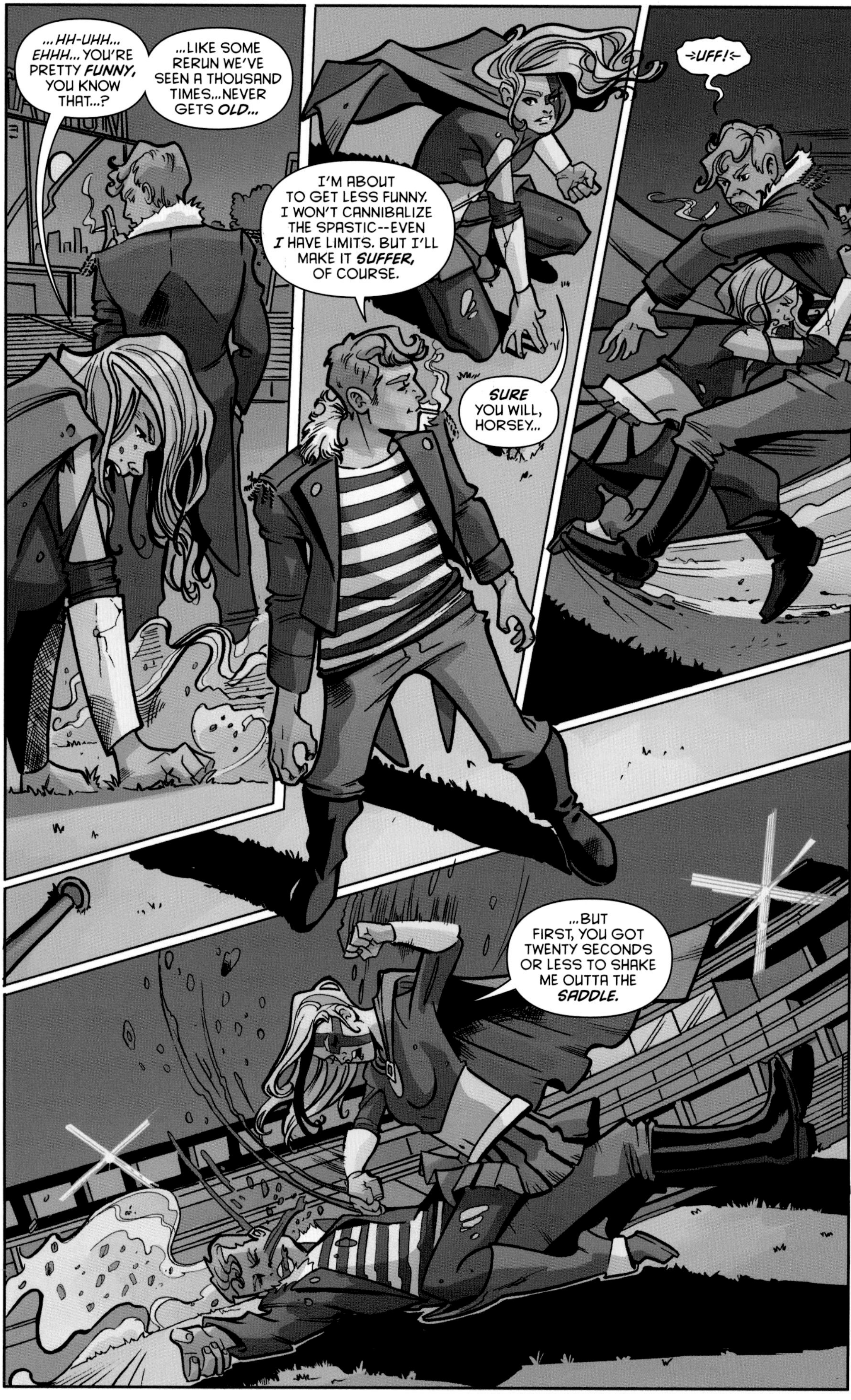
...HH-UHH... EHHH... YOU'RE PRETTY FUNNY, YOU KNOW THAT...?
...LIKE SOME RERUN WE'VE SEEN A THOUSAND TIMES...NEVER GETS OLD...
I'M ABOUT TO GET LESS FUNNY. I WON'T CANNIBALIZE THE SPASTIC--EVEN I HAVE LIMITS. BUT I'LL MAKE IT SUFFER, OF COURSE.
SURE YOU WILL, HORSEY...
UFF!
...BUT FIRST, YOU GOT TWENTY SECONDS OR LESS TO SHAKE ME OUTTA THE SADDLE.

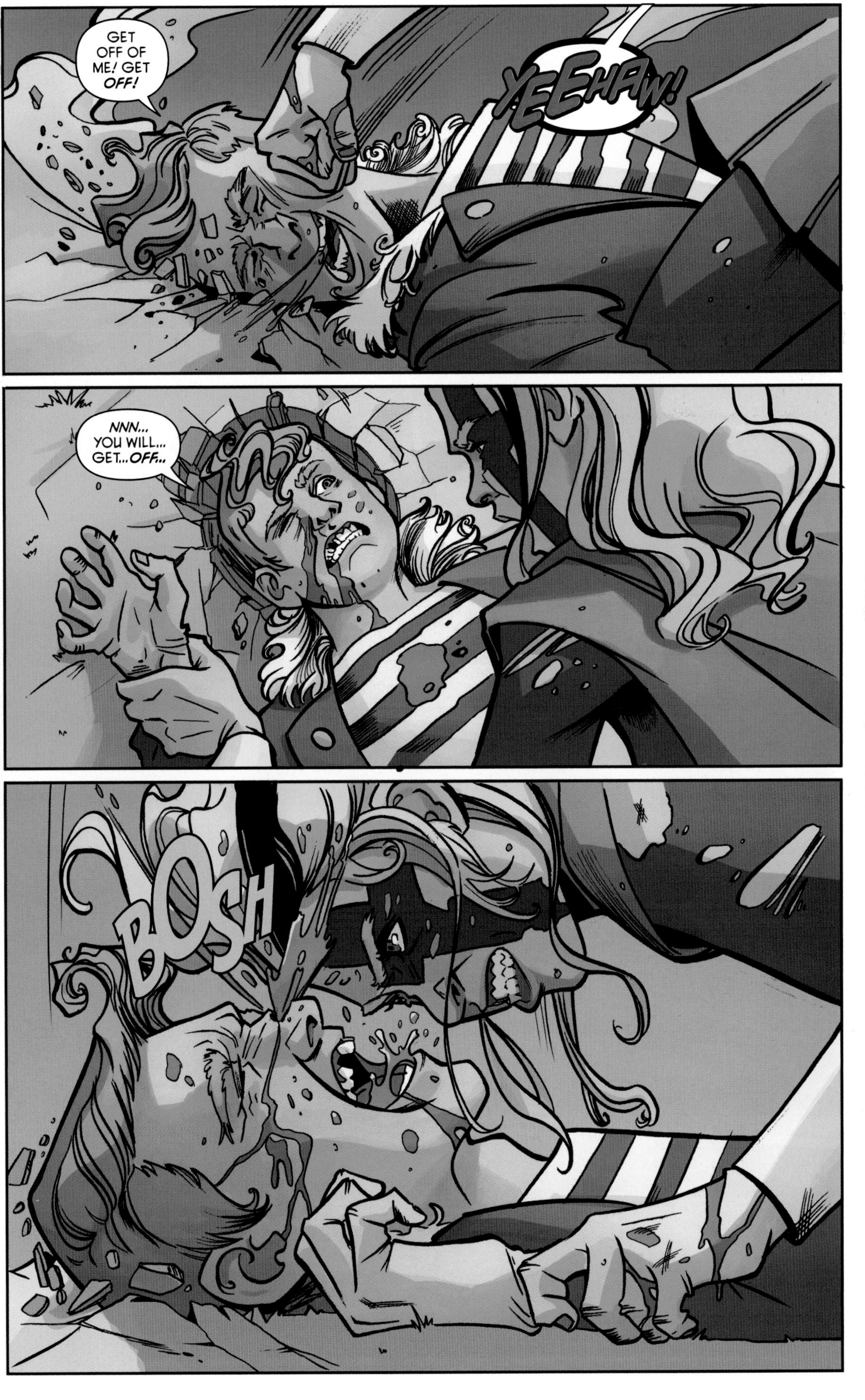
GET OFF OF ME! GET *OFF!*
YEEHAW!
NNN... YOU WILL... GET...*OFF...*
BOSH

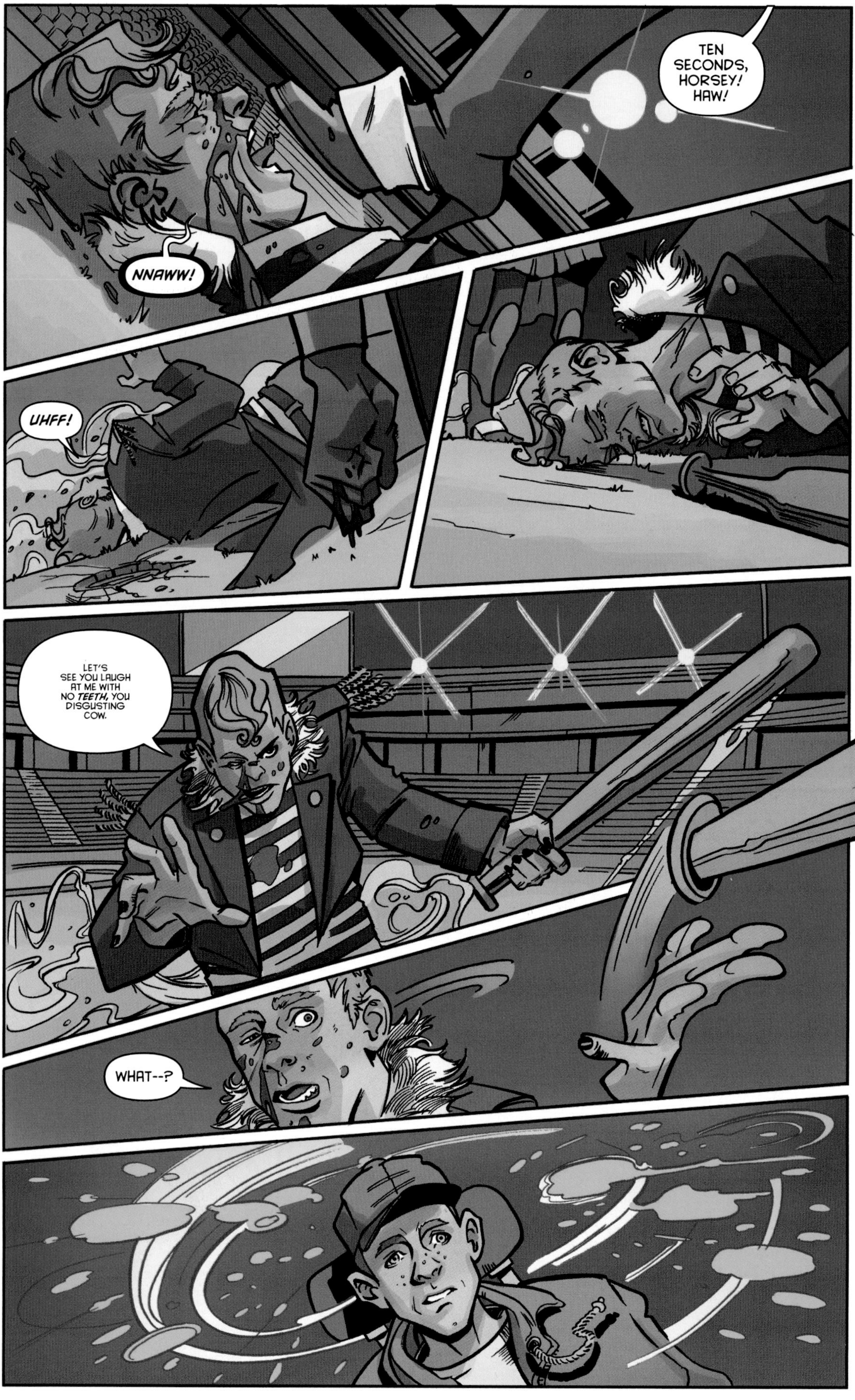
TEN SECONDS, HORSEY! HAW!
NNAWW!
UHFF!
LET'S SEE YOU LAUGH AT ME WITH NO TEETH, YOU DISGUSTING COW.
WHAT--?

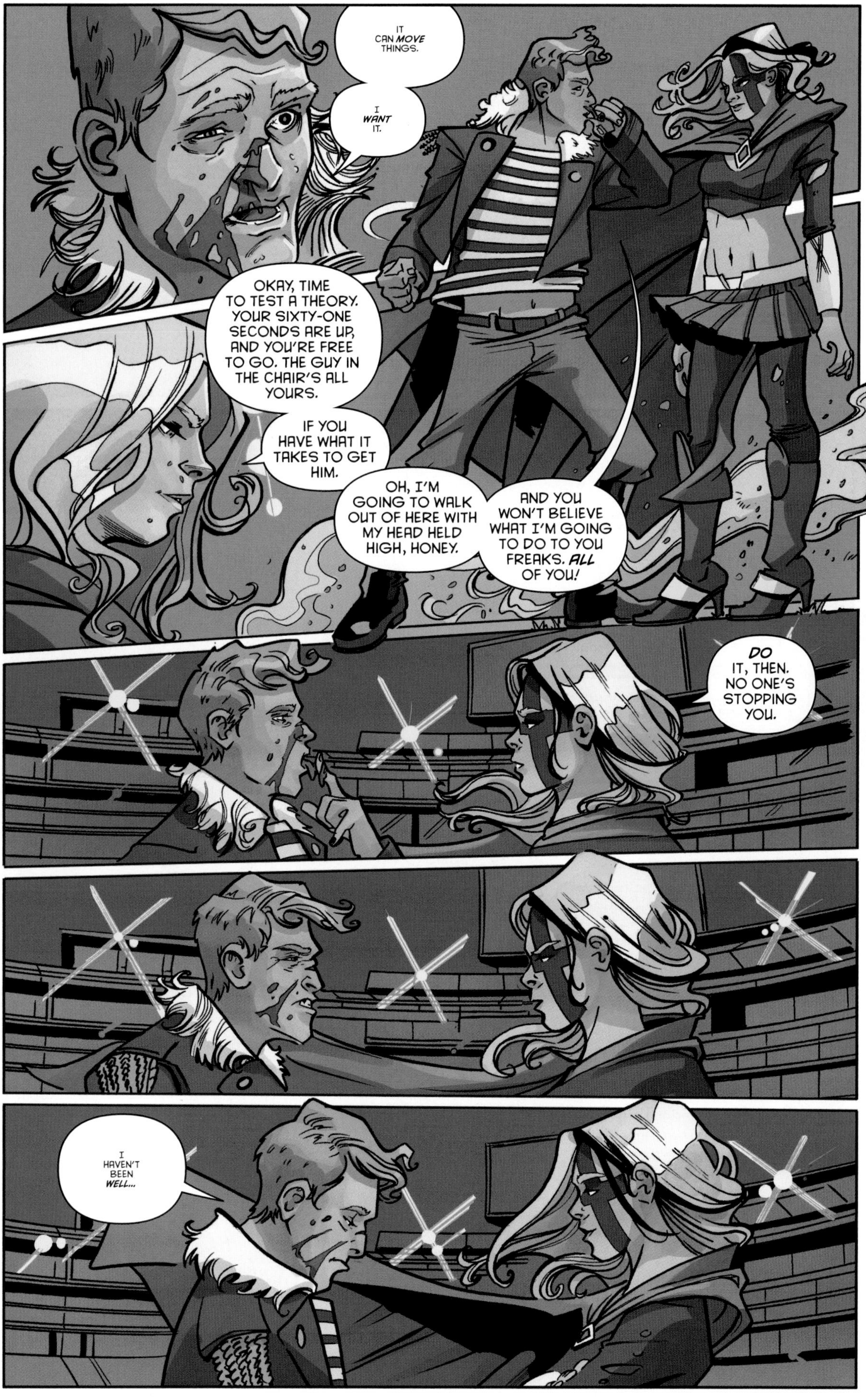
IT CAN MOVE THINGS.
I WANT IT.
OKAY, TIME TO TEST A THEORY. YOUR SIXTY-ONE SECONDS ARE UP, AND YOU'RE FREE TO GO. THE GUY IN THE CHAIR'S ALL YOURS.
IF YOU HAVE WHAT IT TAKES TO GET HIM.
OH, I'M GOING TO WALK OUT OF HERE WITH MY HEAD HELD HIGH, HONEY.
AND YOU WON'T BELIEVE WHAT I'M GOING TO DO TO YOU FREAKS. ALL OF YOU!
DO IT, THEN. NO ONE'S STOPPING YOU.
I HAVEN'T BEEN WELL...

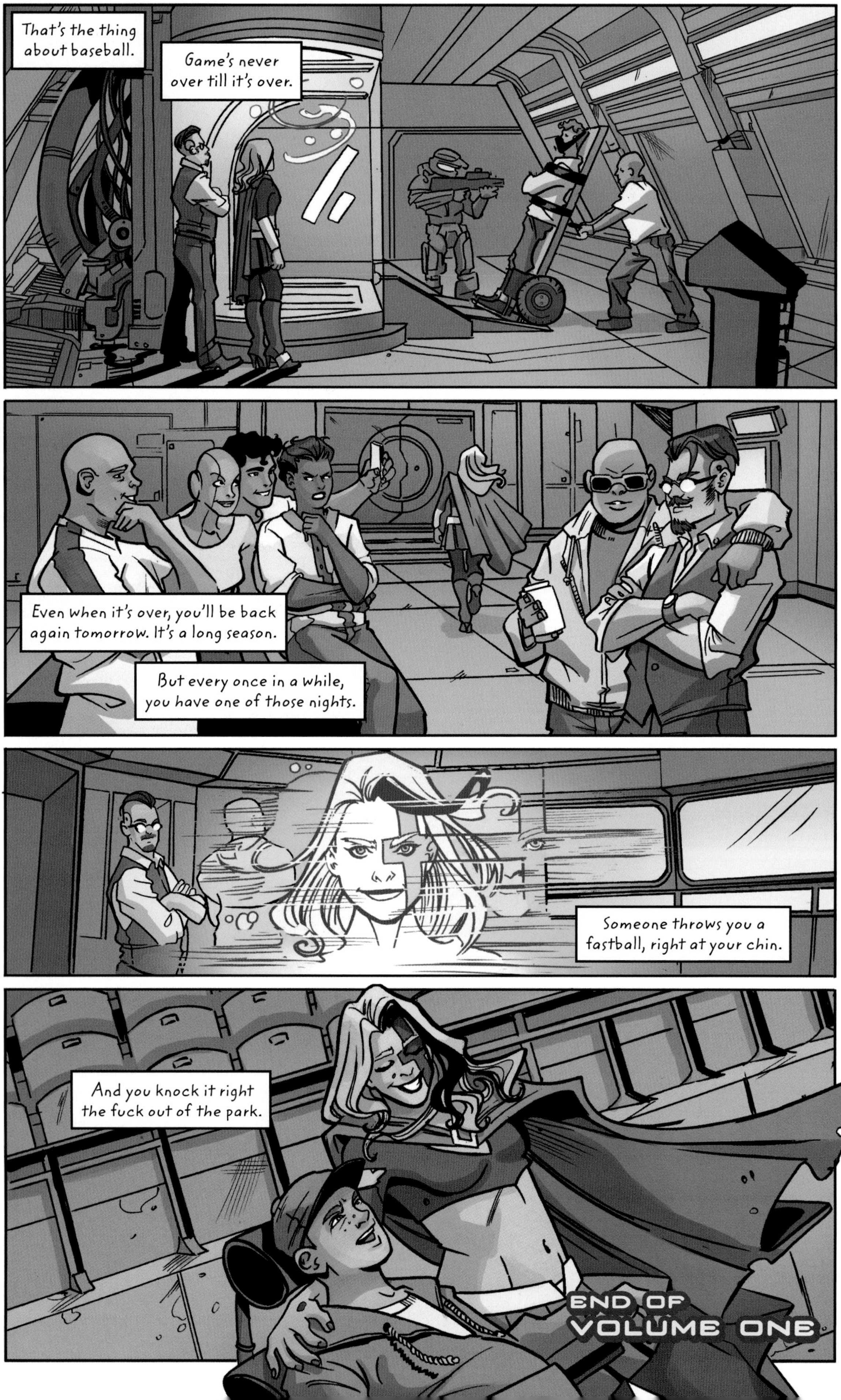
That's the thing about baseball.
Game's never over till it's over.
Even when it's over, you'll be back again tomorrow. It's a long season.
But every once in a while, you have one of those nights.
Someone throws you a fastball, right at your chin.
And you knock it right the fuck out of the park.
END OF VOLUME ONE

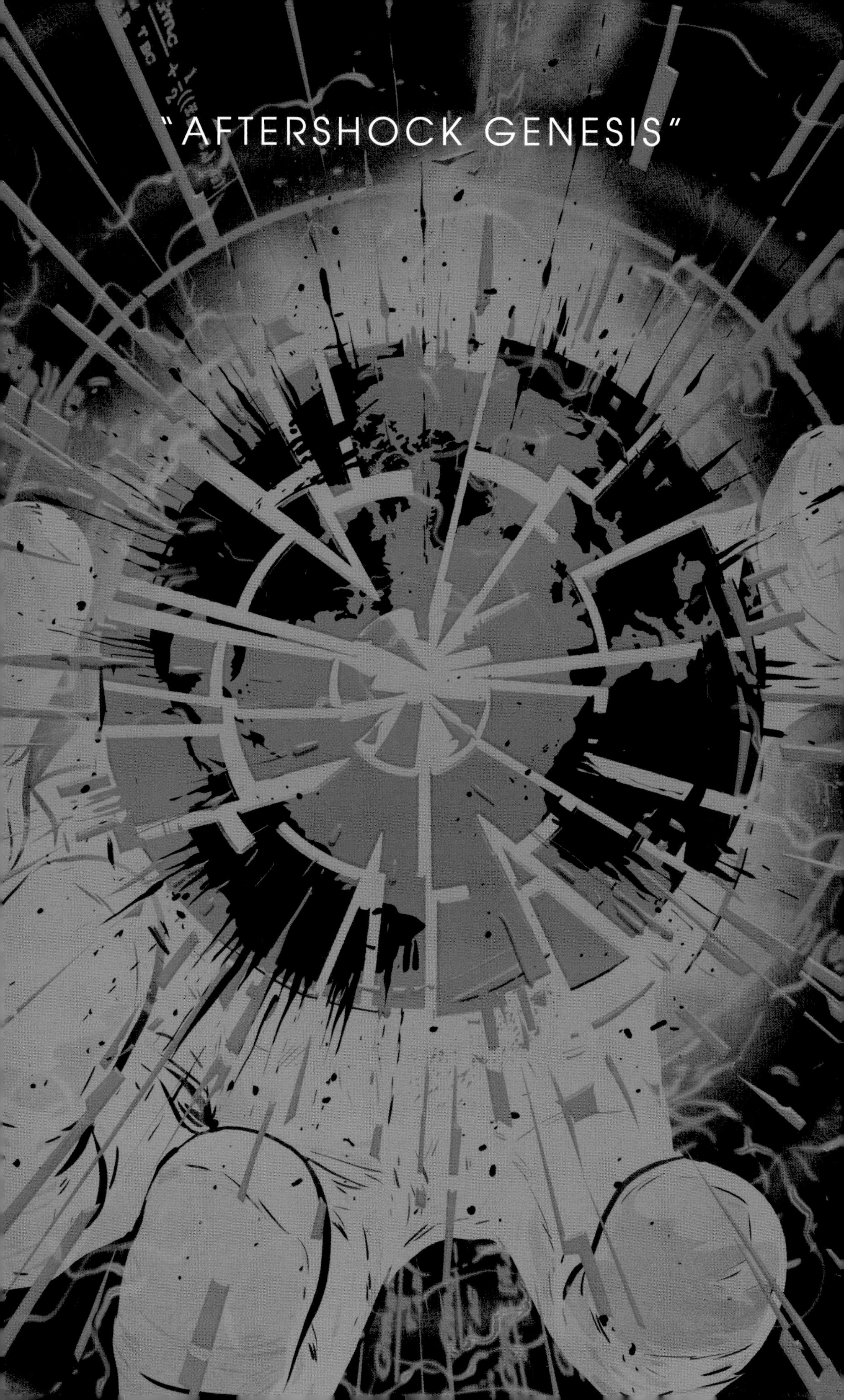
"AFTERSHOCK GENESIS"

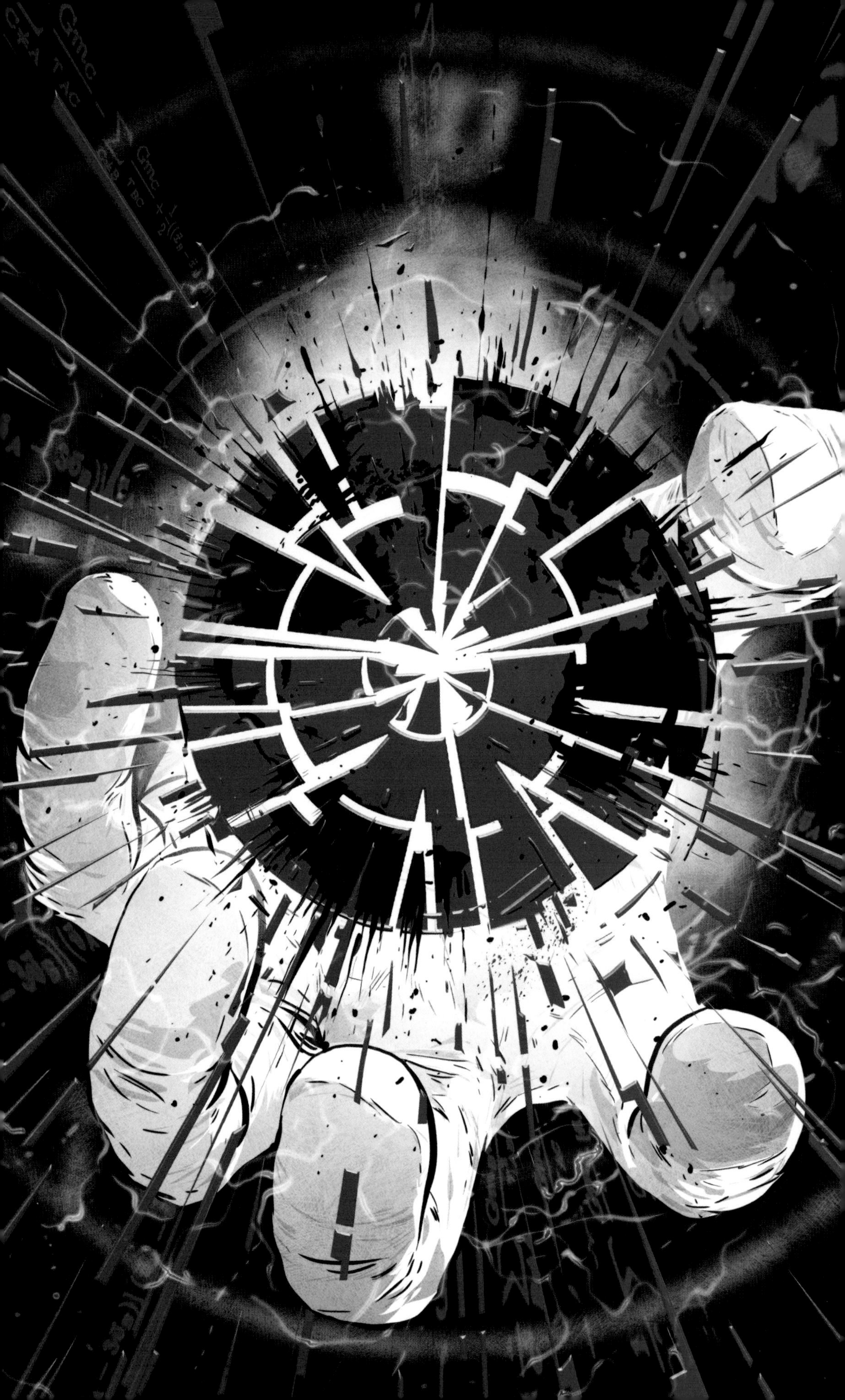

Presenting an EXCLUSIVE short story from ALTERS a new series from AFTERSHOCK COMICS...

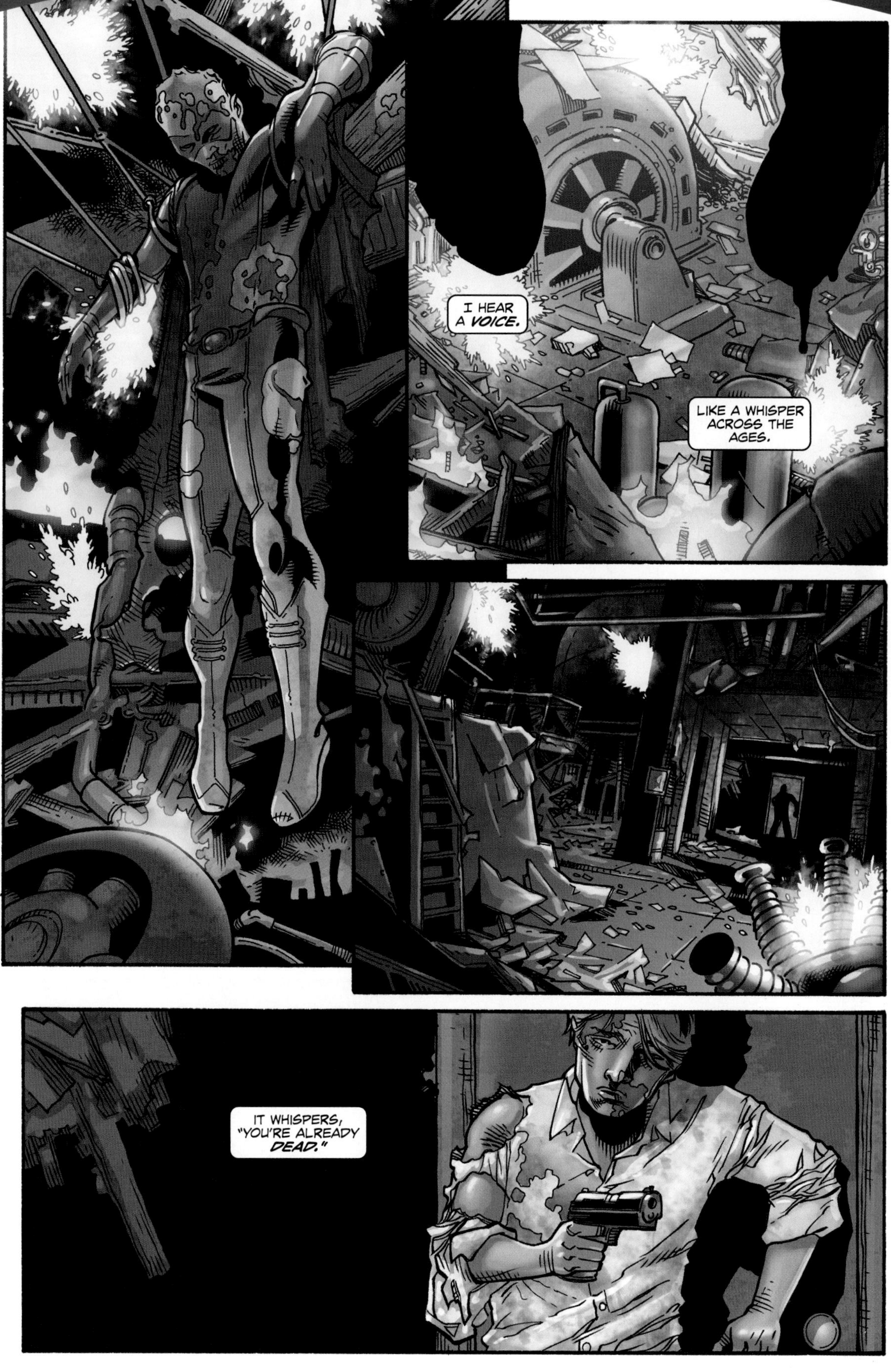
I HEAR A VOICE.
LIKE A WHISPER ACROSS THE AGES.
IT WHISPERS, "YOU'RE ALREADY DEAD."

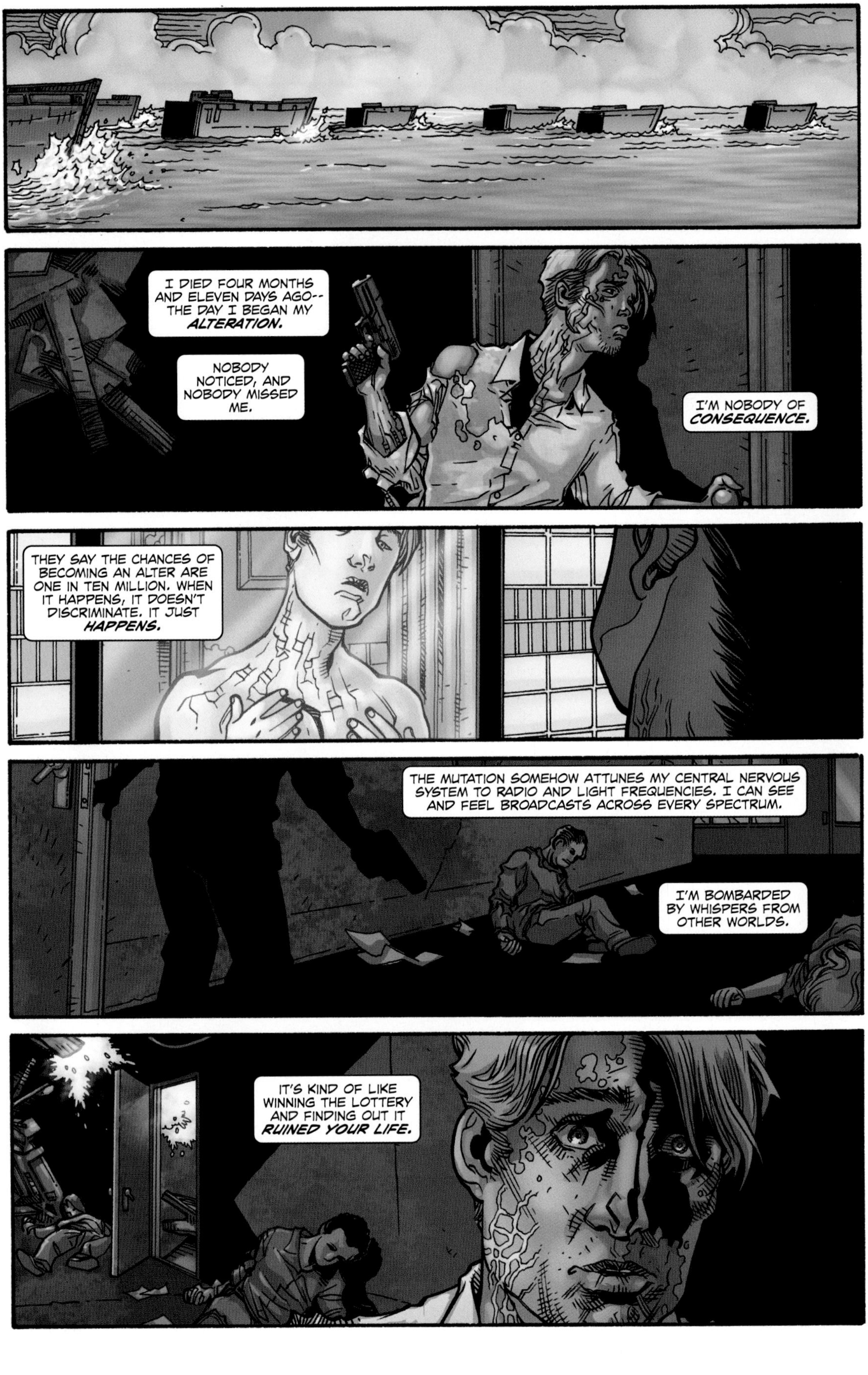

I DIED FOUR MONTHS AND ELEVEN DAYS AGO-- THE DAY I BEGAN MY *ALTERATION.*
NOBODY NOTICED, AND NOBODY MISSED ME.
I'M NOBODY OF *CONSEQUENCE.*
THEY SAY THE CHANCES OF BECOMING AN ALTER ARE ONE IN TEN MILLION. WHEN IT HAPPENS, IT DOESN'T DISCRIMINATE. IT JUST *HAPPENS.*
THE MUTATION SOMEHOW ATTUNES MY CENTRAL NERVOUS SYSTEM TO RADIO AND LIGHT FREQUENCIES. I CAN SEE AND FEEL BROADCASTS ACROSS EVERY SPECTRUM.
I'M BOMBARDED BY WHISPERS FROM OTHER WORLDS.
IT'S KIND OF LIKE WINNING THE LOTTERY AND FINDING OUT IT *RUINED YOUR LIFE.*

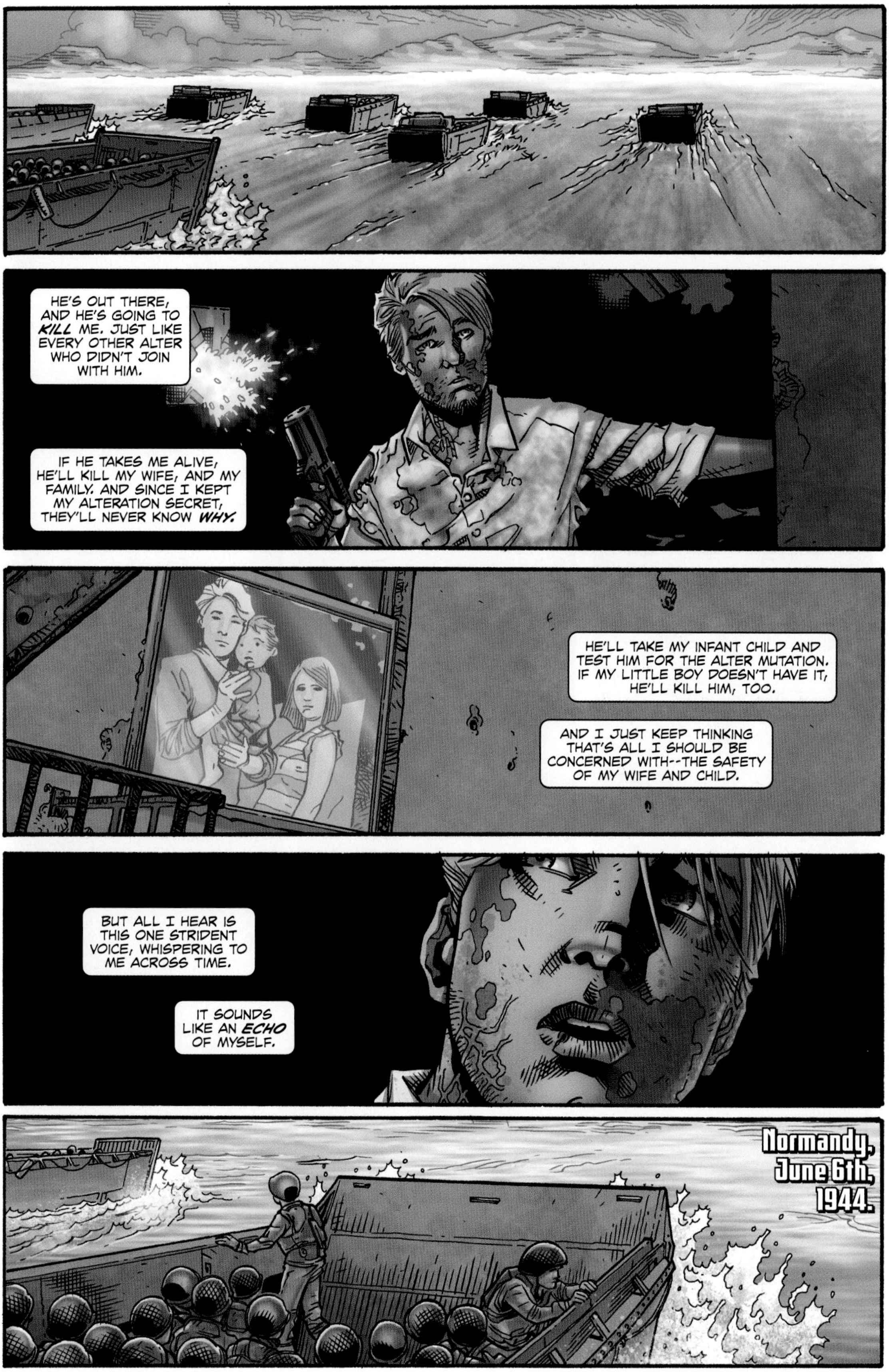
HE'S OUT THERE, AND HE'S GOING TO KILL ME. JUST LIKE EVERY OTHER ALTER WHO DIDN'T JOIN WITH HIM.
IF HE TAKES ME ALIVE, HE'LL KILL MY WIFE, AND MY FAMILY. AND SINCE I KEPT MY ALTERATION SECRET, THEY'LL NEVER KNOW WHY.
HE'LL TAKE MY INFANT CHILD AND TEST HIM FOR THE ALTER MUTATION. IF MY LITTLE BOY DOESN'T HAVE IT, HE'LL KILL HIM, TOO.
AND I JUST KEEP THINKING THAT'S ALL I SHOULD BE CONCERNED WITH--THE SAFETY OF MY WIFE AND CHILD.
BUT ALL I HEAR IS THIS ONE STRIDENT VOICE, WHISPERING TO ME ACROSS TIME.
IT SOUNDS LIKE AN ECHO OF MYSELF.
Normandy, June 6th, 1944.

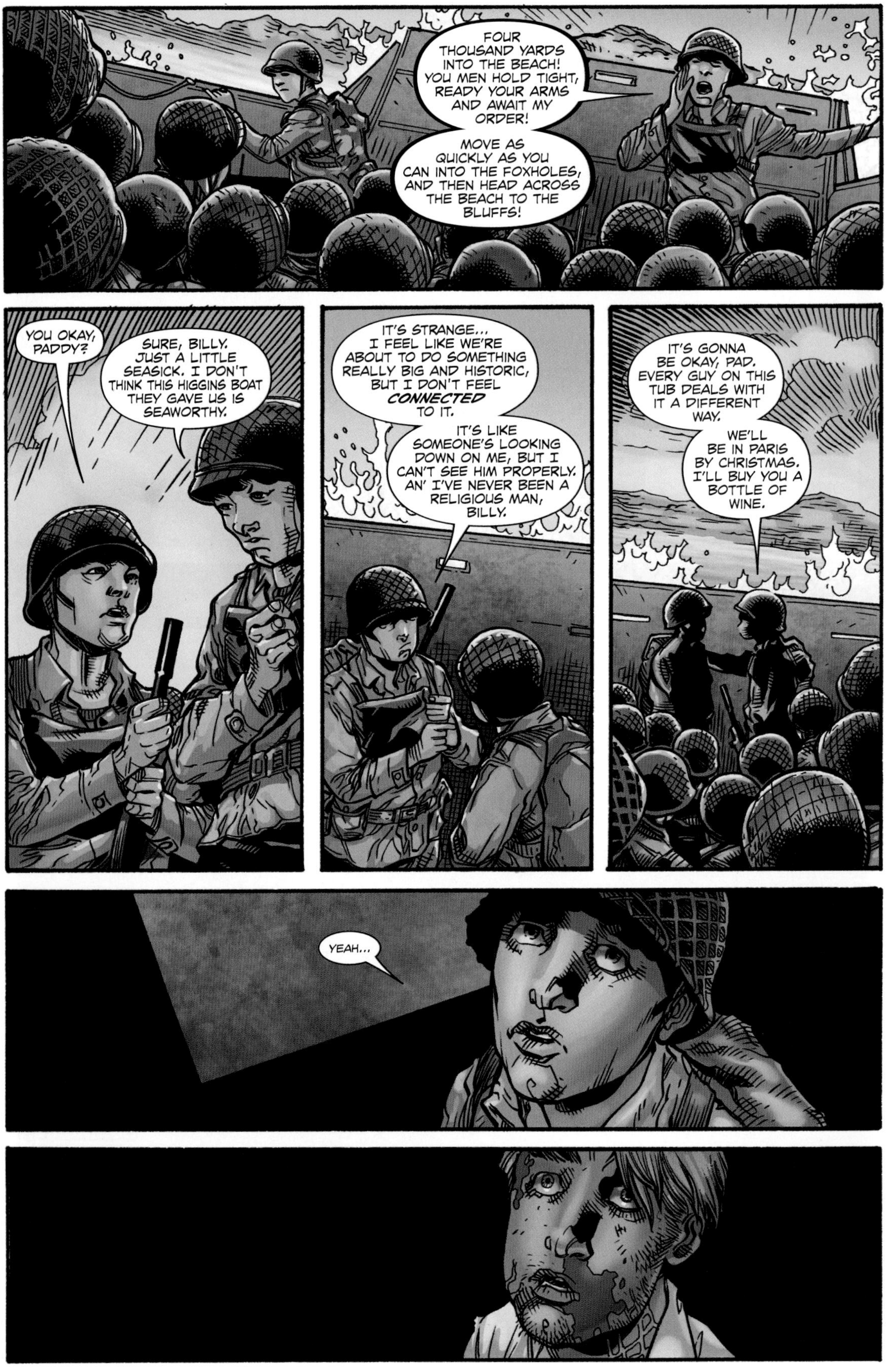
FOUR THOUSAND YARDS INTO THE BEACH! YOU MEN HOLD TIGHT, READY YOUR ARMS AND AWAIT MY ORDER!
MOVE AS QUICKLY AS YOU CAN INTO THE FOXHOLES, AND THEN HEAD ACROSS THE BEACH TO THE BLUFFS!
YOU OKAY, PADDY?
SURE, BILLY. JUST A LITTLE SEASICK. I DON'T THINK THIS HIGGINS BOAT THEY GAVE US IS SEAWORTHY.
IT'S STRANGE... I FEEL LIKE WE'RE ABOUT TO DO SOMETHING REALLY BIG AND HISTORIC, BUT I DON'T FEEL CONNECTED TO IT.
IT'S LIKE SOMEONE'S LOOKING DOWN ON ME, BUT I CAN'T SEE HIM PROPERLY. AN' I'VE NEVER BEEN A RELIGIOUS MAN, BILLY.
IT'S GONNA BE OKAY, PAD. EVERY GUY ON THIS TUB DEALS WITH IT A DIFFERENT WAY.
WE'LL BE IN PARIS BY CHRISTMAS. I'LL BUY YOU A BOTTLE OF WINE.
YEAH...

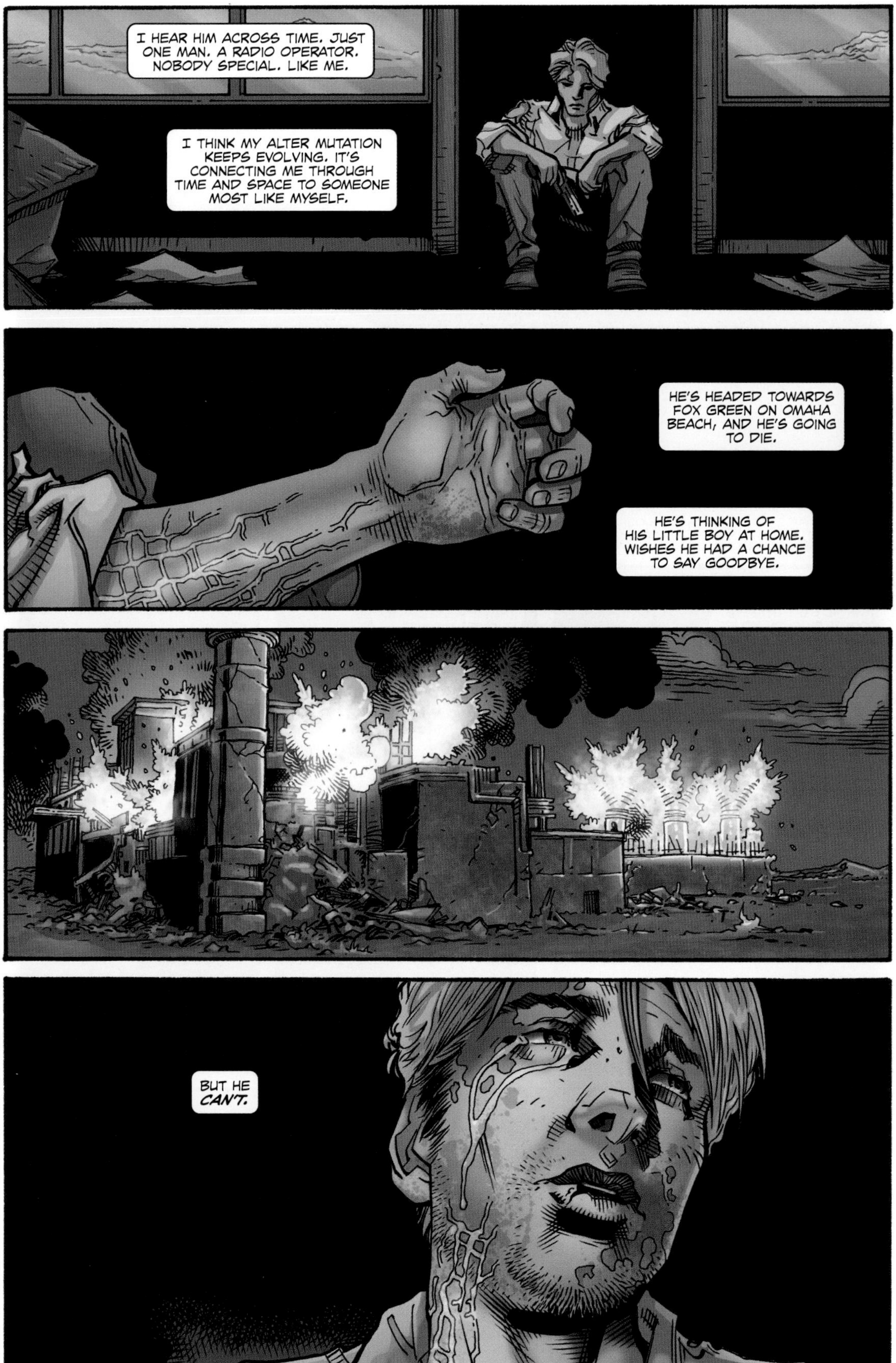

I HEAR HIM ACROSS TIME. JUST ONE MAN. A RADIO OPERATOR. NOBODY SPECIAL. LIKE ME.
I THINK MY ALTER MUTATION KEEPS EVOLVING. IT'S CONNECTING ME THROUGH TIME AND SPACE TO SOMEONE MOST LIKE MYSELF.
HE'S HEADED TOWARDS FOX GREEN ON OMAHA BEACH, AND HE'S GOING TO DIE.
HE'S THINKING OF HIS LITTLE BOY AT HOME. WISHES HE HAD A CHANCE TO SAY GOODBYE.
BUT HE *CAN'T.*

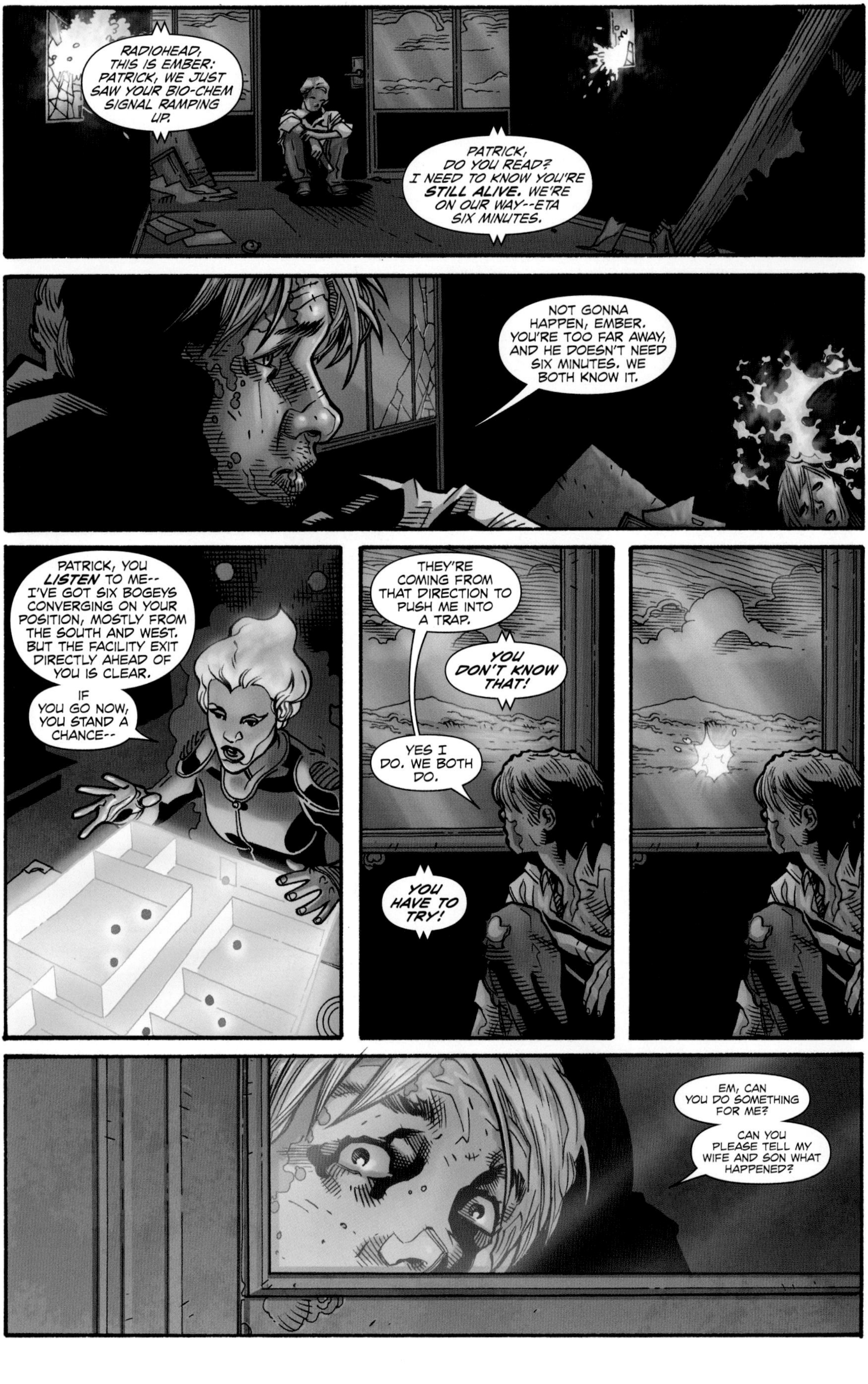
RADIOHEAD, THIS IS EMBER: PATRICK, WE JUST SAW YOUR BIO-CHEM SIGNAL RAMPING UP.
PATRICK, DO YOU READ? I NEED TO KNOW YOU'RE STILL ALIVE. WE'RE ON OUR WAY--ETA SIX MINUTES.
NOT GONNA HAPPEN, EMBER. YOU'RE TOO FAR AWAY, AND HE DOESN'T NEED SIX MINUTES. WE BOTH KNOW IT.
PATRICK, YOU LISTEN TO ME-- I'VE GOT SIX BOGEYS CONVERGING ON YOUR POSITION, MOSTLY FROM THE SOUTH AND WEST. BUT THE FACILITY EXIT DIRECTLY AHEAD OF YOU IS CLEAR.
IF YOU GO NOW, YOU STAND A CHANCE--
THEY'RE COMING FROM THAT DIRECTION TO PUSH ME INTO A TRAP.
YOU DON'T KNOW THAT!
YES I DO. WE BOTH DO.
YOU HAVE TO TRY!
EM, CAN YOU DO SOMETHING FOR ME?
CAN YOU PLEASE TELL MY WIFE AND SON WHAT HAPPENED?

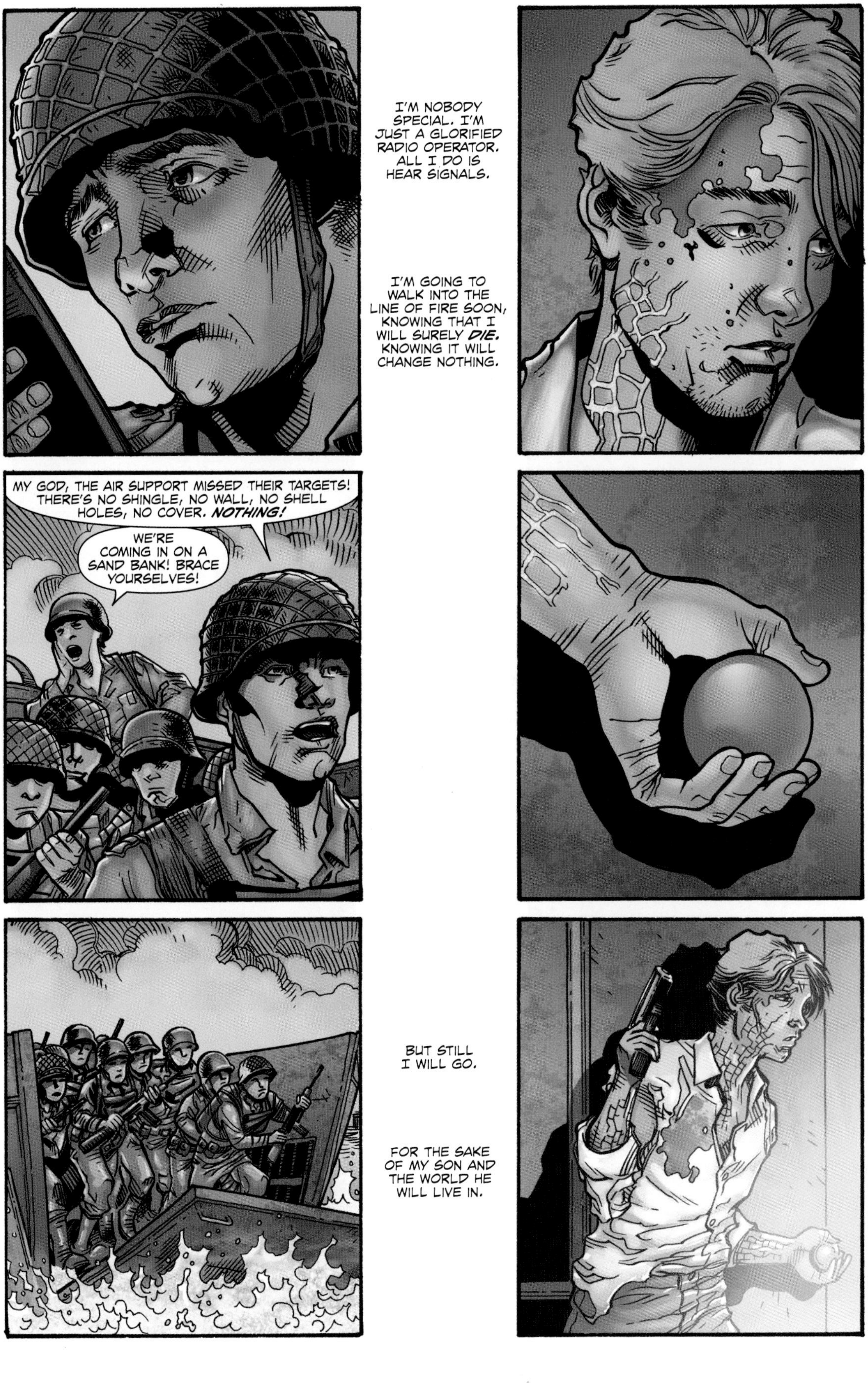
I'M NOBODY SPECIAL. I'M JUST A GLORIFIED RADIO OPERATOR. ALL I DO IS HEAR SIGNALS.
I'M GOING TO WALK INTO THE LINE OF FIRE SOON, KNOWING THAT I WILL SURELY DIE. KNOWING IT WILL CHANGE NOTHING.
MY GOD, THE AIR SUPPORT MISSED THEIR TARGETS! THERE'S NO SHINGLE, NO WALL, NO SHELL HOLES, NO COVER. NOTHING!
WE'RE COMING IN ON A SAND BANK! BRACE YOURSELVES!
BUT STILL I WILL GO.
FOR THE SAKE OF MY SON AND THE WORLD HE WILL LIVE IN.

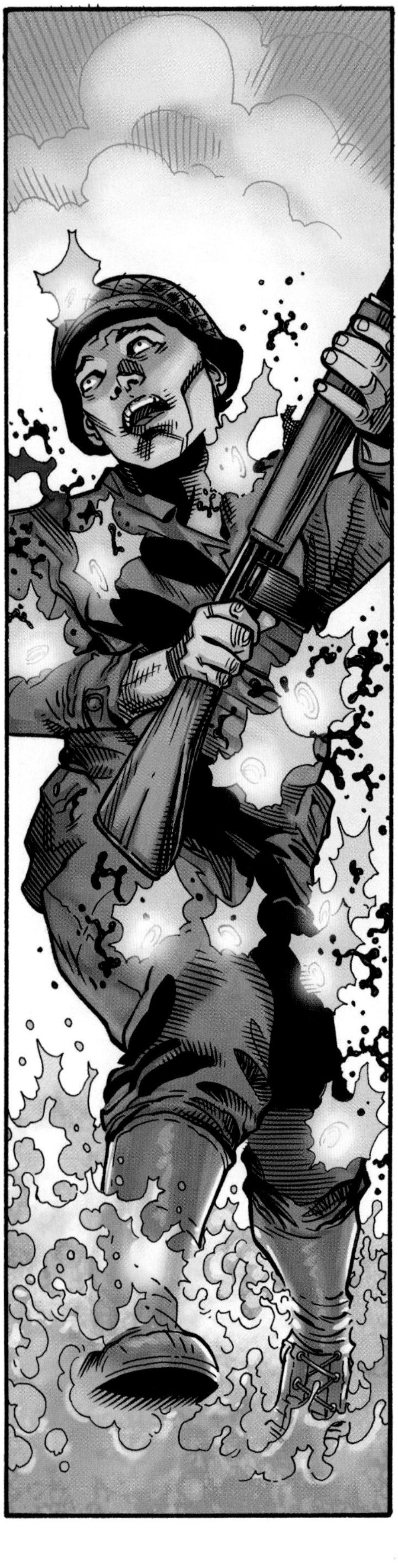

THOUGH WE ARE NOT SPECIAL, WE FIGHT FOR WHAT IS RIGHT AND JUST.

IN THE MANNER OF THE HEROES ***BEFORE*** US.

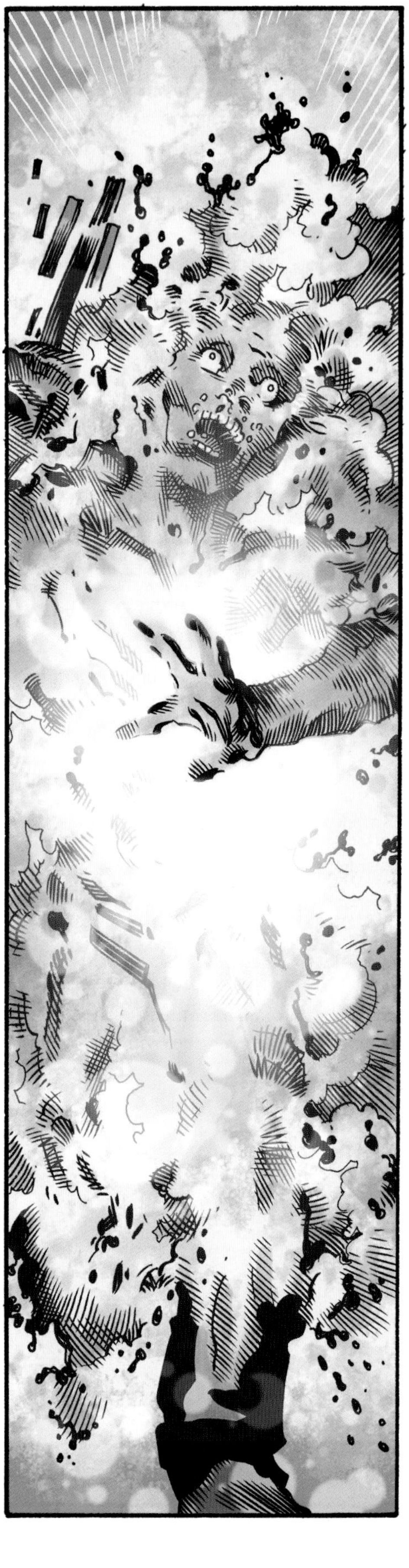

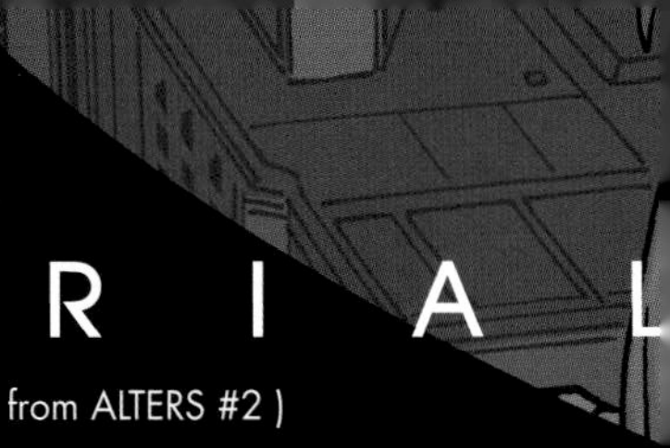

DITORIAL

by PAUL JENKINS (from ALTERS #2)

S is not just about people who are trans, or people born with cerebral palsy, or abou essness, or Alzheimer's, or any of the other challenging subjects we're going to address durinç ne on the stands. ALTERS is about all of us, and it belongs to all of us.

I took on this project, I knew it would be a challenge. It's perfectly understandable that some eaders would be concerned that Chalice is being written by a middle-aged white guy. I wen is book knowing that my job is to work hard, listen hard and research diligently. Each issue o S is read by at least six different trans consultants who have helped me learn more with each d script. It has always been my intention for this series to be inclusive and representative, and creative team to be as diverse as the book's subjects. I'm the token middle-aged white guy or m. The wonderful Leila Leiz (with whose art I hope you are falling in love) is a Frenchwomar n Italy. Our colorist, the talented and hilarious Tamra Bonvillain, is a trans woman. She and ou , Ryane Hill, turn what Leila and I do into a beautiful finished package. And the amazing Bria eze provides us with covers.

art of each issue I'm going to include this editorial section, which I'd like to use as an opportunit nect readers with some of the people who are helping me with the book. I want you to hea oices too, and I'd like to share some of the things I am learning along the way. My first guest i a trans woman who was one of the first people I reached out to for my research. Kelly's beer the transgender community for about eighteen years, and tells me she has been happily in c nship since 2004. I'm grateful that she agreed to be included in this first editorial page.

Paul: *When I was first making the commitment to writing about a trans character a the central focus of ALTERS, I felt a little lost. I've had my own personal experiences and relationships that helped inform me, but I found very quickly that I had a lot to learn. So reached out, rather blindly, and got in contact with you via a website. What did you thin when some random guy contacted you for help writing a comic, and do you have any thoughts on the differences between a trans writer working on this type of character, and c cis guy like myself having to approach it from a perspective of intense research?*

Kelly: *I was glad to be contacted and happy to help. I've long thought there was c huge amount of untapped material about transgender experiences. There is a difference in perspective between a trans and a non-trans writer in that a trans writer has probabl experienced feelings personally, but I think a non-trans writer can do the subject justice.*

Paul: *I think so too, otherwise I would have been very reluctant to move ahead with the series. Even so, I feel I have learned a huge amount over the time I've been working on the character of Charlie. One thing that struck me early — and it's quite a difficult subject — i the general public's heightened interest in the topic. At times, I feel the creative materia pertaining to trans issues is going to help a lot of people to understand something tha may be difficult for them. At other times, I feel the exploitative nature of some material car be borderline repellant. What are your thoughts on the proliferation of "trans" stories ou there? And how are you feeling personally about the way things are being reported — i the visibility helpful, or destructive?*

Kelly: *Well, I like to be optimistic about the future. Things have improved; it's much easie to get information today than it was in the 1970s or 80s. The internet is responsible for a lo of that. On the downside, right-wing groups have discovered we exist and have picked u as the newest enemy. All things considered, the visibility has been helpful as more inclusive legislation has passed and more organizations include us in their non-discriminatior policies. Things are better today, even if some negative things have happened as a resul of our new visibility, like North Carolina's HB2. I hope this will come back to haunt the people who passed it. All in all, having more information is better, as the old days were dark indeed.*

Paul: *As I've had a number of discussions with people from all walks of life, I've come to realize that some people are slightly confused by transgender issues. One way of couching it is to say that so many people clearly have no particular issue with any other human being*

and are more
than happy to be accepting,
but express to me that they have a sort of
knowledge gap in understanding why or how a person
transitions. I remember that you put me at ease in our first discussion because you were so
open about your own transition. In your opinion, when will we truly have arrived in terms
of understanding and acceptance? And what's the path that will take us all to that goal
together?

Kelly: I suppose we will have truly arrived when being transgender isn't viewed as being
a big deal, when there are no societal obstacles to being one's self. As best as I can tell,
education is the path to that.

Paul: I'd love to get there sooner rather than later, as I'm sure many people would agree.
But there is a poor signal to noise ratio at the moment — with the U.S. election cycle, people
seem to be losing their sanity. I agree with you that education is the key. If only people
would allow themselves to become educated.

Kelly: Hmmm…people only hear what they want to hear. I would want to say, "Being
transgender is not a choice or an illness." But convincing people that is true is another
matter.

Paul: I'll ask the same question of everyone creatively associated with the book: If you had
one thing to say to say to everyone, and they were forced to hear it, what would you want
to say?

Kelly: I'd like to say, "love your neighbor," and "do unto others as you would have them
do to you," but that has never been much followed either.

So. A couple of pieces of business before I sign off for this month. I'd like to express a special thanks
to my friend, Liz Luu, who was instrumental in helping shape the story of Chalice. Liz is a talented
young creative working at Cartoon Network — you will see her listed as Special Character Consultant
in the credits, and I have spoken of her frequently in numerous interviews about the book. Liz had
an idea for the trans character in this book that was far better than the one I had originally intended,
and I asked her permission to include some of her ideas in this series. She graciously agreed, and
for that I am truly grateful.

Every month, I'm going to sign off by describing something significant I have learned during the
research or writing of ALTERS. One of the most important things I've learned so far is the specific
damage done when we mis-gender someone who has gone to the trouble of telling us who they
really are. Mis-gendering is more than just rude, it can also be dangerous: it suggests that the person
in question is merely "dressing up," and it can lead to direct attacks, both emotional and physical.
Everyone knows who they are, deep down – it's wrong to question someone's fundamental identity.
So I'd like to request that as people review new issues of ALTERS they remember to always refer to
Charlie as "she" or "her." Charlie is female because we the readers know she identifies as a woman.
No matter how she's dressed or who she's told about her trans identity, we know she's a woman and
she should be referred to accordingly.

Until next time!

PAUL

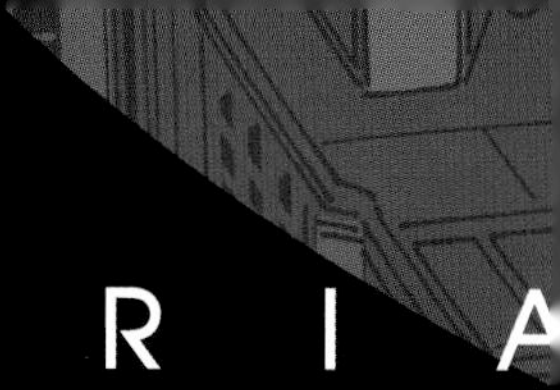

D I T O R I A

by PAUL JENKINS (from ALTERS #3)

o issue #3 of Alters, everyone.

d, we're going to continue with our back-page editorials, where we'll be pretenc ats, thanks to the magic of the Internet! My guest this month is Maeve Baruk, a een giving me some very welcome editorial advice on the scripts, and who is a consultant. At time of writing, we are in the aftermath of the recent election, wh and difficult for just about everyone in the world. While I rarely talk publicly ab portant to address some of the concerns that women like Maeve are dealing wi to make sure that all voices are heard, even the less strident ones.

Paul: *So Maeve, tell us a little bit about yourself. How did you first become aware of Alters?*

Maeve: *I am in my mid-30s, a Jill of many skills by habit, and an activist by necessity. I first became aware of Alters while a friend was discussing their disdain for the common narrative and plot arcs transgender people overwhelmingly ge written and wrought into, in most media.*

Paul: *I'm trying to run a line between simply making a story about a coo character, and also adding to the ongoing conversation we're having abou nclusion and acceptance in our society. This comes obviously from the point o view of a person who is not trans, yet feels that, as human beings, we are all ir his conversation. After such a difficult and divisive election recently, how do yo think that conversation is going?*

Maeve: *The conversation has evolved from complex into a few iterations tha are more complex and manic. The qualms about cisgender writers writing ransgender characters have been mostly overshadowed for the moment. There are well-founded fears that there will be a more zealous legal attack on not jus ransgender people, but other minorities, following suit to the bigots emboldened by the election and appointments of anti-minority people. The conversations stil iltering around about transgender portrayals are still heavily discussing that we're oft depicted in rather rubbish ways; either as a token to seem relevant and "on the pulse of things," or as a cliché joke and/or plot twist. There hasn't been enoug change out there to really catalyze a significant shift in discussion yet. As far as I've seen, anyway.*

Paul: *Yeah, I agree that change can be pretty slow at times. Let me ask you thi question: in your opinion, is it possible for "imperfect" stories portraying tran characters to still help by expanding the conversation to new audiences? I have hought about this long and hard myself; when we began this project, I understood hat some of this would be a learning curve for me. I know from experience tha you cannot please all of the people all of the time, and have accepted that fo years. But I felt it was important for me to listen carefully and not just jump ir with both feet, hence all of the people helping me as consultants. As the stor has progressed, I am becoming painfully aware that transgender stories are "en vogue" right now, something that is difficult to me for two reasons: (1) Alters has been many years in the making and just happens to be coming out now, and (2 Alters happens to focus on Chalice at the moment, but will move to focus on othe characters in time. So as I look at the proliferation of stories revolving around tran characters, I wonder if this can be seen as a positive thing, or are there too many negatives? What do you think?*

Maeve: *To certain extents, it
is possible. When possible, I try to reach out to
talk to cisgender authors and ask if I can bend their ear for a
moment to fill them in on what*

*they conveyed vs. what I think they were trying to convey. Much like the first
conversation I had with you about Alters #1. My honest thought is that the dice
are still rolling down the table at the moment as to whether or not it's positive or
negative. I don't like to cast judgement before I've finished the second page of a
book, unless the writing is utter rubbish.*

Paul: *I am almost excited for the time when Chalice happens to be in the Alters
series and we rarely have to mention her in any other context than being one of the
main characters. For now, we are doing her story, though. Will we all need to get
to the stage I mention here, where there is little conversation to be had, or do you
think we need to discuss this topic for some time to come?*

Maeve: *There will be a point where the aspect that she is transgender needs to
not be mentioned. This won't need to be mentioned at that point as it would have
no bearing on the conversation or story. Similar to how if a conversation strikes
up about Wonder Woman, how often does one talk about her hair color or if she
writes with her left hand or right?*

Paul: *I ask the same question of everyone I put into the book: if you had one thing
to say to say to everyone, and they were forced to hear it, what would you want
to say?*

Maeve: *I'll dance on this question a bit. You can't really force someone to hear something. I'd rather tell
people to respect each other, and have everyone understand that killing & screwing each other over is
pointless & shortsighted. People can accomplish much, much more if they'd stop trying to build a throne
on the bodies of others.*

Thanks again, Maeve, for helping me with Alters and for being the subject of this month's editorial page.

So what have I learned lately? During the writing of this issue, I had to create a scene in which Charlie
makes a choice to come out to her brother, Teddy. In speaking with the various people who consult on
Alters – and with plenty of others who have been through this particular scenario – I have learned that this
happens differently for different people. There is no one way, and no one predictable reaction. I suppose
we must collectively hope that each person in this situation is met with an embrace of compassion and
acceptance. Because hey… if you can't accept the reality of another person's life, why should anyone
accept yours?

I wish you all peace, love and happiness.

PAUL

E D I T O R I A L

by PAUL JENKINS (from ALTERS #4)

I'd like to thank all of you — our readers — for your tremendous support of this series. We've received a ton of emails, positive comments, and a tanker full of compliments about the book. A few have expressed their concerns about our subject matter, and I hope we've done a little to address those worries. Hey, we were even targeted during a North Carolina signing by those wacky funsters at the Westboro Baptist Church, so I think we must be doing something right.

This month, I'm talking to our very own colorist, Tamra Bonvillain. For any of you not paying attention, I felt very strongly that our series should be written, drawn, colored and lettered by a very diverse team of creators. Tamra is a fantastic colorist with many impressive credits to her name, including *Rat Queens* and *Devil Dinosaur*, to name but a few. She is also a trans woman, and I've had the good fortune to be able to send her my scripts for review, as well as check out her wonderful work on the series every month.

Paul: Tamra, for those readers who may be unfamiliar, tell us what other projects you've been working on lately, and some others you've been known for in recent years. Also, I know you've been pretty busy lately. What's your work day like?

Tamra: Aside from ALTERS, I'm currently working on Moon Girl and Devil Dinosaur and Great Lakes Avengers for Marvel, Angel Catbird for Dark Horse, and Wayward at Image. I also did an arc of Rat Queens at Image. My days can vary pretty wildly. It mostly depends on how the schedule aligns. Sometimes book deadlines fall on or near each other, so those weeks tend to be busier than ones where the deadlines are more spread out. Some days I might work less than or up to eight hours, and other times I'm working for 24+ hour stretches. Ideally, I try to keep schedules spaced out enough so I can work 8-10 hours/day and keep a consistent sleep/work schedule.

Paul: I follow you on Twitter, so I know you've been catching up on semi-awful 90s TV shows during the last year. Star Trek: the Next Generation had its moments but it's pretty dated at this point. Is this a hobby or something you have on in the background while you're working? Because I think if I had it on, I'd never get a thing done...

Tamra: Oh, for me, once I have any big problems figured out about palettes or technique, mostly for new books or some wildly different scene in an existing book, I can color pretty much on autopilot. I tend to get distracted and want to check the internet, and TV, podcasts, etc. weirdly keep me focused in on my work. It occupies that part of my brain that wants to wander around looking at other things. Because of that and the long hours I work, I'm constantly looking for content, so something like TNG was perfect. It's really low-key and easy to follow while I work. Although, as I went deeper, it did tend to slow me down a bit as I was always searching for screenshots to share of all the weird shit that happens in that show. I've taken a little break from that while I get caught up again, but I'll probably work through the other series as well when I run out of other things to watch.

Paul: I think it must be different being a writer. I can't get anything done at all if I listen to anything with words. I pretty much listen to New Age and Chillout-type music when I'm working. I feel like an aging hippy, which seems fair because I am becoming an aging hippy, I suppose. So, let's talk about ALTERS a little bit. Most of my research for Chalice has involved talking to trans people about their experiences and trying to glean what I could. If something struck me — an anecdote or a point of view I hadn't considered — I'd usually ask the person who'd given me the piece of information if I could use it in a story. I have been really surprised by how much I did not know, and also struck by how various peoples' experiences are quite different. I remember when you and I first started talking about this project, you told me something pretty interesting: since you spend so much time indoors being nerdy and working late into the night, you were not sure your personal experience was much in line with that of many other trans women. That made me smile. Is that still the case, and what do we have to do to get you out and about?

Tamra: Hmm, I don't remember what I was on about exactly, but I socially transitioned while working in comics, which is pretty much me sitting at home all day. Since I'm not leaving the house to go to work every day, it greatly limits my encounters with the public that others would deal with on a more constant basis. So, I feel my experience there is pretty different. I don't deal with harassment or anything like that, and if I did, it would be isolated incidents rather than being caught in work/school situations where I'd feel more trapped and have to deal with those same people consistently. I do try to get out to a few cons every year, and I'm working on getting back to doing more social things in my daily life.

Paul: It's funny...I learn more with each conversation. My discussions with you really led me to spend less time on the story of Chalice's personal life, and more towards just giving her hero stuff to blow up. That's a good thing, by the way: I now think I can tell her story quite slowly, over a longer period of time. And that means I can cover so much more than if I were to condense it. It's not condensable (if that is a word). What do you think about this? Would you prefer it see it more condensed, so that the story of her transition is addressed, or are we on the right path? Either answer works...

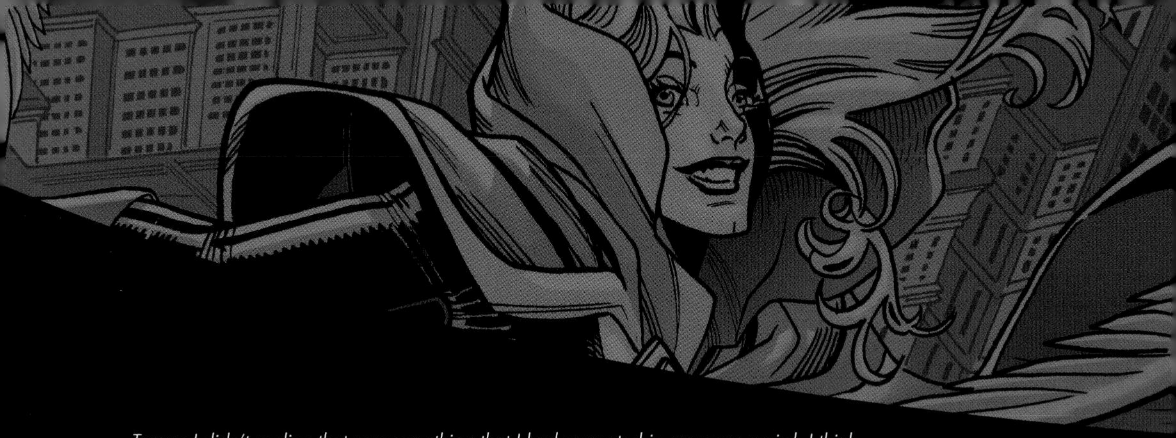

Tamra: I didn't realize that was something that I had prompted in any way, weird. I think it's probably better being spaced out. It gives a context to everything. Might seem weird to just front load it with a bunch of family drama, and then more or less move on. It makes more sense to me to have all the aspects of her life more integrated and happening at the same time.

Paul: Obviously, we live in interesting times. I'm personally a bit concerned about Mike Pence in terms of his past approach to issues such as LGBT rights and so on. Yet I seem to remember Donald Trump having no particular issue with trans people, and once going so far as to tell Caitlyn Jenner she could use whatever bathroom she chose in his building. What the fuck is going on? Are we going forward, backwards or sideways, in your opinion?

Tamra: Way backwards. I don't care what words Donald Trump has said when his actions speak for themselves. The fact that Mike Pence is his Vice President at all is bad enough, but most (or all?) of his key positions right now are being filled with people that have an anti-LGBT history. Currently Title VII and IX are interpreted to cover gender identity under sex discrimination, giving trans people protections under the law in employment and schools, but that is an interpretation that I highly doubt will be continued with his administration. Without this interpretation, less than half the states explicitly protect gender identity in their non-discrimination policies. More "freedom of religion" and bathroom bills are being proposed. Whether Trump truly believes these things or not is unimportant to me, because he's enabling these people to attack us. And, of course, this is just on LGBT issues; he's dragging us backwards in so many other ways, as well.

Paul: I ask the same question of everyone I put into the book: if you had one thing to say to say to everyone, and they were forced to hear it, what would you want to say?

Tamra: I am terrible at these questions, but juxtaposing it next to the Trump thing makes me think something along those lines. I am at a loss for words, or useful ones at least. I just generally want people to see the humanity in others that are unlike them or people in need. But, it seems we don't even recognize the disadvantages people face, let alone want to help them. I don't know how to package that message in any way that reaches people it hasn't already, but if I could, I would.

Thanks, Tamra, for taking the time to speak so thoughtfully, and for being awesome!

So, what have I learned this month? As I mentioned, I rarely comment on politics. But of course, politics have dominated our conversations these last few months, so I feel it would be remiss if I didn't address one particular aspect that concerns me, which Tamra and I addressed above.

Tolerance, communication, open-minded discussion…these things do not take place over the course of one single day. One act of tolerance does not make you tolerant, or open-minded: a lifetime of it does. I feel it is our collective responsibility to watch carefully and to respond accordingly, because we've taken quite a few steps forward on LGBT issues in the last few years, and there is just no sense in going backwards. If any person in our society ever feels marginalized, intimidated, worried, bullied…I mean, we make sure in our elementary schools that these things do not happen…I'm sure as hell our nation's chief executive has a responsibility to protect all citizens. We all have a responsibility to look out for each other, Republican, Democrat and Independent alike.

I wish you all peace, love and happiness.

Paul

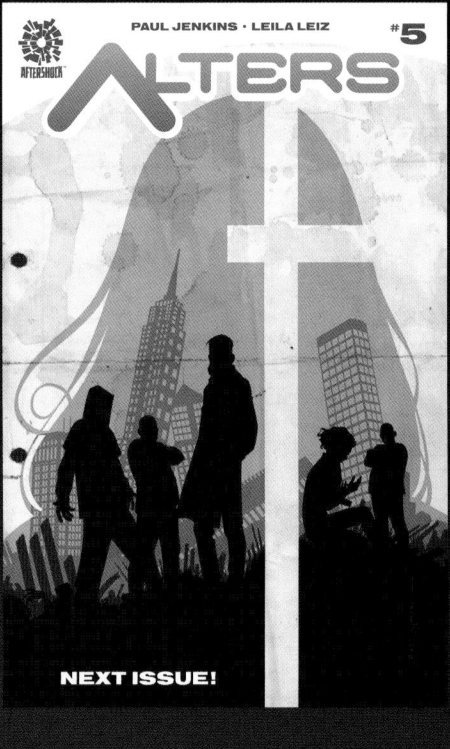

PAUL JENKINS · LEILA LEIZ
#5
AFTERSHOCK
ALTERS
NEXT ISSUE!

E D I T O R I A L

by PAUL JENKINS (from ALTERS #5)

So here we are at the end of our first arc. I wanted first to thank our amazing creative team: Leila Leiz, Tamra Bonvillain, Ryane Hill and Brian Stelfreeze. I hope you'll agree their work has been stellar. I'm oh-so-proud to be a part of it. Thanks, of course, to our ace editor, Mike Marts, and to Joe, Lee and Jon from AfterShock for taking a chance on our series. We're gearing up for the second story arc, where I'm planning to expand the group a little bit and explore some of the other characters in better detail. Chalice will continue to play a major role, so we'll hopefully get the best of both worlds.

I was contacted recently by this month's interview subject, Sabrina. She is the proud mom (and, trust me, a genuinely awesome person) of a young trans woman named Kuyo. They had become fans of our series, and simply reached out to express their thanks for the subject matter. This type of positive response means a lot to me — I consider my job a privilege, and even more so when someone is emotionally affected by the work.

Paul: Sabrina, from a mom's perspective, tell us a little bit about yourself, your daughter, Kuyo, and perhaps a little about your family's involvement in the LGBTQ community. You told me offline your grandfather had been involved in LGBTQ issues in the past...?

Sabrina: Kuyo's twenty-three now. She was reborn to her real self when she came out, aged fifteen. She had seemed so sad for a couple of years, which really concerned me. But no matter how much I asked, she kept telling me everything was fine. The day Kuyo told me she was now my daughter, you can't imagine how she glowed. I told her, "Just don't look better in my clothes than I do. And don't ask me for makeup tips (because I don't wear any)." I asked some trans friends — also, my own mom — how I could best be supportive. I was just told to love my daughter, and to be there any time she needs to talk. So, it came naturally. We went out shopping together, and I bought her the clothes and other stuff she needed. I was so happy to have my daughter healthy and happy, though some members of our family didn't know how to accept her true self. Luckily, we have ties in the LGBTQ community dating back to my grandfather, so we weren't going in blind. My grandfather, Elliott Blackstone, is known in the community for fighting for equality back in the '60s.

Paul: I'm grateful that you reached out via Twitter to express your support of the book. I appreciate all feedback — negative and positive. But there are times when someone is emotionally affected by something we're doing...makes the long nights worth it.

Sabrina: Kuyo and I have found an awesome, supportive community, which is how we heard about the launch of ALTERS. We told the guys at Red Pegasus here in Dallas about the series, and they jumped at the chance to carry it. I was worried it might take the trans aspect and drive it into the dirt, but I was pleased with the way it was written, and how it didn't exploit that aspect of Chalice. It's more of a "so she is a super hero in training, and, oh yeah, she happens to be trans" kind of thing. We're hooked, so we buy one copy each.

Paul: Very cool. I feel as though this experience writing Chalice has been one of the most positive of my career, one that I have learned from, and one that has given me a different kind of connection to fans. I know you are both excited about ALTERS, and that makes us even more proud of the series. How did you feel about having a trans character who's prominent in a series like this?

Sabrina: Kuyo said it best, "It's great to see and experience the life of a young transgender woman through an unfiltered lens." Chalice has the chance to do for young trans people what Wonder Woman did for strong, independent women. (Paul: I hope that's true, but it might take a few years on that one!) Young trans kids are under a new spotlight on issues ranging from bathrooms to mis-gendering. What was once behind closed doors for those transitioning is now more open: Are you being pushed? Are you being held back? Where do you go to the bathroom? Where do you shower? The suicide rate in transgender youth and adults is at a new high. So, hopefully, ALTERS is another stepping-stone. Chalice's character suggests it's not about the label, it's about the person behind the label (or mask in her case).

Paul: We never set out to be crusaders, as I've mentioned a number of times. Instead, we aim to tell a decent story about people dealing with certain disadvantages, and let the "crusading" take care of itself. But I've seen how deeply people are affected by the subject matter...

Tamra: When my daughter came to me and told me who she really was, I was so happy, because the son I was losing to depression became my daughter, glowing with happiness. Parents need to talk to their kids without judgment, to educate themselves on teens today. There is no set gender anymore (not that it wasn't like this sixty years ago, it's just "out" now). If I could go to every parent, I'd tell them, "Put your feelings on the back burner and love your child. Learn who your child is. Don't force them to be "normal" because there is no normal." I'm a parent. I'm supposed to fix things when my child is sad, not add to the problem. Kuyo and I agree there should be lots more support groups. We need public speakers who can educate not only teens, but also their parents and other family members. People need to learn to look at things from both sides of the table. We need PSA videos, and information taught in schools as part of the curriculum.

Paul: Couldn't agree more. God, I love my two boys so much it hurts. Those two little buggers (and Nigh Perfect, my lovely wife) are everything to me. I know that most parents feel this way about their children. I want my boys, more than anything, to be healthy and happy, and to be good people. I also want the little one to stop whacking me in the groin at every opportunity, so we shall see how that goes.

Finally, I ask the same question of everyone I put into the book: if you had one thing to say to everyone, and they were forced to hear it, what would you want to say?

Sabrina: I would say, "Shut up and love each other." If I could take the fear from these kids who are trying to talk to the people who are supposed to love them unconditionally, I would. Life is hard enough without these stupid issues and rules they want to put on our children. Let our daughters and sons be. Let them become who they truly are, and not who you think they should be. Peace, love and harmony is sadly lacking in this world today, so put down your hatred and let me love you.

Fuckin' A — right, Sabrina. And as an aside here, I also had a chance to chat with Kuyo before I transcribed this editorial. I wanted to concentrate on her mom's perspective because that was new to these editorials. But I think Kuyo had the best response to the final question. Her family is Scottish by descent, and their family motto is, "Do well, and doubt not." Kuyo told me she'd want to express that sentiment to others, if she could. Fuckin' A — right again.

So, what have I learned this month? Well, I am beginning to see that there are so many individual stories, yet so many repeated patterns. I hate the fact that any group of people might be dealing with issues of increased depression and might be more at risk for suicide. Think about that. We owe it to each other to listen and learn, and try to understand each other's points of view. Not because I am a fucking hippy but because, hey…being nice to people is more fun than being shitty, isn't it?

Look, think about it this way: imagine you decided to talk to a stranger about, say, homosexuality. Or racism. Or homelessness. Now, imagine that once you said your first sentence, the stranger replied that their son is gay, or that they were once homeless, or that they happen to be married to a person of a different race. Well, if you knew in advance, and it would have changed the way you made your first statement, you may want to think about the way you're having conversations in general. Just a thought, right?

I wish you all peace, love and happiness. Do well, and doubt not.

Paul

issue 1
variant cover
BRIAN STELFREEZE

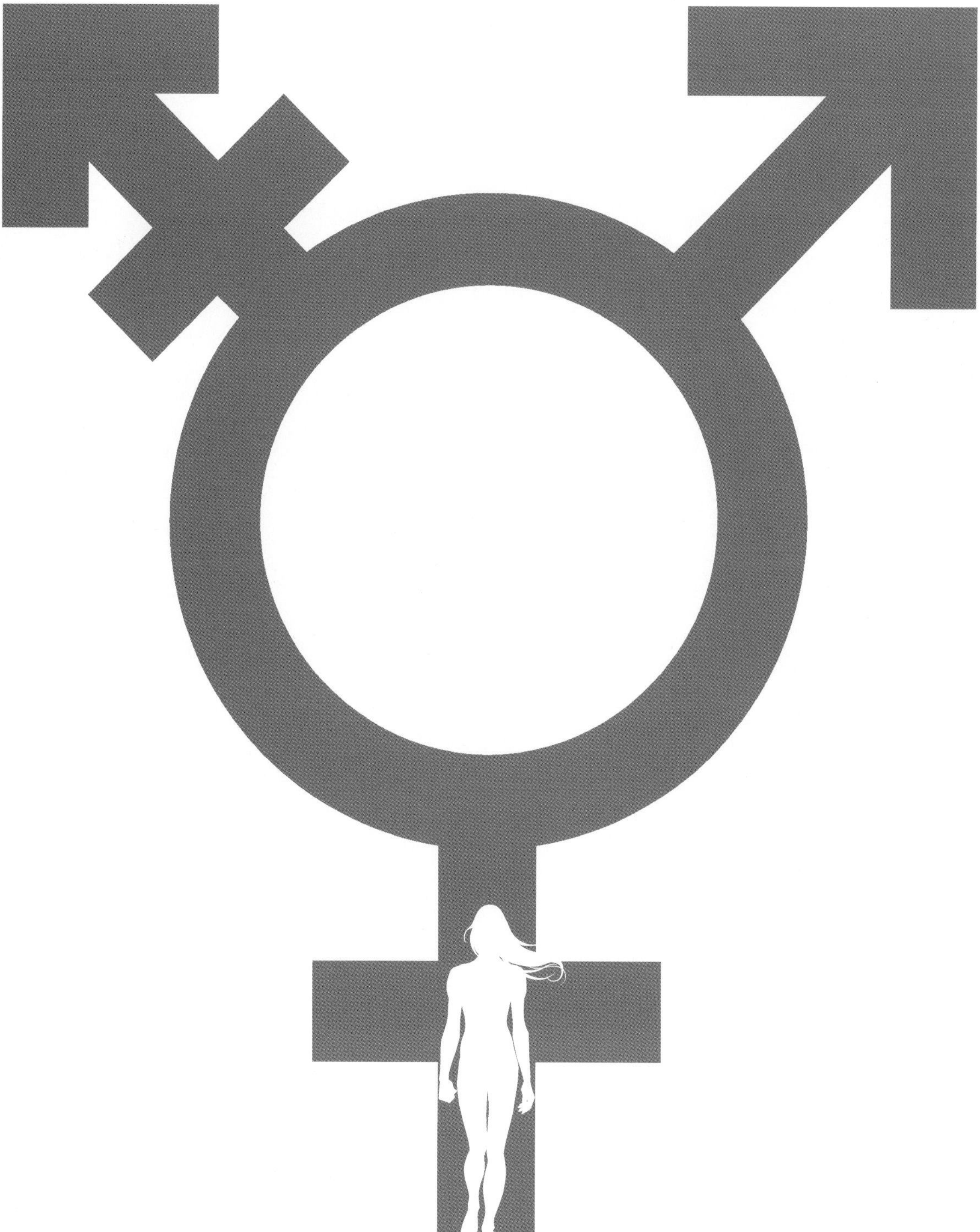

issue 1
variant cover
TONY HARRIS

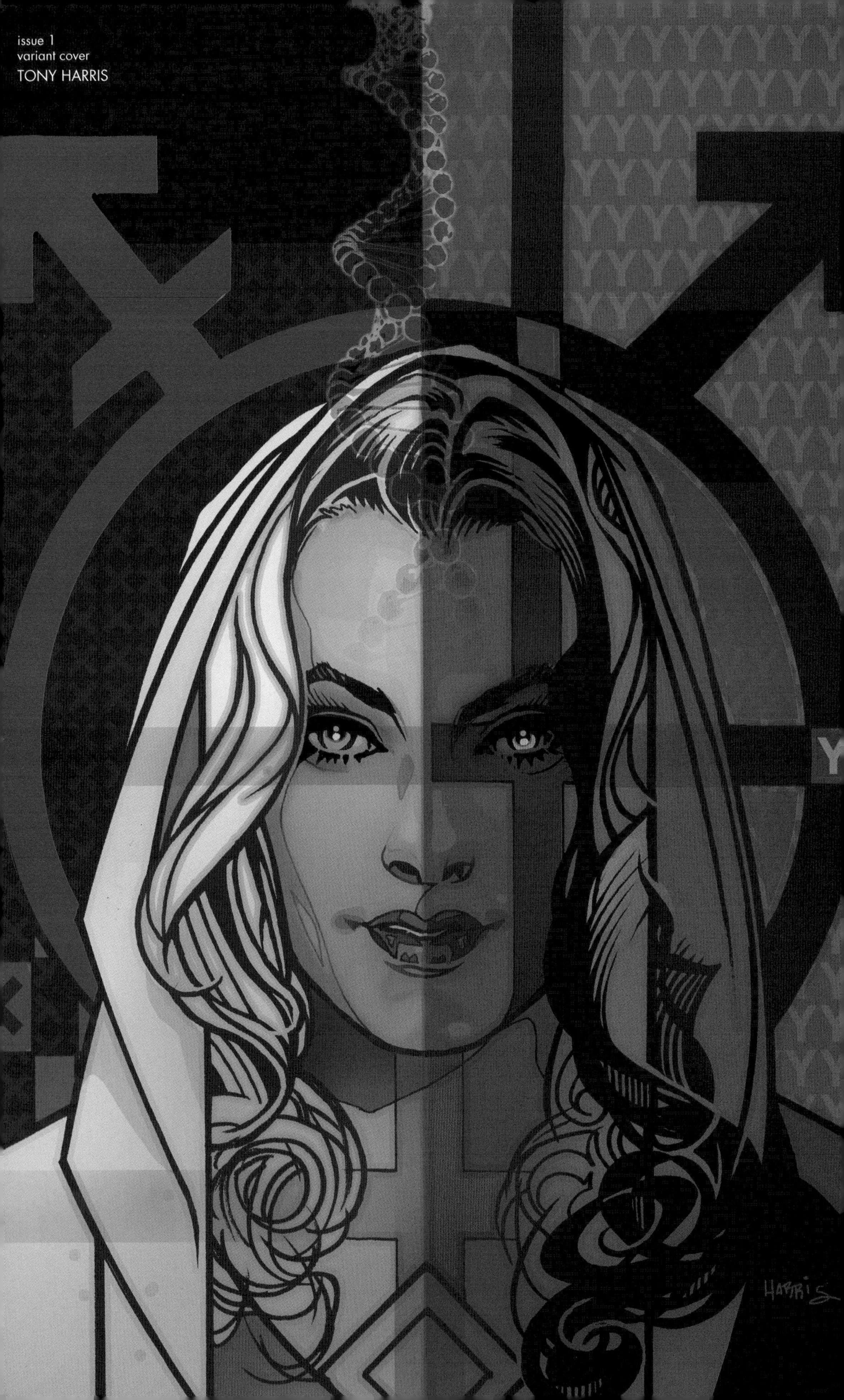
HARRIS

issue 1
Laughing Ogre incentive cover
CHRIS SPROUSE &
GABE ELTAEB

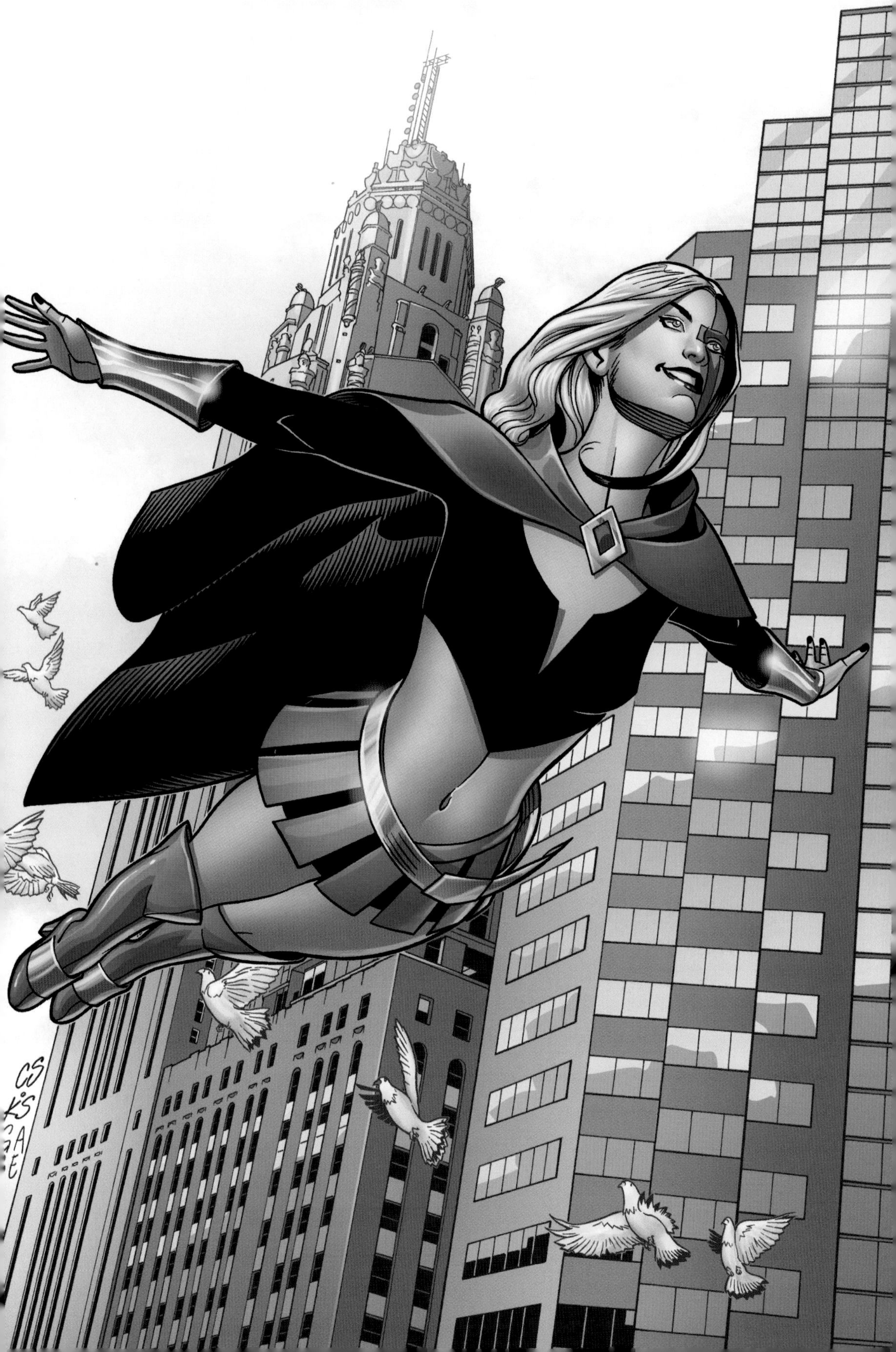

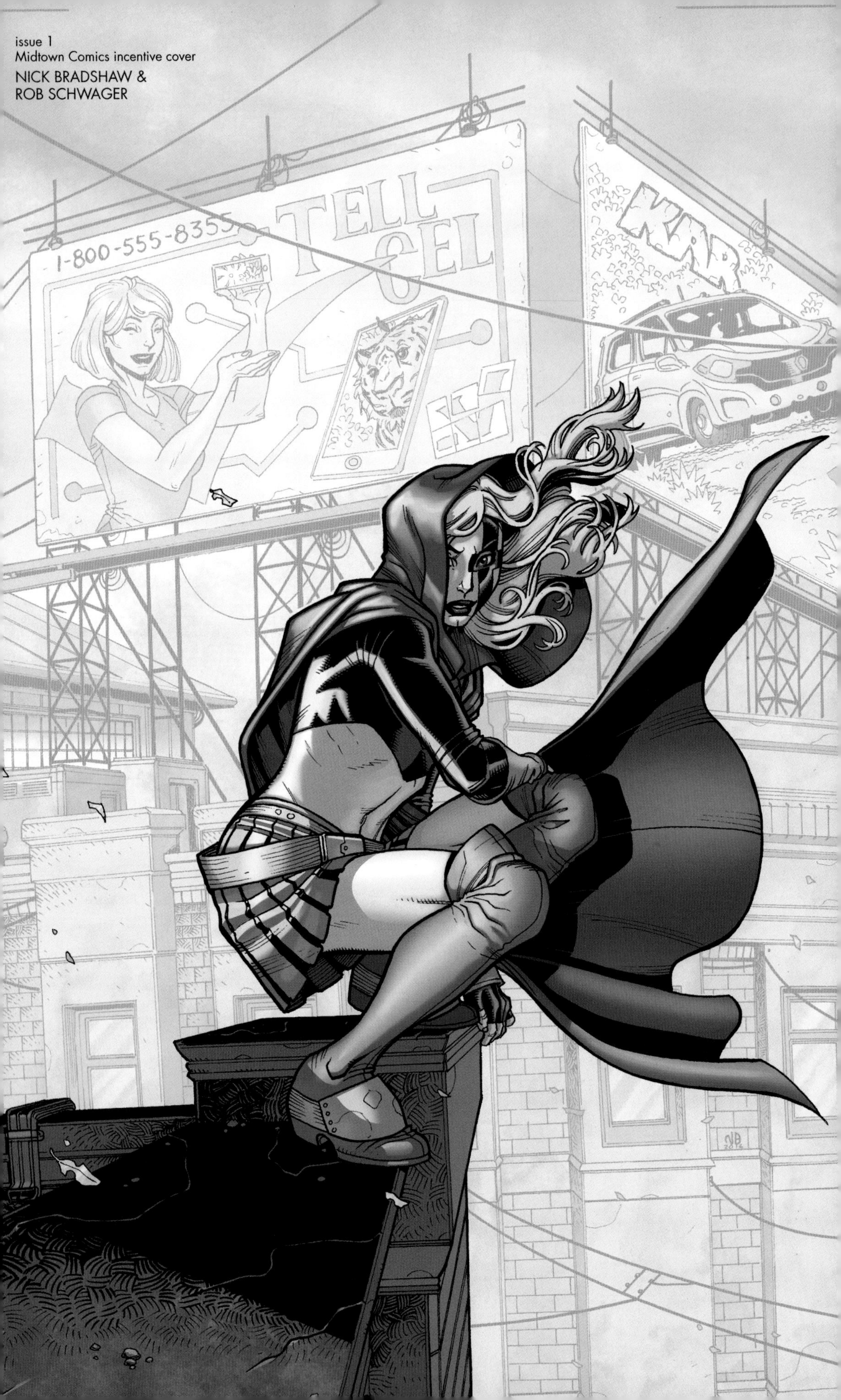
1-800-555-835
TELL
CEL
KAR

issue 1
Midtown Comics incentive cover
NICK BRADSHAW &
ROB SCHWAGER

issue 1
Ssalefish incentive cover
RICHARD CASE &
GREG SMALLWOOD

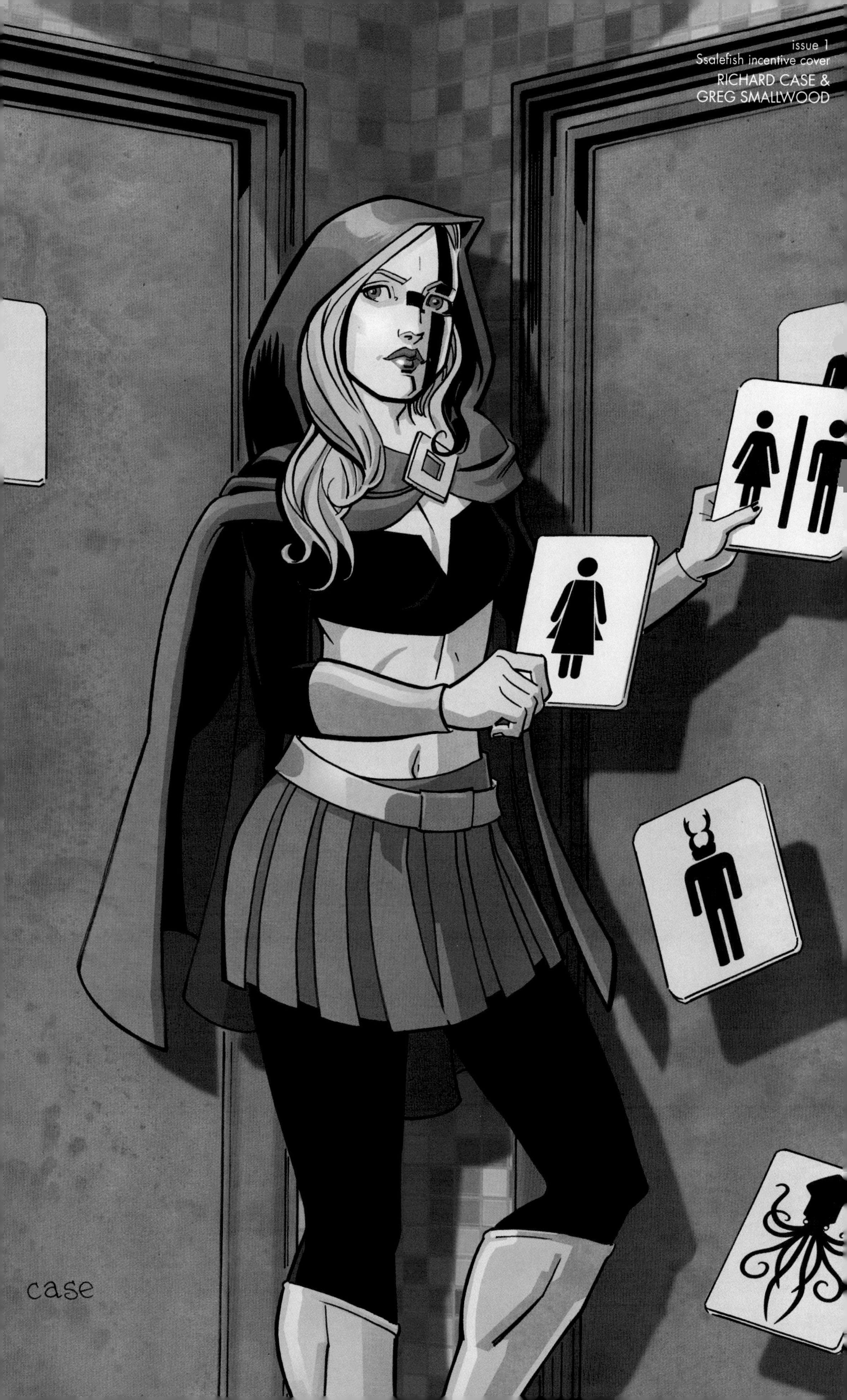
case

issue 1
Cards, Comics & Collectibles incentive cover
JOHN McCREA &
MIKE SPICER

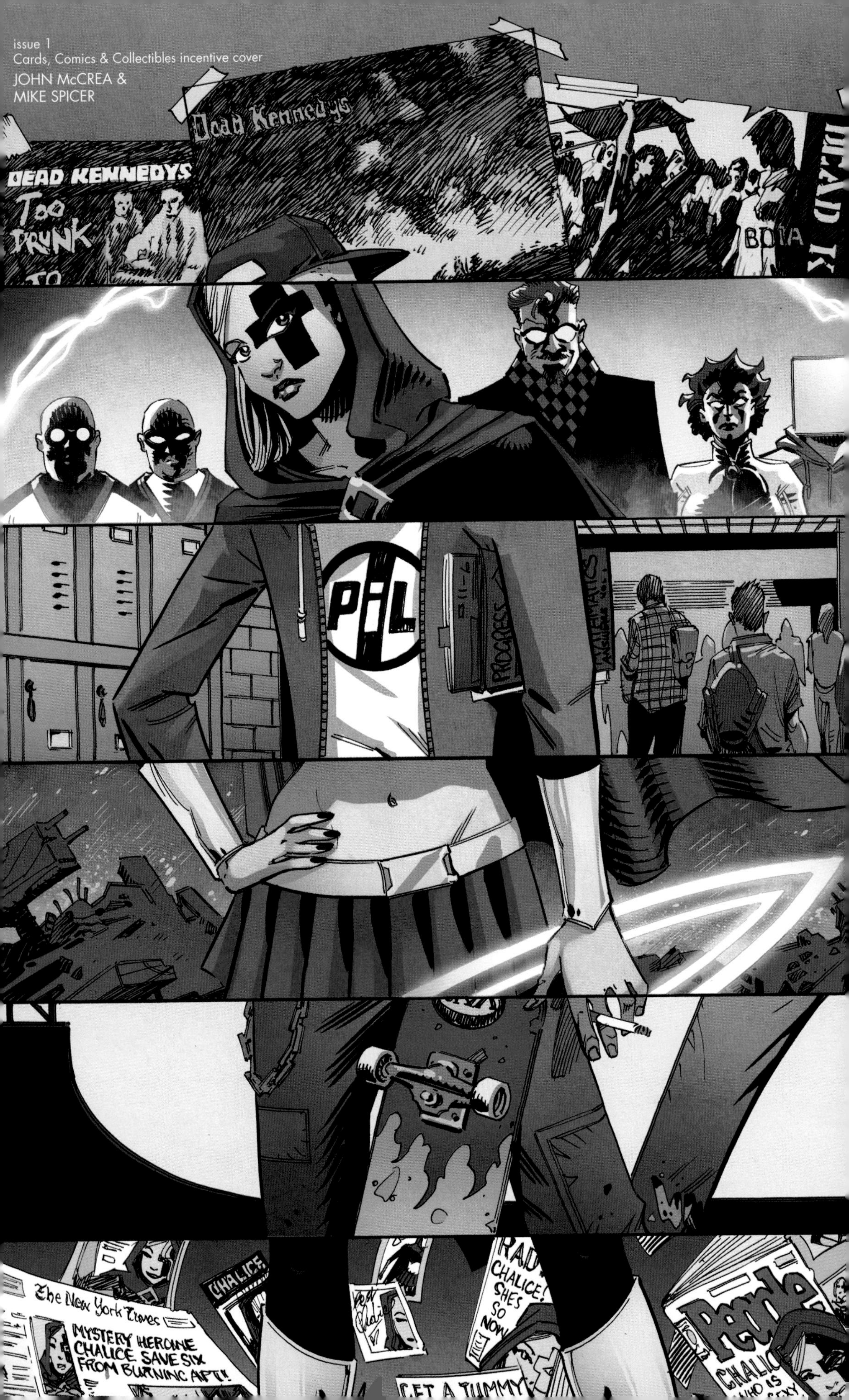
DEAD KENNEDYS
TOO DRUNK TO
Dead Kennedys
PiL
PROGRESS
The New York Times
MYSTERY HEROINE CHALICE SAVE SIX FROM BURNING APT!!
CHALICE
CHALICE! SHES SO NOW
People
CHALICE
GET A TUMMY

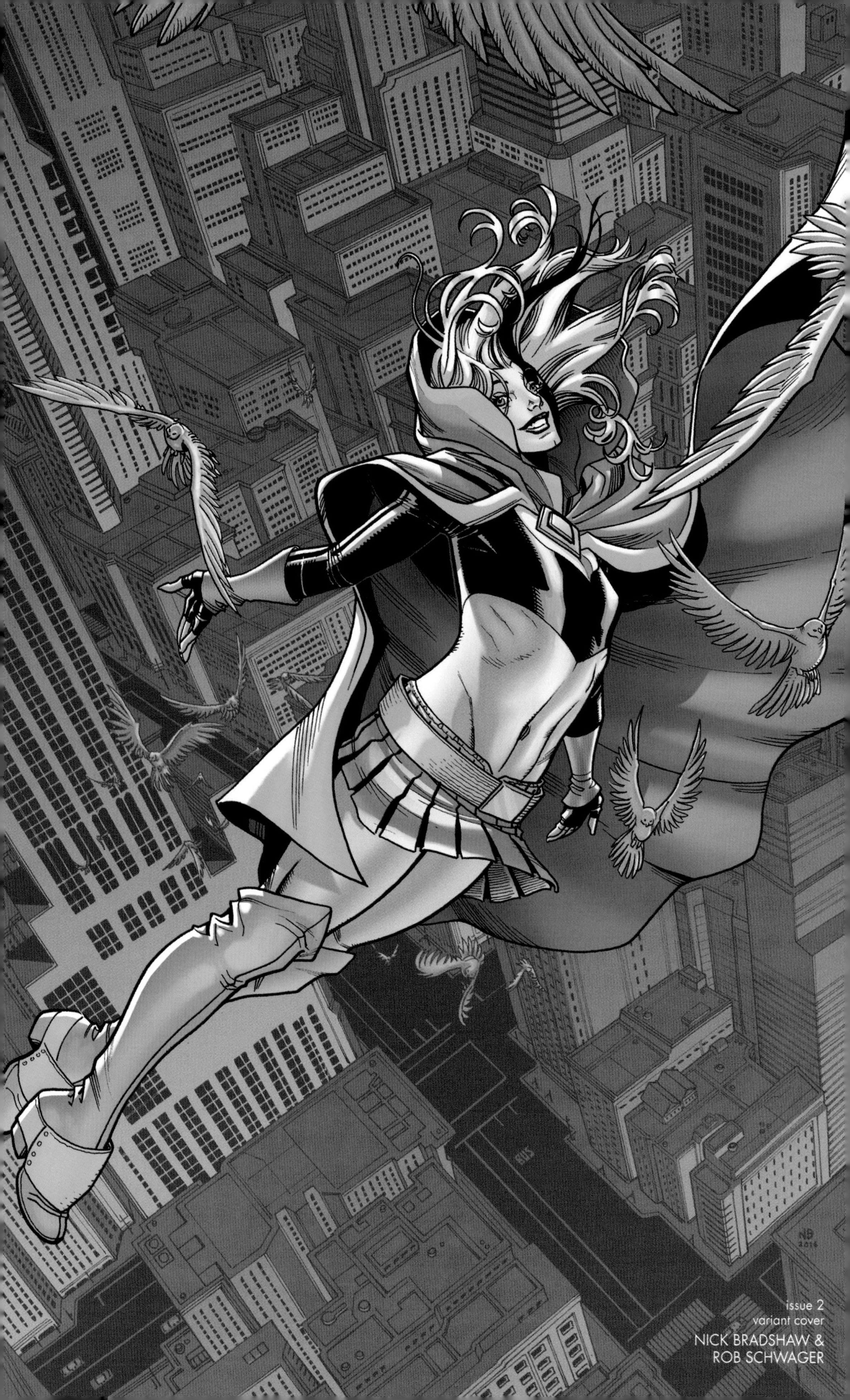

issue 2
variant cover
NICK BRADSHAW &
ROB SCHWAGER

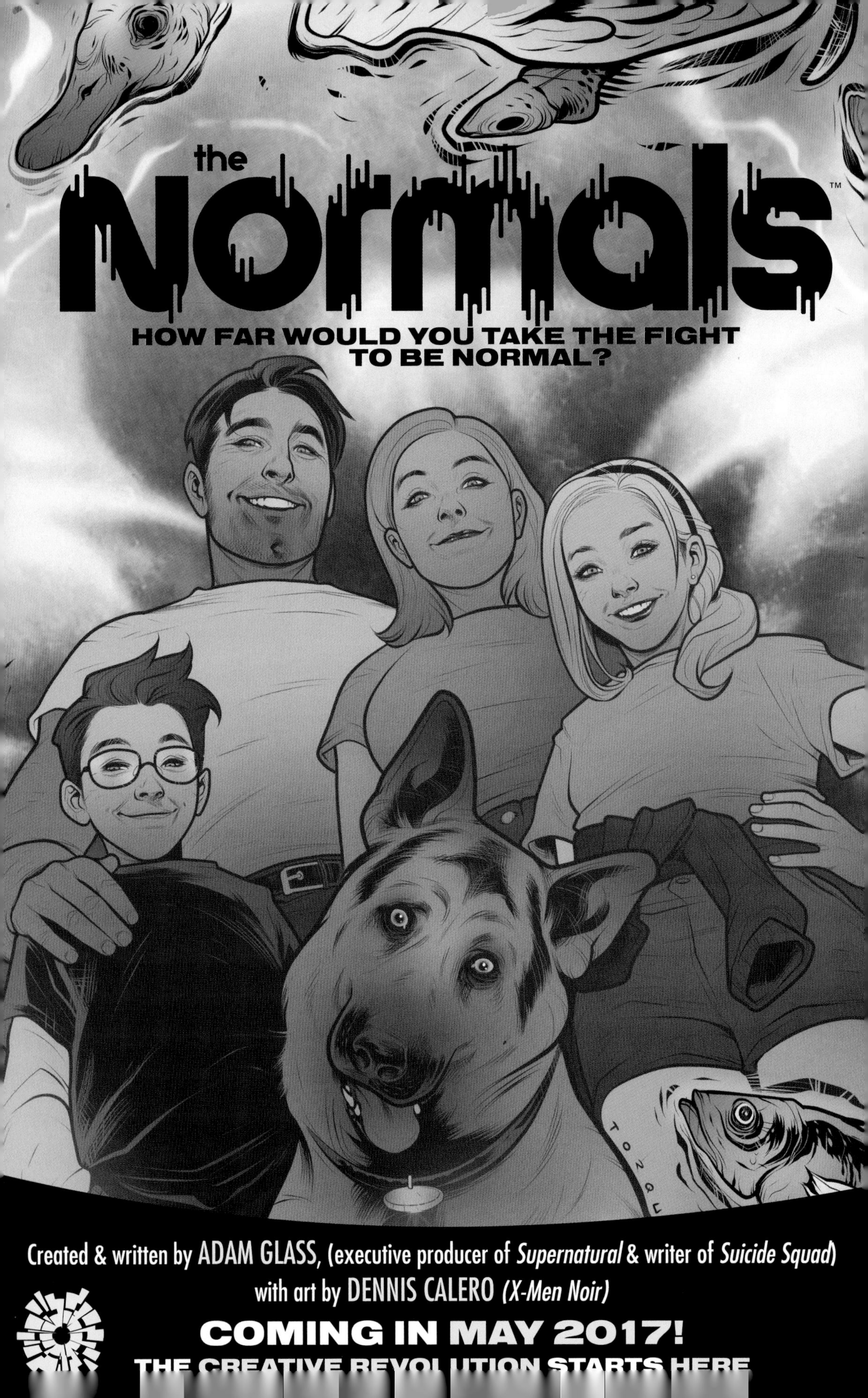
the Normals™
HOW FAR WOULD YOU TAKE THE FIGHT TO BE NORMAL?
Created & written by ADAM GLASS, (executive producer of Supernatural & writer of Suicide Squad)
with art by DENNIS CALERO (X-Men Noir)
COMING IN MAY 2017!
THE CREATIVE REVOLUTION STARTS HERE

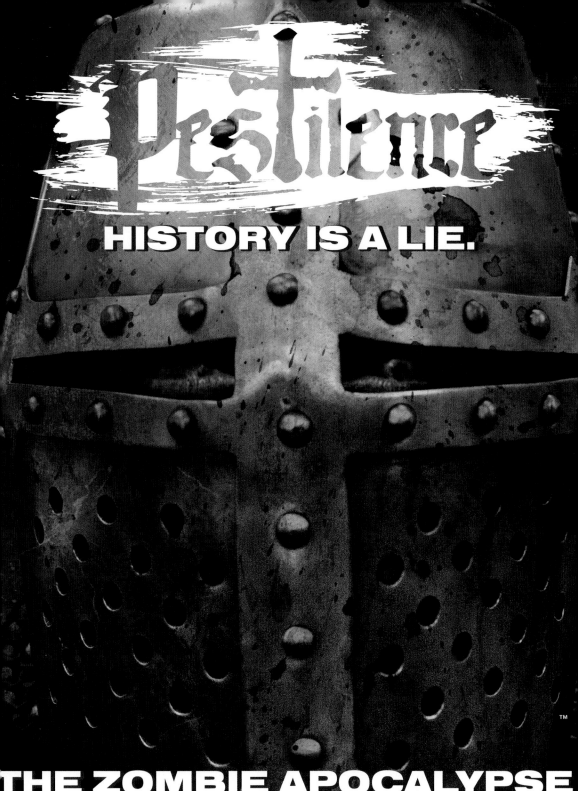

PESTILENCE

HISTORY IS A LIE.

THE ZOMBIE APOCALYPSE ALREADY HAPPENED.

Written by the master of mayhem, FRANK TIERI, *(Wolverine, Deadpool)* with art by OLEG OKUNEV and covers by TIM BRADSTREET *(The Punisher, Hellblazer)*!

COMING IN MAY 2017!
THE CREATIVE REVOLUTION STARTS HERE

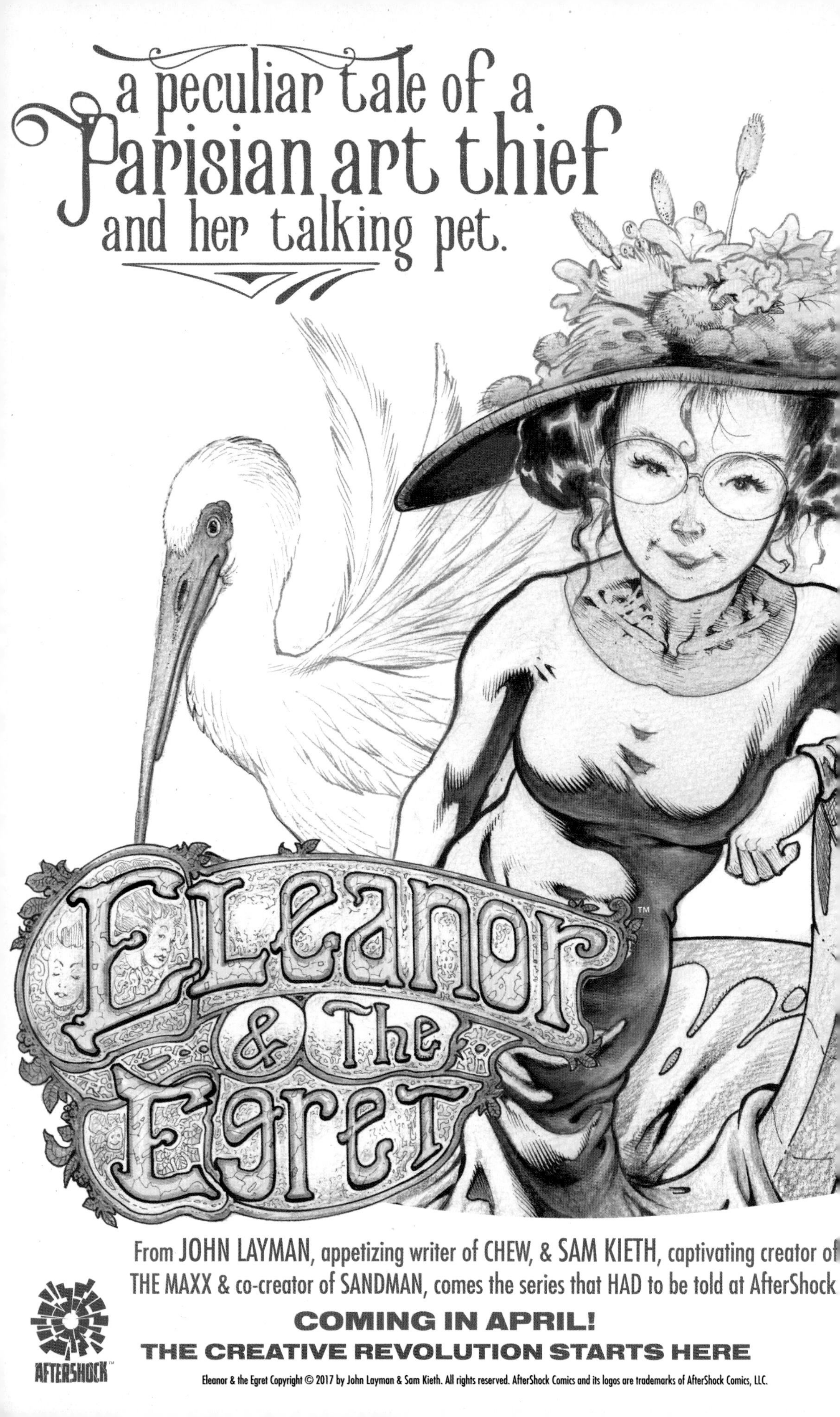
a peculiar tale of a Parisian art thief and her talking pet.
Eleanor & The Egret™
From JOHN LAYMAN, appetizing writer of CHEW, & SAM KIETH, captivating creator of THE MAXX & co-creator of SANDMAN, comes the series that HAD to be told at AfterShock
COMING IN APRIL!
THE CREATIVE REVOLUTION STARTS HERE
AFTERSHOCK™
Eleanor & the Egret Copyright © 2017 by John Layman & Sam Kieth. All rights reserved. AfterShock Comics and its logos are trademarks of AfterShock Comics, LLC.

Paul Jenkins has been creating, writing and building franchises for over twenty years in the graphic novel, film and video game industries. Over the last two decades, Paul has been instrumental in the creation and implementation of literally hundreds of world-renowned, recognizable entertainment icons.

From his employment with the creators of the *Teenage Mutant Ninja Turtles* at the age of 22 to his preeminent status as an IP creator, Paul has provided entertainment to the world through hundreds of print publications, video games, film and new media. With six Platinum-selling video games, a #1 MTV Music Video, an Eisner Award, five Wizard Fan Awards, and multiple Best Selling Graphic Novels, Paul Jenkins is synonymous with success. He has enjoyed recognition on the New York Times bestseller list, has been nominated for two BAFTA Awards, and has been the recipient of a government-sponsored Prism Award for his contributions in storytelling and characterization.

Paul's extensive list of comic book credits include *Batman* and *Hellblazer* for DC Comics; *Inhumans, Spider-Man, The Incredible Hulk, Wolverine: Origin, Civil War: Frontlines, Captain America: Theater of War* and *The Sentry* for Marvel Comics; and *Spawn* for Image Comics.

LEILA LEIZ artist
🐦 @LeilaLeiz

Born and raised in Italy, Leila is a self-taught artist who has seen her lifelong dream of working in American comics come true. After working for several years at European publishers like Soleil and Sergio Bonelli, Leila has made the exciting jump to AfterShock Comics, where she begins her new adventure on Paul Jenkins' series, ALTERS.

TAMRA BONVILLAIN colorist
🐦 @TBonvillain

Tamra Bonvillain graduated from the Joe Kubert School of Cartooning in 2009. For the next four years, she worked at Spiderwebart for Greg Hildbrandt and Jean Scrocco doing design work, retouching paintings, cleaning/scanning drawings and other various tasks. While there, she began coloring in her off hours, eventually moving back near her hometown to pursue coloring full time. She is currently coloring *Strayer, Rat Queens, Wayward, Moon Girl and Devil Dinosaur, John Flood,* and more.

RYANE HILL letterer
🐦 @Ryane_Hill

Ryane Hill is a native Californian living with her husband and two French Bulldogs in the beautiful Pacific Northwest. After years of working in the background as a production assistant, and gaining experience with both lettering and design, she is extremely excited to have the opportunity to work with AfterShock Comics on ALTERS.